DAVE WORKMAN

Muse Harbor Publishing

SURREALITY
A Muse Harbor Publishing Book

Published by
Muse Harbor Publishing, LLC
Santa Barbara, CA

Publishing History
Paperback edition: March, 2021

ISBN: 978-1-61264-208-6

Visit Muse Harbor Publishing at
www.museharbor.com

Please direct questions or comments to:
info@museharbor.com

v.2.2

For Karma Christine Salvato

"Jump and you will find out
how to unfold your wings
as you fall."

— Ray Bradbury

AUTHOR'S BIO

For many years, Dave Workman served as a Los Angeles-based film critic. When not writing fiction, he currently functions as a graphic designer and book editor. Dave's professional blog, *Rules of Engagement*—words of encouragement for aspiring novelists—can be found at **www.MuseHarbor.com**. You can also find Dave's two crime thrillers, *On The Rocks* and *On The Edge* for sale on Amazon. His newest novel, *Like A California Dream,* a modern Hollywood fable, is slated for release in 2021.

Surreality is Dave's first collection. He lives in Northern California with his wife, author Eileen Workman.

ACKNOWLEDGEMENTS

Thanks to Giselle Embry, Patty Haugen, and Eileen Workman for their feedback and proofreading skills, as my fingers and brain often work independently of each other. Thanks to Chris Wozney for her editorial support and keen eye. And a hat-tip to the usual literary faces; Ian Wood, Stephen Vessels, Amanda Creighton and Eileen among them, for keeping me motivated and, when lacking motivation, politely persecuted. Thanks to Sima Walker for clarifying those many delicate distinctions between Persian and Arabian cultures and to Ciscandra Nostalghia for the use of her eyes.

Fiction by Dave Workman:

On The Rocks

On The Edge

Surreality

Like a California Dream
(Coming in 2021)

On The Run
(Coming in 2022)

AUTHOR'S PREAMBLE

❧

If you were to ask me about the meaning of life—at least the meaning that defines *my* life—I'd tell you this: It's sitting down at my laptop to blindly delve into a new story, staring at a blank page that offers both infinite emptiness and absolute potential. I'll sit for a few moments (or a few days) until eventually some deep-down synapse sparks, my brain rattles and hums, my fingers tingle, and I begin to write a cogent thought or two that an instant before did not exist.

I typically have no idea where my first few ideas are going, although occasionally I'll have a hazy purpose in mind. Maybe I've visualized a vague, distant end game. Most likely I've concocted a fragmented idea for a short story, so I'm willing to invest a thousand or two words, charging head-first into the unknown.

Over the years I've written a few hundred first lines. Jotted down dozens of short story concepts that go nowhere fast. Tapped out a few thousand words that remain mired in uncertainty. My problem is that, according to my wife, I can't write a *short* short story to save my soul.

Those ideas that do gel gradually morph from vague notion to potential short story to unwieldy first chapter, at which point I suspect a novel is brewing. A few million synapses then decide to reroute those pages into my PENDING NOVELS folder—a whole different purgatory—and where most ideas will linger unceremoniously evermore.

Then there are those few stories (three, actually) that have managed to thrive and survive in their original, elongated, yet somewhat truncated form. When I do finally reach that final page, I'll discover a word count that falls suspiciously between a marketable short story and a fully developed novel.

Presented here are a novelette, novella and quasi-novel—a *trilogique*, if you please—three plump orphans deserving of a good home. I love these stunted newborns no less than my bona fide novels. I do not perceive these efforts as ugly stepchildren, but as uniquely different mutants. Think of a full-blown novel with all the boring parts removed.

Because I'm conscious of the value of writing a creatively provocative first paragraph (not necessarily edgy, although seductively inviting), I'm also curiously aware of my own inception process before those initial few words ever make it to the page. For a novelist, there's always an initial *"What if...?"* moment that slowly evolves—for me, usually while showering away all the hot water, strolling through the redwoods or bicycling along the Iron Horse Trail. My favorite percolation process occurs while driving up (or down) Northern California's coastal Route 1. Cruising along the Pacific Coast Highway has become my favorite contemplation zone. Even if nothing fully develops, I've allowed myself a magnificent, Zen-like paradise in which to unwind. Some people do yoga. I drive through seaside towns like Cambria or Gualala or Mendocino. And I feel whole again. Occasionally, I'll even discover the genesis of a new story.

But I digress. From whence do *these* particular tales arise, you might ask? (Or not. But I'm telling you anyway.)

The Hole is a story about…a hole. A simple enough premise to have come and gone in a flash, I suppose. Not long ago, I was tasked (because I'm married) with planting a young grapefruit sapling in our backyard. I recall a cloudless, blue sky and I believe a Negra Modelo or two may have been previously consumed. I also remember being utterly unmotivated, and after hoisting those first shovels filled with dirt, I watched the little hole began to collapse in on itself. Ah, but what's the purpose of a glorious summer afternoon if not for idly leaning on one's shovel and daydreaming? And thus *The Hole* was born. The story refused to die after the first ten pages, nor after another 20 or 30…and so here it is, in all its glorious holiness.

I've been privileged with the opportunity to travel to places like Costa Rica, St. Thomas, Barbados, Chichén Itza, Hawai'i and Tahiti, and I admit to having an affinity for anything even remotely resembling a tropical paradise. I'll also admit a fondness for 1930s Americana—not the most pleasant of times if one were to consider The Great Depression, The Dust Bowl, and with both Europe and Asia under siege; the likelihood of global war all but inevitable.

And yet, shameless film fanatic that I am, the early 30's heralded Hollywood's Golden Age; Tracy & Hepburn, Gable & Lombard, Powell & Loy, Bogie & Bacall—not to mention classic thrillers like *Dracula, Frankenstein, The Black Cat, The Mummy* and *The 39 Steps*. Spooky stuff. To this day I'll skip a decent sleep to catch a late-night, cable-rich glimpse into filmdom's reflection of that era, even if such celluloid realities are the echoes of a screenwriter's personal fantasy.

A literary Renaissance during that same period—Steinbeck, Hemingway and Faulkner; Pearl S. Buck, Margaret Mitchell, P. L. Travers and Gertrude Stein; fringe elements like Tolkien, Trumbo, Kafka (and hundreds others)—had also begun to transform modern fiction. *All* of which is to say that my brain feels quite at home in the 30's

Several years ago, I came upon a vintage photograph—a grainy, B&W image of a dilapidated thatched hut tucked beneath a bevy of coconut palms, the picture taken on some nameless South Pacific island shortly before WWII. Two bare-chested U.S. sailors sit on a log in front of the hut, smiling toward the photographer. A small wooden sign over the doorway, barely visible, simply reads: TATU.

That image lay simmering in the back of my mind until I realized I could no longer ignore its impact on my psyche— and so began *The Tattoo*. The story, a tale of a hard-drinking mariner and an island girl, not only reveals my love of the South Pacific and my affection for all things Hitchcock (as in Alfred) but also my attempt to recreate the stylized prose of that turbulent period. Because, why not?

One final note: San Francisco natives will encounter my colloquial (and reviled) use of *'Frisco*. Do realize that *S.F. Chronicle* columnist Herb Caen did not proclaim his staunch interdiction of the word until the early 1950s, so my story falls well within the proper timeline for its accepted usage. So, please, no hate mail.

My wife is also a writer. Eileen's a philosopher of sorts, a deep thinker and voracious reader who often wakes me during the wee hours to ponder insoluble questions, such as the

meaning of life, what comes next, where do our thoughts reside, and a host of similar pre-dawn head-scratchers. (My favorite among her ubiquitous 2AM comments is, "We are all taste buds on the tongue of a living Universe.")

Eileen and I have long discussed—often during the light of day as well—a myriad of confounding philosophical concepts. *The Eternal (Book 1)* is my attempt to capture as many of those conversational snippets as possible, then weave them together in a logical and stable fictive home. Just how or why a 100-year-old Chinese woman got involved—I don't choose my characters so much as they choose me—remains a mystery. But I believe every word she has to say.

Don't be confused by the story's *Book 1* addendum. I'm not leaving you in the lurch. *The Eternal (Book 1)* is a complete, fully formed story: a hero's journey sort of tale with a beginning, middle, and a definitive conclusion. *The Eternal (Book 2)** will one day be an entirely separate story—one that already percolates within those deep cerebral recesses— and will offer a separate plot line that forms a conjoined, if somewhat unconventional, complete novel.

Then again, don't you find convention depressingly overrated?

— Dave Workman
The Sea Ranch, CA
November, 2020

---

* You'll find an excerpt from The Eternal (Book 2) at the end of Surreality.

The Hole

SUNDAY

HENRY DOOGAN AWOKE EARLY, the summer sun hinting of a beautiful morning as it crested the hilltops to the east. A quiet and practical man, Henry preferred his chores over and done with, favoring his afternoons for reading, or for meandering beach walks with his wife, Emma. He wore wire-rim spectacles and had dressed haphazardly on this particular morning, in faded chino shorts and a tattered T-shirt, his favorite bucket hat and a scuffed pair of unlaced work boots.

Emma watched her husband putter from the kitchen window and thought every day should be so perfect. She smiled as Henry duck-walked a young sapling midway across the yard. Emma would be able to see the orange tree blossom from the kitchen window over the sink, and she delighted to imagine its fragrance soon filling the cottage.

She dabbed a dishcloth over a fat, ceramic gnome and replaced the figurine on the sill, exactly so. Emma wasn't particularly fond of bric-a-brac, but Henry had bought the bauble on their first anniversary and she had vowed to keep it forever. Now, almost twenty-five years later, she couldn't picture her kitchen without the little fellow.

Emma noticed—as she did every morning standing at the sink—the missing tip of her left pinky. The accident had occurred when she was quite young, the result of an ice-skating outing with her older sisters back when their family lived cross-country, near Stowe, Vermont. She and Henry had been in California since her college days, and Emma had not felt the sting of winter or the bite of a skate blade in a very long time. Warm winters were the best revenge, Henry occasionally told her, aware of his wife's preoccupation with her loss. But being a precise woman, Emma was constantly aware of the slight asymmetric imbalance of the missing fingertip. She was an *artist* after all, and occasionally sensed her life as being a single brush stroke from perfection.

Nevertheless, Emma freely admitted that she and Henry lived an otherwise blessed life, in a perfect little cottage—their *dream home,* she often remarked—quite sure that Henry felt the same. She typically painted three or four days a week, watercolor seascapes mostly, and sometimes acrylics if she was feeling adventurous. Emma did not consider either Henry or herself as being even remotely retired (Emma still 16 months shy of her 50th birthday) so much as damn fortunate. Several years ago, Henry's successful architectural firm had been acquired by a larger, even more successful competitor. The Doogans had unexpectedly found themselves with a sufficient nest egg and a strong resolve to spend their days enjoying a peaceful, stress-resistant lifestyle.

Emma loved the morning fog, the smell and taste of the Pacific coast. The unassuming seaside village of Santa Rosarita stood a scant five-minute's stroll from the ocean's edge. Often times, after supper, she and Henry would sit on their porch listening to the rhythmic rumble of waves, content to observe the sun's lazy descent toward the horizon, seemingly as endless as the days ahead of them.

After nightfall they'd sometimes linger; Henry with his pipe and a snifter of brandy, Emma sipping a glass of sherry or herbal tea, awash in the warm breezes. They were often aware of the crickets and plump toads croaking out their peculiar love sonnets under the blanket of darkness. To Emma, *this* was the meaning of life.

She fisted her damaged hand and glanced again at Henry, crouched in the yard, freeing the tree's roots from a small black tub. She noticed the remnants of a morning chill in the air and stepped to the back doorway.

"Darling? Would you like some coffee?"

Henry paused and straightened. Arching his back, he looked skyward. "Some tea, actually. Earl Gray, please, if you wouldn't mind."

"Of course not." She turned toward the stove, loving Henry with every fiber of her being.

EMMA PUT THE KETTLE ON, brought a ceramic mug from the cabinet and cut Henry a lemon wedge. She returned to the open doorway, aware of the spindly tree lying on its side, awaiting its permanent home. She watched Henry bring a shovel from the shed near the garage and move to a bald swatch of dirt; they'd never been able to grow grass on the spot and Emma was happy to hide the blemish beneath the sapling.

Henry looked up. He tapped the tip of his spade upon the bare spot. "About here then?"

Emma stepped into the yard and squinted, judging distances with an artist's perspective—sufficient space from the white picket fence that separated Mrs. Peroni's property and plenty of growing room between the sapling and the budding lime tree that Henry had planted last spring.

"Yes, dear," she told him. "That would be perfect."

"You know what they say. Ask once, dig twice."

"I believe the adage is measure twice, *cut* once."

Henry rubbed his hands together and firmly grasped the shovel. "Well, the motivation's the same."

She stepped back and watched Henry poke at the dirt a few times, as if judging his adversary.

"Should we soak the ground first?" Emma asked.

"No need. Soil's as soft as a pillow." He tamped the spade

with one unlaced boot and hoisted up a small clot.

She remembered the tea and turned for the kitchen—but heard Henry grunt his surprise. She peered back over her shoulder.

"Odd," he remarked.

"What's?"

Henry's gaze remained locked between his feet. "The hole. It, um, seems to be digging itself."

"Oh?" She paused mid-step. The little half-moon slice of earth appeared alive with subtle movement. For an instant Emma thought the sides of the hole were simply falling in. She moved closer to Henry and noticed the bottom of the hole sinking as well, not unlike the sand near the throat of an hourglass trickling relentlessly downward.

"What have you done?" she asked in mock horror.

"No idea." Henry scuffed at the hole with the toe of his boot, as if such intervention might cease the flurry of motion.

"You've discovered a squirrel's burrow," Emma supposed. "A mole's tunnel perhaps?"

"Or an old clay pipeline caving in on us," Henry mused. "Although I'm not aware of any existing infrastructure down there."

They stared in fascination, neither speaking while small clots of clay tumbled into the deepening cavity. The dirt at the bottom continued to descend, as if falling into some unseen chasm.

A minute passed before Emma realized the hole, whose circumference had now formed a perfect circle, might easily swallow a large grapefruit. She glanced at the lime tree, midway across the yard.

You had no problems with *that* one, did you?"

"No," Henry said. "None at all."

In another few moments the size of the hole doubled

and then, gradually, doubled again. "Well, there we go. Job done." Henry picked up the sapling and dropped it into the empty socket. A perfect fit.

"Bravo," Emma said, about to praise him further, but the oddest sensation silenced her. The little tree spasmed and slowly descended another several inches into the earth.

"Henry?"

He shook his head, anticipating her question, unable to fathom the mystery either.

"Perhaps we've uncovered the relics of an old oil field," Emma said, recalling a smattering of rusting derricks she'd sometimes glimpse along the coastal Cabrillo Highway. "What else could it be?"

"A sinkhole," Henry offered.

"A what?"

"You know, a *sink*hole. Those huge pits you hear about suddenly appearing in places like Florida and Mexico. Remember that massive hole in Guatemala a while back? I think it was hundreds of feet deep."

"Oh, Henry—*no!*"

He put an arm around Emma's shoulder and gently squeezed. "Don't worry. That was an anomaly. If we have to, we'll buy a bag of topsoil down at Cambria Nursery."

They watched the hole expand and continue to swallow the tree. The shrill whistle of the teakettle finally snagged their attention. Emma frowned. "We should call someone."

"Who?"

"Mr. Avalara might know what to do." The landscaper had sculpted their yard years before and had nurtured it with loving care ever since. If anybody could resolve the matter, it would be Miguel Avalara.

"Good idea," Henry agreed, reaching out to rescue the sinking sapling. They walked together toward the kitchen. "Although I don't believe it can grow much larger. This isn't

Guatemala, dear. Water's usually involved. Broken mains or bad drainage. Tropical storms. We live in a coastal desert."

"Desert or not, I don't want our yard ruined."

Henry nodded from the doorway and glanced back, shocked to note that the hole's surface had expanded to the circumference of a garbage can lid. His brow furrowed. "You *might* want to tell Mr. Avalara to hurry."

THE LANDSCAPER SOUNDED RELUCTANT over the phone. "A busy schedule this morning," he told Emma, but when she said *sinkhole*, repeating the word several times, he'd been swayed.

"Never seen one," he admitted.

By the time Miguel Avalara arrived, both Emma and Henry had lost their sense of unruffled curiosity. "Thank you for coming," Emma told him in halting Spanish. (Miguel had encouraged Emma to push past her own discomfort with her rusty Spanish, and their conversations often transpired in his native tongue.) He wiped his work boots respectfully on their front door mat, smelling faintly of chili tamales and cut grass.

"You won't believe what's happening in our yard," she added in English, as if the urgency of the situation might be more obvious in her own language.

"Don' think it could be no sinkhole," he replied cautiously in his own heavily accented English.

She led him through the cottage. The landscaper hesitated at the doorway, seeing Henry standing in the backyard, peering down into the dark cavity, holding a tape rule. Mr. Avalara opened his mouth, closed it again, and stared.

Henry glanced up and said, "Good morning, Miguel," shaking his head with mild annoyance. "The damn thing's nearly twice as large as when my wife called you. I just measured it again. Fifty-two inches, side to side."

"Chihuahua," Mr. Avalara replied, drawing the word out under his breath, one syllable at a time. *Chiii-huaaa-hua.* Disbelieving and at the same time fascinated. He stepped into the yard, eyes wide, moving like a man transfixed.

The two men stared in silence for several moments, watching large clumps of dirt topple inward and spiral downward, as if devoured by some unseen demon.

"Sinkhole," Henry muttered, as if already certain.

"Si, *si,*" Mr. Avalara said. "But here? In Santa Rosarita?"

"Are you aware of any old water pipes? A high water table in this area? Is there any reason for this to be happening?"

"No, no. Not much rain lately. Solid ground—" Mr. Avalara stomped his foot twice, hard, to punctuate the remark. "—an' mostly bedrock. Not soft soil, like down in La Conchita. Good clay an' pumice here. Nice hard earth."

Henry had to admit that the dirt surrounding the hole did look firm and dry. Softball-sized rocks, porous and grey, appeared and, one by one, fell to the bottom of the pit. Within moments, each had sunk from view.

"*Is* it a sinkhole?" he asked.

"I don' know." Mr. Avalara said, stepping back cautiously as the edge of the hole encroached upon the tips of his boots.

Henry looked up, seeing Emma in the doorway, her face drawn and twisted. He smiled at her, but the gesture failed. For the first time, Henry felt the kind of dread that intelligent people harbor toward irrational mystery. This was beyond any logic, and his uncertainty turned to uncharacteristic anger. "Then I guess it's best we find out."

Tom Harding, a San Luis Obispo County deputy sheriff, comprised half of Santa Rosarita's entire part-time police force. Emma didn't know who else to call and Tom seemed a sensible, levelheaded sort; not yet thirty, he commanded a quiet air of authority. Rudy Tamalack, eighteen years older, served as the town's other officer, but twice divorced and an excessive cigar smoker, Emma suspected the man lacked proper judgment.

Even though crime was non-existent in Santa Rosarita, Emma assumed Tom to be the sort capable of holding his own in places far more hostile, like Santa Barbara or Ventura. Besides, first selectman Vincent Santiago was seldom around and rarely accessible; either deep sea fishing off the Channel Islands or gambling at the Chumash Casino, so Tom seemed the obvious first choice. Emma picked up the phone once again.

Henry and Emma waited on the front porch, drinking iced tea under the pretense of normality. Emma felt relieved to be away from the backyard, as if this particular nightmare might be confined there and might just as mysteriously cease in their absence.

Tom Harding's white Jeep Cherokee swung around the cul-de-sac and stopped in front of the cottage's short driveway. "He'll know," Emma said, more to herself than to Henry, although she felt mildly irritated when Tom lingered officiously inside the vehicle.

"A hole?" the officer asked finally, stepping from the vehicle and peering over the open door of his Jeep. Emma and Henry glanced at each other, sensing young Tom's skepticism regarding the need for official intervention.

"Rather *large*," Emma called back. Henry noticed the vestiges of Emma's New England childhood lilt emerge whenever she was upset.

"And you want it arrested?" Tom grinned at them as he walked up the stone walkway. He was a tall man with broad shoulders and the chiseled face of an athlete.

"Police humor," Emma mumbled under her breath.

"A coin toss between you or the fire department," Henry said quickly, if only to keep Emma from saying something she'd later regret. "Unfortunately, you lost."

To his credit, Tom nodded solemnly. "Why don't I take a look?"

THE FORTY OR SO MINUTES they'd lingered on the porch had been an emotional respite. Both Emma and Henry were appalled to discover the speed at which the hole had continued to consume their yard—so much so that neither heard Tom mutter "*Christ almighty!*" upon seeing the crater.

The Doogan's yard was modest. Barely fifty feet separated the back of their house from the little white fence that bordered Mrs. Peroni's backyard, a similar width dividing them from neighboring cottages on either side. Emma had planted a vegetable garden at the yard's south end—safely distant from the hole, thank goodness, and far from Mrs. Peroni's lofty Jeffrey pine, easily a century old. The tree blocked sunlight for much of the morning.

During those forty minutes, the hole's diameter had expanded by at least two feet. Mr. Avalara, still puttering about, had brought Henry's nine-foot aluminum ladder from the garage, and had uncoiled the garden hose, as if preparing some Don Quixotesque assault against such a perplexing opponent.

"Was it a meteor, Henry?" Tom asked suspiciously.

"I'm afraid we birthed this puppy ourselves," Henry admitted. "I was planting a tree this morning, and the hole literally began to dig itself."

"You drawing well water?"

"On the county main, like everyone else in the village."

"What about septic?" Tom asked. "You got a leach field buried back here somewhere?"

Henry shook his head. "Nothing."

"And you're sure about that?"

"The cottage is only three years old, Tom. We've been living here the entire time."

"Ever since TMA purchased Henry's company," Emma thought to remark. "We saw the house go up ourselves."

"I watched them bulldoze and grade the lot. To my knowledge, there's nothing subterranean on the property."

Mr. Avalara said, "S'cuse me," and stepped between the two men, standing over the hole like a gun fighter, pistol gripping the nozzle-fitted garden hose. He stared down into the pit with a squinty-eyed disapproval. The bottom had to be at least eight feet deep by now.

"You gonna fill 'er up, Miguel?" Tom asked.

"This deep, should be clay," Mr. Avalara said. "The hole, it *should* fill up. Before you arrive, I let the water flow a good long time. The water, it jus' disappear, like down a drain."

The landscaper fingered the nozzle and the men watched a steady stream vanish beneath the churning floor of loose topsoil. Emma moved beside her husband and said, "It doesn't even look wet."

Tom glanced at the aluminum ladder lying on the grass, a few feet away. "You go down there yet, Miguel?"

"*Me?*" Mr. Avalara's expression darkened. "No, no, I don' go down. *Es el agujero del diablo,*" he added cryptically.

"Devil or not, I suppose I should take a peek," Tom said. "See if I can find anything—hell, I don't know, anything *unusual* at the bottom."

"You think that floor's stable enough?" Henry wondered as Tom moved off to grab the ladder. Mr. Avalara shut the nozzle and backed away, as if retreating from an awakening bear.

"I guess there's only one way to find out," Tom said. Henry side-stepped to help heft the weight of the bulky nine-footer, still unsure of the deputy's wisdom.

But Emma, either by quirk or by happenstance, prematurely answered Henry's question herself. She'd been standing at the edge of the hole, staring after the two men, when a sizable patch of sod under her shoes loosened and gave way. She slid into the abyss with a surprised chirp.

"Emmie!" Henry called. Suddenly fearful, he snatched the ladder from Tom's grasp, whirled and thrust it down into the hole in a single fluid motion. He slid more than climbed its length, his heart racing.

Emma wasn't hurt—she'd managed to clutch a fistful of the pine's exposed root system on her descent, breaking her fall. Yet by the time Henry touched bottom, her left foot had already been tugged under the churning soil.

"Darling?" she said, embarrassed, but also pleased that her husband and not Tom Harding had come to rescue her. She wrapped her arms around Henry's neck and kissed his cheek as he hoisted her up the ladder. Tom grabbed for her wrists, lifting her out of the hole in a single, splay-legged pirouette. Henry scrambled up and tugged several times at the ladder before he finally dislodged it.

"You're okay?" Tom asked.

"Clumsy," Emma replied, pushing long stands of hair from her face. The gnarled roots had left a nasty scratch on her chin. "Although I found nothing unusual to report," she added, brushing soil from the knees of her pants.

"You're sure you're okay?" Henry pressed, adjusting his spectacles.

"I'm fine, darling. None the worse." She laughed nervously, then tilted her head, as if recalling the wisp of a distant memory. "Except that it seemed to be pulling at me from below. And would have gobbled me up, had it more time."

"It?" Tom asked suspiciously.

"Oh, and it made a sound," Emma said.

"A sound?"

"Like a whisper," she said, turning to stare curiously into the hole, trying to recall the ambient hiss, *a whisper* the best description she could muster.

"You scared the crap out of me," Henry admitted.

Tom exhaled sharply. "I think we should be more—"

"Darling, look," Emma said to Henry, pointing, aware of the little white fence that separated their yard from Mrs. Peroni's.

Both Henry and Tom turned to watch the fence begin to sag, the slats slowly tipping inward, less than a foot now from the hole's expanding rim.

"Here now!" echoed a distant voice. Claire Peroni's screen door swung open. Orange haired and nearing ninety, Mrs. Peroni ambled from her kitchen doorway with a fuzzy-slippered, slow-motioned intensity.

Emma had been expecting their neighbor for some time now. She'd already seen Mrs. Peroni peeking from behind her curtained windows, the old woman likely considering the Doogan's problem to be none of her business—although the encroaching hole had become very much her business.

"What's going on? What are you people doing?" she called suspiciously.

As if this is our fault? Emma thought, then suddenly wondered if somehow it might be.

"Stay back, Claire," Tom warned. "We're not sure of what's happening yet."

"Well, keep it out of *my* yard," the old woman insisted, frowning at the hole from a safe distance. Tom and Henry stared at each another in befuddlement.

"Damn," Tom muttered, fishing a cell phone from his pocket. "We're going to need more people. Hopefully *some*body who might know what the hell is happening."

By one o'clock that afternoon, after a half-dozen phone calls to various local agencies, consensus decreed that who the hell *might* know would be the eggheads over in the Soil and Earth Sciences Department at Cal Poly, thirty or so miles to the south. Fortunately, Tom Harding knew someone who knew someone who knew Dr. Francine Conrad, a graduate professor of geology. Tom left a message with Dr. Conrad's machine, inferring that she'd best get her ass up to Santa Rosarita ASAP.

Nobody at Cal Poly might have cared on this perfect, sunny Sunday, except that Tom had captured several images on his cell phone camera and sent them to Dr. Conrad as evidence. Ninety minutes later, two SUV's filled with Cal Poly's curious elite arrived in front of the Doogan's cottage. What they found in the backyard filled them with a particularly chatty sort of awe.

After a meticulous overabundance (Emma thought) of photographs, soil samples and text exchanges, the geologists finally took measurements—on their *smart* phones no less—and determined the chasm's size to be 10.815 feet in diameter by some 10.64 feet deep. *A volume of just over 180 cubic feet,* Dr. Conrad noted to herself, barely aloud. She was a stout, stern-faced woman, sixtyish, who moved about the yard with an air of brisk authority. Several of the dozen people around her carried video equipment. Others continued to fiddle with various gauges cabled into laptop computers.

The hole had maintained its cylindrical precision, small boulders and root systems protruding here and there, but otherwise the chasm's walls appeared remarkably smooth. The floor tapered slightly, churning and gulping dirt and stone in a gradually descending spiral—a *Fibonacci* spiral, one of the geologists casually remarked—and nobody from Cal Poly appeared ready to repeat Emma's descent to the bottom quite yet.

Within the hour, the hole had reached a depth of approximately 14 feet.

Tom Harding had been busy on his phone most of that time, appearing alternately weary and perplexed, finally glancing toward Emma and Henry, the couple standing grim-faced in the kitchen doorway. "Uh oh," Emma whispered with sudden foreboding, watching the young deputy move toward them with an unpleasant expression.

"I know what you're going to say," Emma said, "and the answer is no."

"This is for your own good, Emma. It's dangerous here."

"I'm not leaving this house, Thomas Harding. You'll have to arrest me, because that's the only way I'm leaving. Kicking and screaming and making a terrible ruckus."

Tom attempted to stare her down, but Emma didn't blink. A few of the Cal Poly people turned to observe the confrontation, but the deputy had neither the time nor the inclination to pursue the matter. "*Damn* it, Emma, not a single step into this yard. Not one toe. That's non-negotiable. Understood?"

"Understood," she said with a solemn nod, gracing the officer with a polite smile. She was unaware of Tom's gaze briefly touching upon Henry who, unlike his wife, realized that any subsequent encounter would not end so graciously.

Emma made a pot of coffee for anyone wanting a cup and heated water for Henry's tea, then planted herself at the kitchen window, next to her chubby gnome, somberly watching the hole expand like a black stain across her yard. She couldn't help but perceive that the chasm looked somehow *hungry*.

By SEVEN-FORTY-FIVE that evening—the sun moments from setting against the clear amber horizon—first selectman

Santiago appeared on the scene, trying to appear suitably in charge and yet completely overwhelmed by the situation. Santiago shuffled after Tom Harding like a lost puppy. Several others from who-knew-where meandered about, two or three in military uniforms, a few others in business suits, all in various stages of curiosity and suspicion. Stern and officious looking men, Emma thought. Three large generator-fueled floodlights had been delivered and triangulated in the waning daylight. Trucks dislodged other instruments in the driveway; big, bulky things that Emma regarded as disturbingly ominous.

By now, the hole measured thirty-four feet in diameter, having gobbled slightly over 900 feet of surface area. To Emma, it appeared that a quarter of her yard had disappeared. From her unwavering vantage point at the kitchen doorway, she watched her little lime tree dip, shudder and finally drop away. Amid the shrill scream of chainsaws, a cutting crew from CG&E eventually topped the giant Jeffrey pine—now a scant yard from the northeastern edge of the chasm. Somebody-or-other of importance had worried that the tree might topple sideways, taking out either Mrs. Peroni's home or the Doogan's. While Emma appreciated their concern, she felt its loss far more irreplaceable. She watched the top third of the tree tumble into the hole and, a short while later, the middle third fell as predicted. *Funny,* Emma thought. *Tomorrow, we'll have morning sunlight.* And then she cried.

Another hour passed and additional people arrived. In the waning twilight, Emma found it impossible to see who was who, but she assumed they were all important in some way or another. Flashlight beams crisscrossed the darkness. Half the throng took up residence in Mrs. Peroni's yard (the old woman had been safely relocated hours before) and additional floodlights were being hastily erected on her property. The little white fence had been completely removed, mostly for convenience but also, Emma realized, because its continual, post-by-post capitulation into the growing chasm had proved a distraction. An ominous one at that.

She knew that the governor had been notified and overheard that a California National Guard convoy had arrived in neighboring Cambria. Two vehicles from the CCSD Fire Department waited out front in the cul-de-sac, although Emma wasn't certain why they were necessary. The hole certainly wasn't belching *fire*.

While a variety of conversations and general confusion kept Emma both curious and distracted, Henry wandered from room to room, discreetly removing various articles. He gathered up several photos—last year in Rome with the Orlandos, pictures of their parents and Emma's sisters back in Vermont. Henry also furtively grabbed Emma's paint box, favorite easel, and three small, blank canvases. He snatched the laptop from his office, seized a bulging accordion folder of essential paperwork and contracts, including their passports and insurance documents. With methodical deliberation, he filled two large suitcases and their overnight travel bags with clothing, transferring the items without a word into the trunk of their Volvo.

The distant sound of rotor blades snapped Emma from her trancelike fascination at the window. She gazed upward, seeing nothing against the darkened sky, although there was no mistaking the sound of the approaching helicopter. She leaned forward, craning her neck to finally glimpse the aircraft descending, positioning itself above the hole. An instant later a powerful spotlight, far more illuminating than those stationed in the yard, blazed from the craft.

Emma was shocked to realize just how frighteningly big the chasm had become. Only a few feet of turf remained between the pit's northern rim and their garage. Less than six feet separated the advancing edge from the kitchen doorway. A good third of Mrs. Peroni's lawn had also fallen away. As Emma watched, several of the old woman's rose bushes disappeared from view.

First selectman Santiago's voice bellowed from another room, raising itself over the sound of the overhead rotors. "I said *cement* trucks. Why can't we use cement trucks? Fill the damn thing in?" A pause. "Well, what about dynamite?"

She sensed a presence close behind her and turned to see Henry, quite solemn, and Tom Harding nearby, also looking grim.

"Emmie," Henry said, reaching gently to take her hands. "We need to listen to Tom."

"Do we now?"

Tom nodded. "I hate to say this, but you and Henry have to leave. You can't sleep here tonight. We don't know how long the structure will remain intact."

"Tom, I won't have—"

He raised a stern finger. This time Emma capitulated, closing her mouth with a quivering lower lip.

"This isn't coming from me," he said gently. "This is straight from Sacramento. We've already procured a hotel room for you, over at the Del Mar Vista, courtesy of the state."

"Henry, don't let them *do* this," she whispered.

"It's for the best, darling. Tom's right. The truth is, we may lose the cottage."

Emma hiccupped a sob.

"This monstrosity might stop growing at any moment," Henry said, "but we won't know until it does."

"Look," Tom said, "if it comes to—well, if we're forced to abandon the structure, I'll give you a call. Unofficially," he added, "as a friend."

Henry nodded. "Thanks, Tom. I appreciate it. Let's get out of the way, darling," he said softly. Emma squeezed her eyes shut, aware of the cacophony of sound in the darkness behind them, and without a word allowed Henry to lead her through the cottage.

MONDAY

HENRY'S CELL PHONE CHIRPED from the bedside table. They'd both been subliminally anticipating the sound. Emma never slept well in hotel rooms and she'd barely been able to quiet her mind through the night's excruciating string of endless minutes. Not yet six-thirty, the faintest haze of morning daylight seeped through the curtains.

Curled in a fetal ball beneath the starched white sheets, Emma heard Henry say, "Yes, of course we will. We'll be right there." His words reminded her of a man who'd lost a friend or loved one—and so unlike Henry to sound helpless, the forlorn cadence of his voice bringing her to tears.

In the Volvo, they held hands without speaking. Two Highway Patrol cars blocked Tully Lane, rack lights animating the early twilight in dancing pastels. Their street wasn't long; three homes lined the left side, three on the right, their own cottage occupying the far end of the cul-de-sac. In the brightening murk, Emma could see something awry—the little house's roof sagging grotesquely near the center pitch.

She was afraid they might not be allowed to pass, but one of the Highway Patrolmen said, "Mr. Doogan?"

Henry nodded.

"Please follow me."

Police cars and several fire vehicles crowded the sidewalks. Tom met them at the foot of their driveway. He looked tired, his chin stubbled, his once crisp tan uniform dirt smudged. A sweat stain formed a dark V against his neck and back. "I'm so sorry, Emma. Henry. There was nothing we could do."

They heard the noise of timbers twisting, wrenching. The little house gave a shudder. The roof dipped more precariously near the center, wood crackled, and the entire rear section collapsed. The façade jolted backwards, as if being pulled inward by some gigantic unseen hand.

Glass tinkled and broke and Emma put a hand to her open mouth.

"How big?" Henry asked.

"Ninety feet across. Maybe a hundred by now. All I can tell you, it's *huge*."

"Has it slowed at all?"

Tom shook his head. "On the contrary, its growth rate has been accelerating. Shit, Henry, it just keeps—*swallowing* everything. The Cal Poly people have dropped seismic devices, but they're not telling us much. Less and less, it seems, as this thing progresses. We've turned off gas and water to the entire village. We've evacuated everybody within two hundred yards of the epicenter. I'm not sure what else we can do."

Henry nodded.

"The National Guard will be here at seven-thirty. Listen, I don't think you should hang around too long. I wanted you and Emma to be able to say goodbye. But now I need you to go back to the hotel. I'll call you the instant the situation appears to be stabilizing. Mr. Santiago has some forms you need to fill out. Contact your insurance company. I don't think—"

"Is this an act of God?" Emma asked, not speaking to anyone in particular. "I don't think we're covered by acts of God. I wonder if this *is* an act of God."

Tom shook his head. "Emma, I honestly don't know what it is."

The remaining structure cracked and splintered. The

last piece of the roof collapsed, pulling most of the façade to the ground. Dust plumed from where walls once stood. Only the front porch remained intact.

"Darling," Henry said, "it's time to go."

EMMA AND HENRY secluded themselves in their hotel room for the remainder of the day (the Del Mar Vista safely distant in neighboring San Simeon), numbly watching old movies on TCM and occasionally surfing the local news stations, but by Monday evening, the network affiliates were as of yet unaware of the hole eating through their village. Emma had tried unsuccessfully to catnap throughout the afternoon, Henry wandering to the window every now and then, peeking through the curtains without a word. *Waiting for the hole to appear,* Emma suspected. They'd ordered pizza for lunch and picked at leftover pizza for dinner, but otherwise the day passed uneventfully. Neither mentioned the prospect of ever actually *leaving* the village; Emma because she couldn't fully believe their cottage was gone and Henry because he knew better than to pop that particular bubble.

TUESDAY

EARLY TUESDAY MORNING, the *Santa Rosarita Sink-hole* made CNN Headline News. Shortly thereafter, the channel preempted normal programing for a Breaking News report. Helicopter cameras captured the yawning pit from various angles high above the village. Emma could no longer recognize their street. She saw no trace of their cottage. Mrs. Peroni's house was also gone, as was the Vargas's home—their neighbors to the south. Two others as well. Where those five homes once stood, only a yawning black chasm remained. Tully Lane ended in a jagged edge of crumbling asphalt, void of vehicles. It appeared as if the entire village had been evacuated.

A man wearing a blue FEMA jacket officiously told a CNN reporter, "What we're possibly seeing here is a unique example of pre-volcanic seismic activity. Traditionally the Earth's crust is forced upward by magma rising in the mantle, or else elevated by cooling lava flows to create igneous rock formations. Mount St. Helens, for example, or Kilauea. Japan's Mount Fuji. Those peaks typify our definition of what a volcano would appear to be. In this case, it's feasible to assume that an enormous flow of core magma has found a soft spot or perhaps a capture chamber in the upper mantle. This is obviously causing the ceiling, the top layer of crust, to collapse as the magma rises. The activity we're witnessing is still in early development, but we should not discount the possibility of an eventual eruption."

"My God," Emma said. "A volcano birthing in *our* backyard?"

"Someday we'll have an incredible view," Henry replied with the hint of a smile. Despite her anguish, his comment prompted a sudden laugh. Emma reached over and squeezed his hand.

Later that morning, the networks began mentioning the Santa Rosarita sinkhole, although they imparted no new or relevant information. Emma and Henry watched the stories repeat themselves, interspersed with happy commercials about toothpaste and tomato sauce and women's designer jeans.

Emma finally stood up with a flourish. "I don't want to stare at this damned television set another second. Let's go home, Henry. Or as close to home as they'll let us."

"You sure you're up for that?"

"I have you, dear. What more do I need?"

"Agreed."

"I want to see this wretched hole for myself."

HENRY EXITED THE HOTEL parking lot and turned the Volvo onto the two-lane Cabrillo Highway that meandered the narrow grassy corridor between the sloping foothills and rock-strewn Pacific coast. They traveled less than a hundred yards before encountering two Humvees straddling the road, an oversized STOP sign positioned with unmistakable intent. Several soldiers—carrying *guns*, Emma observed—milled about, warily eyeing their approach.

Henry gazed past the roadblock, the empty road ahead. Usually on weekday mornings a steady stream of locals occupied this stretch of highway. He realized a similar barricade must be blocking the northern approach to their village as well, up near San Simeon. Henry could glimpse several hillside rooftops above the Monterey pine forest less than half a mile ahead. From here the village remained a picture-perfect community.

A soldier stepped toward them and raised a gloved hand.

Henry leaned out the open window and smiled at the young corporal. "What can we do for you?"

"Do you have business in Santa Rosarita?"

"We live here," Henry said.

Lived here, Emma thought morosely beside him, wondering if that was an important technicality or not.

"Can I see your driver's license please?"

Emma leaned toward the window as Henry fumbled for his wallet. "We know about the *hole*."

"Yes, ma'am."

The soldier briefly studied the license. Emma wondered if he knew that Tully Lane no longer existed. For the first time since she was a child, Emma contemplated telling a lie.

She smiled at the young man. "We're here to pick up my mother. She's quite elderly. She's living at the Atria Hills Assisted Living facility on Ocean Crest Drive."

Henry regarded her with a raised eyebrow.

"Mr. Atkinson is the manager at Atria Hills. He's insisted that we take her right away and move her to a safer location. You understand the urgency, don't you, sergeant?"

"Corporal, ma'am."

"An oversight, I'm sure," Emma said politely, not at all distracted by Henry's pained expression.

The soldier returned Henry's license. "I'm allowing you to pass this checkpoint, but I'd advise you to leave Santa Rosarita as quickly as possible. You may encounter police or National Guard roadblocks ahead and whether or not they let you through—well, that's up to them."

"Thank you," Henry said, counting the seconds until one of the Humvees pulled aside. He waved absently to the corporal and steered the Volvo through the checkpoint.

"My God," Emma said quietly. "They're carrying weapons, Henry."

"I suppose there's always a chance of looting."

"Well, they certainly won't be getting *our* good china," she said, verging again on tears. Emma's hand fluttered helplessly, motioning for Henry to hurry on.

They were stopped again at the Santa Rosarita exit, where Mulligan Road veered inland from Cabrillo Highway toward the village square—twelve tree-lined blue and white wooden structures that included three restaurants, a bar and grill, a wine-tasting room, two gift shops and a drug store. Emma counted *five* Highway Patrol cars blocking the bottom of the exit ramp. The dozen or so milling police officers looked even more grim-faced than the soldiers.

The closest cop shook his head and frowned. "Sorry, folks, you'll have to turn back."

"We *live* here," Emma told the officer.

"The town's been evacuated, ma'am. The highway's closed ahead as well."

"Can't you make an—"

"Henry?" called a voice. They shifted their gazes and saw Tom Harding amid the knot of policemen, stepping forward with an affable wave.

"Thank God," Emma breathed.

"It's okay," Tom said to the frowning officer. "Give us a moment, will you?"

Henry stepped out of the Volvo and the two men shook hands. "My Lord, Tom, what's happening?"

"The situation's not promising," he said quietly. Emma had stepped from the car as well, noticing that Tom had changed his clothes since their last meeting, and had maybe snatched a modicum of sleep. He looked suitably official today, clean-shaven, wearing his tan Smokey hat and mirrored sunglasses that winked back glimmers of morning light. A *professional* air amid all the Highway Patrol officers. Emma liked that. Liked knowing that Santa Rosarita had credible supervision.

"No one's getting through?" Henry asked.

"Cabrillo Highway's detoured north of Hearst Castle. To tell you the truth, we're not sure if there's going to *be* a highway much longer."

Henry and Emma glanced toward the ribbon of asphalt jutting between the town and the rocky bluffs that framed the ocean. Emma put a hand to her throat. "You mean the hole's going to reach the coast?"

"Appears that way."

"Those cliffs are granite," Henry said. "How in hell could it eat through solid rock like that?" Something large and considerably heavy rumbled and splintered, thundering from the direction of the village. A cloud of dust mush-roomed above the trees and rooftops, then dispersed on the gentle Pacific breeze.

"We expect the hole's southwestern perimeter to en-croach Pico Beach early this afternoon, by one or two o'clock," Tom said. "I suspect most of Santa Rosarita's going to become a lake shortly thereafter. That's our best guess."

"The town's been evacuated?"

"Pretty much empty, except for the geologists and civil engineers. We even have some NASA people on the ground. The Cal Poly people say the growth rate's still accelerating. What they're doing—well, it's all Greek to me, but we've lost nineteen structures already and that's in—"

"No, Tom, that *can't* be true," Emma cried out, staring past the deputy's shoulder, for the first time in her life frus-trated by the thick legion of trees shielding the village from the highway. "This morning on TV. We saw only five or six homes gone!"

Tom lowered his voice. "That was *yesterday's* feed, Emma.

The governor doesn't want people—" Tom's gaze darted toward the milling policemen, his voice a whisper. "Look, they don't want to start a panic. They've been replaying the loop since yesterday morning. There's no more Tully Lane, no more Elm Way. Not much of Ocean Crest or Dutch Arbor either. Almost a quarter of the town's gone. What's left are the homes on Pacific Drive, Sycamore and Laughlin, whatever remains of Mulligan and the highway."

"Just how big is it?" Henry asked.

Tom let escape a ragged rush of breath. "A few minutes ago, somebody mentioned the chasm as being over 500 feet in diameter."

"Five hundred?" Henry said, stunned. That's—" Using his architect's knowledge of spatial dimension, he quickly calculated. "—four and a half acres!"

"My Lord," Emma said, clutching Henry's arm, visibly shaken. "Somebody on TV mentioned a volcano."

"Nobody knows *what* it is," Tom said, "and I suspect nobody's going to know for a long while. But when it hits the ocean—they're anticipating some sort of tidal surge. A tsunami. It's probably going to take whatever's left of the village. Even the Guard's been given orders to pull out, once a shore breach appears imminent."

Tom glanced back toward the village. "Listen to me—there's nothing left to see. I suggest you get yourselves a healthy distance away from here until this thing stops."

Emma began to speak plaintively, but Henry's attention wandered, his gaze contemplating the scraggly slopes rising up a half-mile behind the village. Slightly to the south, Pino Caido Mill Road twisted and climbed into the Santa Lucia foothills. He and Emma had driven it many times before, never accelerating too quickly up the snaking ribbon of aging asphalt. Emma had occasionally painted Pacific sunsets from a dusty turnout above the village. Henry knew the old road was rarely used and little known, dead-ending at an abandoned lumber camp about four miles further east. Folks wanting to reach Highway 101—either heading toward Los Angeles or San Francisco—took Route 46 through Cambria or Hearst Castle Road to the north.

"No, no, Tom's right, dear," he said, brushing Emma's arm, silencing his wife mid-sentence. "We'll be leaving now. Thanks for everything."

She glanced at him curiously but, knowing Henry all too well, Emma simply offered the officer a mute smile.

Tom studied them from behind his mirrored Ray Bans. "Don't do it, Henry. Whatever you're contemplating, I'm sure it's dangerous. We've had no fatalities thus far and I don't want you two being the first."

"We'll be careful," Henry promised, stepping around the Volvo's open door. He dropped into the driver's seat, waiting for Emma, then quickly backed the car onto the empty highway. Emma cast a curious final glance at Tom, the deputy's expression dubious.

"Well?" she asked impatiently, once Henry had pointed the Volvo south

"The mill road," Henry said.

"My God, yes! But Mulligan's blockaded. How do we even—?"

"Remember the firebreak, south of Becky Farber's property? We walked it last year."

"Picking raspberries," Emma said, nodding.

"If you recall, it connects to Pino Caido at the foot of the mountains."

"Yes, *yes*," Emma said. Henry slowed the Volvo. She looked back, aware that they were beyond sight of the police cars. Ahead, no more than a half-mile, she saw the Humvees at the National Guard checkpoint.

The little unmarked dirt road jutted off to the left, unobtrusive and unguarded, shrouded in thick patches of berry bramble.

"Won't the soldiers see us turning?"

"They'll probably assume we're an official vehicle, doing something suitably officious."

"And if they don't?"

"Being the military, I suspect they'll have to wait for orders. They won't abandon the checkpoint."

Henry's logic made sense. He braked, carefully checking the empty stretch of highway before turning onto the dirt road. Emma held her breath, gazing south, expecting a flurry of motion. But the soldiers remained at their post.

The Volvo bucked and shook for several minutes as Henry traversed the rutted trail with methodical deliberation. Eventually the firebreak swerved upward and turned onto paved and pitted asphalt—Pino Caido Mill Road. Henry accelerated into the foothills with a racing heart, the Volvo's tires squealing. Emma realized this was no time to be squeamish. No time to be lecturing Henry about slowing down or minding the sharp curves. Henry was already her hero.

THE OLD MILL ROAD twisted and turned inland. For much of the drive they were unable to glimpse either the ocean or Santa Rosarita below. Emma recalled a specific turn-off, a narrow patch of grass that afforded a magnificent view of the Pacific. The spot couldn't be much farther ahead. She fidgeted, itching with anticipation.

"Almost there," Henry announced, the road veering sharply to the west. Free of impeding forests or slopes, both the ocean and the village emerged below them. The grassy overlook appeared on their left.

Emma barely waited for the Volvo to stop. She dashed around the car, excitement and fear churning within her stomach like a bad meal.

She'd always been captivated by the gently curving horizon; an endless, sapphire blue realm that reached to the sky. But today, she looked down and gasped. The gaping hole astounded her.

"My God, Henry. I had no idea!"

"No idea," he echoed, his voice strangely devoid of emotion.

The chasm appeared nearly a quarter-mile in circumference, Emma estimating the missing expanse that stretched between Nuevo's Drug Store and the Seaside Café, a distance she'd frequently walked. From this height they could peer several hundred feet into the unfathomably smooth, cylindrical cavity that the hole had become. They spotted a dozen or so distinct striations in the layers of earth and rock—eons of geological history implausibly visible to the naked eye.

They could hear a distant, continual rumbling of loosened soil and the gnashing of falling boulders echoing from somewhere deep below the shrinking remnants of Santa Rosarita. Every few seconds, a fresh vertical slice of earth peeled away and slid downward into the abyss.

Some hundred so feet beneath the hole's surface, a coal black impression of an ancient ship began to materialize, its mast a stump but otherwise distinctly a sailing vessel. A priceless secret buried for centuries, Henry realized, below their very noses. It looked like a Norse longboat—impossible, wasn't it?—but too quickly the rotted timbers splintered and the ship disappeared into unseen depths.

"Isn't it odd?" Emma remarked. "This large, yet the damn thing's still perfectly round. That doesn't make sense. A hole this size should be anything but *tubular*, Henry. It's too damn perfect. Like some invisible drill boring directly into the Earth."

"Exactly what I was thinking."

"A black hole?" she wondered aloud.

"I believe a black hole would have consumed the entire earth in a flash," he told her, wondering if black holes even existed. But he was fairly certain that *any* sort of cosmic collision would not exhibit such slow and methodical destruction.

"This is so surreal, Henry. Beyond comprehension," Emma said.

His thoughts too chaotic for words, Henry merely nodded.

After a moment of further contemplation, Emma said, "I think—I think we should have dinner in Cambria tonight. Wouldn't that be nice?"

Henry wasn't certain if the vision below had proven too overwhelming for Emma's mind to cope, or if she had merely grown hungry. Emma's thoughts could often turn on a dime. Startled into silence, he said nothing until Emma's gaze met his, her expression cautiously expectant.

"All right," he agreed with a forced smile.

"Maybe we can stay a few days in one of those little waterfront motels on Moonstone Beach. I'd like that."

They leaned against the Volvo's hood and watched a single row of military helicopters arrive and hover for quite some time. One maneuvered ominously low, disappearing into the hole for several minutes before eventually reappearing, rapidly gaining altitude. Emma's gaze followed the craft and then drifted to the horizon. How complacent, how normal, the distant world seemed—until the echo of rending wood and shattering glass pulled her attention back to the gaping pit. She shuddered, imagining half the village already in shambles, deep within the bowels of the earth. She pictured her fat kitchen gnome lying in tiny fragments and put a hand to her lips, biting hard, not wanting Henry to see her cry again.

The helicopters finally departed, having accomplished nothing that either of them could fathom. Like bees, Emma thought, scurrying from a honey pot they could not possibly hope to access.

For the next few hours she and Henry watched the gradual disintegration of Santa Rosarita from their hillside perch. Home after home capitulated, as did the quaint blue and white buildings that constituted the center of town, first along Main Street and then Pacific Drive, until little of the village remained. The café was one of the last structures to fall.

From this height, they were aware of how quickly the hole's growth appeared to be accelerating, the chasm easily half a mile in diameter by now. Huge portions of land tumbled, the advancing rim greedily erasing the existence of everything in its way. Emma watched an entire house collapse in a handful of seconds.

"The National Guard's leaving," Henry said, pointing.

The Cabrillo Highway roadblock was indeed dispersing, the Humvees heading south.

"I can't believe they're abandoning us," Emma replied, her tongue clicking.

"Probably setting up a barricade near the park."

San Simeon State Park stood at the north end of Cambria, less than two miles down the highway. "There's no other access north of San Simeon Creek Road," Henry said. "They'll set up there. Not a soul will get through."

Emma nodded, briefly silent, looking at Henry with dismay. "Do you think they'll evacuate Cambria?"

"I don't believe so. My Lord, I can't imagine a sinkhole *that* large." He stared off to the south, then added, "No, no, darling. Cambria will be safe."

Shortly after one o'clock, the western edge of the hole encroached upon Cabrillo Highway. For a brief while the asphalt held, but cracks and depressions quickly formed, several yards of pavement twisting downward like hot taffy. Eventually, the road tumbled.

"Good God, that was fast," Henry said.

They could see how trivially small an area remained between the chasm's western edge and the granite cliffs rising beside the ocean. Soon a large section of solid ledge cracked, falling away with an enormous rumble. Seagulls took flight, circling and crying their alarm.

Emma stepped closer to the cliff's edge. "Henry, it's almost to the beach."

Henry stepped beside his wife. He noticed the upper strata of the hole turning pale brown, then nearly white. A streaming cascade of sand fell into the abyss.

The ground shook beneath them. They glanced at each other and waited.

"Earthquake," Emma remarked finally.

"The tremors are only going to get worse," he supposed, watching the hole's curved rim advanced along the beach. A wave broke upon the soft sand, then another. A third, finding no shoreline, lapped at the nothingness and spilled downward. Other waves rose slightly, then dropped into the depths. Within moments, a steep V formed by eroding sand funneled a solid sheen of water, like a slender Tahitian waterfall. The width of the downpour expanded, several feet wide, eventually several yards, tumbling with graceful nonchalance into the chasm on whatever mysterious journey toward its unseen bottom.

"What now?" Emma asked.

"Like Tom told us, darling, Santa Rosarita will very soon be a lake. Although I suppose a cove or bay would be more technically accurate."

"Rosarita Bay," she whispered absently, as if in hopeful anticipation.

Henry could only imagine the volume of water already consumed; easily thousands of gallons a second, he estimated. Soon the hole had cut so deeply into the Pacific that the width of the falls dwarfed even Niagara. A rainbow arched majestically above the carnage.

He waited, expecting any second to see a frothing blue surface rising out of the blackness—*ending* this nightmare, Henry hoped, once and for all.

They watched for another several minutes in vain. "No, this isn't right," he said finally. "A hole that size should have filled by now."

"Where's it all going? The water?" Emma asked.

"Underground tunnels maybe," Henry speculated, not quite believing his own assumption. A large, fat-bellied helicopter approached again from the north and hovered. Something dropped from beneath its fuselage, a small drone of some sort. A dozen antennae protruded from the device and they stared, fascinated, until the gismo descended below their view.

"They still don't have a clue, do they?" Emma remarked.

The aircraft banked and veered away, retreating again to the north.

"I don't think—"

The ground shuddered again, a much stronger tremor. The mountains groaned and shook, sending small rocks clattering around them.

"My God, Henry," Emma said, pointing. He followed her gaze. They'd been so transfixed by the waterfall that they hadn't noticed the hole's progression toward the foothills. A quarter mile farther north, the rim had reached the base of the Santa Lucias. Henry wasn't worried—a great deal of rock remained between the mountains and the expanding chasm, but Emma grabbed his arm and said, "Henry, our little *road!*"

He observed the hole's edge advancing toward the dirt firebreak. Barely a half-mile separated the chasm and their escape route. Under the circumstances, he felt it best not to linger.

"Time to go, darling."

They stood and the ground shook a third time. Against the foothills to the north, a landslide of loosened soil slid into the abyss.

Henry drove with caution, painfully aware of the seconds ticking away as the Volvo snaked down the mill road. Small stones and pebbles trickled from the higher peaks, several pinging the hood or rattling against Henry's door. Finally, he veered onto the dirt road toward the highway.

The hole was no longer visible behind a gently sloping carpet of sage and grass. Henry's gaze darted repeatedly to the edge of the road. He worried that, too late to react, the chasm would abruptly appear—the road ahead crumbling—and devour the Volvo. But within moments they had traversed the firebreak without incident. A gradual upward slope brought them to the edge of the Cabrillo Highway and Henry braked the car. From here they saw the missing stretch of asphalt and the absent crescent of ocean; an optical illusion where both earth and sea had vanished. Whatever disruption that was occurring on the sea floor had created a monstrous swell of surf, rising precipitously before disappearing into the void.

Emma squeezed his hand anxiously and Henry swung the Volvo south toward Cambria, accelerating gratefully onto the empty highway.

HENRY'S ASSUMPTION had been correct. A National Guard barrier had been erected at the northern edge of Cambria. The soldiers seemed surprised to see a car approaching from Santa Rosarita and waved them through without comment.

Emma was startled to glimpse a big, armored monstrosity of a tank with a long gun barrel sitting idly at the side of the road. South of the barricade, several TV trucks and a dozen Highway Patrol vehicles lingered in disarray. The frenzy of people that Henry and Emma expected to find here was conspicuously absent.

"It's a different world," she remarked.

Emma noticed a smattering of sails on the distant horizon, as if this terrible thing that had devoured the village did not exist here. She shivered, imagining some hapless sailor confronting the gaping chasm, swallowed into the abyss before he could even begin to maneuver his craft to safety. But the Pacific remained in blissful repose. Looking back to the north, she saw fingers of rock descending into the sea. Higher outcrops of grassy foothills prevented the curious from gaining any real knowledge of what lay beyond. Maybe the Cal Poly people, or the media, had assured the town that such a catastrophe could not possibly stretch this distance. Emma took momentary comfort in that notion, half able to convince herself it might be true.

"To Moonstone?" Henry confirmed.

Emma nodded and forced a smile. "That would be lovely."

A two-lane ribbon—Moonstone Beach Drive—veered off the Cabrillo Highway and draped the coastline for several miles. A host of casual, pine-shrouded hotels flanked the road's inland edge. To the west, the beach remained pristine, a simple wooden boardwalk snaking along the edge of the cliffs. Henry and Emma had walked these beaches countless times. The town, a thriving artist's colony, had sold many of her watercolors and several of the gallery owners warmly welcomed her work.

Emma realized she could not bear the thought of losing Santa Rosarita *and* Cambria. The hole, she knew, would have to stop short of this town. If not, she feared the loss of her sanity.

A few sightseers strolled casually along the beach and many of the hotel lots appeared full. Henry felt as if he had awoken from a nightmare, once again embraced by the idyllic reality that he and Emma had shared for so many years.

"Here?" he suggested, coming upon a terra-cotta colored hotel he knew Emma had enjoyed in the past.

"A little farther south," she suggested.

Henry nodded, aware of her concern. He drove on and they chose one of the more modest lodgings at the farther end of the beach.

He parked the Volvo and took his time lugging most of their possessions into the room. Only then did Emma notice that Henry had packed her paint kit in the trunk. Her eyes brimmed with tears.

"A necessary item for any bohemian's journey," he told her.

Emma kissed him fiercely.

They had not eaten since early that morning—Earl Gray and leftover pizza crust. "Do you want to dine inland?" Henry asked, feeling the first pangs of hunger beginning to stir.

"Let's stay on the coast." Emma's brow furrowed. "I want to keep an eye on things."

They walked the hundred yards or so to a wooden planked restaurant overlooking the Pacific, selecting an outdoor patio table where Emma could indeed keep an eye on things. The descending four o'clock sun threw a silver sheen against the horizon. A scattering of patrons conversed quietly at the tables around them. A seagull squawked overhead.

"It's all so... so horribly *normal*," Emma said, inhaling

a breath of salty air.

The waitress appeared. "Beautiful day, isn't it?" She smiled at them.

Henry returned her smile, aware of his wife bristling. Emma stared at the young woman for a long moment and said; "Tell me, do you even know what's happening up in Santa Rosarita?"

"You mean the sinkhole? Yes, isn't it *terrible*." The waitress continued to beam at them, as if that was that. Henry and Emma glanced at each other, perplexed by her innocence.

"Would you like a cocktail?" the young woman asked.

Frowning, Emma said, "Don't you think it might be—"

Henry raised a finger. "A bottle of your best Sauvignon Blanc, please."

Emma cocked an eyebrow and Henry winked at her. "Every sunset deserves a celebration, dear. Wouldn't you agree?"

She held her tongue, eyeing the ocean again, which continued its seemingly untroubled existence beneath the blue veil of afternoon sky.

They ate calamari and salmon steak over asparagus, sipping their wine, aware of the horizon turning ochre, then tangerine, then a fiery blood red.

"It *is* a beautiful day, Henry," Emma remarked finally.

They started back toward their hotel, Emma slightly inebriated, resting her head on Henry's shoulder. She felt drained of energy, as if the past three days had been a marathon and their hotel room, just ahead, the finish line. She closed her eyes, content to let Henry guide her way. For a minute or two, safely cocooned behind her own eyelids, she managed to forget about the hole.

They made love later that night, with the windows open and the surf crashing in a rhythmic pulse only yards away.

They lingered, lost in the unhurried pleasure of each other's company. Afterwards, in the dark, Emma softly sobbed. Henry wrapped his arms around her and whispered soothing assurances, waiting until she had cried herself to sleep. He slept as well, and soon enough his dreams consumed by those same horrors that now plagued his waking life.

WEDNESDAY

HE AWOKE TO SOUNDS of hubbub in the street, people chattering and cars passing hastily outside their window.

Emma opened her eyes to find Henry, wearing only his boxers, standing at a window, peeking through the curtains. Alarmed, she sat up. "What's happening?"

"A commotion, it appears."

"Is everyone leaving? Is it an evacuation?"

"No. People appear to be heading north."

"*North!*" She flung the covers aside. "The hole, Henry. Maybe it's stopped growing."

He shrugged. "I believe we should go find out."

They dressed quickly and stepped from their room, the warm, salty air reeking of promise. Small knots of people hurried north along the road, some gesturing, some calling loudly to others. Henry and Emma walked to the cliffs above the beach, aware of a distant throng of bystanders crowding granite outcrops much further north.

"Oh, *no*, Henry," Emma said, pointing.

Well below the horizon, not far beyond the rocky shoreline, they watched a tremendous, frothing current surging in the direction of Santa Rosarita. Loosened fronds of seaweed drifted north. The waves that normally tumbled so uniformly upon Moonstone Beach pulled slightly, as if sucked from beneath by an invisible force.

"It's still expanding," Emma moaned.

"Why in God's name are they heading north?"

"Excuse me, do you know what's happening?" Emma asked a passerby.

The man offered an animated shrug. "I heard the military's pulled out. The road's open through to Santa Rosarita."

"Really?" Emma frowned, knowing that couldn't be true. The road to Santa Rosarita no longer existed. "Something's not right," she told Henry.

"Let's take the Volvo and see for ourselves," he suggested, aware that they would be far safer on the road than on foot. Emma nodded excitedly.

They hurriedly returned to the hotel and Henry grabbed his car keys, then waited impatiently as a half-dozen vehicles zipped by, heading north. They made the far end of Moonstone Beach Drive within minutes. The small park at the northern edge of the Cambria was already crowded with hundreds of onlookers gazing toward the horizon.

"Should we stop?" Emma wondered.

"We'll have a better view further ahead. Especially if the roadblock's gone." Henry pulled onto the coast highway and accelerated quickly as cars behind him blared their horns. The road snaked ahead through a thick outcrop of pine forest, the roadblock was longer evident, the tank and Humvees gone. Cabrillo Highway appeared wide open.

"I don't understand," Emma said.

"Perhaps they've moved the blockade." Traffic threaded as far north as they could see. Henry was aware of the absence of oncoming traffic, the southbound lane suspiciously empty. "Maybe it *has* stopped growing," he offered.

"I want to see for myself."

Unfettered by oncoming traffic, several cars behind the Volvo swerved and sped dangerously past on Henry's left. Within moments a steady stream of traffic occupied both the north and southbound lanes. Returning would no longer be an option, and Henry's foreboding returned.

A half-mile later, around a bend in the highway, they came upon a stalled line of automobiles. Henry braked, as did the cars rushing past on his left. He heard tires squeal behind him and a cacophony of irate horns. Directly ahead, the Cabrillo Highway had become little more than a confused parking lot. A half-dozen cars had attempted to veer off the asphalt and sat mired in the sandy, grass strewn embankments on either side of the highway.

Henry regarded their own unfavorable vantage point with a touch of anxiety; a slope gradually rose ahead of them, blocking any possible view of the hole's approach. They could glimpse the rush of frothy ocean directly opposite his window, but otherwise they were blind to what might be happening over the hill.

"Can we turn around?" Emma asked.

"Too late," Henry said, peering into the rearview mirror. Two long lines of traffic had already closed in behind them. As he watched, several other vehicles attempted to U-turn. They too quickly sank into the sandy scrub.

"Shit," Emma said with uncharacteristic frankness.

Henry unlatched his door. Startled, Emma reached out and clutched his arm.

"No use just sitting here," he told her, nudging his glasses. He waited until Emma nodded in sullen agreement.

They stood beside the car, taking stock and inhaling exhaust-infused air, aware of the nervous murmur of the people around them. Henry cocked his head, cognizant of the gently crashing surf—but also conscious of an ominous, barely perceptible hiss, like air escaping from a valve.

Far behind them they heard an abrupt squeal of brakes and the inevitable crunch of metal. A horn blared for several tortuous seconds.

"So much for any chance of a hasty retreat," Henry remarked.

"Should we abandon the car," Emma wondered, "and hoof it back?"

He wasn't certain, although he knew the Volvo was no longer an option. His curiosity piqued, Henry motioned toward the slope ahead. "Why don't we take a look first?"

Hesitating only a second, Emma nodded and reached for his hand. Together they wove their way through the stalled traffic, moving past groups of people also proceeding northward on foot. They topped the slope, disappointed to discover an even larger hill directly beyond, its crest crowded with spectators. Henry started forward but Emma's grip quickly anchored him in place. He sensed her resistance and nodded to himself. *Close enough.*

From their current vantage point, they could see the partially eaten Santa Lucia foothills far to the northeast, rising above the coastal meadows. Every few seconds slivers of solid rock crumbled and slid from view with a loud, echoing crackle that sounded like thunder.

Ahead, to the west, Emma could likewise discern the hole's edge—the Pacific Ocean bizarrely ending in a half-moon sheen of falling water, a deluge that dwarfed any waterfall she could have ever imagined. Like some apocalyptic Bosch painting, the sea simply fell away into the void. Thick curtains of mist rose above the rim, concealing much of the distant horizon.

Henry's attention, meanwhile, had remained on the automobile-cluttered highway. The crowded ridge ahead gave him a certain measure of relief. Several people stood atop their cars, some taking photographs. Selfies. Mementos. Henry considered *that* endeavor particularly absurd.

A flurry of overhead movement snagged his attention. He squinted skyward and watched a squadron of helicopters approach from the north. The eight aircraft broke formation and hovered—*like numbers on a clock,* Henry realized, aware of the circle in the sky gradually expanding, the aircraft likely revealing the hole's perimeter. He frowned to himself, noting the proximity of the nearest aircraft—almost directly overhead.

Amid distant screams and cries of alarm, a surge of panicked motion convulsed the ridge line. People began to run from the slope, scattering willy-nilly around the twin lines of stalled traffic. Within moments, the crest had been abandoned.

Despite the curious stillness of people chatting incessantly around them, Henry realized the merging crowd would prove chaotic. "Time to go," he told Emma, tugging at her hand, leading her through the milling uncertainty of lingering onlookers. Once clear of the crowds, Emma began jogging back toward the Volvo. Henry followed. A steady trickle of latecomers from Cambria stymied their retreat; dozens of people moving excitedly northward in the direction of the advancing hole.

Emma reached out several times, saying, "No, no, go back. Please, go back!" The people she touched wrenched away, their inquisitiveness bordering on hypnotic frenzy. Henry saw the fear in their eyes and recognized the insatiable urge that compelled them to glimpse what he had already seen. He knew that if someone had attempted to divert his curiosity twenty minutes ago, he would have ignored their warning as well.

They reached the Volvo, ensnarled in the surrounding stalled traffic.

"Henry?"

He shook his head. "We don't have a choice, Emmie. We'll have to head back to Cambria on foot."

She nodded and they broke into an easy jog, occasionally weaving through knots of uncertain pedestrians. They'd covered barely a quarter-mile before Emma slowed her pace. She glanced over her shoulder, huffing, and Henry realized that she'd been crying.

"My God, Henry," Emma said breathlessly. "What's going to happen?"

"I honestly don't know."

"It's *not* a sinkhole, Henry. It's something else. Something horribly else."

Something else indeed.

They began to run again, and almost immediately heard a siren approaching from the south. Henry could see a red SUV in the distance, a giant Ford Expedition with oversized balloon tires bouncing through the sandy chaparral along the side of the road, headlights flashing, roof rack blinking red and blue.

He would not have given the vehicle further notice had not Emma suddenly stopped short, waving her arms frantically. Henry looked again, noting a small oval of surprise on the driver's face.

Tom Harding.

The red Expedition swerved toward them, the siren's piercing wail abruptly whining down to silence. Tom scrambled from the driver's seat, stood and waved to them from outside the driver's door.

"Emma! Henry! Come quick."

They ran toward the vehicle. "Oh, Tom! *Tom!*" Emma said, shaking her head. "There's nothing you can do up there. Turn around."

"Get in."

They did so, gratefully, Emma in the back seat and Henry riding shotgun. Tom looked gaunt, austere; as if all traces of his warmth and personality had drained from his persona.

"She's right, Tom," Henry said. "There's not a thing you can—"

"Listen up," he snapped. "There's something you both need to know."

Henry closed his mouth.

"The hole. It has no bottom."

Henry and Emma glanced at each other, their expressions wavering between confusion and disbelief.

"NASA's been dropping sensors every couple of hours. Around midnight, they dropped a drone almost two vertical miles. Then it disappeared."

"Crashed?"

"According to the NASA people, impact sensors would have transmitted some sort of data analysis, if even for a fraction of a second. That didn't happen. It didn't crash. It didn't land. It ceased to—to *be*. Early this morning, the last drone descended. This was a live video feed—nearly three miles deep. A device the NASA people expected to retrieve. Three miles down and it vanished."

Emma reached out and touched his arm. "It doesn't make sense."

"Dr. Conrad says a hole this deep, at sea level, should be radiating a slight amount of ambient core heat. Something tangible," he said. "An instant before the transmission ended, the reading dropped to zero."

"Centigrade?" Henry said. "*Freezing?*"

"Or else immeasurable. Something beyond our ability to record."

"And the ocean?" Emma asked.

"A hole that size, consuming that much water, should have filled up within the first half-hour. They're saying—" Tom hesitated, frowning toward the unseen chasm. "They're saying the Pacific's already dropped several inches. The entire fucking Pacific Ocean, Emma. It's falling into nowhere."

Emma glanced at Henry, then back at Tom, her mind unable to accept the officer's words. "I don't understand."

"No one does."

"But...what's going to happen?"

As if in response, the ground trembled. The idle row of

cars beside them skittered and bounced on the pavement. Several people hurrying past them staggered drunkenly.

"There's more," Tom said. "The hole's growing at a rate of—hell, I don't remember the technical terms. *Exponentially*, I guess. But as of this morning, the circumference was expanding about three miles an hour. Twice the speed of last night. Three miles an hour," Tom said again. "That's about walking speed. What happens when we can't outrun this thing?"

Henry opened his mouth but couldn't find the answer. He watched the crowd— most running or jogging now, but a few on bicycles—pass the red Expedition, fleeing toward Cambria. Far to the northeast, a gigantic pillar of Santa Lucia mountainside tumbled. The resulting grumble shook the vehicle.

"Jesus," Henry said. "We've got to move."

"Yeah, let's roll," Tom agreed. The SUV fishtailed as he spun a tight 180. Tom floored the vehicle, barely a moment before he grimaced, his eyes on the rearview, his foot mashing hard against the brake pedal.

"God*damn* it."

"What's wrong?"

Tom hadn't taken his eyes from the mirror. "Henry, you and Emma need to bail out."

"What?" Emma asked from the back.

Henry turned to look behind his wife and saw a white minivan maybe thirty or so yards behind them, weaving precariously through the narrow embankment beside the highway. The van lurched sideways, snagged a rocky outcrop and spun its wheels. Doors swung open and several people—Henry saw children—spilled from the vehicle.

"Good Lord," he whispered.

"Now, *please*," Tom said.

They stepped from the Expedition. Henry glanced again

toward the stalled minivan. *There's no time,* he wanted to say, but he could muster neither the words nor the cowardice to say them. He slammed the door.

Once again, the big Ford spun a tight half-circle in the sand, then braked. The passenger window descended midway. "Henry? Don't stop at Cambria. Get as far away as you can, as fast as you're able. Come back only when you're absolutely sure it's safe."

Henry nodded and watched the SUV surge forward, cutting through the bramble, gaining speed. The people standing beside the stalled van waved frantically. Henry felt Emma's hand tugging at his sleeve; they began jogging again toward the highway, peering back every few seconds as the Expedition advanced toward the van. They scrambled up an embankment toward solid pavement. Emma stumbled on a loose stone, slipping, cutting her knee. Henry groped for her, helping her to her feet. When they looked back toward the hole, the white minivan and Tom's SUV had vanished.

"Oh, *Tom,*" Emma whispered, then turned again and ran.

THE STALLED COLUMN OF AUTOMOBILES trailed another quarter-mile on the highway toward Cambria. Emma saw several people sitting in their idling automobiles—*waiting for what?* she wondered in amazement. Waiting to be *rescued?* Emma stared at their vacant expressions, horrified to realize that she found no pity for these people, these strangers without enough sense to flee. She felt no heartfelt yearning to pull them from their automobiles, shake them and point them back toward safety.

Or had they already accepted some inevitable fate that she could not comprehend? Is *that* what she saw in their frozen gazes? Pity for her—pity for anyone who still considered running to be a viable option? A car horn blared behind her, its sound quickly fading. Emma imagined both automobile and driver tumbling into the void.

She and Henry finally reached the tail end of the traffic jam. A serious accident had occurred—an SUV lay flipped on its roof, broken glass strewn about. Several other cars sat crumpled and damaged, all abandoned now, effectively gridlocking the highway. Just behind the accident, a tow truck tugged a midnight blue BMW from its sandy lair. A small knot of people lingered near the truck—awaiting their own vehicles' imminent liberation from the embankment, Emma assumed. Further south, the highway, by now devoid of traffic, lay tangled with scattered throngs of people scurrying both toward and away from the advancing hole.

She cast her gaze over the Pacific, startled to notice an enormous frothing wave, a tsunami perhaps fifteen feet high, stretching far to the north. She stared, aware that the wave didn't appear to be moving toward them, its crest instead *bending* to the north, creating a wall of water that swirled at least partially around the expanding hole, like tub water spiraling down a drain. No less startling, the clouds above the hole had begun to mirror the same spiral vortex, as if the hole exuded a palpable force above the ground as well.

Ahead, the group awaiting the tow truck's progress met them with anxious glances. Henry quickened his pace, gesturing to a large, bearded man giving the driver a wad of cash. A skinny mechanic in faded overalls struggled to unhook the man's BMW from the truck's towline, the vehicle straddling the highway.

"Excuse me," Henry said. "Our car's trapped up ahead. Can you give us—"

The bearded driver shook his head, waving off Henry's advance. "We all got troubles, buddy."

"Please, just into Cambria?" Emma pleaded.

But the bearded man had already turned away.

"*I* can give you a lift."

Emma turned toward a thin Black woman watching them, clutching a purse tightly with both hands. The woman nodded toward a Honda, mired only a few feet from the edge of the highway. The mechanic, towline in hand, was moving quickly toward her vehicle, gesturing to the truck driver with a flurry of hand motions.

Frowning, Henry watched the bearded man climb into his car. The BMW's engine purred to life, the driver returning Henry's gaze with an angry glare.

"Thank you so much," Emma told the woman. "You don't know how much we—"

Tires squealed. Emma's gaze followed her husband's, in time to see the blue BMW abruptly back-ending off the highway, its rear wheels spinning a foot or so above the embankment. The bearded man accelerated, and the car's engine screamed, the BMW going nowhere. They could hear the bearded man's muffled howl of rage.

"Hurry, *hurry!*" a waiting women sobbed.

Henry's attention shifted. The hole had begun to munch away the top of the nearest slope—creating an odd optical illusion that he had no time to further contemplate, the chasm's leading edge perhaps no more than a hundred yards away. Bits and pieces of visible ground disappeared every few seconds. A small oak tree toppled. Two automobiles at the lip of the remaining highway upended, then slid into the abyss. Henry felt an icy shiver float up his spine. *Too close,* he thought. *It's gotten too close.*

The skinny mechanic, glancing furiously toward the approaching abyss every few seconds, secured the towline to Honda and waved to his partner. The little car crawled easily out of the soft sand and coasted midway across the highway.

"Two hundred dollars," the Black woman said to nobody in particular, fishing through her purse.

"No, no, please allow us," Emma insisted.

The mechanic popped the towline and the freed Honda coasted several feet down the empty highway. The skinny mechanic gestured again, calling to the driver, "We got time for one more, Curtis! Come on, gimme some slack, gimme *slack!*"

"We better go," the Black woman said.

The bearded man had already scrambled from his BMW and advanced upon the mechanic with a menacing stride. "You're not finished! Get my car on the fucking *road.*"

The mechanic, hook in hand, was directing the tow truck driver with a series of hand motions. "You're done, mister."

"I paid you!" the guy yelled.

"Yeah, well get in line. You'll pay us again, too."

The bearded guy grabbed the mechanic's shirt, pulling him nose to nose.

"Wait your turn!" the mechanic screamed, attempting to break away.

Henry heard the fear in their voices, could see it in their eyes. The bearded guy clenched a fist and popped the mechanic in the jaw. The mechanic went down, eyes rolling.

The tow truck driver yelled "Hey!" and jumped out of the cab. The bearded man spun around, fist cocked again. Henry watched the truck driver raise an arm—fleetingly aware of the pistol—then blinked twice as the little gun made a hollow, metallic *pop.*

"What?" Henry said, unaware he had spoken aloud.

The bearded man staggered backwards, arms flailing like a broken marionette. A ribbon of blood corkscrewed below his left shoulder. He fell against the side of the overturned SUV and slid to the ground. He stared curiously at the pavement between his outstretched legs.

"My God," Henry breathed.

The ground around them rumbled and shook.

"We gotta bail, Curtis!" the mechanic yelled, scrambling to his feet. The tow truck driver remained frozen, staring in disbelief at what he'd done.

The mechanic grabbed the driver's extended arm. "Curtis! Let's bolt, dude!"

The hole's edge yawned closer, now no more than seventy, sixty yards away. The air crackled and hissed around them—the approaching cacophony of sound unlike anything Henry had ever heard.

"C'mon, c'mon," the mechanic screamed. "There's no time left! Hop on, we're getting the hell outta here." Those still remaining for their stranded cars clamored toward the truck.

The bearded man moved his mouth, but no words came.

"Can you walk?" Henry asked, his attention drawn to the cascading flow of blood drenching the bearded man's shirt, his expensive grey slacks. Another stain had begun to pool on the asphalt. Henry crouched and gently touched the man's knee. "Can you stand up?"

The man said nothing. Henry stared into his vacuous gaze. He had never seen a man die and the moment struck him as utterly surreal.

"Henry?" Emma asked curiously, her voice ethereal, floating anxiously behind him.

"He's gone, Emmie."

"We need to leave. *Now*," the Black woman insisted.

Henry stood, shaking his head, still contemplating the bearded man as he and Emma climbed into the back of the Honda, aware that the man would be alive had he not poked his shovel into the soft soil a few days before. The Honda lurched forward, gaining speed, maneuvering around knots of people hustling back toward town. Henry glanced back to see the blue BMW and its dead driver disappear from view.

They drove several moments in silence, the woman glancing repeatedly into the rearview. "My name's Kayla," she said finally. "My husband's stationed at Point Magu. He'd blow a fuse if he knew I came all this way for a look," she said, but with a dry tone that implied she would have done it anyway.

Kayla asked them where they were headed. To the hotel, Emma assumed, although without their Volvo, that was a silly assumption. Henry asked if she would mind dropping them on Main Street.

Emma glanced at him with a raised an eyebrow and Henry said, "I recall seeing a car lot near the corner of Main and Bridge. That might be our best bet."

Kayla nodded solemnly and peered a final time into the mirror, sighing with visible relief.

THE CAR DEALERSHIP stood where Henry remembered. He thumbed through his wallet, talking stock of their resources. About three hundred dollars and several credit cards. Sufficient, he thought. Certainly for a down payment. Kayla pulled into the lot, smiling wanly as they climbed out.

"Can I give you some money?" Henry asked, feeling embarrassed, but wanting her to know they'd appreciated her kindness.

Kayla shook her head. "I'm a good Christian woman, just doing what the Lord would expect of me."

"Thank you." Emma squeezed the woman's hand; they said goodbye and watched Kayla pull into the empty street without a backward glance. Toward Point Magu, Emma assumed, or hopefully somewhere *much* farther south.

A sign above the asphalt lot at the corner of Main and Bridge proclaimed, "Honest Dan's Used Cars." Perhaps two-dozen cars of clean but dubious quality dotted a larger, mostly empty parking lot outside a small white office. Colored balloons fluttered in a gentle westerly breeze.

They found a single employee inside the office, a middle-aged man with a large gut, wearing a plaid jacket. The quintessential used car dealer, Henry thought. The man sat at a metal desk, scribbling on a large cardboard sheet. Most of the office lights were out.

The man looked up, smiling pleasantly. "You folks in need of a car?"

"That's right."

"Get caught up in that mess to the north?"

"Yes, we did," Henry replied.

"Hardly the first. Sold off half my inventory in the last half-hour. Thought I'd seen my last customer."

Henry realized their impending transaction would likely be expensive.

The man stood. "I'm Dan," he said. "Honest Dan, the sign says. More like Skedaddlin' Dan if you want to know the truth." He smiled again. "Any particular color you have in mind?"

When Henry and Emma glanced warily at each other, the man allowed himself a laugh. "Sorry. A pitiful attempt at humor, I'm afraid. Help yourself. You'll find keys in the ignition. Jump in whatever you fancy and then get yourselves the hell out of Dodge."

"Pardon me?" Emma said.

"Pick one," Dan said with an affable wave toward the lot. "Doesn't matter to me. Most of 'em got at least half a tank."

"I don't understand," Henry said.

Dan laughed again. The sound struck Henry as genuine, not that of a man not hiding a pea, asking them to choose a walnut shell for a price.

"Look, folks, I'm walking out that door in a minute or

two and don't intend to return. Don't expect anything to return to. So help yourselves to whatever you find on the lot, okay?"

Dan held up the cardboard sign written in thick black marker: FREE CARS! KEYS INSIDE. TAKE ONE AND HEAD SOUTH!!!

"Tell you what. Come back in a week. If the lot's still standing, we'll negotiate a sweet deal, how's that?"

"You're *giving* us a car?" Emma said, still not comprehending.

"Don't know what I'm giving you," Dan said. "A head start maybe. I've got a low mileage Lexus out there, and brand-new tires on the Subaru. Gas might be a factor if you're looking to get out of California. Me? I'd take the SUV. It's a Volvo, only three years old. GPS is wonky—still waiting on a part," he said with an apologetic frown, "But otherwise it's in good shape."

"A Volvo?" Emma asked hopefully.

"There's an old Camaro 8-ball if speed's of the essence, but she sucks gas like a Hoover." Dan moved from the desk and taped the cardboard sign to the door.

"You'll have to excuse me. I'm off to fetch my wife. We live off the 46. I suspect we'll be heading somewhere else PDQ."

"The hole," Emma said. "You don't think it's going to stop growing?"

"I'm not about to take any chances. I got a brother, lives south of Cheyenne. I think we'll keep an eye on it from up in Wyoming for a while. Listen, I'd stay off the 101 South. Traffic's congested all the way into L.A. You won't even make it through Santa Barbara."

Henry nodded. "Are you sure we can't give you—?"

Dan held out one hand, a halting gesture like a traffic cop, and Henry closed his mouth. "Two kinds of folks you'll likely meet at a time like this," Dan said affably. "Those who tend to give and those who tend to take. I'd like to believe I'm one of the givers."

Dan smiled again and continued through the door. "Like I said, keys are in the ignition. Good luck to you both."

They watched Dan walk across the lot and jump into a burgundy Lincoln.

"I don't know whether to laugh or cry," Emma said.

From the north came a resounding echo of stone cracking—a loud boom that rattled the windows and shook dust from the ceiling of the little room. Emma grabbed for Henry's hand. "Let's go."

They found the Volvo, an unobtrusive silver-blue SUV hatchback that Emma liked immediately. As promised, they found the key fob on the front seat. Henry got in and the car purred to life.

"Will we miss having GPS?" she wondered.

"There's only one direction that holds my interest—and that's *east*," he said. "I don't think we'll have any trouble in that regard."

"What about our things?" Their hotel room was a mile or so away, uncomfortably toward the north.

"It would be wise to fetch them," Henry told her. "We have all our clothes, toiletries. My cholesterol pills. Your oils. Basically, everything we own."

"Is it safe?"

"Good God, let's hope so," Henry said, nervously nudging his glasses up the bridge of his nose. He accelerated the new Volvo, cautiously swerving around those people on foot—mostly heading south—but finding few cars and almost no traffic. He pulled into the hotel parking lot and said, "Can we be packed and out of here in two minutes?"

"It's a skillset I believe we ought to hone," Emma replied tartly, already midway out the door.

THE CHEVRON STATION at the south end of town had closed but, as promised, the Volvo's tank was half full. Two hundred miles, Henry figured, give or take. They sped south on the Cabrillo Highway and turned east onto Route 46 at the edge of town. They passed sloping green meadows and spindly forests, anxiously aware of the Volvo being one of the few non-emergency vehicles they'd seen on the road. Emma turned on the radio and found a slew of emergency broadcast channels announcing major traffic jams on both Highway 101 and Route 405 to the south. Similar congestion bottle-necked the roads heading north toward San Francisco. Looters had been arrested in various abandoned areas and National Guard troops were being deployed in several cities. Emma discovered an intermittent jumble of evangelists spouting Bible verses and celebrating the coming apocalypse with a blustery, told-you-so cheeriness.

"The good Lord never mentioned a *hole*," Emma shot back at a smarmy voice repeatedly touting God's promise to smote sinners. She thumbed the radio off in a huff and for the next several miles they traveled the road in stony silence.

Route 46 eventually merged with Route 101 North, where they lingered in near-standstill gridlock for a desperate ninety minutes. Three miles later, at Paso Robles, Route 46 again branched eastward. Henry maneuvered the Volvo amid a frenetic stream of traffic, passing miles of farmland and sporadic cattle ranches.

Emma eventually turned to Henry and said, "How far have we gone?"

"From Cambria?" He glanced at the odometer." Just about forty-two miles."

"Do you think it's safe to stop?"

"I don't think so, Emmie. Not yet. Not until we've had confirmation that the hole's no longer expanding."

She nodded slowly, watching the passing scenery for another few minutes. "Do we even know where we're going?"

Henry laughed uneasily. "No. I don't have a clue."

"How unlike us."

How unlike us to have dug a hole that's swallowing up our lives, he thought, but decided to keep it light for Emma's sake. "Do you have any recommendations?"

"I don't. I'm not fast on my feet. I'm not cut out for—for this sort of nomadic behavior."

Henry's gaze drifted to the distant green hills. "It's pretty, you know."

"What's?"

"All of it. The mountains. The pastures. We're *tourists,* darling. Had we taken this road a month ago, I wouldn't have bothered a passing glance. The beauty would have swished by in a blur. Now, every mile feels priceless."

"I don't think I'm capable of enjoying this, Henry. Not now. We're not tourists. *Orphans,* perhaps."

"Life's a journey, isn't it? What else would you call this moment?"

She nodded, aware that her husband's words had placated her rising panic. Emma had never thought of herself as a pessimist and felt embarrassed that she'd been reduced to seething over her loss.

"We've never been to Sedona," she offered abruptly.

"Arizona?"

Emma nodded. "Red rock canyons. Remember that National Geographic special we saw last month? It's a very spiritual place. It would be a lovely setting for me to paint."

"We'll have to take Route 5, then drop down and connect with Interstate 40. I wish we had GPS now. We'll have to skirt the Mojave. We won't make much headway today," Henry said, aware that the waning afternoon was already upon them. "Likely we can be there tomorrow."

"Thank you for bringing my paints, Henry. You're the

sweetest man who's ever lived."

"Some things neither God nor giant pits shall cast asunder."

She reached for his hand. Quietly, she said, "Maybe I should paint the cottage. A tribute of sorts."

"That would be nice."

They found an open Texaco station near Blackwells Corner, a little oasis a dozen miles farther east. *The middle of nowhere*, Emma thought. She scoured the station's attached convenience store with a keen eye, purchasing a bag of pretzels, several fresh apples, protein bars, vitamin pills and plenty of bottled water.

Henry filled the Volvo's tank and spent another sixty dollars on necessities; a flashlight, first-aid kit and a pocket knife, thinking about the future for the first time since leaving Santa Rosarita and realizing how unprepared he and Emma were to leave the life they'd always known. Almost an afterthought, Henry asked the woman behind the register for a road map.

"Map?" the woman replied with a crooked grin. "Never once got asked for a map in the eight years I've worked here. Earlier today, I coulda sold a couple of dozen easy—but no, we don't sell maps. But a word to the wise? Stay off Route 5. Been listening to the emergency band since this morning. A coupla big-rig accidents south of here. Too many crazies on the road, I guess. Too much commotion. You want my advice?"

Both Henry and Emma nodded vacantly.

"Forget the 5 and get yourselves along to Route 99—another forty or so miles down the road. Head south to Bakersfield and then hook up with Route 58. From what I hear, it's slow-an'-go but still moving. Once you hit Barstow, take either 15 North toward Salt Lake or eastbound Route 40 all the way to the Atlantic."

They thanked her and left. A few miles later, they crossed over Route 5 and Emma confirmed the woman's sage advice. The highway traffic below them had stalled, bumper-to-bumper as far south as she could see.

"We're not prepared for this sort of thing," she said, barely above a whisper. She wondered if they were all little more than rats scurrying to-and-fro aboard a sinking ship. She closed her eyes, not quite sure that the darkness behind her eyelids was the safest of places to be at the moment, but aware that she had nowhere else to hide.

As PROMISED, Route 99 proved hectic. The Volvo maintained a mostly steady 40 mph pace for much of their trek to Bakersfield. In three hours they made Barstow—by now the eastern horizon beginning to darken. Henry glanced at his watch, suddenly aware of his own fatigue. They'd put almost 260 miles between here and whatever it was that had eaten its way through Santa Rosarita. A safe enough distance, he hoped. For now.

"I believe we should find a motel, hunker down early and try to get a full night's sleep," he told Emma.

"Are you sure, dear?" she asked cautiously. "We still have a few hours of daylight remaining."

"I think it would be prudent. I'm not sure how safe the roads will be after dark. Not to mention that the later we stop, the less chance we're likely to find accommodations. Besides, part of me wonders if we'll wake tomorrow morning and discover this whole nightmare over. Until then, I think we could use a good recharging. Maybe a stiff drink to boot."

"Whatever you think is best. Truth be told," Emma said, staring out the window, "a nice pinot noir wouldn't hurt."

By the time they reached Barstow, a dry, dusty old mining and pee-stop town, traffic had slowed considerably, a

complication that only reinforced Henry's determination to
settle down for the night. They found a comfy-looking Best
Western on the eastern edge of town within easy access of
Route 40. Henry felt better about leaving the bulk of Barstow—with its tangle of converging roads—behind them.

"In case a quick getaway is in order," he told Emma. She
promptly agreed.

Henry's decision to stop proved prudent. Inside the lobby, a half-dozen people preceded them at the check-in desk
and within minutes a dozen others, wide-eyed, exhausted,
waited behind them as well. *Funny,* Emma realized, that nobody spoke. No casual smiles. No idle chitchat about the
weather or travel destinations. *Is it that all we're so afraid,* she
wondered, *or merely the standard societal procedure for polite
people in peril to remain quietly aloof?* Either way, Emma realized that she was in no mood for small talk either, and stood
morosely silent beside Henry until the hostess waved them
to the counter.

By happenstance, a manager appeared from a doorway
behind the counter, surveying the crowd that now extended beyond the front doors. "Only three rooms remaining,
folks," he announced. "I'm sorry, but most of you will have
to look elsewhere tonight."

Amid the moans and grumbled curses behind them,
Henry and Emma exchanged a relieved glance. Without
a word, the hostess stoically accepted Henry's Visa card.
Watching her check them in, he suddenly wondered how
much longer his credit would be accessible. Tomorrow, before they left town, he'd try to find an ATM and withdraw
as much cash as possible.

Once inside their room—their earlier thoughts of alcohol and food all but forgotten—Emma couldn't help but
hurry to turn on the television. They sat at the foot of their
bed and watched a video drone replay the collapse of the

sprawling Hearst Castle from several hours before. They stared into a receding tunnel of raw earth before darkness engulfed the chasm. A swirling mist blanketed most of the waterfall that fell into the void at the hole's western edge.

A somber female voice announced that hole had consumed much of the Santa Lucia range. Cambria was gone. So was San Simeon. Morro Bay was being evacuated.

"It's a weapon of some sort," Emma said. "Something the military was testing."

"In our backyard, darling?"

Emma put a startled hand to her lips. She'd forgotten that this monstrosity was indeed *their* hole. It seemed a lifetime ago that Henry had been planting her little orange tree.

"Is it our fault, Henry? Did *we* do this?"

"I don't see how. Had a meteor fallen directly on our heads and destroyed the cottage, the entire village—well, I don't see any difference. I wouldn't consider it *our* meteor."

"Do you really believe the hole has no bottom?"

"I can't imagine that. I think we simply don't know what's down there."

Emma fell silent. Then, "Is this the end of the world, Henry?"

"Not at the moment it isn't."

"We were much too complacent. *I* was much too complacent," she amended. "I should have done more."

"You're a good person, Emmie. You've done so many selfless and noble things as long as I've known you. I'd even dare to call you inspirational."

Emma shook her head. "I'm glad now," she said, her eyes filling with tears. "Glad that we never had children. That we never could. I would be a basket-case, watching this unfold with children about."

"Harsh reality has never spared the young," Henry offered, "but I'm glad too, dear. Happy it's just you and me.

Like Bonnie and Clyde," he added with a soft smile.

She smiled too; despite the fear roiling about her stomach and the aching despair of watching this thing on television, eating away so many people's lives.

A grim-faced woman appeared on the set, explaining that much of Los Padres National Forest had flooded. The tsunami that had risen the day before continued to spill millions of gallons into the low coastal areas north of San Simeon.

"At least three thousand are feared dead," the reporter continued. "Another hundred and fifty thousand are missing and unaccounted for. However," she added officiously, "with such a massive exodus from the Pacific Core Breach, it is impossible to determine how many people are on the road, seeking shelter to the east. Cell phone service west of the Southern Rockies is sporadic and vast areas are reportedly without service."

Neither of them had heard a death count before now. Emma thought of Tom Harding again, the deputy's face drifting into memory and Emma suddenly appalled that she'd barely given his death a second thought. Mortified by her own callousness she began to cry, silently mourning Tom. Mourning the three thousand nameless others.

Emma's slight frame convulsed, bathed in the glow of the harsh television light. Henry draped an arm around her shoulder and when he was certain she had finished, he said, "Are you hungry?"

"Not at all."

"Then I think it's time we get some sleep, darling."

Eventually she capitulated and closed her eyes, sleep intermittently coming and going before the new day dawned.

THURSDAY

BY MORNING, PASO ROBLES, Atascadero, Morro Bay and Lake Nacimiento were gone; San Luis Obispo was threatened and mass evacuations were underway far to the south and east. Some 995 square miles of California's land mass had been gobbled by the hole. An equal swatch of ocean had likewise disappeared. The hole's circumference had doubled over the last eight hours—meaning its surface area had *quadrupled*—and its growth rate continued to accelerate.

Numbed to the carnage, Henry and Emma lay in bed, sipping on motel-room coffee and listening to the drone of CNN. A reporter mentioned the Pacific Core Breach several times that morning, a phrase Henry remembered from the previous night. Someone had actually *named* the wretched thing, as if somehow a label made its existence more palatable to the masses. More easily digested. Less lethal.

Measurements taken in San Francisco Bay and in Los Angeles Harbor revealed an eight-foot drop in water level, grounding freighters and beaching fishing fleets. The Pacific coastline was being redrawn almost hourly, the newscaster said, and recent Atlantic tidal surges in Nova Scotia, Bar Harbor, Cape Cod and Miami had flooded enormous tracks of land. Westbound tsunamis in the northern Beaufort Sea and south of Cape Horn had killed or displaced thousands.

An estimated four hundred and fifty thousand people had been displaced and the forced evacuation of millions would soon begin in San Francisco, Sacramento and Los Angeles. Head counts, body counts, the MIA—existing statistics were unreliable and new data would no longer be forthcoming. The disaster was progressing too swiftly, said the newscaster, to be tracked with any sense of accuracy.

"This is bigger than the Ebola outbreaks," Henry remarked. "Bigger than the Indian Ocean tsunami, the Fukushima 'quake, even the damned virus. Bigger than all of those catastrophes combined."

"Maybe those were merely test runs," Emma said. "Maybe the cosmos has been planning its retaliation since God knows when."

"Retaliation?"

"For our apathy. Our ungratefulness. Our disrespect toward a planet that has nurtured us for eons."

He might have smiled a week ago at his wife's sudden consternation. Emma was not a rebel. She was considerate but not fanatical. They recycled, but not meticulously. They turned off lights and turned down heat and, long ago, Emma had eschewed paper and plastic bags, cycling through several sturdy canvas sacks to cart their groceries home from Soto's Market in Cambria.

So Henry found it odd that Emma viewed the hole as some type of cosmic retribution, or that the earth might implode beneath them to spite their species' gross negligence. He found perverse humor in the way his wife sometimes attempted to grasp at straws—yet he soberly reminded himself that he could offer no more rational an explanation.

They remained in a trance-like stupor in front of the TV until Emma glanced up, aware of morning sunlight beyond the window and noted the time. "It's already past nine," she said, startled.

"So much for our early getaway," Henry replied, well aware that he'd spent close to twenty minutes standing beneath a steaming shower earlier that morning—and giant holes be damned.

"Why don't I take the helm," Emma suggested with a

firm resolve, beginning to gather her belongings. "I'm sure you could use the respite. You can spell me behind the wheel this afternoon, if you'd like."

"Alright," Henry agreed and followed his wife dutifully out the door. The hotel's parking lot, crowded the previous evening, lay empty—the Volvo the sole remaining vehicle. Glancing around, Henry discovered the little town all but abandoned, chagrined to discover his resolve crumbling like a sand castle beneath a brisk onshore breeze.

They made the Arizona border, just east of Needles, a few hours later. Traffic had proven surprisingly light for much of the way, although Emma felt a sense of solidarity among the few other vehicles occupying the same stretch of highway. She'd been relieved to have left California behind. Traffic maintained a steady pace and Emma noticed the Highway Patrol occasionally pulling speeding drivers over and ticketing them. She felt a burst of optimism to observe such a normal slice of life.

SHE CAME UPON THE TWO HITCHHIKERS a little before ten. Henry had been napping off and on in the passenger seat, his nylon jacket rolled into a ball against the side window. He awoke, sensing the Volvo braking.

He sat up and snatched his glasses from the glove compartment. Emma smiled timidly. "Oh, hush," she said. "It will be alright."

Hush? Henry wondered. The Volvo stopped. Before he could fully grasp the situation, Henry heard the sound of footsteps slapping against asphalt. The rear door popped open and dry heat washed through the car's interior. He peered back to see a young couple, barely out of their teens, both in blue denim; a bespectacled girl with long auburn braids and a scruffily bearded boy, dreadlocked, wearing a loose-knit rainbow-colored snow cap.

"Blessings," they chirped in unison, smelling faintly of pine and cinders, of too many unwashed days on the open road.

Henry stared at Emma who warmly replied, "Hello."

"Thank you so much," the girl said.

"You're most welcome." Emma cast a brazen *see there?* look at Henry before pulling back onto the highway.

They introduced themselves as Victoria and T.J. They'd hitchhiked from Escondido, a small city east of San Diego. Coincidentally, they too were on their way to Sedona. Victoria told Emma and Henry that they hadn't caught a ride since yesterday morning.

"Everybody's afraid," T.J. said.

"Afraid?" Emma asked.

"Of me and Vicky being part of the Apocalypse."

Henry shot Emma a dismal *see there!* look of his own.

As if reading their silence, T.J. laughed. "No, man, not like literally. But the Core Breach is something new and unexpected, so it breeds fear. People see me and Vicky on the side of the road and since we're new and unexpected, they're afraid of *us* too."

Emma glanced pleasantly into the rearview. "Well, we're quite delighted to meet you. There's bottled water, crackers and fruit in the back. Help yourselves."

They did so, timidly at first, then more eagerly. Spurred on by Emma's polite encouragement, they buzzed through several pieces of fruit and several bottles of water without speaking. Henry realized they'd likely been on the verge of starving and felt a sense of compassion chip away at his lingering pessimism.

"You two have family in Sedona?" he asked.

"In a way, yeah," Victoria replied, she and T.J. gazing curiously at each other. "I mean, I *guess* that's what we are. Well, soon enough, anyway."

"We're heading to the Red Rock Circle Jump," T.J. added.

"Circle Jump?" Emma asked.

"There's going to be a thousand of us," Victoria said excitedly, "and maybe more."

"Red Rock Canyon, man," T.J. said. "It's south of Sedona but an easy hike from town. And not a coincidence that it's arriving at the stroke of midnight."

"A full moon, too," Victoria remarked.

"A full moon at the stroke of midnight," Henry echoed. "Sounds rather ominous." He turned in his seat to see both T.J. and Victoria frowning—not angry expressions, but the two hitchhikers sharing a subtle disappointment.

"You, um, *do* know about the hole?" Victoria asked suspiciously.

Despite their sour expressions, Henry couldn't help but smile. "Yes, my wife and I have made its acquaintance."

"You know about the timeline, don't you?"

"Timeline?" Emma asked. She unconsciously slowed the Volvo, her gaze in the rearview intently focused on the young couple.

"Its ETA," Victoria said.

"The leading edge," T.J. added. "It's been tracked on like a thousand different Websites. The hole's leading edge will reach at Lake Havasu by tomorrow morning. ETA for Sedona is 11:58 tomorrow night. And thanks to you, we'll be ready."

The car was silent for a long moment. Emma spoke first. "Victoria, what's a Circle Jump?"

But it was T.J. who replied, his brow furrowed, eyes blazing belligerently. "We're not going to run from it anymore."

"We're gathering with people who believe the Core Breach is something cosmically significant in our lives," Victoria said. "Like a new beginning. A rebirth. The Circle Jump, it's like a consecration."

"Oh, Victoria," Emma whispered softly.

"We're gathering on the eastern rim of the canyon to hold hands and sing. Whatever happens—we'll all going to experience it together."

Henry cringed. "You're can't be serious."

"There have been several Jumps already," Victoria said. "One in Big Sur, another one near Ojai. Others are scheduled in Taos, San Antonio and at Shambhala Mountain."

"You're *throwing* yourselves into this thing?" Henry asked, incredulously.

"No," Victoria said. "We're *communing*."

Henry barked out an uncharacteristically harsh laugh. "Well, you're crazy, the two of you."

"And you're not?" T.J. said. "Trying to run from it? To where? What happens when you get to Mexico or Canada or Florida and there's nowhere left to escape—you and fifty million other people squeezing into that last little speck of solid ground? People are going to be clawing and pushing and killing each other over a few inches of concrete. Tell me that's *not* crazy?"

Henry closed his mouth, pondering T.J.'s words and his own burst of anger.

"It could stop expanding," Emma offered softly, with a hopeful smile into the rearview. "At any second, this entire horrible nightmare could end."

"It won't," Victoria answered.

"How can you be sure?"

"We've heard that the Breach has no bottom."

Emma and Henry exchanged another glance.

"It's some sort of consciousness," Victoria said. "It's not even a hole, not in its own dimension."

"And what dimension is that?" Emma wondered, one eyebrow curiously arched.

"It's hard to explain. We're not even sure ourselves, but

it's something I want to believe. That I have to believe. You've heard of Eduardo Fuentes, haven't you?"

"We haven't," Emma admitted.

"He's a Brazilian base jumper."

"A what?"

"He parachutes. But instead of jumping out of airplanes, he jumps off skyscrapers and bridges. He jumped the Colca Canyon in Peru last year. Blyde River in Africa. He jumped the hole yesterday morning."

"He had a GoPro mounted on his helmet, and a microphone," T.J. said. "We watched him jump."

"You couldn't really *see* anything inside the hole," Victoria added, "but Eduardo documented the experience for several minutes. We listened to his podcast."

"The last thing he said," T.J. told them, grinning at Victoria, "he told everyone that he didn't feel alone. He felt safe and that, whatever the hole was, it was somehow aware of him."

"He was laughing when he said it," Victoria added.

"Like the Breach wasn't some horrible, evil thing."

"And you believe that?" Henry asked.

"It's what a lot of people believe. So instead of fearing it, we've chosen to embrace it."

"Good Lord, but that's insanity," Henry said. "What proof do you have?"

T.J. shrugged. "Proof? When was the last time you saw God, huh? There's a lot of people running around, praying right now to a God nobody's ever seen. What's the difference?"

"Some might call that *faith*," Emma ventured.

"And that's what Vicky and me have. Faith. Total belief in something that's real and here and now. Something that maybe just misunderstands us or isn't even aware that it's hurting us."

Henry said nothing, staring ahead at the passing landscape. He couldn't dispute T.J.'s logic. He and Emma were not practicing Christians; as of late he wasn't sure they could call themselves practicing *anything*. He'd always felt they were spiritual people, respectful of humanity, of nature, aware of the intrinsic difference between right and wrong. He doubted he could still tick off all Ten Commandments, but he felt confident that he and Emma had violated none of them. If any God, Christian or otherwise, discounted their respect for life on Earth, Henry knew that Emma would have a few choice words for that particular entity at whatever eternal gate she happened to confront.

They continued their drive toward Flagstaff with little more than polite chatter between Emma and Victoria. None of them again mentioned the hole. Emma and Henry switched seats at Ash Fork. The desert had gradually given way to green pine forests, exquisitely beautiful country, each of them lost in their own thoughts. Henry turned the Volvo south and veered onto Route 89A, a magnificent ribbon of two-lane asphalt that snaked down through a red rock canyon.

Silent all the while, Henry had tried to concoct a dozen different strategies to keep these two wayward kids from throwing themselves into the chasm, but none of his thoughts gelled. He still could not quarrel with T.J.'s oddly profound logic; that if current circumstances persisted, sooner or later they'd have nowhere to run. A week or two from now, if the hole continued to exponentially expand, *then* what?

The sandstone canyon walls grew steep. Beneath the early afternoon sun, the wind-sculpted outcrops appeared to pulsate with a majestic chalky rust-red glow. Victoria and T.J. *oohed* and *awwwed* from the back seat, holding hands and sometimes pointing with childlike exhilaration. Henry found it hard to believe that they were on a suicide mission.

A few miles further south, traffic slowed to a near crawl. Small knots of hikers trekked along the edge of the highway, heading south toward Sedona. Before long, the trickle became a single, steady stream on either side of the road. Victoria's excitement bordered on the sublime.

"There, man!" T.J. said, pointing toward a turnout ahead. The canyon widened to reveal a meadow filled with ramshackle tents and smoldering campfires. A road sign pointed to Slide Rock Picnic Area. Hundreds, maybe thousands of people, milled about.

"The rendezvous!" Victoria chirped.

Someone had bothered to construct an enormous quilted banner that read: *Red Rock Canyon Circle Jump* in large, cheery letters. Henry edged off the highway, careful not to bump passing limbs or backpacks. He nosed the Volvo between a haphazard clutter of cars and vans. Their windows down, they could smell chicken cooking and heard wisps of joyous music; mandolins and flutes and, further off, the rhythmic beat of many drums, the meadow vibrating with a palpable, carnivalesque excitement.

"Oh my," Emma said, unprepared for such revelry.

The people streaming past the Volvo were mostly young, smiling and laughing. Henry spied a bare-chested, long-haired young man standing amid the crowd, who held a large square of cardboard over his head that read FREE AYA-HUASCA!

"I don't want any," he heard Victoria whisper fiercely. "I want complete awareness, T.J. I want to be in total communion when we jump!"

Henry found a vacant patch of dirt and braked the Volvo. Victoria and T.J. spilled from the car and stood for a moment in silent gratitude, their young faces lifted upward, bathed in sunlight. Henry watched them with a quiet reverence—admittedly the closest expression to prayer he had observed in a long time.

Emma stepped from the car. Henry remained unmoving, fixed in his seat, hands knuckle-white on the Volvo's steering wheel. He simply could not accept T.J. and Victoria's intentions. Capitulation had never once entered Henry's mind.

Emma, Victoria and T.J. stood in a long embrace beside the car. Henry heard both women simultaneously laughing and crying and, to his surprise, saw T.J. stepping around the car. The boy thrust his palm through the open window.

"Hey, thanks for the ride, man."

Henry realized that he could not ignore the gesture. He nudged his glasses against the bridge of his nose and stiffly obliged T.J. with a firm handshake. "Look, I apologize for my attitude, son. I cannot fathom giving up. My instincts are geared toward survival. I don't know how to act otherwise."

"No worries. When your time comes, you'll know what to do."

"Well, I certainly won't be *jumping*."

T.J. smiled. "Maybe we all jump, sooner or later, in our own way. We'll meet again." He squeezed Henry's hand warmly and trotted back toward Victoria, who affably waved goodbye. Henry managed a feeble smile in return and watched them wander off, arm in arm, quickly lost amid the denim and the sun-drenched sea of flowing hair and colorful hats. For a second Henry felt consumed by the energy that cracked and sizzled around the Volvo and, in that instant, he recognized the strength of its vibrant potency. He reached for the door handle, but Emma's door suddenly pulled opened, his wife sliding brusquely beside him.

Henry shook his head. "I don't under—" but silenced the thought, aware of Emma's tears. She grabbed his hand

and clutched tightly. He continued to watch the milling crowd, aware that T.J. and Victoria had already passed from their lives. Henry reached up and stroked Emma's hair.

When she was ready, she dried her eyes and regarded Henry with an embarrassed smile. "She called me *mother*."

Several minutes lapsed while Henry zigzagged his way clear of the haphazard parking area, and finally nosed the Volvo back onto the highway. They continued their descent into Sedona. Quite a few vehicles and a steady stream of hikers approached from the south as well.

"A thousand people?" he remarked. "There's got to be double that number already milling about. You mean to tell me all these people are simply going to jump to their deaths?"

Emma said nothing.

"Well it's crazy," Henry whispered to himself with a deft jut of his chin. "It's just insanity." They continued in silence toward town.

DOWNTOWN SEDONA appeared unexpectedly small to Emma. The main thoroughfare consisted mostly of brown and ochre-colored storefronts, adobe (or faux adobe, she suspected) boutiques and hotels peeking from behind clusters of pine and mesquite. Art galleries and trendy boutiques proliferated. Normally teeming with tourists, she presumed, the town appeared largely abandoned, most of the shops closed, storefronts dark, ominous. She saw clutters of cars parked around a smattering of Mexican restaurants and pubs—*typical*, she thought, although not disparagingly. She noticed numerous sandstone buttes in the distance and thought them breathtaking. Once upon a time she and Henry might have lingered amid such splendid beauty, but time was a luxury they no longer owned. She felt the weight of a sudden, dreadful despair, certain that these timeless formations would soon fall away into the cavernous void.

Henry turned off the highway, cruising past numerous other vacant storefronts. Aware of his wife's gaze flitting to the dashboard, he said, "We're well below a quarter tank."

She nodded with tightly pursed lips.

"Finding fuel is our primary goal."

"And we'll need a place to stay, Henry. Do you think the hotels have all closed?"

Before he could answer, and with an almost magical precision (in Emma's mind), the Arroyo Grande Hotel appeared on their right. Henry slowed the Volvo.

"Happenstance?" she wondered.

"Or divine intervention. Let's take a look."

The place appeared clean and tidy, the grounds meticulously manicured, the façade—Sedona's quintessential reddish-brown adobe—unremarkable but inviting. It was the sort of place Emma knew they would have chosen on an ordinary weekend here, shy of luxurious but comfortable. They saw only a few vehicles littering the parking lot and Henry braked the Volvo in front of the lobby.

"I see a light," she said. "Look there, someone's inside."

Henry locked the car. Emma slipped her hand into his and they passed through double glass doors into a room of dark wood and large prints of painted ponies and desert sunsets. The indoor air felt refreshingly cool—a welcomed blast of normality. Behind a dark wood counter, they encountered a pony-tailed, gray-haired man of about sixty, Native American, wearing a coat and tie.

"Good afternoon," he said pleasantly. A small brass name tag identified him as Roca.

"Hello," Henry said. "Might you have a room available?"

"A great many." Roca's voice carried both irony and a weary mirth.

"Do you have something around back? Away from the

street for one night."

"Fifty dollars, if you're paying cash. One hundred if you're paying with a card."

Emma wrinkled her brow. "Seems remarkably inexpensive."

"Two-fifty's the usual rate. Wasn't sure anyone would be showing up today," Roca said. "Yesterday by this time I would have turned you away. No rooms available until first light this morning. Night before last, I turned away maybe three hundred folks."

"We've always considered ourselves stragglers," Emma said with a smile.

"Are you folks here for the, um, jump?"

"Just passing through," Henry said without expression.

"Heading east?"

"That's right."

"Stay away from Albuquerque. Dallas and Houston, too."

"Oh?"

"Many of the major cities east of here have closed all access roads. Can detour around, of course, but the populated areas are keeping the Californian refugees out."

Refugees? Emma wondered.

"Wichita, Denver, Kansas City," Roca continued. "Too many people pouring in over the last few days, cleaning out stores, supplies. There's been some violence. A lot of killing, from what I hear."

"Thank you," Emma told him. "We'll keep that in mind."

Henry remained quiet, T.J.'s words—*People are going to be clawing and pushing and killing each other over a few inches of concrete*—already haunting him. He took his time, fiddling with his wallet, reluctant to part with his carefully hoarded cash. He handed Roca his Amex card.

"Oh, and I have to warn you," Roca said, "you'll be fetching your own towels and clean linen from the laundry room, just behind the office, first floor on the left. We still have electricity, hot showers, TVs and a nice sauna by the pool. Kitchenettes available in each room. You'll probably have trouble finding a restaurant open. I suggest you buy what you need in town, heat it up in your room. We used to offer a continental breakfast, but…" Roca's voice trailed off with a quiet acceptance.

"Are you alone here?" Henry asked.

Roca nodded. "Owner and manager. My nephew's keeping up with the maintenance, at least through tonight, but the staff's either long gone or home with their families. Didn't seem right, keeping people to work at a time like this."

"You happen to know any gas stations open around town?"

"Here and there," Roca said, "although fuel will be expensive. Tell you what. Get yourselves over to Heacliff's Hardware, just off Brewer Road. About half a mile north. Daryl Heacliff's a local; he'll stay open as long as he's able. Get yourself a siphon, a couple of sturdy flat-head screwdrivers and a few ten-gallon aluminum cans. All these folks heading off to Red Rock, they're not coming back. They're driving over in droves and they won't be using their cars again. Siphon as much gas as you can before you head out of town."

"Thank you," Henry said, unsure if he meant it or not. The world around him might already consider them refugees, but even so, he wasn't certain if he could stoop to petty thievery. Henry recognized his own reluctance as utterly naïve.

They checked in but decided not to loiter. Best not to unpack the Volvo either. Henry wanted to find gas sooner rather than later, and certainly before dusk.

But Roca had been wrong about Heacliff's store—they found the place closed and dark, its plate glass façade protected behind iron mesh. Further down the street Emma spied a Shell station, lights on, a one bay garage and tiny convenience store attached. Henry coasted to the nearest pump with a relieved grin.

"I'll check out the cuisine," Emma mused, spying a *One Dollar Jalapeño Donuts!* sign in the window. Henry nodded and swiped his credit card at the pump, then stiffened in horror.

"Holy mother of God."

Midway to the station, Emma turned.

"Twenty-five dollars a gallon."

"You want to try somewhere else?"

Henry shook his head, aware he'd find no place less expensive; he snatched the pump handle and reluctantly began filling the tank. "Wait a sec," he called. "I'll come with you. Let's see what *else* they can soak us for."

They found the station curiously unattended and frowned at one another. Henry called *"hello?"* and listened to the silence. He peeked cautiously into corners, but the station was empty. He shrugged to Emma and walked to the attached garage. The bay was vacant as well.

Henry returned to the convenience store. Emma had begun to fill a small canvas bag with water bottles, packages of dried fruit, crackers and nuts. She had thus far avoided the jalapeño donuts.

"They sell road maps," she shouted joyously.

Henry called out for an attendant one last time, then plucked another satchel from a rack next to the register and moved to the humming refrigerated case along the back wall. One section had been depleted. *No beer,* he realized. No ice either. He did notice three bottles of an unknown

Chardonnay—$3.49 a bottle—and contemplated the label with the disdain of a man who appreciated good wine. He nevertheless confiscated all three bottles. He added several cans of fruit juice and V8, several more bottles of water, and then strolled to where Emma waited at the register. He peered behind the counter and saw several crumpled Budweiser cans scattered on the floor, near a waste can brimming with empty Modelo bottles.

"What do we do now, Henry?"

"I'm not sure. I suspect the proprietor may be on a bender."

"Should we leave money?"

Henry couldn't remember stealing anything in his life, but he said; "I think the price of filling up more than compensates. Here, give me your bag. I'll put these in the car. Let's fill up two more. Two apiece."

"Henry?"

"We're not in Kansas anymore, darling. I suspect the rules of the game have changed. Unfortunately, I don't know what the new rules are yet. But let's err on the side of survival at least."

He walked to the car and placed the two bags in the back seat. The pump had cut off. The Volvo's tank had taken almost thirteen gallons. $324.88.

Henry returned to the convenience store and with sudden inspiration veered again toward the yawning garage bay. He found screwdrivers in an open toolbox, but no gas can. No siphon either. He did find a coil of clear plastic tubing and realized, in a pinch, he could fashion a crude suction device. He found an empty cardboard box and collected a roll of duct tape, cutting shears, several nylon straps and two cans of motor oil. In a metal wall cabinet beneath a crumple of dirty rags he discovered a small, grease-stained .38 revolver. He stared at the weapon for a moment of befuddled contemplation and then picked it up, aware that the gun felt profoundly odd in his grasp.

Emma would have been appalled of course, but he recognized their present situation as dire. He glimpsed bullets in the cylinder's visible chambers, although his knowledge of revolvers had now peaked. He grasped the concept of pointing and shooting—although he could not imagine himself ever *doing* so. Still, he could comprehend the potential depravity of a panicked population and to ignore the weapon on moral grounds seemed absurd. Henry snatched several rags and wrapped the little gun, pushing it to the bottom of the box. He would tell Emma at some point and trust she would not argue with his having taken such a precaution.

She met him in the doorway with two satchels filled with groceries. "Maybe we should take another palate of bottled water?"

"Yes, my love, let's take as many as we can fit."

"I feel downright sinful."

"That will change," Henry told her, "when you see the Visa bill."

THE ARROYO GRANDE HOTEL proved sufficiently comfortable that evening. Lying on a turquoise-and-peach quilted king-sized bed, they munched on nuts and sipped cranapple juice and, as had become their custom, watched CNN, contemplating the horror that had by now preempted all other programming.

The Pacific Core Breach had become television's solitary story—the ultimate reality show. A sequence of live satellite feeds from a hundred or so miles above Earth revealed a global anomaly that could no longer be considered an aberration, but rather its own epochal event. As if the earth were some cosmic apple being cored by an omnipotent, cosmic hand. An unseen voice announced the hole's circumference as having doubled over the last six and a half hours—and its growth rate continued to accelerate.

Against the chasm's expanding rim, they watched towns and forests, roads and mountains crumble and fall into the void. Without commercial interruption, they witnessed what the distant cameras revealed. At the top left of the screen, a massive, curving waterfall tumbled into an incomprehensible depth, its girth spanning hundreds of miles before vanishing behind an impossibly concave horizon.

"I don't think I recognize *any*thing of California," Emma remarked.

"There, near the bottom," Henry said. "That coastal dogleg to the southeast. Isn't that the L.A. area?"

"Los Angeles no longer exists, Henry. That's Baja, *Mexico.*"

What had once been the Sea of Cortez had become a sliver of receding water—little more than the width of a lake—between the Baja peninsula and inland Mexico. The peninsula itself had greatly expanded, having reclaimed many square miles of the dry Pacific shelf.

"Los Angeles is gone?" Henry said incredulously. "Yesterday morning it hadn't even reached San Louie. Can the hole possibly be expanding *that* fast? My God."

The satellite feed changed abruptly. They saw an unrecognizable land mass amid a deep blue sea. A new unseen voice said; "What you're looking at were once the seven Hawaiian Islands, four now as dwindling Pacific levels have connected Oahu, Lanai, Molokai and Kahoolawe. Much of Niihau and Kauai have been rendered uninhabitable, as surging eastbound tsunamis have passed over low-lying areas. Several dozen new islands have appeared on or near continental shelves. There has been no recent word from Japan and Malaysia. We've had reports that dry sea beds presently connect much of the Philippines and Indonesia.

"The Pacific's sea level has dropped one hundred and thirty four feet by last official estimate, although that figure is hours old and, at this point, the world's sea loss must be assumed to be far greater. What was once the largest ocean on the planet may soon be reduced to a series of large salt-water lakes, separated by newly surfaced mountainous land-masses.

"We've had no further ground reports of the Breach's leading edge as communications southwest of Las Vegas are non-existent. We've had no contact from California since three forty-five p.m., Pacific Standard Time. We're fairly certain nothing remains of the state south of Eureka. Nothing of southern Nevada. Seattle remains the only major West Coast city not yet on the federal evacuation list."

The screen blinked and from another orbital angle Henry and Emma peered into the expanding black pupil of a pristine blue-green iris. The similarity struck Emma with a physical jolt. "It's like an eyeball staring at us. Good Lord, Henry, turn it off. Please, turn it *off.*"

"There have been no confirmations," droned the TV's unseen voice, "of the Earth's axis having tipped six degrees to the southwest since yesterday morning, although if that's been su—"

Henry's thumb found the remote switch and the room blinked into darkness.

FRIDAY

DESPITE THE UTTER CERTAINTY of the hole's encroachment, Henry and Emma awoke late Friday morning, shocked to find that they'd slept almost ten hours. They decided to leave the TV off and, as previously proposed, Emma reconfirmed her desire to paint, a notion that struck them both as completely rational. He recalled those sublime days *before* the hole's appearance, when he and Emma would sometimes ponder as to how they'd spend their final days together, philosophizing over a glass of Merlot or two how important those last hours would be.

"I wish only to be at my easel when the meteor strikes," Emma would sometimes remark. "With you at my side, of course." It had always been a meteor in Emma's mind; not a flood or nuclear war, and neither of them had ever thought to consider a *hole*.

Henry surprised himself, driving leisurely that morning toward the majestic red rock formations that surrounded Sedona. That Emma *wanted* to paint filled him with a joyous sense of tranquility. The rising sun proved warming and comfortably familiar. Both nature's abounding silence and the absence of humanity's often boisterous presence provided a splendid ambiance.

They drove to an isolated area that afforded a splendid view of Cathedral Rock, an outcrop of red-brown sandstone that Roca had suggested they visit the night before. Henry helped Emma unpack her easel and paints, dismayed to remember that he had procured only three small canvases. At the time it had seemed a sufficient quantity. Emma, hugging him tightly in the dry Arizona air, told him that remembering her paints *at all* was a gift she would never forget.

She set up her easel and stripped off her cotton cover-up. Emma wore lavender running shorts and a black Lycra tank top. She had often admitted her preference for painting naked if not for the fear of being carted away to the loony bin by some startled forest ranger.

Ever the artist's husband, Henry had accustomed himself to solitude while Emma mixed and dabbed a multitude of colors to concoct a coherent image. Emma loved Henry's company, although of course she could never bear for him to *observe* her create. So Henry found a suitable rocky outcrop nearby and, using his canvas jacket as a pillow, opened one of three novels he'd taken from their home library. At the time he had considered the action little more than a dare—an in-your-face challenge to the chasm gnawing through his backyard. He had relished the idea of replacing each book in its proper gap. How brazen a gesture that now seemed.

Over the last few days, he'd come to consider the possession of these novels a personal triumph. Reading felt as essential to Henry as art did to Emma. If this were to be his last day on earth, lounging beside his wife amid the stone formations, he could imagine no greater joy.

The only flaw in Henry's scenario was the bottle of gas-station Chardonnay that he and Emma sipped leisurely from plastic cups. He found the flavor somewhat brackish.

Since neither of them had ever visualized getting plastered in their final hours, they acknowledged that the wine *was* a rather pleasant perk, if barely more tolerable than sweetened grape juice.

"The end of the world," Henry supposed with a sigh, "does come with certain drawbacks."

Emma painted in silence for well over an hour before

dismissing her canvas with the inevitable tongue-clicking that Henry had come to recognize as the sound of dissatisfaction.

"Problems, my love?"

"Just changing my mind," she admitted, brushing loose strands of hair from her eyes and discarding her efforts with an air of nonchalance, although Henry knew better.

He put aside his novel. "Might I take a peek?"

"It's not finished," she told him, and in a tone that implied she'd rather he not. Henry smiled and returned to his book, allowing his wife sufficient time to work in solitude.

But curiosity eventually took hold and Henry stood with the pretense of stretching before venturing a bold step toward the spot where Emma had tilted the offending canvas against the trunk of a mesquite tree. He nudged his glasses to the bridge of his nose and peered at what his wife had created.

She had completed much of Cathedral Rock, capturing its presence exceptionally well, he thought—although the top third of the canvas remained bare. A fundamental rule that Henry had learned years ago was *sky first*—and he cast a curious gaze upward. He saw almost immediately what he'd failed to notice this morning.

Bands of puffy white clouds had formed a series of distinct east-west striations amid a deep turquoise blue. To Henry's casual glance, the clouds had assumed an intriguing yet unremarkable pattern—although he understood Emma's visual repulsion. The hole was sucking *everything* toward its unseen advance. Henry envisioned an intense white vortex somewhere over the horizon, the hole absorbing the very sky from existence.

Had she not sobbed, he would not have looked, but Henry turned to glimpse the rough, charcoal likenesses of Victoria and T.J. scratched against her second canvas. Emma stared at her work with a hand trembling against her lips.

"I want to leave," she whispered. "We don't belong here."

He nodded without a word and moved to pack her easel. Emma reached out and touched his shoulder. "That's not necessary. I won't be painting again. Not the world as it is now." She looked skyward. "Not what it's become. It's time for us to go, Henry."

They found no reason to return to town. Henry had fully packed the car earlier that morning, suspecting that quick getaways would be something of a necessity in the coming days. They hiked back to the Volvo without speaking and drove east.

Emma discovered Schnebly Hill Road would take them five miles to Route 17—which merged with 89A just south of Flagstaff. With the map unfurled, she'd been adamant about *not* returning the way they'd come. She did not want to chance passing in such close proximity to the Circle Jump or to the children they had left behind to perish there. What the map didn't divulge however (and to Emma's immediate horror) the road's rather tentative existence slowed their impending escape. Schnebly Hill proved little more than an unpaved, rock-strewn trail that wound tortuously through the rugged highlands. The Volvo bounced and bucked for a half-hour before spitting them out on the highway.

A few minutes later, speeding north on Route 17, they encountered a whitewashed billboard, splashed in angry strokes of red paint. Emma audibly gasped her amazement.

DO NOT STOP IN FLAGSTAFF

NO GAS / NO FOOD

NO SYMPATHY

Aware of his wife's expression, Henry reached out and patted Emma's knee. "Don't worry. I believe Route 40 will bypass the city proper. We'll leave them alone. We have plenty of food and a full tank. Sufficient fuel to get us into New Mexico."

Emma pondered the map. "Gallup should have open stations, don't you think? It's a small town. Maybe they're still friendly."

"One way to find out," he supposed.

A few miles later, they came upon a second sign tacked to a slender post—a small cardboard square, hastily erected, scribbled in magic marker.

Jesus Loves You!

"Talk about mixed messages," Henry thought to remark.

"Well, you'd think people *would* be civil to each other in times of crisis."

"Some are," Henry suggested.

"Obviously some *aren't*."

"Fear does that. Can't really blame them, darling."

"Fear or indifference. People have gotten so used to passing by strangers in need."

Henry said nothing.

"Why is it," Emma wondered, "that we're so horrified by a plane crash in our own town and less so by one across the state? And even less so by a crash across the country? If people are killed halfway around the world, we barely take notice. Why *is* that?"

"We can't mourn everyone, I suppose. Eight billion people? We're not capable."

"If there *is* a God, he should have made us capable of greater empathy. We'd have no wars. No starvation. No poverty. Why wouldn't a sane God do such a thing?" They rode another several moments in silence. She brusquely turned on the radio, pushing knobs, hearing alternate bursts of silence and static.

Then, suddenly, a woman's voice, speaking without inflection, without emotion: *"...Blyth, Ehrenberg, Cibola, Yuma, Wellton, Someton, Cuervos, San Luis Rio Colorado, Big River, Parker, Poston..."*

"What on Earth?" Emma said.

Henry shook his head.

"...Tonopa, Goldfield, Wheaton..." The list went on for a solid minute.

"Towns," Henry remarked finally. "I think it's everything the hole's recently consumed."

"...Lovestock, Battle Mountain, Fallon, Fallon Station—"

Emma snapped the radio off, content to let the silence wash her troubled mind.

As ANTICIPATED, Route 17 connected with Route 40 via deserted cloverleaf. Henry headed east, skirting Flagstaff, the town passing immediately on their left. They peered intently for the expected fortifications; barricades or roadblocks or gun-toting cowboys on horseback. But nothing appeared unordinary.

"It's so tranquil," Emma remarked.

"Maybe just good PR," Henry replied, referring to the paint-splashed billboard. "Not too many passersby willing to take a chance of dropping by for lunch."

Flagstaff swiftly disappeared behind them, although occasional homes and small businesses dotted the surrounding landscape. Pine forests eventually reclaimed the gently rolling hills on either side of the highway. The few cars they encountered here were hitched to trailers or laden or with rope-cinched trunks overflowing with possessions. Not far ahead, an old, primer-blotched Chevy Impala had broken its rear axle under the strain of a load. Three burly men stood glaring beside the vehicle.

"Oh, dear," Emma said, reaching for Henry's hand. "Should we do something?"

Henry said nothing, surprising himself at how easily he steered around the Chevy. "They're not stranded. Look—" Henry pointed. "Houses there and over there. Dozens of homes. There's a gas station. This isn't the middle of the desert, darling. They'll work it out."

They drove another mile in silence, until Emma said, "Are we really different from the people who painted that sign?"

"I'd like to think so," Henry said, not quite certain at this point. He glanced in the rearview and said, if only to convince himself, "Had we been in the Mojave we would have stopped. At least offered them food and water."

"I know," Emma said. "I'm not blaming you. Truth is, I secretly hoped you *would* drive past, because I couldn't blame myself for that. Those men back there, I guess they're no different than a plane crash halfway around the world. I feel nothing and I hate myself for that, Henry. I absolutely hate myself."

They drove through Winslow without stopping. Twenty minutes later Henry discovered an open Chevron station adjacent the exit ahead. Aware that they'd already put a hundred miles behind them, he decided to stop. "Let's top off the tank," he told Emma. "One never knows what lies ahead."

She nodded her agreement.

A thin man with a limp emerged from the station, a shotgun hanging loosely under one arm. He warily eyed the Volvo coasting toward the pumps.

"Henry?"

"It's okay. He could have waved us along if he wanted."

Henry braked a good twenty yards in front of the man who begrudgingly signaled them forward. Henry obliged, his window descending, both men peering at each other with distrust.

"You have gas?"

"A hun'ert a gallon," the man said with a curt nod. *"Cash."*

Henry realized that amount would eat up a hefty chunk of pocket money, but he didn't see what other choice he had. Prices would likely increase steadily, day by day. Perhaps even hour by hour. "Okay."

The proprietor stepped back to let the Volvo roll forward and stop. "You pump, I watch."

Henry did as he was told. Neither man spoke, Henry's gaze overtly aware of the shotgun—at one point the barrel rising slightly, the man's finger moving toward the trigger. Henry felt a momentary tingle of dread, but the man made no other threatening gestures. He watched the proprietor's gaze drift now and then toward Emma, still in the car. Henry could only assume that they presented a rather harmless pair.

The tank took almost six gallons. Henry diligently counted out six 100-dollar bills and said; "Keep the change," in the most cynical voice he could muster.

The man nodded, grim-faced, toward the Volvo and said, "Tell the missus I woulda took you out first."

First? Henry frowned and watched the proprietor retreat into the station like a spider, lurking behind tinted windows, biding time until another unwitting motorist bumbled into his lair. He was unable to make sense of the attendant's parting words—until he slid behind the wheel and saw Emma gripping the little revolver he'd found yesterday.

"Good Lord, Emmie."

"Drive, Henry," she said, her voice wavering. She waited until he'd sped from the station, back on the highway, and then placed the gun in the glove compartment.

"I, um, found that in Sedona," he told her.

"Yes, I assumed so. I went looking for the cashews. Imagine my surprise."

"I'm trying to," Henry said with a sidelong glance.

"You *should* have told me."

"Apparently I didn't need to."

"It's been in the glove compartment since this morning. Little good it would do us sitting in a cardboard box in the back."

When Henry didn't comment, she said, "I'm not oblivious to what's happening, you know. I'm not some old-fashioned B-movie princess likely to swoon at every turn. I pointed the gun quite deliberately at that station attendant and, had he threatened you, Henry, I'm fairly certain I would have used it."

"Fairly?"

"I believe so, yes."

He smiled. "But you let him take almost a quarter of our cash."

"I'm not indiscriminate, you know. Your life is priceless to me. I'm not sure all the money in the world is going to do *any*body any good." She tut-tutted disapprovingly. "I can't imagine how that poor man's going to spend it. If he's here now he'll be here tomorrow. Before he knows it, his fortune's going to be at the bottom of a very large hole, and him along with it."

"I sense a moral there somewhere," Henry said, "although we've got less than two thousand in cash remaining."

"We have plenty of food. We have enough fuel to get through New Mexico, and well into Texas. We'll cross the next bridge when we come to it."

Texas, Henry thought dryly. Emma with a gun, driving through Texas. What metaphorical bridge could possibly materialize in Texas?

FOR AN HOUR OR SO Henry had been aware of the skies darkening behind them in the review mirror. "Storm's building back there."

"I can't imagine what sort of horrific atmospheric conditions we left back home." She grew silent again, and Henry realized that was one conversation she did not wish to have. Home was a concept best left forgotten.

He warily checked the mirror again and said, "Are you getting hungry?"

"I am. An early supper?" Emma's attitude brightened and she graced her husband with an increasingly rare smile. "You need a good stretch and I certainly need to pee. If you'd like, I'll drive for a while afterwards."

Henry proceeded another few miles, until he found a desolate crossroad—Xavier Ranch Road—a strip of rutted asphalt stretching across the landscape as far as they could see, seemingly heading nowhere. He exited Route 40, the terrain mostly flat, occasional rocky granite outcrops rising like mythical castles from the desert floor. He located one formation that would nicely conceal them from the highway. Keenly aware that the Volvo contained a small fortune in gas, Henry could only assume that certain people were desperate enough to kill for it.

Emma wandered off amid the towering fingers of pinkish-gray rock to find a suitable bathroom. Henry felt safely cocooned between the sloping walls and, curious, he discovered a crooked crevice stair-stepping one side of a boulder that might give him a decent view of the highway. He carefully made his way a dozen or so feet upward, grateful to find a flat perch that overlooked the surrounding terrain.

Henry saw Route 40 devoid of traffic—but his brain instantly dismissed that realization, his thoughts instead focused on the distant horizon, his gaze searching the sky above the ragged peaks of whatever mountain range they had crossed an hour or so before.

He had been wrong about rain clouds. A wide, darkening V hovered above the horizon, as if the hole had begun to suck the very blueness from the sky. The late afternoon sun burned brightly against the upper edge of a brooding cadmium funnel, not quite yet black, bordered on either side by a fluttery white mist. He noted again that even the clouds were being sucked downward toward the edge of what he assumed to be the advancing hole.

Aware of his tenuous stance upon the boulder, Henry spread his feet apart, his legs braced, cautious of the wind slapping at his back, as if some physical entity were pushing him with steadfast determination. The rocky outcrop whistled softly from various crevices.

The ominous sky and heft of the wind threatened to crack Henry's resolve. An instant of mindless fear rumbled through his psyche. He might have succumbed to blind terror had Emma not appeared below him, asking; "What on earth are you *doing* up there?"

He forced a smile. "Keeping an eye on traffic."

"Can I look?"

"It's slippery," he lied, beginning his descent, hoping to spare Emma from similar dread.

"Do you hear the wind?" she asked. "Sounds like a kettle about to boil. Like a hundred kettles."

"Yes, it does."

She reached up, touching his calf. "Careful, darling."

They wolfed down a meal of packaged apple pie and dry roasted peanuts, sipping bottles of mango-flavored fruit juice. When they finished, Emma gathered their trash in a plastic bag, a habit Henry found utterly charming, under the circumstances. He looped the Volvo back toward the highway and accelerated. Emma peered over his shoulder to the west, and gasped.

"Henry?"

"I know," he said. "I've seen it."

He pressed his foot to the floor, shooting east toward Albuquerque.

THEY CROSSED INTO NEW MEXICO less than an hour later. They'd been mostly silent, Emma pressing her head against the window, feeling the subtle vibrations of the world slipping past—perhaps for the last time—watching the desert gradually turn a vibrant, passionate yellow, its arid beauty both stark and glorious. Emma regretted that she had never before appreciated such beauty. Only now could she see it for its worth. She felt aware, too, of the need to appreciate its grandeur, to not miss this moment by too busily mourning its imminent demise.

They passed Gallup without stopping—Henry now convinced the hole was closer than he'd thought possible—and sped past several other, smaller junctions as they climbed through the mountains. Oddly enough, during their last 90 minutes on the highway, Henry had encountered no other traffic. Not a single automobile, and Henry thought that odd. Emma had been silent most of that time, she and Henry holding hands as they had done for most of the drive from California. They considered the gesture a tenuous yet important bond, physical compensation for their occasional lapses of verbal communication. They were aware of each other's pulse threading through their entwined fingers, connecting them on a far deeper level and infusing them with an unspoken hope for their future.

Not long afterwards, Henry noticed a teal-colored blouse tumbling along the center of the highway, followed by a billowing ochre scarf off to his left that barely touched the hot desert floor. For several minutes, various snippets of color fluttered past on the steady westbound wind. Every so often the Volvo shuddered as the velocity of air rushing past intensified, which did not bode well for their journey east.

The Volvo crested a rise and headed downward again, into a sparse valley a mile or so wide. Still, they encountered no other traffic. He worried that maybe they would find Albuquerque deserted.

He shifted into neutral, coasting as long as he could, conserving every possible drop of fuel. Topping the last of several hills, he spotted a stalled school bus straddling the road a mile or so ahead.

He saw no milling passengers, no movement or signals for help. A breakdown, most likely, and a possible source of fuel. Henry noticed a cascade of colorful clothing strewn about the highway and assumed this to be the source of the afternoon's parade of debris. He understood the logic of those on the bus; jettison everything too heavy to carry. The last road sign had indicated Albuquerque still 60 miles away.

Henry shifted into drive and Emma stirred from her silent regard of the desert, suddenly cognizant of the abandoned vehicle. "Could they have run out of fuel?"

"Possibly. Or broken down. If that's the case, it's good news for us if they still have…"

But Henry closed his mouth, stunned into sudden silence. Less than half a mile remained between the vehicles, and he could more clearly make out shapes beneath the colorful garments cluttering the road.

"Henry?" Emma whispered—the ground littered not with articles of clothing, but with human bodies. They could see bullet holes peppering the side of the bus, sunlight glinting off shards of glass that lay beneath the shattered windows.

Henry lifted his foot from the gas pedal, slowing the Volvo to a crawl.

"Turn around," Emma said with a quivering voice.

"Turn around, Henry."

He braked and sat in cautious silence.

"I don't think it's a trap of any sort." He craned his neck to scour the surrounding landscape. Several buildings, warehouses of some type, stood several miles away to the north. Henry saw no other structures close enough to identify. The desert loomed around them, flat, strewn with scraggly bits of vegetation. Nowhere a person might hide.

"Albuquerque's on the other side of that bus," Henry said gravely. "I don't see what other choice we have."

"Someone might be waiting *inside*," Emma reminded him. She fumbled for the glove compartment, withdrew the gun and placed it on her lap. "Alright, but slowly. Dear God, let's be careful."

Henry eased forward, the speedometer barely registering their crawl. About fifty feet from the bus he stopped again.

"Wait here, Emmie."

"And perchance watch you gunned down in the middle of the road? I think not. We'll go together, Henry. Like always."

He nodded. No use arguing. They stepped from the car, leaving the Volvo's engine purring. The odor struck them immediately; a sweetly sickening scent carried on the hot breeze. These people had been dead for some time. Bullets riddled the twenty or so bodies—old women and middle-aged men mostly, Native Americans or of Mexican descent—left to bloat and decay under the hot sun.

"My God," she said. "Who could do such a thing? For gas? Food? Not for money, certainly not now."

"Maybe it's a warning."

"A what?"

"Telling anyone on this road not to come closer. Not to continue."

"*Why?*"

"A thousand different reasons," he said, his voice trembling. But none he could understand.

Henry remembered seeing an exit off the highway a few miles back, a small, barely noticed slash of asphalt cutting through the desert to the north. "I think we should backtrack," he said. "Detour around whatever's ahead."

The notion of turning back filled Emma with dread, but she could not deny that this terrible thing *was* a message. These people had been killed to dissuade others from approaching.

"We can't just leave them like this," she said.

"I don't know what else we can do. Burying them seems absurd under the circumstances. In a day or two, the hole will accomplish a far more thorough job than we ever could."

Emma nodded without another word. Henry eased the Volvo across the weed-choked median strip and turned back west, leaving the dead where they had fallen. Ahead, the dark funnel loomed fatter and far more ominous than he remembered seeing only hours before.

"Good Lord." He gunned the Volvo, no longer content to coast.

Emma remained silent for several minutes, finally turning to him, her words a hot reproach. "We humans aren't fit to live. Not a species that so indiscriminately kills. Maybe *that's* why the hole has come for us—to swallow the abomination that we have become."

THEY FOUND COUNTY ROAD 12 and turned north. The landscape appeared cast in an eerie pallor, the desert floor radiating an odd, grayish-yellow hue. They headed due north on the bumpy, two-lane slash of asphalt. Orange and pink mesas rose many miles ahead of them. To the west, the distant tailbone of the Rocky Mountains remained intact, concealing any hint of the oncoming monstrosity.

Emma unfolded the map and told Henry that the road would connect with Route 509 and eventually link with 550, another forty or so miles to the north. "We'll cut a wide path around Albuquerque and head east on Route 84 north of Santa Fe." She glanced at the gas needle, relieved to notice the Volvo's tank remained more than half full.

The drab desert floor gradually gave way to patches of tall yellow grass, yucca, and clusters of gnarly mountain oak, fragile signs of encroaching life. A herd of elk meandered in the distance.

A strange purplish glow of dusk advanced from the east as well. Emma had hoped to reach Santa Fe before nightfall, but now she felt uncertain. To the west, the afternoon sun already lay partially within the inky, funnel-shaped V looming over the mountains. A few days ago the western horizon would have majestically bled orange, pink or crimson; now an impossible darkness surrounded the sun's hot yellow glow, creating a halo, its light pulsating in slow, steady waves.

Emma realized that few humans had ever seen a bright sun against the shrouded blanket of night and for an instant her brain refused to accept the illusion. She did not dare to admit that the vision was indeed quite beautiful. Despite the horrifying implications of what she witnessed, a portion of her artistic brain perceived the image in all its breathtaking splendor, a once-in-forever glimpse of a cataclysmic event beyond her mind's ability to fully grasp.

"Do you see, Henry?" she asked in awe.

He nodded. "A full sun, shining in a midnight sky."

She gripped his hand tightly. "It's bigger than us. Larger than our puny little brains can conceive. We're like insects caught in a giant headlight. We can't begin to understand what's bearing down on us. We're just..." Emma shook her head, on the verge of weeping. "Just tiny insects," she whispered again, her voice drifting off, her mind unable to wrap itself around the anomaly she felt certain would sooner or later consume them all.

They came upon a beige Toyota 4x4 around the next curve. The battered, rusting pickup had pulled to the side of the road, its hood raised. Thin traces of steam rose from the radiator, trailing away on the prevailing breeze. A young dark-skinned couple stood beside the car, while a throng of young children—Emma counted seven girls and a boy—milled about. The youngest appeared no older than four or five, playing alone in the flat bed with a ragged cloth doll. She smiled a gap-toothed smile as they passed.

Neither Emma nor Henry spoke for the next quarter mile. Finally, Henry's foot eased off the gas pedal.

Emma cleared her throat.

"You don't have to say it."

"I haven't uttered a word, dear."

He checked the rearview mirror and exhaled sharply, braking the Volvo to a hard stop. He cranked the steering wheel and swung the car in a tight U-turn.

"Maybe we can help."

"It's a *desert*," Emma said. "No amenities nearby."

"You knew I couldn't just drive on."

She smiled at him, a presumptuous little expression that Henry both disliked and loved. "Of course I knew."

"And if I'd continued?"

"Another mile," she told him, still smiling, "and I would have taken your little gun from the glove compartment and shot you in the foot."

Henry returned her smile, finding the comment so deliciously Emma.

As they approached the Toyota, the woman's eyebrows rose in curiosity. Her companion frowned, his hands fisting as the Volvo slowed.

Henry lowered his window. "Can we help?"

The couple looked at each other with puzzled expressions and Henry immediately understood that they spoke no English. Emma leaned over, her chin on Henry's shoulder, and repeated the question in her halting Spanish.

"*¿Necesita ayuda?*"

The young man's hands relaxed. He responded with a jumble of words that Emma translated. "He says it's a broken water pump."

"Hold on." Henry swung the Volvo into the hard, grassy earth behind the Toyota.

"They may be hungry," Emma said.

"Let's see what we can do."

The couple introduced themselves as Luis and Dominica, then hurriedly ticked off the children's names in Spanish. Neither Henry nor Emma registered the names—except for the youngest, whose name was *Emma*. Luis and Dominica lived in Pescada and were on their way to her sister's ranch. Five of the children belonged to Dominica's two sisters, who lived farther north near Navajo Lake.

Emma asked cautiously if they'd been on Route 40 toward Albuquerque. They shook their heads, Dominica telling them that they usually took Bluewater Road up through Thoreau, to 371. They'd heard that bandits were stopping cars and stealing gas and money, so they'd decided to detour. Very few people took this road, Dominica said, now that the borax mine had closed.

"How far to Navajo Lake?" Henry asked. Emma translated. Another sixty or seventy miles to the north, near the Colorado border.

"Are there any major highways near the lake?" Emma asked the couple in Spanish. "Any major thoroughfares to the *east?*"

Luis and Dominica looked at each other, eyebrows furrowed, then shook their heads.

"*Nada,*" Dominica said.

Luis spoke with dismay, staring at Emma with a mute, forlorn expression.

"He's saying something about twisting mountain roads." Emma shook her head. "A whole lot of nowhere."

"Seventy miles," Henry said sullenly.

"Into the mountains."

"Apparently so, darling."

They studied the surrounding terrain in silence. The flat, gently sloping landscape stretched away to the west, dotted with squat trees and a smattering of lower foothills, eventually rising into tall, jagged peaks. Only empty desert lay behind them. Fingers of encroaching forest grew to the east, a wide, flat-topped mesa not far beyond, no more than three or four miles away.

Henry's gaze returned to the jutting landscape ahead. Navigating such terrain at night would be slow and treacherous. He doubted they'd be on their way east again any time before morning.

"There's something else," Henry said.

"I can do the math, darling."

"We can fit Luis and Dominica in the backseat with maybe two or three of the smaller kids." He glanced dubiously at the Volvo. "One up front with you. Four in the back with the groceries?"

"We'll have to jettison the luggage."

Henry nodded. "I'm thinking about our rations. Our water. Do we leave most of it behind?"

While they talked, Dominica began sobbing. Emma reached out and hugged her—offering empathy for a stranger in the way only another woman could provide. Luis began to speak in a heated rush and Emma, without looking at Henry, said, "He asks that we please take the children. He and Dominica will remain here."

"Well that's ridiculous," Henry said, angrily pushing his glasses along the bridge of his nose. "We're not leaving *any-body*. We'd never be able to find this ranch of theirs, nor the lake for that matter. We're not even sure what roads are open that far north."

Dominica began to speak through her tears, a halting soliloquy. She folded her hands as if in prayer, resting her fingertips beneath her chin. When she was finished, Emma said, "The ranch has been their family home for generations. They wanted the children to be with their mothers, for the families to be together one last time."

"Good God," Henry said, chagrined.

Emma patted Dominica's shoulder and, eyebrows clenched, said, "You and I need to chat, Henry. Let's feed the children first. I'm sure they're hungry."

The children were indeed hungry and ate ravenously, with innocent abandon, even as the sky darkened around them. Their laughter calmed Emma. She and Henry lingered a while, masking their apprehension for the children's sake. Finally, she reached for Henry's hand and led him along the edge of the asphalt road. For several minutes they chose to simply walk, their fingers intertwined, each of them silent.

He already knew the purpose of this little stroll, and Emma knew that he knew—one of the many reasons she loved him. All that remained was the formal acknowledgment of their unspoken agreement. She smiled and squeezed his hand.

"It's beautiful here, don't you think?"

"Yes, magnificent."

"I never truly appreciated the desert until now."

"We've always been coastal creatures, my dear."

"Navajo Lake. What a pretty name."

"It is, yes." He offered her a sidelong glance.

"The most important thing we can do right now," she said, pausing to inhale a deep breath, "is to get those children home to their parents. A few days, a week, whatever time they might have left."

He said nothing.

"I'm tired of running, Henry."

"I know."

"You do?"

"Leaving Victoria and T.J. behind—it changed you somehow. Maybe changed both of us. I think they were smarter than us."

"Not smarter, just better prepared," Emma said. "Sedona *was* their time. And now it's time for us. This should be our choice, not the decision of some infernal hole in the ground."

"In our *yard*," he reminded her.

She laughed, which made Henry laugh, and they knew the decision was made. They fell quiet again, until Henry said, "Would you care to join me for an intimate little Circle Jump, my love?"

She hugged him, her heart brimming. "It would be my honor."

"And you're sure about this?"

Emma nodded. "We'll keep enough food and water for—how long? Three or four days?"

He glanced at the brooding western sky. "Less than that, I suspect."

"The hard part…." She looked over her shoulder with a frown.

"Is?"

"Getting Luis and Dominica to agree to this."

"For the children," he reminded her.

"For the children."

The couple resisted—*no, no, no!*—Dominica and Luis

tearfully pleading that this was not what they wanted. Emma soothed them with her gentle logic. Eventually, they relented. While Emma convinced them, Henry removed two bags of food supplies, their two plump overnight bags and suitcases, making sufficient room for all the children. He snatched the flashlight and utility knife from the glove compartment, and the revolver of course, knowing that Emma would be appalled if he'd left the gun in a car filled with so many curious little hands. He heard her voice soothing the young couple in Spanish, reminding them of how *necessary* it was for the children to be with their families, for as long as possible.

"*Para los niños,*" she told them once again.

Henry and Emma watched the Volvo crest the next rise. It stopped for almost a minute, brake lights glowing. Finally, the lights blinked out—and just like that, Luis and Dominica and the eight children were gone. Henry turned to survey the vast and empty desert around them.

"Well then," Emma said with a resolute nod. "On to business." They stared at the broken Toyota and found no reason to linger.

"Where do you think we should we should make camp?"

He pointed to a small grove of twisted oak on a rocky mound some forty yards off to the east. "Let's take the food and find shelter. I'll come back for the luggage."

They trekked the distance, breathing in the warm air perfumed with coleus and pine. Henry realized that the mesa to the east was blocking the brunt of the wind's force, although an ambient whistling above them struck him as ominous. He returned for their suitcases and had barely reached the knot of trees again when Emma pointed.

"Look," she said.

Henry glanced at the black horizon and watched the yellow sun graze the distant peaks. Advancing shadows cast an odd golden mosaic against the landscape around them.

Quite soon the sun descended behind the mountains. Around them, the pale golden hue of dusk darkened and then, as if a switch had been thrown, the fullness of night was upon them. Remnants of color splashed the upper face of the distant peaks, but those colors quickly vanished. A myriad of stars blossomed overhead, pulsating, as fiercely white as Emma had ever seen.

They set up camp as best they could, Henry's flashlight playing a slender beam here and there while they fluffed sweaters and jackets into makeshift beds. They eventually snuggled together amid the trees, Henry's back pressed against an old stump. They munched on dried fruit and peanuts, listening to the wind howl its resonant, somber tune high above them. All in all, Emma considered, not a bad little spot to spend the night.

"They told me they'd pray for us," Emma remarked. "Dominica and Luis."

"Really?"

"I don't think anyone's prayed for us in a long while," she added.

"Well, the timing's not bad. I don't mind having prayer or two on our side."

She gave him a squeeze. "We did a wonderful thing for those children."

"I believe we did."

"Even if they only have tonight, Henry, only an hour together, that's worth everything we could have accomplished in our own lives. Maybe *that's* what's important now, in the grand scheme."

"I suppose the things we value have always been subjective. Yesterday, our money. Today, our moments."

"Henry, *look*," Emma said with newfound fascination. Where the sun had descended, the night sky had abruptly come alive with thousands of slender tendrils, a spider's web of flickering purple light.

"What could it be?" Henry wondered.

"A lightning storm?"

"None like I've ever seen. Electrical, maybe. A type of aurora perhaps."

"It's beautiful," she whispered. Distant filaments danced and frolicked, perhaps dozens or hundreds of miles in length, so numerous that the ground around them pulsed in a chalky violet hue.

"I'm not afraid," she said after a long silence.

"We've always believed in a forever more, you and me," Henry told her.

"I still do."

"So whatever fate we confront, we'll face it together."

"When the time comes, Henry, hold me as long as you can?"

"I promise." He kissed her forehead, breathing in the scent of her hair. He closed his eyes, wondering if he had the ability to remain strong—if not for himself, then certainly for Emma's sake. When he opened his eyes again, the horizon spun in a dizzying mandala of electric purple light.

They watched the sparking filaments dance late into the night, huddled together beneath the dry wind. Henry and Emma eventually grew weary, closed their eyes and slept, both dreaming of far-away worlds of unimaginable beauty.

SATURDAY

THE GROUND TREMBLED and the echo of falling giants shook them awake. In the predawn haze, they rose stiffly to discover that the western peaks had vanished overnight. They could still see the rolling slopes of the closer foothills, but the enormous, jagged walls of granite had disappeared. In their place, Emma and Henry observed only an inky black void of perpetual night, sprinkled with the glow of countless stars.

"Do you see, Henry? Do you *see?*"

"I do," he said, filled with an adrenaline rush of dread.

"Could it have been so near, all this time?"

"If the hole's been growing exponentially," Henry said, "by now it must be expanding at incredible speed."

They stared toward the horizon, aware of the distant, ambient grumble of the chasm's approach, punctuated by the incessant crack of stone toppling into oblivion.

They stood together, Henry's arm around Emma's waist, feeling the desert floor throb and tingle beneath them.

"Did you ever stop to wonder," she asked, "why it picked *us?*" Emma put a hand to her throat. "Maybe we ran too fast, or maybe we weren't meant to run at all. Maybe it's been after us all this time."

A tremendous boom of thunder rocked the ground. A hillside shuddered and dropped from view. Henry's grip tightened around his wife. He noticed a distant herd, elk or deer, bolting toward them through the predawn murk—then suddenly they too were gone.

"I want you to know a secret," Emma said. "I've always fretted about which one of us might die first. I never wanted it to be you, but I never wanted it to be me either." She smiled wanly. "Do you think this might be God's way of answering my prayers?"

"If so, the Almighty might want to work on his methodology. This seems a tad excessive."

"There's a reason for this," she said firmly. "There must be."

"I've wondered why a hundred times." Henry stared into the starry visage to the west. "I've heard theoretical physicists claim that maybe a billion universes exist on a billion different planes. Who know, maybe in each one, the hole chooses a different yard. In some other dimension you and I are on the porch right now, sipping hot coffee and watching rain clouds form against the horizon." He shrugged. "Or maybe this is all a dream. All in my head."

"It's in mine too," she reminded him.

A single tear dropped from the corner of his eye. "If you're a figment of my imagination, darling, you're the most perfect one I can possibly fathom."

The ground shivered and Emma cried out. They clutched at each other, struggling to keep their balance. Henry realized he could no longer discern the slight curvature of the earth. In the distance, treetops fell away. A scant half-mile or so of desert foothill sloped toward them, ribbons of landscape like a giant tapestry unraveling, disappearing with impossible swiftness.

"Do you think it *is* alive?" Emma asked. "Like Victoria said? Do you think it's conscious?"

"I have no idea."

"If it is…? I don't think we should blame it, Henry. I don't want to curse it to damnation. I want it to know that I feel no malice toward it."

He squeezed her gently.

The wind howled at their backs, whipping away their bedding. They leaned against its force so as not to be pushed forward, holding their ground, each of them determined not to relinquish a single inch. The approaching sound thundered like a speeding freight train, and Henry knew they would soon be unable to hear each other speak.

"Should we be afraid?" he wondered, perhaps not intentionally aloud.

"Of course not, darling. It's a silly little hole after all."

The blackness of night—where moments before had been solid earth—hurled down the slope toward them and Emma turned, no longer obsessed by any desire to watch. She nestled her chin tightly against Henry's neck. He felt her breath hotly caress his skin and, in her closeness, found strength.

The sound overwhelmed their senses. Emma felt her husband's arms pull her tight. *A silly little hole, a silly little hole, such a silly little hole,* she thought, clinging to that notion with all her mental capacity.

"I love you, Henry Doogan!" she shouted, not certain he could hear, yet certain that no other words could possibly satisfy her.

Unable to look away, Henry watched the black, impossibly concave horizon snatch away the remnants of all he had ever known. Suddenly the little asphalt road was gone, and the broken Toyota toppled. Henry gazed into a chasm of incomprehensible girth, glimpsing an immense sea of silver-gray clouds far below, a flash of distant lightning seemingly miles beneath their feet. He pressed his face again against Emma's head, kissing her, inhaling the scent of her hair and—

EMMA AND HENRY DOOGAN FELL, bound together by the tenacity of his grip. The sudden rush of adrenaline overwhelmed any attempt at conscious thought. Henry felt Emma's resistance melt, felt her grow limp in his arms. An instant later he too succumbed to dizziness.

Emma was aware of his release, curious to realize that any sense of fear had slipped away. She no longer felt herself falling; rather, she intuited a sensation of being carried upon a cushion of swirling air, not quite floating but not dropping either. Moving swiftly, but without a sense of direction or speed or distance. She reached for Henry, touching him, yet not touching him, no longer able to feel his warmth but very much aware of his presence. As if, somehow, she remained ethereally attached to the lump of living energy that an instant before had been her husband.

Henry thought he might be dreaming. Any remaining residue of panic had dispersed beneath a warm, euphoric wave. The whirlwind noise had dissipated, replaced by a soft tickle of vibration. He tried to open his eyes and recognized vague, swirling patterns in colors he could not identify. The patterns weren't in front of his face; they were *everywhere*, as if he could observe the entirety of his surroundings without turning.

Emma? He could not find her, yet somehow he sensed her closeness. Behind him? Around him. No—even closer. Henry had a distinct impression of Emma's thoughts encroaching upon his, and simultaneously he felt a rush of—what? Her essence? Her completeness. She had melded with that part of him that no longer felt tangible, neither living nor dead. That distinction now seemed a trivial matter that he—*they?*—considered irrelevant. Their conscious selves had somehow shed the physical entities that had once been Henry and Emma Doogan, and instead occupied an immeasurable swatch of space that felt oddly comfortable, and that—much to their delight—expanded with limitless possibility around them.

As if the notion of infinity was no longer such a significant conundrum.

"Henry?"

It wasn't a frightened sound, nor remotely curious. Not even a sound, but rather a *feeling*, a recollection of sound inside his thinking self. And wasn't that the thing about Emma, always a little bit more self-assured, swifter to grasp the obvious? If he could have smiled, he would have. Once again he intuited her voice, her thoughts, soothing and reassuring—Emma's presence permeating, intransitive. If this was to be their eternity, they knew they could loiter here happily.

"Hey, man! *Here* we are." T.J.'s voice echoed impossibly inside them as well, but, wait—not the T.J. they remembered, but the essence of T.J. as a grandfather; a much older man, far wiser. Victoria entangled them in her love.

Their thoughts entwined, their happiness radiating outward in soothing ripples.

Three dimensions? How pitifully few, they intuited.

Only five senses? How laughably quaint a notion.

T.J. spoke again—no, no, not T.J. but rather the hole itself spoke to them, the façade of T.J.'s familiarity no longer a necessity. This occurrence, this manifestation, this intrusion they had once obliquely considered *a hole* gathered sympathetically around them, through them, simultaneously consuming them and consumed by them—with all perception of singularity a hazy memory.

A miscalculation, the voice explained with heartfelt sincerity. *In the quantum emptiness of time and space, an unintended paradox. An infinitesimal speck, inexplicably cleaved, spewing particles shared by two cosmic realms and, in the span of a nano-second, claimed by both.* And then? The voice offered the faintest wisp of apology.

Confusion trickled away, lost beneath a gentle tsunami

of knowing. The quintessence that had once been Henry and Emma Doogan laughed in unison, or rather conjured up the memory of laughter, as they were no longer entities of flesh and blood but of something else entirely.

Something beyond all comprehension, and yet not unworthy of a second chance.

SUNDAY

HENRY DOOGAN AWOKE EARLY, the summer sun hinting of a beautiful morning as it crested the hilltops to the east. A quiet and practical man, Henry preferred his chores over and done with, favoring his afternoons to read, or to occasionally jog a few miles along the beach with his wife, Emma. He had dressed haphazardly today, in torn jeans and an old sweatshirt, his favorite 49ers cap and a scuffed pair of hiking boots.

Emma watched her husband putter from the kitchen window and thought *every day should be so perfect.* She smiled as Henry duck-walked a young sapling midway across the yard. Emma would be able to see the lemon tree blossom from the kitchen window, delighted to imagine its fragrance soon filling the cottage.

She wiped a fat, ceramic frog with a damp dishcloth and replaced the figurine on the sill, exactly so. The piece had been a gift from Henry many years before, a silly and seemingly insignificant gesture, yet she could not picture the kitchen without the creature.

She noticed—as she did every morning standing at the sink—the crooked tip of her left pinky. Emma had been only seven at the time, her older sister inattentively slamming a closet door when the entire family lived cross-country in Vermont.

She stared curiously at her finger, then fisted her damaged hand and glanced again at Henry, his shovel tamping cautiously at a bare patch of dirt near the fence. An uncertain chill crept along Emma's spine and she moved quickly from the sill to the kitchen doorway.

Henry looked up. "Right here then?"

"Henry, no—*wait!*"

It was a silly feeling, and yet quite profound. Most certainly *not* there. Her subliminal mind sensed the decision to be one of utmost importance—not a distance of inches but rather of microns. Of atoms. Of unfathomable fractal points, older than time itself.

"A bit toward me, if you wouldn't mind."

Henry moved and tamped the shovel again. "About here?"

She wasn't certain why, but she nodded, still cognizant of the apprehension that had bubbled up from crevices deep inside her psyche. "Yes, dear," she told him. "That would be lovely."

"Easier done than said."

Emma steadied herself against the jamb, watching anxiously as Henry hoisted a shovel of dirt, and another, and then a third. In a moment the hole was dug, and Henry dropped the little tree securely into its new home.

He glanced up, smiling, and Emma's sense of foreboding dissolved. She dismissed its receding memory and in doing so noticed the remnants of a morning chill in the air. "Darling?" she called to him. "Would you like some tea?"

Henry paused and straightened. Arching his back, he looked skyward. "Coffee actually, if you wouldn't mind."

"Of course not," she said. Emma turned from the doorway, loving her husband with every fiber of her being.

The Tattoo

September 1938

BERTRAM MAXWELL GURLICKY, able bodied seaman aboard the *SS Carmelita*, met Kajina Pwatu, daughter of wealthy sugarcane exporter Anders Pwatu, in The Lelystad Club on the evening of the girl's 18th birthday.

The tiki lounge was an often rowdy but otherwise respectable nightspot on South Sukala Road, close to the police station but far enough from the Pwatus' sprawling plantation for Kajina's parents to have forbade her to attend her own party. The club featured traditional *gamelan* percussion-fueled bands and, on Saturday nights, a tolerable American swing orchestra that would often shake the club's bamboo rafters 'til dawn.

The submissive Kajina, raised by a bevy of Catholic nuns to be properly demure and obedient, was nonetheless bound and determined to begin her adulthood with a gin fizz and at least *one* dance with a handsome British sailor— perhaps even an admiral. She had longed to holiday in London after seeing Lionel Barrymore and W.C. Fields in *David Copperfield* at the Grande Amsterdam Theater in Jakarta the previous year. And touring the British capital on the arm of His Majesty's Pacific Fleet admiral seemed a splendid way to pay a visit.

Bert Gurlicky had been dry-docked on the small volcanic island of Bansaka for the better part of a week, ever since the Carmelita—an 8,500-ton Hog Islander commissioned during The Great War and recently certified by The Scofield Steamship Company out of 'Frisco—had disembarked without the ailing mariner aboard. Gurlicky, fourteen years in the merchant marine and a frequent visitor to the Dutch East Indies since '29, had caught a severe dose of *panchaku* during his latest stay in Bangkok. Dizzy, fever blistered and shivery on the day of the Carmelita's arrival, he'd missed both a raucous shore leave and, subsequently, the ship's departure for Kendari the previous weekend.

Yet sailors shuffled freely to and from the many tramp steamers, reefers and tankers frequenting Pu'a Pu'a Bay. With the bo'swain's approval and a local doctor's prescription for a hot clove and calamus oil treatment, Gurlicky had been confined to a ramshackle bivouac camp for a two week stay. Shipshape and in good spirits soon enough, he nonetheless found himself begrudgingly aground until the next available Java-bound vessel could return him to active duty. The Harbor Master informed him *that* would likely be the Dutch collier *Meisje Zwolle* ten days hence. Gurlicky had traced his finger down a wall-mounted chart in the master's shack and figured to rejoin the Carmelita and her crew by the end of the month, probably in Semarang. Until then, and doctor's orders be damned, he was bound and determined to remain as drunk as possible during his stay in Tangshin, Bansaka's solitary port town.

As luck would have it, Gurlicky had been drinking from a bottle of A.v. Wees *jajem* since four bells, which put a nice sheen on his reality that particular Saturday evening—although he lacked sufficient pocket cash to cover a romp with the cherry-lipped Sareen. Still, action of one sort or another was easily found at The Lelystad. Give Gurlicky a run of lucky sevens or a few decent hands of Pai Gow, and the sweet Sareen might still be his before daybreak.

For the last few hours he had been content to linger at the bar over his gin, chatting with a one-legged mariner named Louie Danforth and a drifter who called himself

Old Smokey. Their conversation navigated from devastating monsoons to past women of their pleasures, rumors of pirates' treasure and women again, recent sea wrecks and back to women.

Gurlicky was keenly aware of the arrival of the five giggling teens, all local girls, decked out in flowing, floral print dresses. He carefully observed a flash of well-toned calves and carefully coifed ebony hair beneath wide-brimmed white hats. The way the manager fawned and prattled over such an unexpected delight meant local girls of some renown, pedigree stock from well-endowed parentage and likely fluent in the King's tongue. Gurlicky and his sweat-tainted entourage, having bellied up to a far corner of the Lelystad's lengthy bar, began a circumspect advance toward the teenaged girls' table as might a trio of plume moths fluttering toward an open flame.

Kajina was telling her best friend Ri-Ri—in *vedy* proper English, no less—of her intention to capture a British admiral's heart this evening. And perhaps of one day seeing Piccadilly Circus and Windsor Castle. "In London, they serve tea and crumpets every afternoon," Kajina told Ri-Ri. "And women sip sherry from long stemmed crystal glasses."

The tan bloused, blue-jean clad Gurlicky was clean and tidy on this particular evening, shirt tucked and boots polished, his dark blond hair slicked back with just enough Murray's pomade to catch a glint from the overhead lanterns. He smelled tartly of juniper berries, already in high spirits.

"...and they ride to the opera in Bentley automobiles driven by chauffeurs," Kajina told Ri-Ri.

Having overheard the young woman's remarks, Gurlicky chose that moment to step from the bar with a confident flourish. "Admiral Pendleton Perkinson Peppersmyth, of His Majesty's Royal Navy, at your service," he said, grinning at the wide-eyed, mocha-colored girl, one of the most beautiful Island lasses he believed he'd ever seen. And Gurlicky had seen plenty.

"Really?" she inquired with a small, astonished voice.

"No, not in the least!" he admitted, acknowledging the deceit with a jovial roar of laughter, a sound so provocative that Kajina found herself suddenly giddy in this tall stranger's presence, even as the other girls shrank back in trepidation.

"An' 'bout as Brit as Babe Ruth hisself!" Gurlicky exclaimed. When he winked at her (another of Kajina's cherished fantasies), she swooned for this stranger, whomever he might not have been. Six foot four, sea tan and brawny, Gurlicky re-introduced himself as "The dandiest sailor t'ever swum the channel 'tween Watpi and Tokua."

"After the Johnny Cristo sank durin' the Bismarck squall back 'n '32," said Louie Danforth, peeking from behind Gurlicky's girth.

"He did so, too," chimed Old Smokey—who didn't know here-from-there, only that Gurlicky had poured him several shots of excellent spirits tonight, and Ol' Smoke wanted to return the favor.

"Chock full o' tiger sharks," Danforth told her, "that blasted canal."

"Twelve-foot swells," Gurlicky added with a swaying arm motion, pantomiming high waves.

"Oh, my!" Kajina said.

At that moment, the Lelystad's semi-professional 9-piece orchestra ventured into a new foxtrot. "Care to cut the rug, miss?" he enquired over the first dubious strains of *Pennies From Heaven*.

"I would be delighted, sir," she replied with a prim smile, while her companions gasped their astonishment.

Kajina's delicate hands felt tiny and fragile in his powerful grasp. While the Lelystad's manager—the bespectacled and badly toupéed Mr. Randolph Moot—kept a watchful eye on the young debutante, Gurlicky proceeded to twirl and dip the girl, leaving her breathless and heart struck in the most earnest of ways.

Nobody could deny that Bert Gurlicky knew his way around a dance floor, at least while remotely sober. By their second hour together, Kajina already through her third gin fizz, the young woman felt as if she had taken flight, her feet barely touching the quivering floorboards.

When the maître 'd rang a large brass bell at quarter-'til-nine, signaling the approach of mandatory curfew for women and children (the Lelystad's casino eager for business, as was the club's more prurient upstairs offerings) Kajina realized her magical evening was sputtering to an end. She was also keenly aware of Mr. Moot placing a telephone call behind the bar. Now that curfew was upon them and her daddy's credit no longer available, Mr. Moot spoke with an animated urgency, one arm waggling about as if leading an orchestra in frenetic tempo—all the while the man's gaze leveled upon Kajina's newfound friend. Most of the town was either beholden to or terrified of her family's wealth and power. And a tardy warning of the girl's behavior was better than none at all.

She begged that they might meet again the following evening, "At the Aswani in Souto," Kajina whispered in Gurlicky's ear, the poor girl already being tugged from behind by Ri-Ri and the others.

"Don't tell a *soul!*" she instructed and Gurlicky agreeably nodded. He watched her unorthodox exit with a wide grin, her friends pulling and giggling, and eventually packing themselves into a big black taxi beyond the Lelystad's torch-lit veranda.

Later that night, and well into his second bottle of

A.v.Wees, Gurlicky found himself swinging at a trio of Aussie marines—gruffly escorted from The Lelystad by the establishment's two Samoan doormen. Gurlicky staggered back to his bivouac with a smile on his face, a foggy memory of Kajina's sweet perfume permeating his gin-soaked brain.

SHAVED AND POWDERED, wearing a white silk suit borrowed from a pal off the Dutch freighter *Valkenswaard*, Bert sat with Miss Pwatu at a small table at the back of the Aswani Eats en Bier. It was a weatherworn and dirt-smelling little joint—pigs grunted in the kitchen—a good mile farther inland along Sukala Road. Gurlicky had reason to suspect young Kajina distancing herself from Tangshin proper, if not from some brash young suitor, then certainly from an overbearing father.

It had been Old Smokey, the previous night, who'd confirmed Gurlicky's suspicion of the girl's lineage—her family indeed the richest on the island. Her grandfather, half Dutch and half Malay, had begun the family homestead in 1897 and had forsaken his own European surname for that of his powerful wife's—Kajina's maternal grandmother. In the years since, the Pwatus had grown increasingly wealthy, both her grandfather and father as rabid entrepreneurs, her grandmother and mother some sort of high-priestess, muckity-muckity types in a mystical religion that Ol' Smoke believed had been outlawed on the island for some reason or t'other. Yet the women still regarded in high esteem, or so he thought.

"Good'n rich, eh?" Gurlicky pondered.

"Rich as rich can be around these parts."

Gurlicky raised a glass to toast himself in the Lelystad's oversized bar mirror. "Reason to pay right proper attention to our newfound little princess."

This evening, inside the Aswani, Gurlicky nursed a

warm Filipino beer. His young companion sipped hot tea with a cinnamon stick. He hoped to probe, gently of course, into just how big his little princess might be. Did she enjoy growing up here on an island? *No, it was terribly boring.* What about her parents? *No, they're terribly boring too.* When Gurlicky pressed, she told him, "Daddy grows *tebu* for money. Mama makes magic spells. And they *never* let me do anything I want."

But Kajina wished to dip no further into her own past. "I want to hear about the world!" she said in a voice that quivered with anticipation. "Where you've been and what you've seen and where you're going next!"

Gurlicky scratched the back of his head as if to loosen a memory. "Well then, lemme think. Started off as a scrubber boy aboard the *Nova Scotia,* six-thousand tons outta Bridgeport. 'Course, that was on the Atlantic side of the globe. We made the New York to Marseille run more'n I care to count. Found myself many a night in Algiers and Casablanca, too. On the Dark Continent, that be."

"Have you been to London?"

"Sure as shootin' I've been to London. An' Bristol, Liverpool, Portsmouth. But London, that's a highfalutin' bit o' real estate alright. Had myself a pint in Kensington Gardens once, a spit'n the wind from where the King was likely havin' a pint of his own.

"Three years aboard the *Duchess of Queens,* I was at the time. Nice thing about them Brits is they *sorta* speak the language, so a fella won't get gypped buyin' a bag 'o chips or a pair of stockings for a lady. Been as far up the North Atlantic as Haugesund, an' a cold slab of rock *that* peninsula surely is. Been south, 'round the Horn, too—twice. Nasty a swell as I've ever seen."

Kajina folded her hands under her chin and damn if Gurlicky didn't see the sparkle in her eyes.

"Spent many an hour anchored in Hong Kong and Singapore. Saw my share of the Philippines, too, these last coupla calls runnin' our fair share of guns an' ammo, I suspect—although nobody ever said as much. But since them Japs started trouble in Shanghai last year, there's been plenty of nerves rubbed raw around these parts. Tricky little people those Japanese, an' good with ships, too. 'Course, what happens 'tween those yellow devils ain't none of my concern. So long as they stay north o' Shantou, ain't my business who kills who, nor o'er what.

"Jarapura, Kenduri, Balikpapan, the Malukas and Jakarta," Gurlicky said, lifting a finger for every port. "Brunei Bay, Kuching, Kupang, Port Moresby, Brisbane—you name it an' I pro'ly been there. The South China's been my bathtub for a long spell."

"I've always wanted to travel," Kajina told him with a faraway look that Gurlicky knew very well. "This island's *kecil*—too tiny for me," she added with a pout. "Nothing but rubber trees and sugar fields and the endless sea as far as far can be."

"Ain't nothin' bad about the sea, miss," Gurlicky replied, although he couldn't argue about the size of Bansaka. "A big an' glorious place, the world she is."

"And you could *show* it to me!" Kajina suddenly sat ramrod straight and eager.

"*'Course* I could. Fetch you a penny from every port."

Her beauty and rapt attention was too much to ignore. Before he could stop himself, Gurlicky leaned across the table and favored her forehead with a kiss.

The touch of his lips dizzied Kajina's senses. "Then take me away from here," she implored, speaking the words before she even realized they'd fled her thoughts.

It was a rare moment in Gurlicky's life that he found himself speechless. He stared at the girl for several seconds before uttering an uncertain, "Say *what*, miss?"

Kajina might have changed her mind—she briefly pondered fleeing from the Aswani in humiliation—but she could be a stubborn girl at times, proud and sure of her convictions. She lifted her delicate chin and said, "I believe you heard me quite well, Mr. Gurlicky."

"I'm a mariner," he managed to sputter.

"And I wish to become a mariner's wife. I want you to show me everything you've seen. I want us to share the world together, you and I!"

Poor Gurlicky's head was in no condition to fully interpret Kajina's words. This lovely young woman of privilege and polish had proposed to him (or so he seriously believed), an offer he fathomed unlikely to cross his bow ever again. When Gurlicky nodded in silent agreement, her words playing over and over in the inebriated lobes of his brain, he honestly believed that her vision of *sharing the world* had been somewhat metaphorical in nature.

THREE DAYS LATER, Kajina snuck away from the Pwatu's plantation in those darkest hours before dawn. Gurlicky had secured a Malay boatman who would paddle them across the bay to Kuni Point, where he was told he could hire an island priest for a half-dollar. And thus, at sunrise, Kajina Pwatu became Mrs. Bertram Gurlicky under a thatched roof, a toothless priest and his semi-toothless daughter smiling proudly as he kissed his new bride on the lips for the first time. Kajina cried and Gurlicky felt to be the luckiest man alive.

Kajina cried again that night, upstairs in the Honeymoon Suite (a private bath and a pleasant harbor view had cost Gurlicky a dollar extra) of the Hotel Tangshin, newly painted and recently fitted with *electric* lights. He had managed to secure the suite for an entire week, having wired himself a hefty advance the previous day. He did, however, have to explain the basic fundamentals of how married couples spent their time under the sheets to the wide-eyed girl. Kajina put on a brave smile and promised she'd *try* to enjoy it. Even after three glasses of strawberry brandy, the entire experience seemed rather excruciating. But Gurlicky was a man who mightily enjoyed his horizontal situatin'. Even more so after a few swallows of *jajem*. The honeymoon lasted until well after midnight, and Kajina had dared not open her eyes the entire time.

But Gurlicky's exile ashore was rapidly growing short. For the first time in his life, Gurlicky found himself chagrined about returning to sea duty, obliged to hop a Dutch coal hauler in five days—and he spent two of those remaining days ashore wondering how to tell his new wife she might not see him for a while.

Meanwhile, Kajina took it upon herself to gift her new husband with the only wedding present she could afford. She had heard of a photographic studio located precariously close to Tangshin's notorious *wharf district*, where sailors often bought risqué photos of the women they had known (many of those same women *also* available down in Tangshin's wharf district). On the fourth morning of their marriage she slipped away, Bert having gone off to the local doctor's office for a lengthy appointment. Some malady he never fully explained to her—a *sailor's* ailment, he claimed. But ample time for Kajina to prove to her Bertie how utterly adult his new wife actually might be.

Mr. Yoshida, recently of Osaka (but having left his homeland suddenly, a pacifist in true Buddhist fashion) was only too happy to oblige the young woman. The man's window boasted not only lovely young island ladies in various states of repose and undress, but also photographs of the freighters and steamers that had graced Pu'a Pu'a bay. More importantly to Kajina, the window displayed a color tint of Japan's majestic Mount Fuji. Meaning, in the girl's mind, that Mr. Yoshida was a *sincere* artist.

Even so, she was quite nervous about giving Bertie a so-called *boudoir* photograph of herself—Kajina draped in nothing more than a loose silk kimono and thatched sandals, a dragon-emblazoned parasol over one shoulder and her hair pinned up in a suggestive geisha bun. Mr. Yoshida puttered about, positioning the kimono dangerously low beneath one exposed shoulder and eventually cajoling Kajina into a provocative gaze as she peered over that same shoulder. It was, he promised her, a most splendid gift for a *hanamuko.*

"No sailor hubby panky-panky!" Mr. Yoshida assured her.

Yet the photo would not be available until the following afternoon. As Gurlicky would not be returning for several hours hence, Kajina swallowed her pride and returned by horse buggy to her parent's plantation—only to find the big house swarming with constables and sweat-soaked field hands, all of whom had been combing the vast jungle to the northeast, expecting to find the poor girl dead and perhaps half eaten by predators. Not only had Kajina failed to inform her parents of the marriage, but she'd neglected to tell them of her whereabouts since Tuesday morning. As if turning eighteen might be reason enough for such mystery, she'd presumed.

Needless to say, her father was not pleased.

Had Kajina married a Dutch sea captain or at *least* a ship's officer, her parents might have received the news differently. But to have married a lowly mariner—an *American* no less!—was beyond their comprehension. Kajina thought it wise, at the time, not to mention Gurlicky by name, only that he was a ruggedly handsome individual who had promised her the world. For several hours, as Kajina wailed in a wicker chair in her father's library, Anders Pwatu paced the halls in a rant, throwing and shattering bric-a-brac against the walls. Her mother remained cautiously quiet, sensing a sort of brooding danger that her husband could not possibly understand. A diviner since childhood, the woman knew that the spirits, speaking to her through a circle cast of various brightly painted chicken bones, did not lie.

Anders Pwatu gradually tempered his anger and Kajina's tears melded into a more reliant pout, aided by an occasional trembling smile. By suppertime, her father had at least considered forgiving his youngest daughter. But surely he must meet this mariner—proper introductions would be forthcoming—and, however belatedly, bestow his blessing upon the marriage.

By the time Kajina returned to The Hotel Tangshin, Gurlicky was several glasses into the gin, having grown both angry and increasingly fearful of his wife's absence.

"Good Lord, child," he said, seeing her step through the doorway. "You can't be running off like that without a word!"

"I'm *not* a child!" she insisted with the slight stomp of one foot. "I went home to tell Daddy of our marriage."

"You did *that*, didja?"

Gurlicky offered the girl a suspicious glance. Although her admission was sufficient to temporarily douse his anger *and* his fear of abandonment, it did pin-prickle him with a completely new sort of dread. He'd been run off before at the end of a gun, and Anders Pwatu struck him as a potentially well-armed man. Gurlicky moved to replenish a glass with several fingers of warm gin. "And how did Daddy respond to ol' Bertie as a son-in-law?"

"I didn't tell him *who*."

"Well now." Gurlicky's dark pessimism brightened. "That was a wise course to set, lass."

"I told him you were a *sailor*. A very handsome one at that," she said hopefully, aware of her Bertie's lingering frown.

He grunted.

"Daddy yelled very loud," she admitted. "But I told him our love was deeper than the highest mountain."

"Is that so?" Gurlicky mused, aware that his new wife sometimes had trouble with her metaphors.

"He wishes to bless our union."

"With a shot through ol' Bert's mainsail, no doubt."

"He wants to offer you a job."

"A what?"

"I told him *no*, of course," she said, positioning another firm pout against her lips. "I told him that you and I were going to leave here, that we were going visit the world. Still," she said, "he wishes to make you his *mandur*."

When Gurlicky raised an eyebrow, she said, "His foreman. In charge of the workers in the cane fields."

Despite a sigh of inward relief, Gurlicky roared, his laughter leaden with caustic bite. "I'm a *mariner*, my sweet dreamer, not some farmhand darky!"

The fact that he would even *think* to utter that word to his *coklat*-skinned wife confused and confounded Kajina.

"I told him. *No,*" she said again, meekly, on the verge of tears.

"And rightly so, my love. Rightly so."

Aware of his wife's sadness (but unaware of his role in it), Gurlicky finally offered a broad smile. "You did fine, girl. And we'll go see the folks ourselves, you and me. I'll tell him exactly that—I'm a sailor! Nothing more an' nothing less."

"I said we'd come tomorrow night?" The girl's frown trembled.

Tomorrow would leave him only two days before he set sail aboard the Meisje Zwolle. Plenty of time, he reasoned. "Tomorrow it is, then. I'll be suitably suave and de-bone-er, a perfect new son for the occasion. Now come over here to your Bertie," he told her, patting his knee with a flat smack of his hand. "The honeymoon ain't over yet!"

EARLY THE NEXT MORNING, Kajina left Gurlicky again, telling him not to fret, only that she had to go fetch his wedding present. She left him between the sheets, one bare leg cast to port, one long arm thrown to starboard, Gurlicky with a tussled head of hair, a snore and a feeble grunt of awareness.

When she returned, no more than an hour later, Kajina was dismayed to discover that Gurlicky had already found his way to the gin bottle. "It's only nine o'clock," she scolded, albeit meekly.

"Sun's over the yardarm in *one* of the seven seas," Gurlicky replied with a wink, feeling his wild oats stirring once again. "Shore time's drinking time by any sailor's clock. So now, what's this present you're all up and excited about?"

She held out the photograph, wrapped in thick waxed paper. She grew nervous watching her husband fumble through the crinkly wrapping. Kajina had been able to afford only a small photo—a *personal* size, Mr. Yashida had opined. Some photographs you didn't want big and glossy—not a pin-up a man could display on his locker door or above his cot for the entire merchant marine to peruse.

"No, no!" Kajina eagerly agreed, shocked to realize that anyone but she and her Bertie might ever lay eyes on the image.

Watching his fingers part the final fold, she worried that Gurlicky would be angry again, thinking the image vulgar or distasteful. She watched her husband anxiously,

Gurlicky's mouth forming a startled oval of surprise, his eyebrows reaching toward his forehead. It was an expression she had not seen before.

Kajina retreated inside the shy island girl of her childhood. "You no like?"

It took another second for Gurlicky to find his tongue, to find his smile and to register his utter delight. He held the photo at arm's length and squinted with pride. "Darlin! You've given me the most precious thing in my life! Next to you, that is."

She graced this news with a giggle and bounded into his arms. "We will be happy forever and *ever!*" she exclaimed with elation.

KAJINA'S WORDS would shortly reflect a bitter irony, as the next morning marked the final moments of the young couple's matrimonial bliss. Over a quiet, in-room breakfast of turtle soup, taro and snapper, Gurlicky—who'd snuck several swigs of gin in the bathroom and wasn't nearly as drunk as he'd hoped to be—finally broke the news to Kajina. Come the day after tomorrow, he would be leaving aboard the Meisje Zwolle. Alone. Gurlicky explained that wives were strictly forbidden aboard maritime vessels. And while he expected to return home every few months, perhaps as long as a week or more, it was best she not too heavily rely on any particular schedule for him.

The poor girl remained frozen in disbelief and dismay. She finally leapt to her feet and emitted a loud wail. "You *told* me you'd show me the world!"

"My stories, lass! Close your eyes and I'll take you anywhere you want. Give you all the good parts and leave out the bad 'uns!"

"That's not fair!"

"Fair as I got," he said, growing surly, astounded to

realize that Kajina had actually imagined otherwise. (The gin clouded his brain with regards to his own culpability in creating her perception.) Gurlicky was unaware that, before meeting him, her entire life had transpired amid a flat, square-mile swatch of sugarcane, surrounded by jungle, a handful of village crossroads and the local Catholic Missionary Church down the road. He had yet to fathom that their one encounter at the Lelystad had been the girl's first experience inside a bar. The entire world, to Kajina, lay *any*where but home.

She continued to moan and Gurlicky did not appreciate the ruckus. It seemed to him—the gin again—that his spoiled young bride behaved in petulant and morose ways more often than not. Certainly not the kind of behavior Bertram Gurlicky ought to tolerate in a wife.

"Enough of yer nonsense, there now!" he shouted finally, banging a fist, although the terrified girl could do nothing more but burst again into tears.

Which of course drove her husband out the doors of their suite (neither of them thought it much of a *honeymoon* suite at the moment), and down a rickety stairway to the street, Gurlicky hell bent on having some peace and quiet, goddamn it.

Kajina could little else but sit and wait for Bertie's eventual return, aware of her solemn promise to dine at her parents' plantation that evening. She hoped Bertie would be home early enough to perhaps buy her a new parasol for the occasion.

GURLICKY FOUND THE LELYSTAD CLUB be his most immediate convenience. He strode to the bar quite out of sorts, where he gruffly waved away Old Smokey, in no mood to share his stories *or* his alcohol today. He ordered a glass and a bottle, the glower on his mug assuring the safe distance of even the rowdiest of the bar's early morning patronage.

He managed to get himself drunk fairly quickly. Yet even inebriated, he found himself filled with inner torment, Gurlicky with the belated recognition of his possible complicity in Kajina's dismay. Drunk or not, he deeply loved his young wife, and it occurred to him that he desperately wanted to make her happy.

Unfortunately, the only course to her happiness was one he could not possibly provide—an open passage around the globe. And strangely enough, the drunker he became the more his heart yearned for her approval. He considered flinging the cursed gin bottle to the floor and returning to his beloved, but he feared that he was already too drunk for Kajina to ever forgive him.

A cup of coffee would do the trick, hot and black. But first, one final glass of gin. And then one more after that. Before he knew it the bottle stood empty, the western horizon beyond The Lelystad's foyer bathed in a brilliant crimson sheen.

Even with darkness falling, Gurlicky continued to adore his wife—loved her with such completeness that he felt his eyes brimming and faked himself a sneeze to wipe away a public sniffle. Reaching for a handkerchief, his fingers discovered a curious square of cardboard and he plucked the unremembered photograph of Kajina from his pocket. His eyes again began to mist.

Suddenly, Gurlicky had an idea—and there's no wisdom like a drunken sailor's wisdom. Gurlicky slipped from his stool, staggering a touch before he again found his land legs. Outside the Lelystad, Gurlicky veered toward the rowdy wharf district, away from the more sedate side of the harbor that housed the Hotel Tangshin and his patiently waiting wife.

Meanwhile, Kajina had all but worried herself sick with

the approach of nightfall. She finally decided to search Bertie out and bring him home. Had she left the Tangshin Hotel a minute earlier, she might have caught sight of the weaving Gurlicky approaching the rickety boardwalk. She might have run to him and forgiven his drunken swagger and begged him back to the room to seduce her once again (as she was growing curiously fond of Bertie's girth and weight). But the girl, having sobbed for most of the afternoon, paused to freshen her tear-stained face.

It was within those lost moments that Gurlicky passed from any hope of redemption.

HE STRODE like a man possessed, moving stridently past the edge of town and down a slope of litter-strewn, raw red earth. He crossed a bridge of loose planking that overhung the rocky shoreline. A number of cramped piers spiderwebbed this section of harbor—fishing wharves that fed many here who could find no job nor any other means of survival; a labyrinth of aging wooden boards held together by rusty spikes and thick strands of twisted hemp. Somewhere in the distance, he could sniff the bitter residue of an opium pipe. Gurlicky sucked in a hot rush of salty air and diesel oil, of rotting fruit and the remnants of the day's human sweat. *This* was the breath of life itself, a balm for reality that Bert Gurlicky wouldn't have traded for all the tea in China.

A deep magenta radiance remained visible in the western sky behind the silhouette of *Bapa Batu*—Bansaka's dormant volcano cone, but that glow would soon be gone. Somewhere far away, a lone flute echoed a somber tune.

Gurlicky sought out a small, wood-framed shack, a storefront little more than the length of his own body (had he fallen prone) amid the cluttered density of those tiny boardwalk shops selling their often-illicit wares. At this hour he passed mostly street-toughened women and those few drunken sailors seeking their favor. He paused before a crooked rectangle of yellow light spilling across the planks. Above the doorway, a weather-worn shingle read: TATU.

A man sat inside, casually perched on a barrel head. He was a bald man with a large head, wearing only ragged pants—a mountainous fellow who Gurlicky suspected might be Filipino, or at least partially so. It was rumored that the best artists in the South Seas had emerged from the Philippines. This was exactly the sort of man Gurlicky had hoped to find.

A half-dozen crude tools lay strewn about a roughly hewn countertop, stained a dark indigo blue. Under the anemic glow of a single bulb, Gurlicky could see most of the man's body covered in swirls of ink. Tribal tattoos. Spirals and intricately repeated patterns, diamonds and stars, long augmented fingers of blue-black ink that appeared to alternately pulse and ripple against the man's glistening skin.

Gurlicky regarded the tattoo artist with a squinty appraisal. "You do good work, *tuan?*"

The man observed him silently for several seconds, then glanced toward the rear of his shop. A single bed sheet served as a partition. He uttered a whistled monotone, a sound one might use to call a dog. The curtain stirred and then pulled aside.

A young woman, thin, light-skinned and naked, stepped into the light. Across her chest and abdomen slithered a dark, intricately detailed dragon, a splendid beast that portrayed both infinite strength and beauty. Two long-tailed macaques frolicked across the girl's shoulder. A python coiled around her left thigh, its head poking menacingly above her navel. Vines laden with fruits and flowers sprang in ink from ankle to hip, while a patch of tall flowers tickled her ribcage. She turned slowly. Upon her lower back a tiger crouched, its expression threatening beneath the glowing light. A hornbill in flight soared between her shoulder blades, its feathered wingtips tickling her upper arms. She completed her pirouette and Gurlicky noticed additional vines creeping up her neck, numerous leaves brushing against her ears. A crown of thorns adorned her forehead. A spiral graced one cheek and a starburst painted the other. Barely an inch of the lass remained unmarked by the artist.

In the shadowy glare of the little room, even as drunk as he knew himself to be, Gurlicky understood that he was in the presence of a master. Swaying slightly, he reached into his pocket and produced the image of his wife. He placed the photograph on the counter. The tattooed man peered at the likeness, then switched on a second, brighter bulb overhead. The room filled with a stark white brilliance.

"Can you reproduce my missus with all her beauty?"

"I can."

Gurlicky grunted and slapped his arm beneath his left shoulder. "Closest to my heart," he said. He saw the gesture as a grand and fitting apology, a belated wedding present to young Kajina—one that would prove to the entire world the full extent of his love.

"Let's get crackin'," Gurlicky said.

The man stood and Gurlicky slumped into place on the barrel head.

"A little gin, friend, to dull the pain?"

The man nodded to the naked woman, who disappeared into the back and returned wearing a sarong, holding an unlabeled bottle with a milky liquid filled to the brim. Gurlicky sniffed the contents, then took a sip and nodded—not gin or whiskey, but with a sharp tang of fermented rice. It would suffice. The proprietor waited until Gurlicky had finished his swig, then took the bottle and began to methodically, delicately, clean his instruments—a series of thin metal tubes, hollow and sharpened to spikes. A wooden mallet lay amongst the needles, its handle darkened with blood and sweat. A few smaller copper needles law strewn about. A tin can partially filled with ink. Nothing more.

The man returned the bottle to Gurlicky, who took a long gulp. He peered at the photograph of Kajina lying on the counter. *Something*, he thought. Something else that he sensed might be missing. It took him a moment to clear his mind.

"Can you give the lass some real bubs?" Although he loved Kajina's small and delicate body, he knew that women longed for big curvaceous breasts and a full-figured bottom. Why, that new *Look* magazine had come out and said as much, all those cheeky glamour pictures displaying a gal's gazoombas sticking way out front, like the nose of a '38 Merc. So why not give the little woman an ample set—at least on his arm. Gurlicky was sure it would make her happy.

The artist paused. "Bosoms?"

"Aye."

"Underneat'?"

"No, no, as brash an' bare as a newborn." *Another* great idea, he decided. "An' make 'em plump, too. Each an over-ripe papaya, ready to burst."

Gurlicky took another sip from the bottle and rested his head against a wooden post. In a few seconds, the man's quick tap-tap-tapping began, and with it the most intense physical pain that Gurlicky ever imagined he might endure, an undulating agony that reached his brain in a series of jagged waves. He felt the warmth of his own blood trickling down to his elbow. Gurlicky reached again for the bottle and closed his eyes, grimacing against the surge of flayed nerve endings.

He would remember nothing afterward but a long and troubled sleep. When he awoke, the bottle was nearly empty and his arm from elbow to collarbone lay swathed in gauzy bandages. The bald man had vanished, but the girl accepted Gurlicky's roll of money without a word. He spied the bottle on the table and noticed two fingers of liquid still swirling about the bottom. He grabbed the bottle, assuming—given the price he'd just paid—that the last swallows were his for the taking.

He staggered groggily into the twilight, clutching the bottle and surprised to find the evening's violet hue no darker than when he'd entered the little room. And yet his entire left arm throbbed incessantly. No doubt the man had done his job. Odd.

A couple of young jibs sat smoking Lucky Strikes on the wharf. Swaying slightly, Gurlicky rubbed a hand against the stubble on his face and said, "What day this be, fellars?"

They smirked, although Gurlicky's piercing stare quickly doused their impertinence.

"It's Friday, cap'n," replied one.

Friday! But it couldn't be. A solid *day* had passed, and Gurlicky with no recollection of food or conversation? His stomach grumbled and his bladder screamed. He glanced again at the last remnants of the bottle's liquid and drained it in a gulp, then suddenly remembered his young wife awaiting him. Perhaps scared to tears by now, and legitimately so. He began to shuffle unsteadily toward the hotel, The Tangshin glimmering brightly across the harbor.

She had been waiting for him, perched upon on a chair with her hands clutched and, upon seeing Gurlicky suddenly in the doorway, Kajina jumped to her feet and wailed in a most depressing cacophony of womanly sounds.

"Now, now," he muttered, her cries splitting his brain

like a dagger. "It's not what ya think, girl. I've not been a cheatin' husband nor a drunken one. I've got a present for you is all. Took longer'n I intended by a sunrise." Gurlicky swayed as he entered the room.

"How could you!" she cried.

"Could I what?"

"You left me alone and ruined—simply ruined—dinner with daddy."

"Dinner?" Several seconds passed before Gurlicky, confused, remembered the missing day and his own delinquency.

He expected another wail, had prepared himself for one in fact, but Kajina suddenly spied his bandaged shoulder and the trickles of dry blood staining his forearm, his hand still tightly ahold of the empty liquor bottle.

"You've been *wounded?*" she asked in a tremulous voice.

"Wounded?" Once again, uncertainty clouded his expression. But the memory of his circumstances returned. "Not wounded, lass. I've brought you a present. A wedding present for your sweet self. 'Tis where I've been all day. And night," he thought to add.

"A gift?" Kajina prompted, momentarily forgetting her anger.

"Aye!" He picked gingerly at his bandage, aware that he'd not yet viewed his own work of art. Aware too that his arm would likely be puffed and bruised. He hoped Kajina wouldn't look fat and saggy against his skin.

Gurlicky stripped away the gauze, joyous to discover his arm remarkably unblemished and his wife's image perfectly rendered and stunningly lifelike. He gazed down at her voluptuous bare breasts with pride.

Kajina screamed.

When she had again found her voice, she moaned; "Bertie, what have you done!"

"I've immortalized your beauty, love!"

She screamed a second time and Gurlicky winced at the sound of her voice. Its pitch and volume cut through his misery and extracted a deeper, more intense agony.

"But people will see!" she howled.

"An' let 'em look, I say," he replied, squinting against the pain, unsure of her complaint. "Next to my heart, you are, for all of eternity."

She stared at the inked breasts—they appeared as two ripe melons, with *nipples* that seemed to actually pucker outward from his flesh.

"How could you *do* this?"

"Do what?" Gurlicky asked, truly perplexed.

"What about father! About mother."

Mother? Father? Gurlicky hadn't quite considered that. "I'll wear a proper Sunday shirt, when we head off to visit the in-laws!"

"Dinner was *last* night!" she wailed.

"Calm yourself, calm yourself," Gurlicky said with a deepening befuddlement, the shouting and crying getting the best of his good spirits.

"Take it off! Take it off!" she implored, staring at the tattoo.

"It's part of me, girl! I'd have to peel away my skin."

"Do it then!"

"Don't be silly," he mumbled, his eyes closed.

With a sob, she rushed past him. The pain tormenting his brain came in swirls and flashes of light that seemed to scramble his every thought. He couldn't bother turning to look, but rather heard Kajina rumbling about the room's tiny kitchen area. It was barely more than a closet with a small icebox and sink, and a cabinet with drawers for utensils and plates. He heard spoons and forks scatter and fall— each sound an intense jab of pain—and Gurlicky forced open an eye, only to discover Kajina rushing toward him grasping a butter knife.

A small part of his brain recognized his wife holding a blade so tiny and insufficient that it would have snapped against his bicep. But the drunken Gurlicky, the mariner who'd fought his way free of harm's way too many times to count, sprang into unconscious reaction. Unaware of the bottle still in his grasp, he swung a powerhouse blow toward his advancing foe.

Kajina saw the glint of glass and, squealing, tried to turn away. She managed only to expose her fragile jaw. Before he could check his swing, Gurlicky heard the bottle crack solidly against his wife's neck. The poor girl tumbled forward to the floor and lay as still as the doldrums on the room's round little porter's rug.

"There now, that was an accident," Gurlicky sputtered, staggering a bit to the left, then to the right. He waited for a moan or wail, but Kajina's silence was as frightening as any sound he'd ever heard.

"Kajina, *darlin'?*"

He noticed the blood bubbling up from within her ear, watching in horror as it pooled and ran darkly down her cheek to her throat, staining the little rug.

"Oh, good Lord above," Gurlicky breathed, only now conscious of the empty bottle in his grasp. He released it as if scalded. The bottle fell heavily, still intact, against the floor.

He bent and, as gently as he could, lifted his wife's tiny frame. Her head lolled. Kajina's large brown eyes stared past him, somewhere beyond the ceiling, seeing what only the dead choose to perceive.

Gurlicky sobbed.

He wasn't certain how long he might have knelt on the floor, holding his wife, but Kajina's small body had cooled considerably by the time he regained his senses and lowered her lovingly to the floor. The bleeding had stopped, although much of his blouse had stained, as had the little rug. Enough blood to engage his mind in a frantic deliberation of what might be done next.

It had been a horrible, horrible accident—of that, Gurlicky had no doubt. He could curse his stupidity, his drunkenness, but not his motivation for striking. Utter self-defense, it was. Foolish, impetuous child! But she was deader than driftwood, and no amount of remorse would bring her back. No amount of sorrow would convince her daddy or the island coppers that he had not struck her in anger or spite. There she lay, cold and still, and yet as lovely as any sculpture chiseled in marble or clay. An eternal beauty she was, his poor, dear Kajina.

He DIDN'T REMEMBER much of what followed that night. He staggered about, turning off the lights, leaving only a single candle to flicker dimly. He rolled his wife in the little rug—she was barely five feet tall, after all—only her feet dangling, and long waves of scented, ebony hair that brushed against his arms. Gurlicky waited for the bewitching hour to arrive. Precisely at two, as effortlessly as plucking up sack of grain, he hoisted Kajina over his shoulder and crept from the room with utmost silence.

Nobody saw him slink through the Tangshin's small lobby or out the doors into the inky darkness. The few lone souls he noticed in the shadows were already drunk or unconscious. He stumbled down the raw red slope toward the Wharf district and found a dinghy tied at the far, unlighted end of the pier. Gurlicky placed his bride with gentle care inside the little boat. Nearby he grabbed a coil of hemp and then chose three heavy stones from along the shoreline.

He rowed without conscious thought—for hours, it

seemed, although he later recalled none of it—knowing only that when he returned to the dock, the dinghy was empty, save for himself and the blood-stained porter's rug. The crack of dawn painted a thin pink stripe against the eastern horizon.

Somewhere, a ship's steam horn sounded. He cast his gaze across the harbor, where the broad beams of at least six freighters lay awaiting the morning tide. The Meisje Zwolle would be among them—the ship his ticket away from this God-forsaken bay and its foreboding secrets.

BERTRAM GURLICKY'S ARM slowly healed beneath the clean bandages that he changed every so often during those nine intolerable days he labored aboard the Dutch collier. The bandage was unnecessary, but it nicely hid the identity of a woman whose disappearance might have been radioed to those vessels recently steaming from Pu'a Pu'a Bay. Yet in the privacy of his bunk each night, Gurlicky continued to marvel at the perfect rendition of his lovely young wife, indeed still so very close to his heart. As if, somehow, the lass might not really be gone at all.

"We're happy, you an' I," he whispered to the splendid inking. "An' I once promised you, darlin'—you 'n I will truly travel the world 'ever more."

By the time the ship made Semarang, Gurlicky had begun to relax his guard. The Meisje Zwolle had put four hundred nautical miles between him and the scene of his misfortune. He rejoined the Carmelita with great anticipation, and to a rousing cheer from his buddies and mates. Had he been seen boarding the Dutch vessel, had Kajina's absence been broadcast, the authorities would unlikely consider his transfer between ships mid-voyage. The Carmelita was not scheduled to return to Bansaka for another eight months and so Gurlicky found himself home free, and delightfully single, once again.

Because the Carmelita was not due to set sail for Sorong until the morrow, his first evening ashore on Java was filled with song and frivolity. His mates had promised to buy the hardworking Gurlicky his fill of whiskey and gin that night. And indeed they did, in a little thatched bar named Club Shishi on Pangapon Road—seven sailors filled with laughter and mischievous bluster. To their envy, Gurlicky finally felt free to roll up his sleeves and flaunt the remarkable image upon his shoulder, introducing the lovely Kajina as a name-less barmaid who had caught his fancy.

"A beauty of a lass, indeed," proclaimed his mate Edward, adjusting his spectacles before raising a glass, impressed by Gurlicky's taste in island maidens.

"Here, here," said the others, and Gurlicky smiled proudly.

It wasn't but a brace of shakes later that the club's *kupu-kupu malam* took notice of the mariners. A trio of young lovelies, sensing an easy flow of maritime money, approached the men with a sashay of slim hips. Each wore a sarong of bright batik, one the color of banana, one of ripe limes and one of *bunga raya*—the local flowering hibiscus. And each girl prettier than the other. Edward, already drunk on Jameson's, proclaimed that they should pool their funds and purchase Gurlicky one last hour of enjoyment, before his life aboard the Carmelita returned to routine drudgery. His shipmates, also drunk, lifted their glasses in agreement.

Gurlicky had no problem accepting such a gracious an offer.

One lass, barely crown-high to his sternum, approached Gurlicky with a gentle cooing sound. "Tanika give you *big* smile!" she encouraged, brushing a slender hand along his arm. Gurlicky could smell the sweet essence of her oiled body and said, "Tanika, darlin', I'm smilin' already."

"Tanika is very much ready to—" But her eyes fell upon Gurlicky's tattoo and, within the span of a single heartbeat, the poor girl shrank back in such fear and horror that Gurlicky could only assume his mates had made him the butt of their mischief.

"Don't be afraid, lass," he laughed. "She don't bite."

Tanika spoke rapidly under her breath to the others. Each eyed Gurlicky with a repulsion that he knew could be no ordinary prank.

"Away with you then!" he told them, dismissing the breath of icy chill that tickled the hairs on his neck. Gurlicky had no need to speak twice. The three women backed away as if from a cornered tiger, trading harsh whispers.

"Well, fancy that," said Edward, staring myopically at their retreat, thumbing his glasses and shaking his head with a look of perplexity. "Our scrip ain't good enough for 'em, eh?

"You catch a word of that?" Gurlicky wondered, knowing that Edward *parlez-voused* more than a fair lick of Island gibberish.

"Hard to say, Bert. Something about a *hantu*—a ghost is what I took t'meaning. They were talkin' about some sorta restless spirit."

"Ah, rubbish," Gurlicky muttered.

"Nonsense," agreed their mate Walt Kiskinski. "Voodoo island bunk is all that be."

"Drink up, gentlemen," Edward piped. "The night's young, the ladies as plentiful as fish in the sea!"

And so the evening continued, Gurlicky and his mates wandering from one bar to another, until the entourage of increasingly drunken seamen returned at last to the Carmelita moments before their midnight curfew. Gurlicky staggered to his quarters—a small metal room amidships, just below the bridge, with lockers lining one wall and two dozen bunks climbing another. Most were already filled with snoring, farting sailors dozing beneath the dull bluish haze of sleep lanterns. Gurlicky stashed his clothes and made his way to the head. As was his nightly ritual, he brushed his teeth, urinated, and then paused to admire his lovely Kajina in the polished aluminum mirror above the sink.

But what's this? he wondered, flexing his bicep, arching his shoulder around toward the glare of the overhead bulb. Was it merely a play of shadow, or had his beloved's smile diminished the slightest bit?

Nonsense! Gurlicky assured himself that his drunkenness had merely gotten the better of him. He stumbled back to his bunk and fell anxiously asleep, where the most unpleasant of dreams swirled around his head—all but forgotten by eight bells, when the harsh reality of morning came far too swiftly for his liking.

OVER THE NEXT SEVERAL DAYS, a strange set of occurrences caused Gurlicky to begin to doubt his own sanity. As the Carmelita steamed a steady twelve knots toward Sorong, in Dutch East Indies, he stole increasingly frequent moments to scrutinize his arm. Where Kajina's gaze had once leveled squarely at whomever might have stopped to admire her plump breasts and teasing smile, her eyes now unflinchingly met his own suspicious gaze. Upon her lips, the slightest of frowns, increasingly prominent upon each subsequent appraisal. Had the Filipino used bad ink? And yet the rendering, however transformed, remained remarkably drawn, each line smooth and crisp, almost photographic in its clarity.

"Ahhh, pure rubbish," Gurlicky muttered to himself finally, shaking off the heebie-jeebies by giving the image a good swift swat. He turned from the mirror with a snort. 'Twas a tattoo upon his shoulder—nothing more, and nothing less.

The SS Carmelita made Sorong two days later. Gurlicky pulled winch duty—meaning four hours of hard labor while many of the sailors disembarked for the nearest saloon. Gurlicky determined this was for the best, deciding to forego shore leave altogether. At least until his good spirits returned. His sleep had been sporadic and an extra few hours of shut-eye would do him a world of good.

Gurlicky found an old jersey and shredded it, then wrapped the material around his beloved, lest her brooding demeanor attract unwanted attention or distract him from his duties. For the next three days while the Carmelita took on cargo, Gurlicky worked and slept and did little else, volunteering for every nasty detail that came over the horn. *A fine sailor, that Bert Gurlicky*—he'd heard the captain declare those words himself, shortly before they cast off again for a nor'eastern swing around the island. The Carmelita would make a brief port'o call in Madang, Territory of New Guinea, before starting the two thousand mile trek to Brisbane for an extended leave while the ship's cracked number two piston coupling was replaced.

Well on their eastbound loop toward the Bismarck Sea, making good headway in fair weather, Gurlicky found himself feeling fit and proper once again. Nothing like several days of sweat and strain to set a man's head straight. Later that evening, aware that ample time had lapsed since he'd last glimpsed his true love, he snuck away to the crew's head and removed the makeshift bandage. What he saw startled him so profoundly that he leapt away from mirror and crashed backwards into the steel bulkhead, trembling in terror.

His precious Kajina no longer harbored any pretense of serenity—instead, her luscious lips had pulled apart in the most heinous of snarls. Even more astounding, the inky folds of her kimono had shifted, providing a degree of modest concealment. Even the girl's gentle repose had shifted, as if she were somehow more crouched than seductively seated. As if, he realized, Kajina were about to lunge at his throat.

"Here now!" Gurlicky managed to mutter. "What are ya doin', lass?"

But his query met cold silence.

Gurlicky clamped a hand over the inking and made his way quickly through the darkness to Edward's bunk. He shook the man awake with a harsh whisper. "Wake up! Quickly now, wake up. Heaven have mercy."

"What, what? Have we run afoul?"

"No, no—*listen*. My lovely Kajina, she's gone an' turned on me like some rabid animal."

Edward raised himself in curiosity, rubbing sleep from his eyes. "Are you daft, mate? I was just about to give Rita Hayworth a good tumble."

"Take a look," Gurlicky implored. He thumbed the flint wheel of his pocket lighter and held the sputtering flame to his shoulder. Kajima's outline twitched and gyrated against the meager glow.

"Aye," Edward said in a curious voice, fumbling for his glasses. "I've told you before, a lovely girl."

"*Look*, damn you!"

The girl's snarl had taken on a wolverine appearance, two fangs visible in her open mouth. In her eyes, an expression of brute savagery. More horrifically, Kajina seemed to have risen higher upon his shoulder, advancing toward his collarbone.

"You see!" Gurlicky cried.

"Aye, a beautiful lass," Edward confirmed with a squint, still groping for his spectacles, lost somewhere amid the folds of his blanket.

"Don't you see her teeth? Her wretched glare?"

"You've been inhalin' diesel fumes, by God." Edward shook his head and yawned. "Best you run topside an' see the doc, Bert. Away with you, now."

"Blast your sorry ass!"

Edward at last found his glasses but, as Gurlicky had already slunk away through the bulkhead hatch, he shrugged and rolled away again to sleep.

They made port late the next afternoon, the Carmelita dropping anchor at the far end of the harbor and maintaining a discrete distance from any prying eyes ashore. As the ship would neither take on nor deliver cargo, the crew quickly grew suspicious. Adding to their misgivings, their stay in Madang was to be brief and thus all shore leave had been denied. The captain and first mate left aboard a military tender flying Australian colors. An outpost had been constructed near the local air strip and scuttlebutt had it that the Carmelita would be returning with clandestine arms and munitions after the ship's overhaul in Brisbane.

The second mate had been left in charge. Percy Marlow was known as a fierce ball-buster, a tough cookie looking for any excuse to impress the captain. *There'll be no slackin' off this evening, fellars,* Marlow announced over the bullhorn, as the Carmelita was to be in spit n' polished shape by the captain's return early the following morning.

The crew, filled with grumble at the second mate's pompous bluster, spent much of the waning twilight swabbing and lashing and repairing frayed cabling. Those topside stared longingly at Madang's flickering lanterns, mourning the forbidden proximity of the harbor's taverns and parlors. The distant echoes of wooden drums and mellifluous *seruling* toyed cruelly with their psyches, much like the sound of a cool waterfall to men sun-scorched in desert heat.

But such was their fate on that night.

Precisely at six bells the next morning, the Carmelita readied for departure. The giant turbines turned over with a cough and a sneeze, the cook stirred a giant pot brimming with lamb and rice stew, and the bo'swain stood foulmouthed with the discovery of seaman Gurlicky absent from his post. He called for a bunk check—woe be any sailor who overslept his watch—but Bert Gurlicky was not to be found. The first mate ordered three short blasts of the air horn and directed all spotters to their stations; best to be certain that the man hadn't stumbled overboard in the night, cracked his head and lay bloated or unconscious at the waterline. But there was no sign of able bodied Gurlicky, and the Carmelita could not wait. Shaking his head in disbelief, the bo'swain listed *Gurlicky, Bertram M.* as AWOL and ordered his status radioed to the Australian MPs on shore patrol.

CLOAKED IN THE DARKNESS of a new moon, Gurlicky had shimmied down the thick anchor line naked as a jay, his boots and clothing bunched inside a lye-soaked canvas sack. (He'd left his dog-tags tucked beneath his pillow, should he find himself apprehended before the night was through.) He slipped into the warm waters and began to swim toward shore, the satchel gripped firmly between his teeth. A fine time to deny a man the taste of gin, because if ever a body needed a stiff drink, it was upon this frightful night. Gurlicky swam for most of an hour, diagonally toward shore and keeping a keen eye on the lights of Madang that eventually passed to his starboard. He scraped his shin on rocks coming ashore—a sea critter had been nibbling at a mole on his right buttock for several minutes—but Gurlicky eventually climbed into the balmy night and shook himself dry the best he could.

He assumed the shore patrols wouldn't be very active this late, the few drunks they might encounter groggy and unfit for a fair fight. Sleepy eyed policemen would light yet another cigarette and wait for the dawn shift. But Gurlicky also knew that any mariner caught adrift would feel the cold reality of an Aussie brig, with hell to pay come morning. He'd face an angry dressing down in front of his mates, a loss of pay and a long stretch of hell before he'd ever see a pub again.

A few sips of *jajem* in some quiet, dark corner was all he needed—a few drinks to clear his head and, by God, soon enough he'd be back aboard the Carmelita, sleeping like a baby and the blasted creature on his arm blissfully forgotten.

But Gurlicky had been wrong about the Aussie coppers. In their crisp beige knickers, and their Springfields fixed with bayonets that gleamed under the glow of scattered oil lamps, they patrolled the outskirts of town in diligent pairs—as if all along they'd been *waiting* for Bertram Gurlicky to try his luck tonight. Those foul wog bastards!

He watched from the leafy undergrowth for several minutes, catching his breath, but the presence of the MPs gave him little space to maneuver. The dirt road that wove through Madang stretched around the shoreline to his left and Gurlicky eventually saw no other choice but search for his redemption elsewhere. Surely a gin-joint or two awaited him beyond the outskirts of town. He turned and found himself walking an anxious mile away from the harbor, the only thought in his head being the taste of gin. With each step, he could sense Kajina's murderous intrusion upon his flesh. He licked his lips, salty dry from his arduous swim, and hastened his pace.

Gurlicky had trod a good twenty minutes before he spied a solitary structure in the midst of a clearing—a long, flat building constructed of concrete and bamboo and swathed in a meager yellowish glow of several lanterns. The dirt road, which jutted inland, offered no further solace, consumed as it was by the total blackness of the encroaching jungle. Deliberating but a moment, Gurlicky cut a lively path toward the meager flicker of lamplight.

On a wide wicker porch, an old woman seated on a rocker regarded him without expression. A large man suddenly filled the empty doorway beside her. He was the biggest man Gurlicky had ever seen in the islands, broad and bearish, his long hair tangled and curly. A machete dangled from the hemp belt of his trousers. In the glow above their heads, Gurlicky spied a single wordless shingle—an image of a dragon and python, entwined, locked in mortal combat.

"Have ye any gin here, miss?"

The woman merely stared.

Quite abruptly, Gurlicky's brain registered a faint, pungent odor. He noticed a bluish mist drifting into the night from the corners of the doorway above the big man's head. He would indeed find no gin here—and yet the place beckoned with a sweet oblivion all its own. Gurlicky had stumbled upon a loathsome *pemadatan*, an opium den where wretched souls came to renounce their free will, their hopes and dreams and, soon enough, their sanity.

Gurlicky had long paid heed to the chilling tavern tales and, as any sailor worth his salt, had dutifully ignored the Siren's song of the Chinese poppy. The evil *candu*. Every mariner knew the substance could destroy a man's mind within a fortnight, for it held the power to become both sacred mistress and inner demon.

But what's old Bertie tonight, if not a wretched soul? he wondered.

"A room," he demanded, "an' a bowl." He waited for the woman's slight nod and watched her rise from the chair, biting his lip with dreadful anticipation. He followed her past the brooding man-mountain in the doorway, listening to the cries of the desperate, the sighs of the contented. He peered into a large, darkened chamber with a high ceiling, speckled with bamboo matts. Twenty or thirty bodies lay sprawled beneath the drifting azure haze. The old woman touched Gurlicky's arm and preceded him down a corridor of straw-matted dirt, lined with six roughly hewn doorways, each swathed in long strands of braided bamboo. She paused beside one such doorway and pushed aside the dry wicker curtain. Gurlicky poked his head into a room about eight-foot square, but its efficiency seemed oppressive and he shook his head. "Larger, missus. I need space to breathe."

The old woman shrugged and ambled on. At the end of the hallway she paused again. Gurlicky elbowed through the curtain, confronting a windowless room about twice as large. He could afford the luxury of a night's privacy and nodded. This would suffice. Two bamboo mats lay on the floor in the far corners, a tin piss pot standing between them. A half-dozen candles hung haphazardly from the walls, otherwise bare, save for a hemp weaving of a tiger's head, half-eaten by moths—its gaze animated in the candlelight. He could smell a lingering, perhaps permanent, odor of urine and sweat.

He chose the mat in the farthest corner and sat crosslegged to wait. Alone now, Gurlicky took a deep breath and decided to peel away the knotted cloth that cloaked his beloved. There, in the flicker of light, he found Kajina a creature truly transformed, a hideous she-beast, barely human. Her savage face had fully risen to the slope of his shoulder, her sharpened fangs but a hand's width from his throat.

The old woman soon brought his bowl and a small, pearl-black hookah. "Hurry, woman! Hurry now," he implored. She set the hookah on the floor and blew gently on a charcoal ember until it glowed a bright crimson. Upon the heat chamber she carefully placed a small metal cup, its bottom peppered with tiny holes. She dropped a brown, oily mass and blew again until it too began to glow. The woman hesitated momentarily, aware of the tattoo on his arm, and Gurlicky watched the pity in her expression melt into horror.

"Away now," he told her brusquely.

She backed from the room, her gaze on the floor, leaving Gurlicky with his inked beloved and with his madness. Midway through the corridor, she thought she heard the man begin to sob with a terrible remorse.

DAWN CREPT EARLY ASHORE the eastern fringes of those islands ensconced within the Southern Seas, the encroaching sun splashing the horizon in an eerie crimson sheen. Overhead birds cried and preened in the coming warmth. Not long after sunrise, an old woman's wail startled those same birds into sudden flight.

A messenger was sent afoot to fetch a shaman from a neighboring village. An old, wizened man appeared shortly thereafter, wearing a brightly woven cloak and feathered headdress. But the shaman stopped several paces short of the bamboo porch, slowly backing away, whispering only *"jahat, jahat, jahat!"*—evil, evil, evil!

Distraught, they sent a 10-year-old girl named Yaloli to peddle her rusting bike into town for medical help.

As it happened, Colonel Frederick Christianson, an Australian military surgeon of regional influence, was touring various clinics around the island. By chance, Dr. Christianson had spent the night at the home of a local medic, a younger man named Kabu who delivered babies and stitched up machete and plow wounds in the area. It was to Kabu's doorway that little Yaloli rode her bicycle and, prompted by the girl's animated pleas, Dr. Christianson agreed to accompany his young companion to a place the natives called *Dragon House*—an all too familiar destination for Kabu.

They took Dr. Christianson's eight-year-old Hudson sedan, Yaloli and her bicycle unceremoniously dumped in the back seat with his medical bag and physician's white smock, the girl yelling, "Segera, *segera!*" the entire bumpy ride.

"We're *hurrying* the best we can," Kabu reassured her. Aware of the reputation of the place, they presumed the emergency to be a likely overdose, although Yaloli's insistence about some night-shrouded devil intrigued them both.

The old woman stood on the thatched porch, her hands clenched, impatiently awaiting their arrival. "What's happened, Serah?" Kabu asked and she began to babble, until Kabu slowed her words with a gentle hand, pressing a finger to his lips. "A deep breath, *nenek*. Take your time. We are here to help. Now...tell us the problem."

A *yanqui!* Serah murmured. She explained that the man had come in the middle of the night, a sailor, most insistent, and had smoked three bowls—

"Three?" Kabu asked, incredulous.

She nodded furiously, holding up three fingers. "Tiga! Tiga!"

Increasingly worried, Serah told Kabu that she'd sent her grandson, Simon Situ, to check upon the American an hour before dawn. But the boy—all six-foot eight, three hundred and twenty pounds of him—had been accosted in the doorway, clocked by a single roundhouse punch to the jaw, his machete snatched from his possession. Simon Situ had staggered back into the hall, moaning loudly. Serah had somehow managed to guide him into an empty room, where he collapsed, unconscious, the old woman quivering and praying for daylight, fearing the devil might come and devour them all.

The two medical men moved cautiously along the hallway ahead of the old woman, Dr. Christianson formally wearing his white smock and carrying the medical bag. Several paces from the doorway, old Serah simply stopped walking and pointed. The men regarded each other cautiously before continuing to the end of the hall. Dr. Christianson fingered aside the bamboo curtain and stood transfixed for a long moment before he managed to whisper, "Sweet Jesus have mercy."

FROM THE POSITION of the severed limb, from the various wall splatters and blood trails, Dr. Christianson quickly reconstructed the events that had transpired. The deceased had attempted to saw away his own arm with Simon Situ's machete and, having failed to complete the task, had begun hacking until he'd managed to shear all but a few threads of muscle and tissue away from the collarbone. The poor devil had then *ripped* the offending appendage from his body and flung it across the room.

In the doctor's mind, there could be no other logical conclusion. He noted no signs of an intruder. No ritual stab wounds from the victor upon the vanquished, nor bloody footprints leaving the scene of the carnage. The skirmish had been confined to a single corner, the apparent result of an addict's insanity. The doctor squatted over the body, seeking either ID tag or wallet. Finding neither, he reached down with thumb and forefinger and closed the dead man's eyes, which continued to peer quite horrifically toward the ceiling—as if *still* seeking escape from this earthly plane.

"There's nothing we can do for the wretch," Dr. Christianson said. Aware of Kabu peeking cautiously through the doorway fronds, he pointed to a second bamboo mat in the adjacent corner. "Be a good fellow and fetch the limb for me, won't you? It's only proper that we inter the body intact." He waited a few seconds before glancing inquisitively at his companion, who'd yet to move. The young medic's expression verged on sheer horror.

Dr. Christianson had known Kabu for quite a few years and regarded him as neither coward nor prone to superstition—but he also understood that certain Island taboos were not to be trifled with.

"No worries, lad. I'll do it." Clutching the mat, the doctor stooped to retrieve the stiff and bloodless arm. Most men would not have not noticed a tattoo beneath the thick reddish-black wash of congealing blood, but a fragment of ink caught his eye. He pulled a towel and alcohol bottle from his medical bag and began to gently swab the area. The inking, he knew, might very well be the sole means of identifying the victim.

"How queer," the doctor remarked. "Tell me, Kabu, have you ever seen a rendering such as this before?"

The younger man finally ventured forward and peered down at the limb.

"No. Nothing ever."

"Oddest tattoo I believe I've ever encountered," Dr. Christianson said, trying to decipher the deft ink renderings of a broken parasol and empty sandals, alongside a discarded kimono that stretched from the man's elbow to his ragged shoulder. "I've encountered girlfriends, ships and anchors. But this, Kabu, seems a mystery to me."

"Some sort a cypher?" the young man wondered.

"Certainly beyond my comprehension," the doctor said. "I'll call for a photographer in town. We can pass the markings along to the local harbor masters and check with those ships in port. We'll also need a proper detail for cremation, straight away."

"And a priest," Kabu said anxiously.

"Yes, and a priest," the doctor confirmed. There were enough bloody superstitions lurking about without adding another to the island lore.

They moved down the corridor together, the doctor fingering his chin in a thoughtful manner. "Have you ever encountered this kind of behavior before? Here, at Dragon House?"

Kabu considered the question, then shook his head. "No, never. I have seen much anger and anxiety in those desperate for the poppy, but never more than a lazy stupor from those within its grasp. This man, he must have been in terrible pain."

"Yes, I agree completely."

From the front porch, Kabu told Serah not to worry—he would return momentarily to tend to her grandson's injuries. The proper authorities would come soon to remove the yanqui's body. Hands steepled in gratitude, the old woman thanked and blessed him. The two men moved along the dirt path and toward the road, brighter now in morning's approach.

"Thank you, Kabu. You've been most helpful. I do believe that's one of the strangest—" But the doctor stopped speaking, his gaze focused. For an instant, he wondered if he might be hallucinating. "Do you *see* her?" he asked with a curious skepticism.

"I *do*, sir," Kabu replied, equally confounded.

A young wisp of a woman, no more than a teen, had emerged from the dark shadows of encroaching jungle. She appeared as if in a daze—and utterly naked!—strolling along the unpaved road as if without a concern in the world, nor without a cogent thought either. Her gaze flitted among the canopy of dense treetops, a myriad of birds calling and whistling above her. The young woman's mouth hung open, as if in true wonderment.

"One of the addicts here?" Kabu offered—although this girl was moving toward the pemadatan, not away from in it.

But Dr. Christianson had not heard, having taken several quick strides forward. Shrugging the medical coat off his shoulders, he approached the waif with great empathy.

"Child, put this on," he said gently, draping the garment around her slim shoulders and closing it around her midriff.

She regarded him with a dazed fascination, abruptly aware of his uniform, of his straight and handsome demeanor. Her eyes ignited. "Are you an *admiral?*" she asked.

Her perfect English perplexed him. She was certainly no native to the region; not dark-skinned aboriginal, but much lighter complected, her hair straight and shiny, with facial features more typical of those islanders farther north. Malays probably—with perhaps some Dutch ancestry.

"Can you tell me your name, Miss?"

She continued to stare at him in vague confusion, until a pair of richly plumed cuckooshrikes flew overhead, snatching her attention.

Dr. Christianson waited patiently. "Might you at least tell me what you're doing here?"

She looked at him again, with all the awe and fascination of a newborn. And then she smiled, a dazzling expression that brightened her lovely face.

"Why, I'm seeing world, admiral. I'm seeing the *world.*"

The Eternal
BOOK I
(The Past)

始

BEGINNING

MY NAME IS MEI XING, and I will soon depart from this realm. I have lived so very long, a life rich beyond reason. I now accept *mìng yùn* willingly, guided by the gentle hand of my beloved. My death will be my husband's ultimate consummation of our love, his final gift to our blessed union. Before my passing, I must reveal a most extraordinary tale. I speak not for myself, but rather of my husband's own astounding journey. This is my gift in return, a bequest to all who are and who will ever be. Only with his consent do I write these words.

ONE

THOSE WHO KNOW ME, know nothing. I have carried my secret in darkness for too many years. Yet mine is a secret that must unfold, for it is truth. Listen, my children, and consider all that has come before us.

I was born in a distant land, amidst the turbulent uprising known as *Yihetuan*. I was birthed in the blood-soaked dirt of Shandong, my father already dead at the hands of the Christian foreigners and my mother soon to become a slave of Yikuang, Prince Qing of the First Rank, a great-grandson of Emperor Qianlong. The prince (I would later discover) was the most unscrupulous of leaders, an insatiable man who traded China's tears for gold.

My earliest memories? I remember a palace—although *whose* palace, I do not know. To a small child, a castle is a remarkable realm, a playhouse of great possibility, ripe with dark, secret rooms and gleaming marbled hallways without end, of pungent spices and swirling colors, of uniformed men and temple priests and silk-draped women of high esteem and confidence.

But I was not a child *of* the palace, simply an urchin within its magnificent folds. One morning, along with many girls my age, I was taken by oxcart to a sailing ship, under the watchful eye of a stooped, elderly gentleman whom I had barely met and did not trust. My sisters and I had been instructed to call this man 'Grandfather Lau' with utmost affection. As the morning sun rose, our sails unfurled. I watched with sorrow as my homeland vanished into the past.

The bright colors of the world quickly disappeared, replaced by the ugly brown wood of our worm-threaded vessel. Ahead, I saw nothing but the tepid grey expanse of sea and sky. I remember vividly the tired moan of old planking, the creak of wet hemp and the wails of my sisters. Even the birds had given up their playful cries, ultimately abandoning us to our providence. I constantly scanned the horizon for the edge of the Earth, eager to plunge toward whatever fate that I imagined would only improve my dismal, mortal existence.

As I feared, the waters did prove endless. Our provisions grew scarce and for several days we were given only cold rice and water that tasted—to the best of my childlike recollection—*green*. Even the sailors grew restless and ill-tempered, and then afraid. Min Min fell sick and Jiang died. Around me, my sisters prayed and wept.

One morning, a sudden brightness illuminated the sky. The overhead sun caressed my face with its warmth. A wind of blessed forgiveness filled our slack sails and our vessel plowed through each wave with swift vengeance. Instead of certain doom, there soon appeared before our mast a fog-shrouded silhouette of low hills and dark forests.

I watched this strange land approach, barely aware of the barefooted, half-naked sailors rushing to prepare the ship to dock. I could soon discern tall, block-like shapes of many buildings behind a gradually receding haze. These were not the ornate, angular forms of those I had left, but stark buildings that spanned a far greater distance than any castle I could ever imagine.

The only word I remember on Grandfather Lau's lips is this: *"Fiscow!"*

And what a wondrous place, this Fiscow. I had never before seen a steamship or a railroad train that belched plumes of blackened smoke. I had never seen pale men or tall women with yellow hair. So many remarkable novelties filled my senses.

My sisters and I were taken from the bustling wharf by a horse-drawn wagon, up a hill and then up a larger hill, along a muddy road to an imposing red brick building with few windows. Men carrying large burlap sacks and who smelled of tobacco and opiate smoke accompanied our wagon, their overseers yelling and cursing, brandishing bamboo reeds—many of my sisters cried—and Grandfather Lau hovered over us with a clucking intensity.

At the top of yet another hill the wagon groaned to a stop. My sisters and I stomped up a lengthy flight of narrow, squeaking stairs. We found ourselves in a perfumed room of silk draperies and satin pillows and alight with many candles. Beautiful ladies sashayed among us, and whose enchantingly painted faces reminded me of the intricate opera masks I remembered from the palace. The ladies delighted in our presence, giggling and singing and purring words of soothing assurance against our ears.

I believed that my nightmare had ended. This was a world of soft musical notes plucked on a stringed *ruan*, of mesmerizing colors and scented fragrances, and I wondered if one of these stunning young women might be my mother.

Perhaps the greatest gift of my childhood was my incomprehension that day; I did not understand my intended fate until many years afterward. But on that day, I did not know such words as *slavery* or *concubine*, only that I was given a clay bowl filled with noodles and onions swimming in a steaming fish broth. When night fell, I slept deeply in a world I believed would at last become my loving home.

Much later I would learn the foreigners' calendar date of my arrival in this rambling city of San Francisco: The 18th of March, 1906.

FOR MANY WEEKS afterwards, my sisters and I were locked in a large, windowless room, with only the glow of many small candles casting ghostly shadows against the walls. Porcelain pots in each corner sufficed for our necessary toiletry needs. We ate twice a day and began to learn basic words of our new language. We shared several enormous straw-filled mattresses strewn upon the floor and, each night, I felt safely cocooned amid the warmth of the others, wondering what excitement our next morning would bring.

But quite soon my fairy-tale reality crumbled. Late one night I was jostled from my dreams by a grumbling tremor. The room shuddered and shook, and I felt myself lifted into the air, only to fall again amidst the flailing bodies of screaming children. Suddenly, the night crashed down upon us, choking our terrified wails into abrupt silence. A ragged cadmium sky appeared overhead, while the floorboards beneath us trembled in agony.

I remember the crack and torque of shrieking wood and I tumbled blindly into an abyss. I most certainly lost consciousness, for when I awoke, the world had again steadied itself. I lay without moving for a long while, listening to the whimpers around me. I called out and eventually we found one another in the dark, five of us, frightened and shivering. Clutching hands, we wove a snakelike path through the debris, the barest hint of morning light leading our way. We stumbled amid the rubble, tripping on the broken, lifeless bodies of my many sisters.

We huddled together in the mud-chilled street, aware of distant shouts and cries in the murky light of an awakening sky. A few buildings around us had likewise ruptured, littering the ground with debris and the bloodied dead. From our view atop the hill, I could see a yellow-orange flicker of many fires in the city below. We held each another tightly, awaiting whatever terrible fate would certainly follow. We did not move or eat for two days, until white men in stiff blue suits struggled up the hill, blowing shrill whistles and calling out for anyone who might respond.

Many years later, as a historian of some renown, I would take keen interest in San Francisco's Great Earthquake. At the time, newspapers reported fewer than 700 deaths in the city. Later revisions would raise the death toll to more than 3500. But among the *gu lei*—the so-called worker *coolies*— I would glean evidence of some 8,000 additional deaths. So many transients and immigrants and undocumented slaves had been buried beneath the rubble, forever entombed as the city rose again above them.

But on that horrible day, I remained miraculously unharmed, a whisper-thin waif of child with only a handful of English words in my brain. Poor Grandfather Lau had attempted to teach us our new language in those weeks before the 'quake. But I never saw Grandfather Lau again. Nor do I know what became of my surviving sisters, although I can only assume that none found so exhilarating an existence as soon would I.

For several days I lingered in one of hundreds of hastily erected army tents scattered throughout the Presidio District, far enough from the smoldering embers of a city I had not yet come to know. Then, one morning, two soldiers brought me before a stunning woman wrapped in white silk, who knelt before me with a most haunting smile and spoke in soothing words I did not understand. An older man, a bearded *guilao* dressed in blue, stood beside her and said nothing. Although the woman confronting me was Chinese, her words were those of this new world, and I struggled to remember my own pitifully few English phrases in return. I bowed, speaking politely and she smiled again, her warm hand feather-light upon my shoulder. When the bearded man nodded his approval, the soldiers turned to leave, and I suspected my life's course had been once again inexplicably altered.

Mrs. Lin Li Muldoon, whom I would learn to call *Miss Lin*, took me into her home as an apprentice pot scrubber, entitled to a stipend of two pennies a week, which I was free to spend or save until my services were proven sufficiently worthy of a real wage. Miss Lin nicknamed me *Marcy*, as she deemed Mei Xing too foreign for American tongues. She preferred that her staff speak proper English, Miss Lin aware that the language of these foreigners represented my future.

Ten of us served in the Muldoon household; cooks, valets, porters—even a doorman. Their sprawling estate had been slightly damaged by the quake, but its hillside location in Presidio Heights had saved it from the raging fires that had destroyed much of the city.

Once again, I found myself wandering amid the princes and princesses of this new realm. Miss Lin's home was indeed very much a castle, tall and immaculate, filled with mystique and so many splendid rooms, long and winding passages, anonymous doors locking their secrets behind thick, brass key plates. Heirlooms of my homeland abounded; paintings and sculptures and tabletop objects fashioned from ivory and jade, gold and pearl. We were forbidden to *touch* and sometimes I would stare at these objects until I cried, for they reminded me of my birth land, of a mother I'd never known.

For many weeks I sat on a high stool in the Muldoon's enormous kitchen, with little else to do but watch and wait. I quickly realized the way to Miss Lin's heart was through stillness and rapt attention to detail, and I was very good at absorbing the duties of those around me. Two mornings each week, the Muldoon's household chef, the robustly rotund Mr. Fréchon, explained every detail of his activities. In the afternoons, I often polished silverware or scrubbed a bevy of large copper pots, enormous vats that would sometimes consume my tiny body. Yet I would scrub and scrub until Mr. Fréchon—muttering *Ça suffit! Ça suffit!*—snatched the vessels from my grasp, my hands raw and red and occasionally bleeding from my efforts.

Most other mornings were crowded with math, English and American history, my studies overseen by Mrs. Livingston, an older woman who had lived in Wenzhou for many years. She spoke Mandarin very well, although she rarely permitted me to converse in my native tongue.

The days and weeks and then months passed in a blur. Eventually, I was rousted at daybreak, expected to perform more rigorous duties. I delighted in plucking feathers from various fowl, tending ovens and dumping ash buckets into an outdoor bin. I sliced onions and peeled carrots and, standing upon a rickety wooden stool, stirred simmering sauces and gravies. Within five years I would be preparing vegetable and potato dishes for the family, and by the age of fourteen I ascended to prominence as the Muldoon's primary cook.

Mrs. Lin Li Muldoon, only twenty-seven years of age when she found me, had once upon a time been a Jiangsu princess who'd fled across the ocean ahead of a scandal that would have severed her head in the lightning flash of a *dao*. Gifted with the perplexing beauty of royal blood and having arrived on these shores with trunks filled with Chinese artifacts worth a substantial fortune, she quickly captured the attention of a local sea captain. Raphael Muldoon was a kind and gentle soul, some twenty years his wife's elder, and quite smitten with his young princess.

Captain Muldoon proved to be a most wonderful man, sea-bound much of the time but who eventually became very much like a father to me. I learned that shortly after their marriage, he and Miss Lin had begun their crusade, frequenting brothels and opium houses, buying up the children of the damned and leading them to freedom. Not far away, on Lake Street, The Muldoon School for Orphaned Children of The Orient housed some 80 students a year, young girls once destined for an otherwise brutal and savage existence.

I was one of the fortunate, quick of mind and spirit, wide eyed with wonder and endowed with a persistent smile despite my perilous youth. In the Muldoon household, I knew myself as neither slave nor servant, but rather as a skilled and respected employee, indentured only by my age and ensured to one day become a free woman who might come and go as I please. And yet I could not imagine parting from the Muldoon family, for I wished to remain within Miss Lin's employ for the whole of my life.

Wished for nothing more, that is, until I met Captain Sebastian T. Renaud.

He was quite handsome, this captain, tall and statuesque, perhaps thirty years old, although he wore his age like a shroud. Clearly a man of youthful vigor, clean shaven and polite, he possessed an extraordinary command of the English language, with a wisdom and ken beyond his years. The first time I gazed upon Captain Renaud my heart swooped as might a dove in flight, and I eagerly absorbed as much gossip as I could from the household staff: That he was a dear friend of Captain Muldoon's who had been a frequent guest in the past. An anthropological expedition to Egypt and Sudan had kept him abroad these last several years. But now, much to my heart's joy, he had returned to California.

An exceedingly intellectual man, as one might instantly

perceive by his grace and air, he nonetheless lacked the excruciating conceit of many who are well-travelled and properly educated. Although quiet and reserved in conversation, he was conversely a fine narrator. Before his journey to The Dark Continent, I learned that the Muldoon's six children and many of the staff would often sit in the parlor after supper and listen in rapt attention as he spoke of ancient wisdoms and cultures.

I was likewise invited to hear the Captain's tales this evening (once the dishes had been cleared) and a thousand questions bubbled forth inside my head.

Yet the first time our eyes met, we spoke not a single word. I had rushed from the kitchen bearing a plum-and-sausage glaze forgotten by one of the servers and perchance the Captain was passing the doorway into the dining room. He paused, mid-step—as I nearly collided glaze-first into him—and I shall never forget the way he gazed at me.

I fell in love with him in that same heartbeat, a profoundly *dreadful* realization, as I knew such desire would burn hollow in my soul for all of eternity. But within the span of that chanced glance, I had discovered a depth to my own being that I had never before known. I returned to the kitchen and wept like the child I knew myself still to be.

And yet I remained a child not without precocious wiles. After collecting my thoughts, I took a perverse delight in tiptoeing from my chores to eavesdrop upon their meal. I learned that Sebastian Renaud was a seaman like Captain Muldoon and that he had served as a cavalry officer during the Spanish-American War. He had raced Peugeot automobiles across Europe and had even piloted those rickety little aeroplanes that buzzed the sky like so many annoying mosquitoes. I realized him to be a man of surprising complexity and wondered if there were *nothing* he might not accomplish.

Upon this particular evening, I overheard Captain Renaud pledge to renew his partnership with Raphael in assailing the city's countless flesh merchants—by purchasing slaves solely to procure their freedom. Apparently, he was heir to a fortune even more astounding than the Muldoon's, and not only would they strive to free and educate younger orphans, but also arrange safe transport home for those older girls stolen from their families.

Freeing immigrant slaves in those early years of the new century proved a difficult process. Despite numerous laws forbidding depravity, the peoples of China and the Pacific Isles were regarded with no less contempt than had been the African races a half-century before. With neither passport nor dowry, without claims of legal passage or citizenship, without hope of returning to their native lands, these wretched children found nowhere to flee. Quite often a freed concubine would scurry back to the only food and warmth she had ever known—into the clutches of her former slaver. The underbelly of the city remained ripe with savagery and a lust for both flesh and money that knew few mercies.

I would discover that, on numerous occasions, Captains Muldoon and Renaud had barely escaped foul play at the hands of slavers who considered them obstacles in their various paths to riches. More than once had they traded gunfire with ruffians who would leap from a dark alley, or might linger in ambush beside some deserted highway, in an attempt to end such meddling in their affairs.

But on that day in the late summer of 1915, I perceived little more but snatched fragments of conversation. I did not know if I would ever lay eyes on Captain Renaud again, and lying in bed that night, I assured myself that I certainly would *not*. How could someone so trivial expect more than what the universe had already graciously provided me?

A miracle occurred however, and one that continues to

perplex me to this day. Upon Captain Renaud's subsequent social calling the following month, he requested a formal introduction! Miss Lin, having found a sea captain of her own, took tremendous delight in his curiosity. I was fetched from the kitchen by two giggling *mui tsai*, my face quickly washed of flour and grease before being paraded into an anteroom with barely time to catch my breath.

Once again, our eyes met; me in my stained cap and apron and he seated in a black gabardine suit, wainscot and polished boots. When he stood, I felt as if he almost touched the ceiling. "It is my pleasure to greet you, Captain Renaud," I stammered in my politest whisper of English.

The captain offered a regal smile and replied in perfect Mandarin, "The pleasure is all mine." Upon hearing these words in the language of my lost homeland (and much to my embarrassment) I immediately burst into tears.

Quite unexpectedly, I was invited to dine at the Muldoon's request, supper delayed those frantic twenty minutes during which I prepared for the occasion—quickly lathered and scrubbed and ensconced in Miss Lin's own lavish, red silk *ruqun*, as I had no finery of my own.

I barely remember the words spoken that evening, nor of tasting the meal that I had spent hours preparing—oyster-stuffed Canadian goose, potatoes au gratin and garlic-rubbed asparagus. I remember only the Captain's gaze as he pondered me from across the table. The meal passed in both a heartbeat and an eternity and, soon enough, Miss Lin rang a tiny silver bell that signaled for tea and brandy in the parlor. I was offered a formal chair and a crystal glass with the smallest sip of Napoleon cognac—and I listened above the sound of my own pounding heart as Captain Renaud wove a tale about the grandeur of ancient Persepolis, the capital of Persia's once formidable Achaemenid empire. While he spoke, my eyes never left the Captain's face and, much to my amazement, his gaze did not stray far from mine. I could scarcely remember but to *breathe* that evening.

Later, we strolled among the Muldoon's moon-soaked tea gardens and Captain Renaud remarked of my beauty— *my what?* I viewed myself as a scrawny wisp of a child, all elbow and kneecap and tooth and nail, the ugly scar of a grease burn upon the back of my hand, and even now I blush at the memory of his words. But in the Captain's presence, I felt not like a raggedy child of skin and bone, but rather that I were the Empress of all China.

Before excusing himself for the evening, Reni (as he was known to his friends and enemies alike) asked Miss Lin for permission to court me. A tradition of formality apparently existed among the educated ruling class, and the Captain proved the quintessential gentleman. The Muldoons, the only real parents I had ever known, obliged with uncontained glee. Taking my hand in his, Reni awaited only my consent. After a long moment's hesitation—my thoughts filled not with coyness but with the sudden fear of swooning in his presence—I managed a nod.

And thus I sealed my fate.

CAPTAIN RENAUD AND I were engaged on Christmas Day and we married eight weeks later. I did not know my birthday, nor even the year of my birth, although Miss Lin deemed me 16ish at the time, possibly 17, and old enough in those days to suitably wed. I certainly ached with the needs of a grown woman and had dreamed of little else but his gentle kisses since we'd met.

Despite my assumption of Reni's Christianity—weren't all *mêiguó rén* the children of the crucified Christ?—he delighted in presenting me with a traditional Buddhist ceremony. "The Lord God is more an expression of morality, a state of compassion, rather than a book of rules," he would tell me on our wedding day. "Men of prejudice can alter the nuance of any good intention, can dubiously re-pen pages of any verse, but the powers of good and evil are those which each man must understand from birth."

Like everything else about my Captain, his beliefs were an enigma to me.

I should note here (for posterity, and no other reason) that I did not consider Reni to be Caucasian. Much like his age, his heritage appeared indeterminable, his skin richly tanned like many a merchant seaman, and yet his eyes blazed a rakish and vibrant copper-green. There appeared a certain Persian regality to his cheeks, a Mediterranean influence to the straight, graceful elegance of his nose, and a slight Asian influence to the corners of his eyes. His hair, cropped short, suggested the color of desert sand, and yet his occasional beard grew darker, a burnt sienna. He might resemble, if but for a single instant, a Cossack or Viking. And yet, awash in candlelight, I might glimpse an Andean shaman, Zulu *inkosi* or Sioux warrior. As if all the world's cultures spun a web of fabric within the man that could never fully confine nor reveal him.

The night of our wedding, we consummated our love in a manner that I shall not attempt, either as a proper lady or matron of certain refinement, to describe. Nor could any words express the feeling of joy and satisfaction coursing through my body, captivating my senses, astonishing my very essence of being. Although my conscious mind had always believed in the notion of love, only now did my heart perceive its jubilant fury. Even the tips of my fingers, the tips of my toes, appreciated its newfound meaning. I realized myself as, forever more, love's unmitigated prisoner.

Perhaps a scandalous admission for a woman well over one hundred years of age, I must pen here that I have nothing but cherished memories of our wedding night, and for so many nights in the many decades that followed. As a child, I had often heard of the lustful and selfish tendencies of American males in their haste for self-fulfillment. But Reni was never less than thoughtful and giving, and exquisitely gentle. He delighted me in ways of pleasure that I did not dream possible, and the purity of our spirits fused a bond that I dare say transcended the physical realm. To this day, I merely close my eyes and drift to that place where memories linger, etched for eternity in my brain. What I knew then, and what I know now; Captain Sebastian Renaud was the first and certainly the last man who would, who *could*, claim my body as his own.

On the evening of our marriage he presented me with a hillside house—number 8 Washington Street—a modest stroll from the Muldoon's own splendid residence. The Captain had barely glimpsed the abode before our wedding night but had deemed it fitting that we begin our life together in a home of our own. Until that very day, and despite whatever insinuation of his immense fortune, Reni had resided in a single room above the Baker Street Gymnasium, a residence containing little more than bed and bureau, an overstuffed bookcase, chair and reading lamp, and with barely adequate space for a steam trunk and coat rack.

But Reni was not a miser, merely a man of practicality. I have no doubt that, upon learning of my impoverished childhood, he had spared no expense in presenting me with a castle of my very own. I could scarcely believe my eyes, confronting a sky-blue Victorian with four flights of stairs and an elevator cage, with white porcelain sinks and running *hot* water in each bathroom. An indoor laundry machine! Electrical bulbs that would illuminate a room with the push of a finger. Perched atop its highest rooftop, the house claimed a railed widow's watch. Many mornings, while my husband lay sleeping, I would sneak up the stairway and find a most peaceful solitude, bearing silent witness to a city not yet awake. Occasionally I would cast my gaze upon the distant waters that had found reason to carry me here and weep tears of boundless joy.

That first day as man and wife, once over the threshold of that magnificent home, I am ashamed to say that I wept and trembled uncontrollably, while Reni stroked my hair and whispered soft assurances.

"Would you rather we live in a tent?" he queried, quite sincere, and I have no doubt that he would have granted me such a wish. But the child in me who'd once romped and explored the endless halls of palace wished to romp and explore once again, and I furiously shook my head. This boundless palace would most assuredly suffice!

THOSE INITIAL WEEKS OF MATRIMONY passed in a daze. I don't think we spent a single instant apart from one another, and come the first warmth of spring, Reni delighted in taking me—first by rail to Cazadero, and then by coach, finally by horseback—upon a marvelous journey through many of the Northern Pacific's most exquisite natural wonders. I had been a child of the city since setting foot on America's shore, and I knew nothing of the majestic Redwood forests and steep canyons, nor of the hot springs and rivers that presented a great and unspoiled expanse. I thought this lush wilderness might reach out forever, its breathtaking vistas unknown to all but an adventurous few.

My new husband proved an expert woodsman and a lover of animal life large and small. Each night we would pitch our tent and eat at the edge of a crackling campfire—mostly fish and rabbit, as Reni refused to kill any larger beast for our paltry needs. Our first evening in the wilderness, as we lay wrapped in a woolen blanket and further warmed by our fire's glowing embers, the sky spewed forth a multitude of dazzling white stars, in numbers too great to possibly exist.

"That bright one there is Rigel," Reni told me, my head nestled against his shoulder. "It's part of the constellation Orion. The other bright star, slightly to its nor'east, is named Betelgeuse."

"Constellation?" I asked, as I had never before known the night sky with such intimacy.

"A grouping of stars that appear together in the night sky, forming an outline of a specific image. Orion is known as *The Hunter*—see there, the stars that mark his drawn bow, his head and legs? It is but one of many familiar faces looking down upon the wayward traveler, providing both direction and companionship. Constellations were well known to the ancient Greeks and Romans, passed down from the Babylonians before them, and from the Samarrans before them. The Hunter," Reni whispered again, stroking my hair, and for the longest time we stared upward in silent reverie. A shooting star seared a path across the sky, punctuating the evening's magic.

"Ah, did you see that? Make a wish," he told me.

"All my wishes came true the instant I met you, dear husband," I replied in earnest, and shivered as he softly kissed the top of my head.

"What is that star's name, over there?" I asked, pointing to a twinkling speck peeking above the horizon.

"Sirius," Reni replied, "in the constellation Canis Majoris. Also named by the ancient Greeks, although also once known as *Ka'alu* eons before the Greeks established their dominance. Throughout the ages, the stars we see now were as familiar to humanity as dots of ink on a paper map. See that small grouping? The Pleiades," he said happily, "and there's Alphard and Regulus. And there, above the treeline, lies the Red Planet, Mars. *Luta'u*," he whispered, a word that, at the time, passed innocently through my head. I took no great notice of any singularity, for not many city folk bothered to look upward in those days to count the stars, much less learn their names.

Safely cocooned in his arms, I embraced the majesty of the heavens, feeling as if his voice were master of all we surveyed. I took comfort in that fantasy, and we slept that night beneath the full mantle of the universe, looking down upon us as would any loving mother.

Yet much too soon, we returned to the overwhelming regimen of my new reality, and I busied myself as would any new, young housewife. Reni remained adamant that I was not to regard my presence as 'silk drapery' in either his life or my own.

"What, then, is to be the driving passion in your life?" he inquired one morning, the question taking me utterly by surprise. But without a moment's hesitation, the answer tumbled easily from my lips—that I wished for nothing else but to emulate the decency and distinction of Mrs. Muldoon, to begin my own school and to spend my days wandering the city's brothels and dark alleys, searching for those unfortunate children like myself.

While my husband commended my gumption, he also fretted over my fate in undertaking such a crusade. I weighed barely seven stone, a slender reed of a being and, in the mirror, not at all unlike the unfortunate girls we would be assisting. Reni feared I might too easily end up in the hands of my former captors.

Realizing such a possibility, he hired two bodyguards—unsmiling, bearlike men from the Pacific island of Manu'a. He ordered these two towering hulks to accompany me on my every excursion from Washington Street, no matter how brief. A prudent decision, as both Arnai and Ra'qit would eventually draw their knives to protect my life in those early days, Arnai once slicing the forearm from a man who'd aimed a pistol at my head. (Ra'qit's great granddaughter recently graduated from San Francisco University with a law degree, the recipient of a scholarship that Reni and I established long ago in my protectors' names, in memory of those who had once risked themselves in loyalty to me. For those who are dear and cherished in the Renaud household, the past is never forgotten.)

WITHIN THE FIRST FEW MONTHS of our marriage, Reni tolerated my appointment of no less than seven full-time housekeepers. "We need but two!" he bemoaned, but after my initial selection—12-year-old Hsiu Mei and younger Wa'lana, both children once bound for prostitution—I'd begged for two more, and then two others. After I smuggled young Yu Yan through a back door as a cook's helper, my husband finally found his voice and said, *"Enough!* I cannot step sideways in this house but elbow some poor girl in the back of the head."

Indeed, this was true. Yet our home boasted of eight bedrooms, and we needed only three; the second as Reni's study and the last, I prayed, would eventually become our nursery. The sweet waifs I employed, and who of course quartered with us as well, had no other option of room or board, and Reni's monthly stipend to each was thrice that of any reasonable employer—sufficient funds for each girl to send home to struggling families, or for her own sisters in need. Thus, each month, we provided a gaggle of children the means to survive, and perhaps to one day prosper.

I knew little of the sordid lives of my husband and Capt'n Muldoon in their endless crusade to eradicate the sex trade within our city, so cruel that serpent with its endless tail. Had I been older, I might have provided more assistance to their cause. But according to Miss Lin's chronology, I remained shy of my eighteenth birthday. I continued to rely on Mrs. Muldoon's guidance and to assist her as much as possible. Had I my own way, I'd have gathered our combined fortunes in a pickle barrel to purchase the entire lot of women destined for misery. I declared so one morning, before bursting into tears, although I'm afraid such a solution was clouded with misjudgment.

"My lovely Mei Xing," Reni said gently, drying my eyes. "Such unprincipled men, these malicious *guigōng*, drunk on newfound wealth, would merely buy larger ships in which to supply their trade, and the unfortunate women bound for this city would multiply as would a plague of rodents after a full harvest."

"They are vulgarians. We should kill them *all*," I blurted.

"Rome was not built in a day, child," Raphael Muldoon remarked in his gentle brogue. "To gamble with feckless abandon for the life of a single child could mean certain death for the poor girl, and for those around her. And to kill a slaver might sacrifice a dozen children in retribution, or a hundred in starvation."

"Far better," Reni agreed, "to save the life of one child than lose fifty. What little we *can* do is far more consequential than what we cannot." To my befuddlement, he quoted Shantideva, disciple of Buddha. "Where would I find enough leather to cover the surface of the earth? Better to leather the soles of my shoes."

Moreover, he spoke these words in the language of The Buddha himself. A most unusual man, my Captain. I vowed never to display such impudence again.

A great war had raged in Europe for years and America's involvement had been anticipated for quite some time. Before our marriage, Reni had spent a large fortune advancing the theories of flight, as the aeroplane was becoming a formidable weapon. He frequently piloted all sorts of flying contraptions and knew well of their potential in the skies above France and Belgium. Reni had once spoken of the "bomber aircraft" being the ultimate assurance that modern warfare could not be sustained.

"How can *any* ground war endure such massive airborne fleets, able to rain their explosives upon regiments and fortifications—upon innocent hamlets and villages as well? Good Lord," he once remarked, "the wayward destruction of a single crowded schoolhouse would stop a war in its very tracks."

Oh, but how wrong my husband would prove to be—and Reni was not prone to underestimating humanity's indifference to cruelty. He abhorred armed conflict, profoundly aware that the mass murder of two armies seldom solved the world's problems. "War is a simple solution in the calcified minds of elder statesmen, seeking voice and grandeur," Reni told me. "And to an angry old man, a naïve young man is often the ideal choice of weapons."

But the tide of war in Europe lapped ever closer to our shores. Not six months after we wed, Reni revealed his determination to volunteer for the American Expedition as an Army pilot. I knew, of course, that a man of such courage and passion could not be swayed from the skies, nor from battle. I had already chosen to live each day as if it was our last, as if each was a singular reward, a brief expression of perfection, never to be repeated.

Too soon, the sun set upon that final day. Captain Sebastian Renaud received orders to embark for New York, and then continue by steamer to England. As strong as I hoped my resolve might be, I sobbed for a life together that I now knew was lost. For how can such profound love exist but in the blink of an eye? My Captain knelt before me, my hands in his, his head in my lap, and he promised to return.

Promised that his word was unlike any other soldier's who'd ever gone to battle. I mustered the confidence to believe him.

Reni extracted my promise to safeguard a talisman until his homecoming—a small gemstone he wore secured upon a leather braid around his neck. Unfastening the band, he placed an amethyst of dazzling and deep violet against my throat. It was a stone such as none that I had ever before seen. This gem was the manifestation of his promise, and each night thereafter I would clutch it tightly as I drifted off into troubled sleep.

I must now speak of an odd occurrence that transpired the day after Reni's departure. That evening, the crystal he'd presented began to lose its deep violet hue, turning a vibrant sapphire. I tried not to attach any significance to the variance, aware that Reni had mentioned no magical quality in the stone. But I quickly found in its proximity a soothing tranquility. I would sometimes stare for hours into its mesmerizing façade. I pondered whether the stone's magic was not of my husband's doing, but of my own. Perhaps its transformation wasn't an omen at all, but rather an assurance.

How tenuously I clung to that belief!

My Captain managed to find time to write a letter every week, at first postmarked from England and later from France. He taught the skills of flying to students even younger than I and eventually led an air squadron of his own. He became a minor celebrity in San Francisco, having shot down eleven enemy aeroplanes over the span of four months. Reni sent me newspaper clippings with his photograph, and also the picture of his tiny aircraft—a flimsy contraption that barely seemed capable of sustaining flight. He shortly thereafter mailed me a British newspaper's front page, with a bold headline: YANK FLYBOY SCORES HAT-TRICK

ALOFT. I did not know the jargons of war and was later told that *hat-trick* was the term used for downing three aircraft in a single day.

It saddened me greatly, knowing how Reni hated to kill. He despised war with such passion. But sometimes, as he'd told me the morning of his departure, one had to define duty by virtue of killing so that many more might live.

One week in early spring his letter did not arrive. For over a month I waited. On a particular grey and rainy day, the postman rang, only to hand me a blue-tinged telegram from Washington. For nearly an hour I refused to acknowledge the post. Finally, I tore open the envelope and read:

```
The War Department regrets to inform you
of the death of Army Air Captain Sebastian
T. Renaud…
```

I did not allow myself the surrender of crying. I so believed his promise to return, and to weep tears would break the bonds of that trust. I clutched his talisman—still a tranquil blue—and stumbled that afternoon to the residence of Miss Lin, where I begged to cook again for her family. She immediately agreed, the Muldoons aware of my need to bury my sorrow behind endless chores and the mundane duties of servitude—although Miss Lin soon insisted that I allow sufficient time to properly mourn. But to divert from this daily routine would mean a capitulation of spirit, a submission of body and soul. And thus I carried on, once again a valued servant, for many weeks to come.

A short while later, in a faded tan envelope that bore Reni's remarkably astute handwriting, yet *another* letter arrived from France. I tore feverishly for the pages, knowing that these would be my husband's final words to me. And yet I harbored a heart filled with desperate hope and courage.

192

The letter read:

My most cherished Marcy —
 Do not despair, for reports of my death are
assuredly premature. How it has pained me
these many weeks, unable to write, as I have
been lost in occupied France all the while.
I regret that my unavoidable silence may
have caused you concern. But I have been
sustained by your love, and your promise of
not doubting my return for a single instant.
My vow remains intact, and I will soon
return into your arms evermore.

With utmost love
And profound longing,
— Reni

I wept with abandon, not only in joyous love, but because I *had* doubted his word, and I felt ashamed of my cowardice. But knowing that he would return to me only rekindled my adoration, and my newfound certainty of his return.

Some months afterward, a second blue telegram arrived from Washington. I immediately tore open the envelope on my front steps. Reading the familiar words once again, *The War Department Regrets to Inform You...* I sensed not the slightest smidgen of fear. I smiled at the postman—I'm sure a most confounding expression under the circumstances—and yet my heart raced with the knowledge that I *would* see my beloved again, if even a dozen such telegrams found me!

Reni's own explanation arrived three weeks later:

My dearest wife —
 Apologies, my beloved, as my hapless
little Nieuport fell afoul of the weather over

Le Coteau and I was forced to land, with extreme
prejudice, once again on the wrong side of the
Seine. The Huns were kind and offered me
biscuits and a nice Bordeaux, but nonetheless escorted me to a prison encampment near
Lyon. My escape was compelled by an excruciating ache to hold you in my arms once again.
I shall explain further upon my return.

With all my love
And sincere longing,
— Reni

And my husband did come home, in the winter of
1917, to a rousing hero's welcome. He had destroyed
nineteen enemy aircraft and America's War Department
thought that he would be of far better service back in his
native country, giving speeches and mounting support for
our recent involvement in this terrible conflict.

Of course, they had no idea that once behind the po-
dium, confronting so many young and eager faces, my
Captain Renaud would decry the atrocity and futility of
modern warfare at the top of his lungs.

"Think about your country, good man!" exclaimed one
beleaguered general, striding red-cheeked upon the stage.

But Reni stood his ground. "To die for one's country
is indeed most honorable," he replied, darting a steadfast
finger toward the general's plump face. "But to die for the
sake of political dandyism is utterly absurd!"

They would have arrested him and thrown him into
prison, if not for Reni's breastplate of ribbons; the *Ordre
National de la Légion d'Honneur*, the Distinguished Service
Order, the Conspicuous Gallantry Medal and the Victoria Cross—not to mention that my husband's companies
in California were supplying the war effort to so great an
extent. His voice silenced behind their steel cages would

prove far more embarrassing. So they relented and released him from duty. President Woodrow Wilson personally wrote a note commending Reni's services. As suddenly as he had gone, my Captain had returned to hearth and heart!

His first night back on Washington Street, the first moment inside our threshold, Reni swept me into his arms, the talisman at my throat abruptly blazing a brilliant violet once again. After we had come to our senses, he listened to my story of the stone's transformation, quite perplexed and insisting that he knew of no special powers it held. He seemed at a complete loss to explain the phenomenon. Although he had owned the piece for many years, he could not remember its origin. Whatever its magic, I silently gave thanks for the tranquility the gem had bequeathed me during Reni's long absence. Perhaps magic ensues not from what we are gifted, but from what we ourselves perceive?

I THOUGHT WE MIGHT REMAIN IN SAN FRANCISCO for the remainder of our lives, but by 1926, various business interests were drawing Reni increasingly southward. One did not typically discuss finances with one's husband in those days, although I had a quick head for numbers—America's loss, its ignorance of the mighty abacus—and I soon became a trusted confidant in many of Reni's affairs. I claimed a flair for bookkeeping and a sharp nose for fickle and feckless schemes, and found my judgment well appreciated. Although Los Angeles seemed a great distance from my home and my work at the orphanage, I agreed that the decision to move was a prudent one.

Southern California bustled with intensity in the mid-'20s. Land barons thrived and commerce proliferated. With prosperity, however, came its subversive underbelly. Greed and corruption quickly presented itself in a sinister new form of slave trade. Young women smuggled from the

Orient were routinely given massive amounts of opiates, then forced to perform heinous acts before a moving picture camera.

I realized our work was far from over.

Reni knew of my heart-breaking sacrifice in leaving the orphanage and, as was his way, he chose compromise. He purchased property in the township of Santa Barbara, midway between our new life and our old. What had once been a quaint fishing village and more recently a silent-movie haven, now afforded us the best of both worlds, as the Southern Pacific Railroad offered daily passenger service that fulfilled our need to visit either city.

In that decade after the War's end, I desperately wished to gift my beloved with a child of our own—but despite our efforts, I mothered no heir. I could not help but feel a crushing sense of guilt and shame. Several of the finest doctors in California explained that the acute malnutrition I suffered as a child was the probable cause of my infertility, and I endured a plethora of supposed remedies, both Eastern and Western. As was his way, Reni seemed not at all concerned with our plight. "The thousands of children that we've delivered from bondage, each and every one is no less than a child of yours. You are cherished more than you'll ever know."

His words brought about a most exquisite sense of comfort and joy, and I wept with abandon.

"When the time is right," he assured me when my tears had run dry.

From that day forward, I strove to dismiss that which was not, and pray for only what might be. To distance myself from my misery, I promised myself to live each moment to its fullest. Barely a month later, and with as much positive puffery as I could muster, I told Reni that I wished for a formal education, a college education—not simply a typing and filing career at the local woman's college, but a bona fide profession. My Captain was elated, of course, and promised to support me to his utmost.

I believed my foundation of knowledge to be impeccable: Astute language comprehension and mathematics skills; knowledge of applied science, and cognitive reasoning. I yearned to know everything about everything! And thus prepared, I set out for a formal education.

While a college education was not unprecedented for a woman in the year 1927, that I was a woman of foreign race and creed created a swirl of local controversy. However, that I had wed the city's wealthiest philanthropist smoothed a great deal of bumpy reluctance, especially when Reni promised to donate a sum sufficient to fund an entirely new department. The Santa Barbara Teacher's College (which would many years later be known as The University of California, Santa Barbara) became a valued haven for me over the next several years. I would eventually earn my Masters and a Ph.D.—and in what other field but world history? Reni's incessant stories about antiquity had sparked within me a burning desire to better understand the past.

In those first dozen years of our marriage, I would press my poor husband to divulge an endless stream of astounding tales of the larger world. The source of his personal treasure trove remained a mystery, and I dared not pry into his secrets. The stories themselves were sufficient.

I was curious, of course. I could not deny that Reni possessed a profound and intimate knowledge of the ancients. He spoke, for instance, of a navigational compass, pointing only south, used by Han Dynasty emperors; of a ground barley, goat cheese and red wine stew that Frankish mountain herders consumed a thousand years later. Of Russia's Peter the Great riding a scarred battle horse named Lisette. How on earth? Yet while Reni both willingly and frequently obliged my requests for such stories, I came to recognize an underlying melancholy in his words, a shadow of sorrow that loomed beneath the surface of his otherwise caring and carefree heart. Reni's unhappiness was not a sadness of spirit—as we were deeply in love, his business ventures were solid, and abundance fell like warm summer rays into our lives. And yet I could not help but feel a chasm existed between our love and Reni's innermost secrets.

A SLIP OF THE TONGUE, a single errant thought, would soon change the fabric of my life forever. Early one evening, late in the autumn of 1934, Reni and I shared a brandy on the upstairs veranda overlooking the Pacific. I remember the sun illuminating the western horizon in magnificent pink and orange hues. Our conversation, as it so often did, touched upon the perverse nature of slavery and on those we hoped to assist. Bondage and servitude had only proliferated during the world's economic collapse, the children younger and younger each year, so seemingly helpless and most without a modicum of hope for the future.

"I have known many faces of slavery in my life, but none so aberrant as this," Reni admitted in the midst of our discussion.

"I've not found *any* form of oppression dear to my heart," I said with some intended irony.

"No, no, you're quite correct," Reni said. "I misspoke. Neither the Negro in the South nor the uneducated immigrant on either shore is yet free of peril, despite this—this illusion of liberty that our Caucasian Christian brethren dare to espouse. That such oppression abounds amid such civility, even in this modern age of radio and automobile and electric appliance, I cannot fathom. Having myself felt the sting of a slaver's whip, I can tell you there is no worse feeling than that of hopeless subjugation. The overwhelming sense of unworthiness, of shame, is absolute."

I said nothing, my brow furrowed. Reni had never mentioned slavery in personal terms before. Might this finally be a glimpse into his inner darkness? Into his unspoken pain?

I waited in silence for what seemed an eternity before reaching out to touch my husband's hand. "Do you wish to reveal more to me?" I asked gently.

Reni shook his head quite emphatically, his gaze lingering upon the painted horizon. Despite his reluctance, perhaps without conscious thought, he said, "I was once held captive by Sh'lomoh ben Dawidh, King of Judah. Today we call him a wise man, but he was driven to lust and arrogance and often to utter irrationality."

Reni took an angry sip of cognac. "I was imprisoned because I spoke a single word of kindness to a young maiden whom the man coveted. Sh'lomoh would seduce any virgin brought before him because he considered his seed the divine extension of Yahweh's love. An absurd notion."

I stared intently into Reni's eyes. "Sh'lomoh?" I asked finally, my voice barely audible. "You speak of…of Solomon, Son of David?"

"Aye, the same."

"Solomon," I repeated, unable to escape the dizzying illogic of this conversation. "The king who offered to cut in half an infant claimed by two mothers?"

"The suggestion was not his," Reni said, "but rather that of a plump eunuch, an oracle who would often whisper in the king's ear. The oracle, whose name escapes me at the moment, was far more cynic than fair man. As I recall, much mead was consumed before the decree. You might say that Sh'lomoh was merely—"

Reni's words faded. I believe only now did he realize the extent of his unfettered thoughts. "Ah," he said finally, regarding me with the most pitiful of expressions. "I appear to have broken the vessel, and so the wine spills forth."

I remember the stillness of that instant; the silence of the night, the serenity of the distant ocean, the crickets suddenly muted, as if the entire world held its breath.

"I am ready to listen," I said softly.

"And I am ready to speak. I suspect that this will be... difficult. For both of us."

"I am your wife," I reminded him.

"Yes. My *bao záng.*"

My heart burst forth with elation, with pride. "I am here for you, dear husband. Always."

"Sh'lomoh ben Dawidh," Reni uttered again, as if remembering a long-forgotten memory. "An intimidating man. He had several growths on his neck and shoulder, each the size of a ripe olive. And only three fingers on his left hand. History omits those details."

He paused, as if in reverie.

I waited, wondering if I were indeed witnessing a glimpse of madness—or else some subliminal cry in the wilderness? I noticed that his snifter was nearly empty. "Shall I pour another brandy, my love?"

"No, no," he said quietly. "I believe you should bear witness without suspecting me of drunken rhetoric. I don't wish for you to ogle me like some startled baboon."

I smiled, amused by the absurdity of that notion.

But Reni's gaze remained solemn. "You have not yet heard my story."

"If you were the devil himself, I could not love you less."

"Not demonic, although I fear you'll decide me delusional. Or worse. Some secrets lay beyond the sanctity of matrimony. Of one's perception of reality."

When I said nothing, Reni found the courage to begin his tale. "My beloved," he whispered, "I am older than time."

So very aware of my husband's tenor, I did not believe him to be speaking metaphorically.

TWO

"I DO NOT KNOW THE YEAR, nor the century, nor even the millennia," he began after a thoughtful pause, once again regarding the waning sun on its descent toward the horizon. "And yet, as God as my witness, I believe that I may have been born fifty thousand years ago—perhaps even eighty or one-hundred thousand. I have absolutely no way of knowing for certain, as many holes exist in my memory. And yet, what I do know is that Sister Earth was a great paradise in my youth, a strange and wondrous realm. My story I cannot prove, but ask only that you hear me out, and decide for yourself that I am not certifiably mad."

Again, I did not speak. Maybe Reni thought me intrepid. My heart raced however; I had not spoken for fear of emitting the shrillest of sounds. I sat, rigid and chilled, and allowed my husband to continue.

"Please understand that when I was born, humankind did not yet know of kingdoms or kings, of priests or sacrifice, nor of politicians and the inevitable suffering they cause. Mine was a world frozen in its own naiveté, a time in which *time* wasn't even the slightest of notions. The Roman Empire is merely two thousand years old, the kingdom of the pharaohs but six or eight. I was born many millennia prior, before the concept of paper or an alphabet to write. Before man rode a horse or harvested grain for bread.

"Our thoughts, our tongues, our needs were incredibly simple. I've read many histories of Upper Paleolithic man over the last several decades—some foolish and others remarkably astute, although I have no idea of our species' birthplace, no early memories of any primitive advancements or philosophies. Nor do I have any chronological references prior to these last few millennia. Some say the pyramids of Giza have seen but five thousand years, others claim ten, and I don't have the slightest of clues. And yet I've admittedly observed these structures in their most opulent glory, adorned with ornately carved wooded balconies cascading with red and yellow flowers, and capped in gleaming silver. But without clocks or calendars, one's perception of time is quite imperfect.

"That I don't know the exact millennia of my birth may sound absurd," he said, "but understand that for countless eons, little change occurred in my life. In those distant ages there were no seasons, nor night and day, as our planet did not revolve around the sun as it now does. I can only—"

I stood suddenly, clutching my throat with one hand, wondering if Captain Sebastian Renaud might indeed be mad. Or worse, that his words were somehow fermenting insanity inside my head. I was horrified to recognize Reni's prophesy as truth—I had acted very much like a startled baboon.

I instantly regretted my lack of faith and struggled to find my voice. "I do not for a moment disbelieve you. And yet I fear that I cannot trust my own ears. No day or night? I don't understand the meaning of such words."

"Yes, of course," he said, reaching out to take my hand. "I'm unforgivably cruel beginning my journey with such aplomb. So many mysteries abound, and each deserves its own proper introduction. Permit me to begin with only the most believable of the unbelievable. When I have finished, if you are comfortable with the veracity of my story, I shall divulge more. But only at the proper time."

I settled back in my chair and managed a polite smile. "Perhaps that is best, yes."

"Allow me to reveal this: In the village of my birth, of my early youth so many millennia ago, little variation parsed one's lifetime nor, I imagine, a hundred lifetimes. Our wants were few, our tools absurdly modest, and yet we claimed all we needed to survive. Had we lacked for anything, I suspect we would have intuited a solution. We used sharpened rocks for scraping and cutting. We knew of hemp thread and needles fashioned from bone or thorn. We molded crude vessels and cups from river clay. We created melodic tunes on reed flutes and drums of hollow wood. We even etched simple forms, that of a gecko or a flower petal or a beetle, into soft surfaces.

"I was a hunter and also a collector of fruit and nectar, as had been my ancestors for what I presume to have been many preceding millennia, likely for hundreds of thousands of years. In what lands, on what continent we lived, I cannot possibly hazard a guess. We existed comfortably in what would be termed by today's anthropologists as a fertile river valley, a mile or two wide and quite flat, bordered by high canyon walls. Our valley lay rich and thick with tall, leafy trees, the soil moist and abundant, and from which sprang a plethora of edible plants and flowers. The air around us remained temperate, neither hot nor cold. The skies never rained, although the occasional breezes were quite damp, and would often soak the surrounding forest.

"I must tell you that, despite many recent suppositions about the physical appearance and predisposition of primitive man—those churlish cartoons of hairy, hunchbacked simpletons one sees every so often in *The New Yorker* or *The Saturday Evening Post*—we were tall and lithe; a fair-skinned, fair-haired people. I cannot speak for all of humanity, of course, but these are the people I remember.

"Mine was one of five villages congregated around a river that forked into three smaller rivers and stood no more than a half-mile's walk from a crystalline white beach. The plateau above the canyon walls and the vast sea lying beyond the river's delta were foreboding, forbidden places. Above the canyon walls lay utter desolation. However, we found the sea a mysterious and mystical place; an expanse of deep blue water that reached the horizon. We would sometimes hide, cloaked amid the forest's edge, and watch enormous, extraordinary creatures breach and frolic in the distant waves. None of us ever dared venture past the beach, as the realm beyond was completely beyond our comprehension.

"Yet our river—our *dae,* a word meaning both water and river—was a primal source of life and abundance. I don't remember its flow ever once raging or depleting. Dae's divergence into three smaller estuaries designated a natural border between our villages, and seldom would we venture beyond those sandy banks, as if subliminally aware of intruding upon another clan's hunting grounds. We did not begrudge our neighbors their land or their existence, and I don't recall any sense of wonder about them, as if curiosity toward others did not yet exist in our collective consciousness. We cherished our familial and ignored all to which, to whom, we were unaccustomed.

"My own village numbered as many as forty of my kinfolk, sometimes more or less, but basically an extended family. I suspect other villages were also aligned around a single matriarch, likely the eldest mother of her tribe. We had no word for our village and simply considered it our home, another concept for which we had no name. Once every two or three years—my best estimation, mind you; perhaps once per *cycle* would be more accurate—our eldest mother, our *mu'ata,* would select two young girls from the village. This was done with great fanfare and anticipation, and the girls would be cleansed in the river and rubbed with sweet herbs and adorned with flowered headdresses. I have a vague recollection of the chosen females giggling with anticipation. Mu'ata would eventually lead her little brigade off through the jungle and return after some while. Again, we had no perception of night or day, nor of minutes or hours passing. We slept when we were fatigued, ate when we were hungry. There were no rules, no clocks, no infernal time whistles, screaming to signify periods of chores or labor.

"But mu'ata would return soon enough through the wood, with two female children from other villages—and never two from the same village, although this realization did not occur to me until only recently. We knew nothing of genetics, of course; only in this century did we begin to unlock the secrets of this marvelous science. I can't even begin to speculate as to what instinctive comprehension lay within our mu'ata's grasp of awareness.

"I do remember these new girls being strangers to each other, both likewise scrubbed and smelling of sweet fragrances. Their arrival caused great commotion; we would shout and hug our new sisters and provide a great feast, then gather around and laugh as they'd point to a rock or a fish and utter words we had never before heard. Our local delicacy was a long-eared rabbit—an animal very much like those of today, yet endowed with sharp fangs and razor-sharp claws. We called these creatures *tu'abi,* and might point to one roasting over our pit, very amused if either of our new sisters would say in return *"laba"* or *"naray."* Once in a while, a girl would also proclaim the creature *tu'abi* and we would *ewww* and *ahhhh* with delight, amazed at such remarkable coincidence.

"The girls, of course, would become part of the village and one day bear children and life would continue until the next exchange cycle. Occasionally, a new sister might wander back to her own village, although rarely as I recall. There was a word for her departure—a prehistoric term for 'homesick'—although I do not remember it. But such things were accepted as the way of life. We had no prisons, no chains, no blame. We did not *own*. We had few expectations of 'what should be' and accepted life as it presented itself to us.

"I have to tell you that I have no memory of our villages ever fighting. We had no knowledge of the insanity of war, nor of the want or lack it creates. Nothing of debit or credit, possession or lust. And in that respect, we were far more intelligent than modern man. Nor did we fear the monster we have since named mammoth—the *mammuthus primigenius*—nor the cat we now call tiger. They were not considered predators, but took from the earth what was theirs to take, as I suppose did we all—man and beast and worm alike. On those rare occasions we crossed paths with an imposing creature, we regarded one other with respect, even awe, and each would turn away, intent on our separate journeys. When I recall snippets of my youth, I might even claim our lives as *idyllic*. We were children of the Earth and felt welcomed in her embrace.

"We were also a hygienic people, bathing in the warm river waters three or four times a day. I suppose some villages might not have enjoyed such close proximity to their dae, but I remember spending long periods—probably hours—sitting idly in the river and allowing the warm waters to cascade over my extremities. Within the river I suspect there existed a subliminal reminder of my mother's womb. I do recollect being frightened of *submerging* completely—as I don't believe I had yet grasped the concept of holding my breath."

Reni frowned. "I'm not sure if mine was a personal fear, or a trait held by my entire tribe. In any event, we were clean, and lathered our hair, which grew long and uncut, with the fragranced sap of a certain plant that grew in great quantities along the banks. We would often tie our wet locks with hemp-like filaments that grew from the same bush. Males and females alike would occasionally take great delight in creating elaborate coiffures using these filaments— although today, I assume such radical stylings might seem ridiculously primitive."

My husband dismissed the memory with a laugh. "We were also an amply fed people. Food proved constantly abundant. As I said, there existed no such concept as winter, no famine or pestilence. We feasted on a particularly large, delectable beetle that roamed our sandy soil in great numbers. We would wrap the creature in palm fronds and roast until tender. We would eagerly consume any number of enormous ants—" Reni spread his hands about six inches apart, and I shuddered. "—that we found quite plump and savory. A sweet taste, as I recall. We snatched with our bare hands a bounty of fat fish in the river, or hurled stones with great precision at small game. We had mastered the use of crude slingshots and could easily kill a squirrel or rabbit from twenty paces. I was considered quite a skilled huntsman in my day, perhaps because I was one of the more adventurous among my clan, not afraid to wander farther distances and finding fresh game where the others did not dare to look.

"Our family shared five or six large structures—not huts, but more like exotic lean-tos with thatched awnings, frond-laced roofs, and each structure with a *cist*—a large pit dug several feet deep, covered with fronds and used to store food for days on end. The village itself was nestled between the river and a deep crevice in the canyon wall that rose a good hundred feet above us.

"The valley itself seemed endless in its breadth, if only because none of us ever found reason to trek far from home. Although the canyon walls were not exceedingly steep, few of our number had ever climbed to the top. The barren plateau above offered nothing of value, nothing even of remote interest. And yet I would sometimes ascend and sit at the precipice for long periods, far above the roof of the jungle, peering down at all I had ever known. I did so simply because the perspective thrilled me.

"To the east and west—and I use these terms merely as a visual reference, my love—but in either direction, the upper plateau extended without deviation, flat and bare, starkly white and lacking any sort of vegetation. A hopelessly inhospitable place. By facing north, I could see my valley for what it was, a jagged crack in the shell of the earth, until it eventually dwindled and became one with the empty horizon. And, of course, by turning south, I could glimpse the endless sea that touched the horizon. So I would sit and wonder, although as often as not, I would lie on my back and stare toward the heavens, and wonder even more. For always, above us, an exquisite—"

Reni hesitated, and in his silent gaze I sensed a remarkable secret, although, such was my own frailty that he would not permit himself to speak further of what loomed above. He offered a simple shrug and said, "Eventually I would scramble back home, the older crones clucking at my adventures. My mothers would scold me with forlorn sounds and send me off to fetch firewood or collect berries.

"In the center of the village and partially protected by a large, sloping boulder on which we often cured meat, an ancestor of mine had once built a fire pit which had continually burned since long before the day of my birth. This fire—our *oht*—was the center of our universe. We had not conquered fire, you see, we merely found magic and fortune in its presence. But how *oht* had first come to the village, no one remembered. A long-dead ancestor I assume, who'd come upon a lightning strike, a smoldering tree or a brush fire, and had intuited its worth.

"I do not ever remember seeing a roaring fire but rather a pit of large, glowing embers and a lick of flame here and there, sufficient for our limited purposes. We made stews and heated certain stones until they splintered, making sharp knives as tools. We boiled bark to tan pelts and baked crude pots in its heat. Its acrid stink repelled larger animals and its rising smoke would guide us home from various wanderings. During those rare periods the wet winds blew—a cool breeze we called *tahk-ahm*—we coveted its warmth.

"When we were not hunting food, we'd forage for fallen branches or dead brush, and a plethora of large yellow leaves from a variety of tree long since extinct, which we would tightly roll to produce a hot ember much like charcoal. We knew how to fashion crude torches and to explore caves with these glowing leaves—or at least to investigate the mouths of caves, as we never ventured too deeply into the perplexing mystery of darkness."

Reni stared into the cloudless twilight overhead. "As hard as it may be to believe, our ancient sky remained a constant, azure blue. I do recollect our moist interludes to be accompanied by a slightly violet tinged sky. I suppose one might consider these periods *seasons*, although how many and how long they lingered I haven't the foggiest notion. But during these times I do recall a deep purple shadow falling amid the canyon walls—and many lightning storms danced across the heavens. Overhead, the wet winds were quite prevalent, and occasionally rustled and swirled both ash and embers throughout the village.

"I remember that a neighboring clan had once fueled their fire with green wood, and during a particularly harsh *tahk-ahm,* their fire sputtered and died. They could find no spark to rekindle the flame. They came to us bearing fruits and berries and the best of their skins, and also brought two young girls although it was not yet a cycle. These children they eagerly offered us in return for a torch. Even in a land without darkness or winter, fire meant life.

"For countless millennia," Reni said, "this was likely how all of humanity existed on Sister Earth. My village, this river, was all I had ever known. That it might change, that it *could* change, was an unfathomable concept to me, beyond my ability to perceive."

"IT WAS DURING THIS TIME OF TAHK-AHM, of the purple shadow, that a sickness struck our village. A great *nu'al* killed many of my clan—and all too soon I lay gasping for breath.

"Nu'al," Reni repeated with emphasis, his eyes twinkling. "So much of my native tongue I have long ago forgotten, but this word remains rooted in my memory. "An abscessed tooth, a broken ankle, a stomach-ache; all were known to us as *nu'al.* Unwell.

"I've come to realize this particular sickness as a type of plague, borne on the breeze perhaps. Its infection spread painful, oozing rashes on the skin and then inside the mouth—and eventually crept down the throat into the lungs. Ultimately, whether virus or bacterial, the sickness swelled and closed the esophagus, and we knew no cure.

"As I lay awaiting death, I remember a blurry, dreamlike image of a man—whom I now believe to have been sort of shaman—who entered our village with shrieks and a horrible wail. He was caked head to toe in river mud, with thick white ash circling his eyes. Feathers and twigs protruded from his mud-hardened hair in a most terrifying manner.

"We had never before seen such a creature. Our village would have driven him away with hurled stones and shouts, this stranger, this intruder, had we not been so affected. But many of our hunters had already succumbed, and so the shaman wandered among us unchallenged.

"I had long before crawled near the fire pit for warmth and hopelessly watched the stranger move to and fro. Quite soon the man stood over me, singing words I had never before heard—vague, complicated sounds, both guttural and discordant. In his hands he clutched a rodent of some sort, its skin burned a charcoal black and its midsection bloated, filled with herbs that had liquefied in tremendous heat. The shaman repeated several sounds over me—a complex mantra—then cracked the creature open and dribbled a greenish, moss-tasting medicine against my lips and into my throat.

"Until that instant, even consumed by plague, I don't know if I'd ever perceived the notion of true *fear*. I watched the shaman repeat this remedy several times among others and then, as mysteriously as he had come, he disappeared again into the wood. After a time, the swelling in my throat diminished, although the shaman's presence continued to terrify me more than death itself. When a semblance of my strength returned, I was able to drag myself to the canyon wall and I began to half climb, half crawl up the rocky facade. I thought if I could reach the sky, somehow I'd be safe from the ghastly presence, safe above the inexplicable horror that had emerged from the jungle.

"I was soon exhausted, of course, and once I reached the precipice I sunk into unconsciousness. I don't know how long I remain incapacitated, but I awoke to the buzz and crackle of an electrical storm."

Reni laughed. "Lightning was an unfathomable mystery to us, but in my youth lightning did not carry the same charge we encounter today. It would descend from the heavens in a dance of multiple blue-violet arcs—sometimes dozens of separate threads that stitched and tickled the surface of the plateau for what might be minutes at a time, burning troughs that stretched maybe hundreds of yards in length. Its presence filled the air with a stinging, acrid odor.

"As I lay vulnerable upon the naked earth, this ominous ballet arced toward me with incredible speed. I tried to move, to heave myself back into the crevice that was my home, but all too soon the lightning was upon me. I remember a brief flash and then blackness, although I distinctly recall an awareness of my own conscious self, of my thoughts drifting through a pleasant and tranquil ether, unencumbered by body or bulk. I remember the feeling of moving freely to-and-fro, driven by sheer thought alone. Very peculiar, to say the least. Even so, I recall having no fear, only curiosity—and a feeling of floating through a chasm of great calm between life and death.

"When I awoke, I lay in a hole—a burial pit at the far end of the village—on the valley floor, surrounded by flowers and clay jars filled with nectar. I sat up and heard sudden screams of distant alarm. My family gathered quickly around me, but with great suspicion. I recognized among them many of those who had lain dying before the shaman's appearance, now quite healthy and apparently robust. I did not understand their fear, but when I rose from the pit the entire clan shrank back in horror, shouting and jumping frantically, in the manner they might react to a stranger's approach.

"Only then did I realize the withered state of the flowers around me, the fermenting nectar, and I believe—having had eons since to consider my plight—that I had lain in a near-death repose for quite a length of time. I was naked, and had been vigorously washed and fragranced, as was our burial ritual. It was tradition, in our village, to lay the dead in open pits until the flesh began to rot, as we could not always distinguish between death and unconsciousness, and we were not a people who threw caution to the wind. But, for whatever reason, the rot and stink of death had refused to claim me. Even the animals that so often came to nibble our dead had remained suspicious and kept their distance.

"I cried out, but my family refused to step forward and embrace me! The few times I moved toward the village I was rebuffed by shouts of fear and anger, and once struck by a stone that gashed my thigh. I retreated, limping toward the jungle, as saddened and perplexed as a small puppy scolded by its master for some unknown grievance.

"I picked berries, then washed my torn flesh in the river. Eventually the bleeding stopped. I fell asleep in the tall grasses beside the bank and when I awoke, the wound had not only closed, but had already begun to mend itself. I had partially eaten a papaya, the fruit still fresh and moist on the ground beside me. My entire universe seemed suddenly quite confounding.

"To pass the time, I stripped leaves from a *tu'ato mala*—an enormous succulent very much like Mexico's agave, yet perhaps thrice its height and girth—each leaf endowed with a spiny tip—the *tu'alo*—that, if properly removed, remained attached to a long, fibrous filament. We would often dry and braid several such lengths into a rope for fashioning straps and various tools, or to thread several skins together into loincloth.

"I should mention that we were not prim or prudish in those days, our furs merely providing suitable padding for our bare bottoms, and to keep the myriad of leaves and branches from poking at our more tender regions." Reni smiled at me. "Understand that we had no such notion as *modesty* at the dawn of humanity. No sense of guilt or propriety.

"And so I sat, by my lonesome, knitting a length of fiber into a slingshot. Once finished, I spent much time hunting our local species of rabbit, several of which I eventually killed and whose skin I fashioned into a suitable garment. All the while I remained confident that my family would eventually find their senses and allow my return.

"I don't know how much time passed, maybe a week's equivalence, but the fears of my village did not subside. Worse, every time I showed myself, our mu'ata would begin to howl and cry, increasingly afraid—quite upsetting to me—and soon I became certain that I was no longer welcomed among my family.

"As I had always been relatively adventurous, I decided to set out and follow the riverbed away from both the village and the endless sea. I thought my absence might calm their fears as well. I had trekked such lengths before, no more than a mile or two I suppose, but never further. I soon found myself travelling beyond any familiar markings. With only curiosity left to sustain me, I moved forth into the unknown.

"I followed a series of sandy riverbanks as far as I was able, but eventually the jungle thickened. This deep within the valley, the overhead vegetation created a darkness I did not trust. As I've said, I had never experienced the blackness of night, and the few caves I had tentatively explored, I had done so by torchlight. But I had no such tool now, and I felt naked without the presence of our perpetually burning *oht*. But I could no more start a fire in those days than I could fly an airplane. For a long time I stared into the deep wood, listening to a cacophony of unfamiliar sounds and wishing that I'd never stirred from my sleep. Wished that I'd remained cocooned forever in that pleasant twilight between life and death."

"You *had* died, hadn't you?" I asked abruptly. "The lightning strike killed you that day on the plateau."

"Aye, I believe I had," he replied stoically, "my body either pierced by a bolt or thrown from the cliff into the valley below. What I know for certain is that the villagers were quite convinced of my demise. My re-awakening proved too horrific for them to accept."

Reni regarded me with a curious frown, and I found it impossible to gauge his thoughts. "I remember my bones aching severely upon my awakening," he said, "although less so soon afterwards. The pain gradually dispersed, all but gone by my fifth or sixth sleep. I believe now that a primordial combination—the herbal remedy that I had ingested, together with the electrical charge of the lightning—produced some sort of chemical reaction within me that has left me with regenerative properties I cannot even begin to comprehend."

"Have you *never* been examined?" I asked. "By a medical doctor?"

"Never. Having been burned at the stake a few times, I've learned to distrust authoritarian wisdom. More recently, as our civilizations have become increasingly advanced, I fear a different sort of medical attention; that I might be taken in secrecy and locked away, prodded and poked, needled and biopsied, forced to spend the rest of my life in some isolated little room while science frets and fawns over me, seeking to profit from whatever magic elixir they might hope to extract from my body. And I do feel pain, my love. Exquisitely so. I simply don't suffer the consequences."

Not wishing to hear further of my husband's suffering, I quickly said; "Please, yes, tell me more of your travels."

"I EVENTUALLY MOVED FORWARD, into the depths of the dark jungle. I must have traversed the valley for the equivalent of several days, curious about flora and fauna I did not recognize and quite content to remain below the plateau. In fact, I'd convinced myself never to return to that featureless wasteland above, as I'd found only pain and misery in its realm. I perceived Sister Earth's stark, white highlands as one might regard a mortal enemy, and one who'd already throttled me good and proper.

"Having travelled this far inland, and being insulated from the ocean winds, the valley grew considerably hotter. The soft, moist sands surrounding my village had given way to hardened rock under foot, and even though the soles of my feet were quite tough, I found myself cut and bleeding on numerous occasions. Fortunately, my injuries healed themselves each time I'd stop to sleep.

"I eventually encountered our river again. The waters had grown wide and shallow, and I followed a sandbar for another half-mile or so. I soon discovered a sizable clearing amid the wood. A trail led away from the riverbank and I was curious, childishly naïve as to where it might lead. I came upon the village soon thereafter.

"The thought of other jungle villages—those I had not already encountered in the delta—had not once entered my brain. Such were the limitation of my primitive world. I entered a scant meadow with some trepidation, moving slowly, and within a few paces, I stumbled upon a land of the dead. Remnants of the plague, of course. I found no burial pits, but rather, on either side of the trail and raised on crude platforms above me, a dozen or so bodies that lay naked and blackened by decay. Numerous sturdy branches had been lashed together, cradling the corpses, and numerous birds of prey feasted on the rotting flesh as I watched. It appeared to me as if the birds were *expected* to pick clean the bones, as if this was an element of their death ritual, much like our own burial beneath the sand.

"I thought nothing abhorrent about this observation. In the days of my youth, death was not treated with dismay or chagrin. It was an often and expected occurrence, at any age. We might miss the companionship of the departed, but we held death's inevitability with no regret or fear. It was as much a part of life as life itself.

"In the distance, maybe twenty-five, thirty paces ahead, I could see several mud and straw huts that comprised the village. My arrival had scattered the birds above me in a great flurry of sound and motion, and so my presence had been noticed. I was greeted by several of the male elders who stood at a safe distance in rapt fascination, but who made no motion to scare me away.

"I wondered if they too had been visited by a shaman—people who, in his wake, felt no dread of a stranger's sudden appearance. Perhaps they considered me a magic being as well. They pointed and made sounds not totally unfamiliar to my ears, and after a brief hesitation I moved forward, into their midst.

"The oldest villager, a man stooped and fragile with age, stepped forward extending an arm, one hand raised in greeting. The gesture was not alien to me, but rather one of communion among my own clan. We would press our palms together, fingertips touching, and in that simple convergence, we could infer if a brother were anxious or calm, happy or ill.

"And so we touched hands, this newfound stranger, suddenly a friend. I felt in the warmth of his hand both curiosity and also acceptance. I smiled at him, which appeared sufficient response. The men surrounded me and, with a series of gentle touches, explored my arms, my chest and neck, my cheeks and hair. I allowed this intimacy with no small sense of relief. Soon enough they led me to their fire, where the flank of a sizeable beast was roasting. I had not tasted meat in many days and I whooped with joy, which caused them to nod and laugh—as if my good fortune were also their good fortune.

"Soon enough, women and children began to emerge from the huts. The village hosted a larger tribe than my own, half again as many people, not even including the dead on their raised altars. I ate my fill around their fire and we took turns naming those things we knew, learning sounds for those things we did not know.

"The males carried tall spears of sharpened wood and clubs of thicker, shorter branches—and they were very curious about my slingshot. I could see no evidence of such knowledge here and, as I had noticed several young females in their midst, I was eager to—well, my love, I do confess I was intent on preening.

"As I'd seen many giant agave plants in the surrounding jungle, I made my way to the closest of these, snapping off the pointed tips and extracting great lengths of fiber. This simple act caused great sounds of awe in the village, and I could see that none of them had yet discovered this *magick*. They watched in fascination as I braided a sling from various lengths and then tamped the thicker, center piece into a flat pouch.

"I selected a suitable flat stone and pointed to a large tree at the edge of the forest—unmistakably my intended target—and I began whirling the weapon with a sidelong wrist flick. I took a forward step, as one's stance was of no less importance than one's release, took steady aim and let fly. One could hear the *whrrrrrr* of the stone's accuracy long before it reached its mark, and my missile rang true!

"Damn if the stone not only struck the tree dead center, but also pierced the bark and lodged there for all to see. The elder shrieked his delight and the entire village scurried to observe the tree more closely. Try as they might, even the strongest among them could not dislodge the stone. They continued to shout, jumping up and down as might a pack of excited chimpanzees.

"This brought great pride to my heart. When I presented my new tool to the elder he wept with joy, touching my nose, my lips and my eyelids with his gnarled fingers and then, taking my head in his hands, he touched his forehead to mine. This gesture extracted a hushed murmur from the others. I took this act to reflect a significant honor. In that moment, I had become an adopted son or an honored member of the tribe. At the time, yes, I was moved by such gratitude, and in all the years that have since passed, I have come to regard this toothless old man as the closest figure to a genuine father as I've ever known."

I took my husband's hand in mine. "And did you?" I asked gently.

Reni's brow creased.

"Impress the local ladies with your display of male prowess?"

When he blushed, I could not help but laugh. It was not a common trait of my beloved to grow flush and I could only guess what his answer would have been. I squeezed his hand and said, "Please continue. I'm intrigued."

"My gift was not without reciprocation," he said. "I'd noticed these people wearing rabbit pelts on their feet—a complete skin on each foot, forepaws tied at the toes and the skin of the hindquarters wrapping the ankle. Although I'd been walking upon harder, rockier ground recently, I had never considered such protection. Simply by pointing, I found myself in ownership of a splendid pair of pelt sandals that were no less a necessity for my further travels than my sling. I have never once felt this village got the better part of our trade.

"I remained in their company for quite a few slumbers—and felt that I could have remained for all my days, had I chosen. But the curiosity that had taken hold of me had not diminished. Before I left, I constructed several additional slingshots, and watched as they fashioned many more of these tools with their own hands. I admit to a great deal of bloodletting. The first several stones released are often into one's own shin or foot or scalp, and many young men suffered for lacking mastery with this new invention.

"But it inevitably came time to leave and when I did so, I was presented with as much smoked meat as I could carry, as well as a new set of sandals. Within the short time I remained in the village, someone had thought to weave heat-strengthened agave threads into the foot pelts. I suspect I was gifted with the first pair of shoelaces to grace mankind. We called out to one another for many minutes as I ventured further and further into the dense canopy of trees, until the village voices no longer carried through the forest.

"Ah, but before I continue, I must tell you of something extraordinary, my love. Quite early in my adventure, I'd become aware of a remarkable occurrence. Dental hygiene in those days was an unknown, although I remember we chewed an herbal root that tasted strongly of mint, and for the most part our teeth did not darken or rot until later in life. However, as a young man, I had lost two teeth here—" Reni fingered aside his lip, tapping a bicuspid. "An errant fling with a sling in my youthful exuberance. I was missing a small sliver of my lip as well. During this part of my trek, I experienced a dull throb and eventually felt the presence of two new teeth sprouting from the gum. By now, my lip had regenerated as well. I did correlate this new growth with my own revival in the grave, yet lacked the innate curiosity to otherwise ponder this strange occurrence."

Reni shook his head. And me? I could do no more than squeeze his hand and marvel at his tale, which he continued after allowing himself a final sip of cognac.

"I soon encountered several other villages. Some were hostile and others welcoming. I continued to trade whenever I could and constructed several additional slingshots in exchange for food. One village had already discovered the axe—*ya'ota,* I believe they'd named the tool, a sharp stone laced to a club, and whose handle had been wrapped with animal skin to absorb moisture. The ya'ota became a welcomed accessory and I marveled its ingenuity.

"In another village I discovered the *pee*—" Reni arched an eyebrow and made a *puh* sound with his lips. "Although my clan had been quite acquainted with *bwuh, bwah, bwah*—this was a consonant, a sound heretofore unknown to me, and I practiced diligently to finally duplicate the noise. For a great while afterwards, I traipsed through the jungle repeating 'Puh! Puh! Puh!' over and over until my lips grew chapped and painful. The sound was quite delightful to me.

"The river had thus far remained a constant companion on my trek. At times it ran deep and narrow, producing frothy rapids that I found quite frightening. Other times it meandered, wide and placid. In one village, situated on the bank of the first lake I ever encountered, the inhabitants frolicked about the water's surface on flotation rafts constructed from lashed wood. They would actually dive *beneath* the surface to fish, a frightening, magical feat in my imagination. To watch a man disappear from view and not resurface for a minute or two, sometimes with a writhing fish between his teeth—that was a most fantastic and impossible feat, beyond all comprehension! Although they insisted that I try, I maintained my cowardice. It would be quite some time yet before I dared venture beneath the waves.

"Eventually, after a trek of several additional weeks, the valley gradually began to taper, becoming increasingly narrow. The forests thinned. The once fertile floor became dry and brittle, strewn with the blanched trunks of stunted trees, long dead. On either side of this gorge, the canyon walls soared increasingly higher and loomed far more ominously above me. This stretch of river raced quite swiftly, its flow producing a constant roar in my ears, and I feared to venture too close to its banks lest I be swept away to my doom. Ultimately, the girth of the river and proximity of the steep canyon walls left no way forward for even the most sure-footed of men.

"I began to seek a way up and over the canyon walls several times, but with no luck. Yet, not once during these failed efforts did I consider returning home. I think—and I'm not certain if this were a gift from the sky or as a result of my travels—but I think my mind had begun to expand, creating within itself an inexorable capacity for searching out and accumulating knowledge. Curiosity had been a vague and sluggish concept in my youth, but my sojourn through the valley had sparked an indefatigable wonder within me, and my village now seemed as inviting as might a kindergarten class to a college student.

"After substantial backtracking through the valley, I eventually discovered a series of cleaved boulders that had toppled in much the same manner as might several dominoes, one partially atop another, a crude sort of natural stairway that presented me with adequate access to the plateau above. Soon enough, I stood on the parched surface, the fragile outer shell of our planet. But I faced a sudden new challenge, confronting an issue previously unconsidered by me. *What next?*

"My darling, you simply can't imagine the enormity of that question! What next? The magnitude of that demand on my brain, to one so primitive as myself, was enough to drive me toward madness.

"As far as the eye could see, the featureless white plain stretched toward the horizon, with only the jagged lip of the canyon offering the terrain any sense of depth or variation. Given the extent of my travels—perhaps fifty miles, were I to hazard a guess—even my once familiar sea was no longer visible. Knowing nothing of perspective or distance, for a long while I pondered its absence. After much consideration, I decided to continue my journey inland, moving along the edge of the familiar precipice. I had no desire to remain on the plateau's barren surface, yet I saw no further encouraging indication of human life below me. For mile upon mile I continued to walk, while the river continued to rage and froth between the valley's sheer rock walls. After a long and discouraging time, I at last accepted the futility of my course.

"Despite my many concerns, I decided to venture away from the valley, so I braced myself to set out across the barren wilderness. Looking out over such a vast wasteland I did not know if it might extend into infinity—a vague notion, as I recall, of being *too large to think about.* I considered traveling only until I grew too tired and stopped to sleep. Should I perceive no improvement in my surroundings, I would turn around and return to the valley's edge. The thought tempered those fears boiling up from the depths of my soul.

"I had been extremely fortunate in one regard. The last village I'd come upon had accepted me with openness and joy. In exchange for a sling and some healing herbs, its people had presented me with a large pouch of tough, interwoven fronds. Amazingly, they had woven a strip in sufficient length to hitch around one's shoulder. I could place a plentiful amount of fruit and cured meat inside this containment. Wrapped within the fronds of the *het-nay,* a strangely fragrant plant that I have not encountered for many millennia, fruit and meat would remained unspoiled for a very long time. My pouch enabled me to transport far more provisions than I would have been otherwise able to carry by hand. An extraordinary concept!

"Armed with ample rations, I found myself moderately confident setting off across the expansive plain. I kept a keen eye out for any threats of lightning, as strikes were often visible in the distance but thankfully none struck in close proximity during my journey. Above me, of course…but, ah! A mystery I cannot yet divulge."

Reni paused, and instead offered me a thoughtful smile. "Shall we say that I was driven forward by an innate sense of curiosity? And so I started across a previously untraveled realm.

"The plateau, white, flat and endless, soon became mesmerizing in its conformity. Although I had walked a great distance, I felt as if I had barely moved across this bleak and foreboding desert. And yet, glancing back, I discovered my footprints gradually disappearing against the horizon. No longer could I see the precipice of my valley, nor the sea, nor any familiar marking whatsoever.

"I did, however, encounter an interesting realization. When I had begun my trek across the plateau, I perceived myself to be walking upon an ocean of coarse white sand. Yet the farther I moved from the canyon walls, the thicker the chalky granules became beneath my feet. Farther still, and these ubiquitous white pebbles began to take on various shapes, quite intriguing until I noticed, within the confines of a bowl-shaped depression on the surface, the crumbling bones of several enormous creatures, monsters I had never before imagined. Only then did I realize that this bleached plateau, as far as the eye could see, was carpeted in various bits of bone, most of which had been pulverized to powder over eons of lightning strikes, or else finely ground by some other means, some long-ago catastrophic condition of which I remained completely unaware.

"Imagine a sailor lost at sea and in every direction only

water. That was my experience, as if I'd been untethered from all of known existence, swimming in a sea not of salty froth, but of bone and sand. And, of course, every few moments, from one bearing or another, I would be aware of various lightning strikes poking the earth, a seemingly endless barrage of energy radiating down from the sky. Strangely, as I continued my trek, these strikes became my travelling companion; a constant, familiar marvel amidst the otherwise monotonous visage of white earth and blue sky.

"I had eaten a good deal of my provisions thus far, stopping finally to sleep inside the bleached rib cage of some great creature whose skull bore three great tusks, each twice as long as my own body. Exhausted, I slept eagerly. And yet, when I awoke again, I quickly dismissed my pledge to return the way I'd come. Plucking a moist fruit from my dwindling supply, I sated both my hunger and thirst before once again wandering off to confront my fate.

"I slept several times again on that bleached plateau and plodded onward. Eventually I noticed a slight variance of shape and shadow against the looming horizon. I hastened my pace and soon became aware of a jagged crease that gradually expanded into a precipice. I had returned to my valley!

"I did not pause to wonder how I'd come upon my homeland again—concepts such as *circumnavigation* were completely alien to me—and it was not until I moved fairly close to its edge that I began to realize this was not the same valley, but another such crack in the world; one far wider than my own.

"I encountered many squat and twisted bushes rooting upon the surface near the precipice, none taller than my waist. Such dry and prickly vegetation! Each plant appeared hopelessly unhappy here, its sparse leaves a sickly yellow-green. I wept with joy at their presence, however, for I had again discovered life and the salvation it ensured. I sat among the brambles and stared down at a distant river snaking through this wonderful, lush gorge with its thick, abounding forests. I began to look for a route downward, which I soon maneuvered, and after much effort I reached the valley floor.

"I quickly became aware of an intriguing variable in this valley. While I eventually recognized berries not unlike those I remember near my village—and greedily ate my fill—I found the vegetation here not nearly as bountiful as that in my own valley. While I had been used to a multitude of plants and fruit-trees offering sustenance at every turn, I found this wood largely barren. As I made my way toward the river, however, I continued to forage until I was eventually able to partially refill my satchel with berries and a small, green, bitter-tasting fruit.

"I advanced toward the river, where I hoped to find an abundance of small fish and snails to sustain myself. I moved through several dense thickets of fat-bottomed trees, still searching for edible vegetation. I was quite aware of the many bird calls above—a cacophony of sounds unfamiliar to my ears. How different, this new valley! My mind did its best to decipher both the similarities and differences. I slept for a short while and then continued my trek toward the life-giving dae, the river I'd seen quite clearly from the cliffside above.

"It was while I pushed my way through one such dense tangle of forest that a sudden silence snatched my attention; surrounding me, bird and insect both had become cautiously mute. Overhead, a rush of wings taking flight warned of a presence, yet before I could react, two men emerged from the foliage and charged at me with crude spears. I had barely time to react before these savages were upon me— men much like myself, yet with faces deliberately smeared in streaks of charcoal and ash.

"I did not understand my transgression. Wherever I had been unwanted in the recent past, shouts of displeasure, hostile gestures, or the occasionally thrown rotten fruit or feces had provided sufficient warning. But these men lunged forward with an obvious, lethal intent such as I had never before encountered.

"Amid the thick undergrowth, their weapons proved unwieldy. I easily parried the spear of my first attacker. My club, with its sharpened stone tightly lashed, found the man's skull and he dropped with a loud grunt. I quickly turned to face the other. Behind me, I heard a triumphant shout and immediately felt a terrible pain between my shoulder blades, a blinding agony that forced a scream of rage from my throat. Worse, from my own chest, a length of sharpened wood appeared as if by magic, and my blood blossomed as would the juice squeezed from a ripe citrus. Just as quickly, the spear retreated from my flesh, leaving a gaping hole."

"Oh, dear!" I cried, most unhappily.

"My entire world winked into oblivion." As he spoke, Reni absently rubbed an area of his chest where I could only imagine that horrible weapon had emerged. "I'd been pierced from behind, of course—and that's all I remember until I again opened my eyes. I had no idea how long I'd been unconscious and could only assume that my remaining life slowly oozed from my body, that eternal darkness would soon come to claim me. My chest ached greatly, and I remember awaiting death with a quiet acceptance, watching insects scurry and crawl upon a broad frond that brushed against the tip of my nose.

"I stared at that leaf for so long that I clearly recall its shape and color to this day. I remember insects marching to-and-fro across its girth, busily undertaking their insect lives. And yet, after a great while, I became aware of my pain gradually fading. I grew weary of waiting to die and gingerly moved a foot, and then a leg, and finally dared to raise a hand to my chest. I felt a slight indentation in the skin, the hard shell of a scab, but I otherwise found no wooden stake nor gaping wound.

"I gingerly sat up and took stock, instantly aware of my nakedness and my missing possessions. I finally deduced that my attackers had *taken* my belongings. This concept seemed quite perplexing to me, as they had been clothed and armed and seemingly well-nourished. For what purpose then did they want more?

"Aware that death had once again forsaken me, I consumed several small slugs and salamanders within easy reach, and felt my strength gradually return. Once again, I spent little time speculating upon the incomprehensible. You must understand, my love, that introspection was not a common human trait in those days. I spent far less time contemplating my inexplicable ability to heal than wondering why those men would have killed me for what little I possessed.

"Eventually, I felt well enough to stand and, before long, I moved with renewed strength and agility—although now with far more caution."

"Did you ever find them?" I asked eagerly. "Those terrible men?"

"I did not even think to look," he replied. "Revenge was a completely unfamiliar notion. To seek them out would have been to search for a flame that had badly burned me. Yet one does not attack fire with vengeance, as one will feel similar pain again and again.

"Ah, but I *did* find my sling, discarded a few paces from where I'd lain," Reni said with a sudden smile. "I suspect these men hadn't the slightest clue as to its purpose, and in tossing it aside returned my most valuable possession.

And so I walked on. With the root knowledge of all I once owned, I gradually replenished my pelts and worldly possessions.

"I did find the river a short while later, and spent several hours simply bathing in its warming waters before continuing my trek upstream. Not long afterwards I came across a village nestled along its languid banks. Amazingly, surrounding several small huts, its denizens had erected a wall. Constructed from river clay and wood, the fortification stood slightly taller than the height of a man. I had never before observed such a structure and squatted amid the foliage, lost in curiosity. Reaching no conclusions, I climbed a nearby tree, as anxious as a child attempting to peek behind the foil wrapping of a birthday gift. From this vantage point I could see several clay mounds rising against the wall's interior. I intuited that the villagers could climb upon such mounds and easily perceive what might lay beyond, while remaining almost totally concealed.

"I remained in that tree a great while, contemplating their need to hide from the forests that sustained them. I finally realized these people were not hiding so much as protecting themselves, and likely from the sort of men who had attacked me earlier.

"Imagine the youngest of schoolboys," Reni said excitedly, "staring at a blackboard, pondering that most perplexing of formulations: 1 + 1 equals...*what?* When my brain eventually completed the equation, I became giddy with rapture. I had discovered within myself the art and science of rational deduction! This sense of logic would serve me well over the years, although that first observation has, to this day, remained dear to my heart.

"I did not attempt to befriend the village. I sensed fear in their isolation and thus trepidation, so I passed them by—as I did the next several villages that I found likewise fortified. Despite its size, the valley remained somewhat barren for many miles; few animals presented themselves and its many fruit trees appeared both stunted and stingy. I wondered if *this* might have been the reason for the aggressive nature of my unknown brethren although, fortunately, as I moved farther upriver, the vale gradually became once again generous in its bounty. Lo and behold, the villages that I soon encountered there lacked fortification. Another observation, another deduction! Whereas a year before I might have walked an entire day with little more thought than collecting firewood for the village, I now walked with an inner purpose of contemplating such fascinating discoveries.

"Many things, old and new to my eyes—types of trees or varieties of fruit, small creatures or birds, familiar things I'd anonymously known throughout my lifetime—I'd begun to *name* these objects, a practice I found amusing. A fruit that tasted quite like a pear for instance, but more reddish in color, I would name *fire-pear—oht-bala!*" Reni laughed. "What a busy place my brain had become.

"This gorge around me, being much larger in scope than my own valley, yielded much greater treasures over time. After a lengthy trek along the river's edge, I came upon an island. Another first! The river forked to either side of the almond-shaped swatch of land no more than a quarter-mile in length. To one side of this island, the river had been tamed by the remnants of an isthmus that had crumbled away, producing a shallow but quite ferocious series of rapids. Yet behind this stretch of churning water lay a large reservoir, as still as any lake. These ingenious people had erected rope bridges connecting their centralized island to either shore—bridges constructed not only from thick hemp, but also of wooden trestle, much like today's railroad ties, that provided stable footing.

"I had never before seen a bridge. I sat in fascination

until a woman emerged from the village and quite capably traversed this scientific marvel into the forest. As I watched her step sure-footedly *above* the rolling river, my heart sang. Think of someone living today who witnesses his first aeroplane aloft, or spies a locomotive passing at full speed, with its trail of smoke and piercing whistle. How incredible that confrontation must seem!

"Seized by such utter fascination, I moved closer and waited. Eventually the same woman returned. I watched her again walk with assuredness across the bridge, even as she labored beneath the hefty weight of numerous fat leaves across one shoulder.

"I could see many huts through numerous trees on the island, perhaps a dozen or so structures. Smoke drifted from several fires. I observed various small animals roaming freely, including a squat and hairless creature I had never before encountered. I would soon discover both the fury and the tastiness of the wild boar, although they remained placid beasts when rooting and unprovoked. It didn't take me long to comprehend that these creatures were held captive by the island itself, and thus easily captured by the villagers.

"After much contemplation, I stood and moved to a trail that presented itself and which directed me to the foot of the rope bridge. For some time I admired the structure's flooring, its cut branches spaced evenly, and I realized that even if one lost footing, by gripping the hand ropes on either side, one could easily prevent a fall into the river. It was a marvelous contraption. A rocket to the moon!

"Eventually I decided to venture forth, advancing only three or four paces over the rapids before backtracking again to the safety of the shore. I repeated this process several times, laughing at my own timidity. The island's edge lay no more than a dozen yards away, and yet I found myself distracted by my increasingly sustainable sense of balance.

Midway across the river, I was aware of the bridge dipping and shimmying with every step, and yet I felt no sense of fear. I began to flex my knees and rock the bridge to and fro, up and down—I must tell you I felt as delighted then as I felt ages later by my first carnival ride—and by the time I came to my senses I looked up to see a handful of village folk standing upon the shoreline, quite perplexed by my display.

"And yet so cheerful was I in my frolic than none seemed to find my presence frightening. I shouted to them in a joyful manner and, at length, the matriarch appeared, older than the others by a generation. After a moment of stern observation, she nodded and waved me forward.

"Thus, I entered *Tu'ulth*, a place upon the land that had been given its own name. I would soon realize that the word Tu'ulth represented both village and island, and also the people I discovered there. The word and its meaning were inseparable, for they were one with the island and all it contained.

"After the usual touching and poking and marveling, I found my sling's ability once again able to amaze those within this village. After I had offered a proper display of its ability, I gave the old woman my weapon. She treated the gift as a great compliment and she spoke rapidly, using a string of unfamiliar words that confounded me. She presented me with a necklace of small pink, brown and white shells. I had come upon a few villages where crude tattoos were prevalent, even some body-piercings, but this was my first taste of fine jewelry. Many of the women and men in Tu'ulth wore unique necklaces, and I would later learn that the various shells symbolized particular skills, indicating a knowledge of stomach-ache remedy, or of hunting ability, or of midwifery. I found the embellishment quite appealing on the others, and I could only imagine that such a piece looked similarly fetching around my own neck."

Reni's gaze twinkled. "Vanity, I can only assume, blossoms with knowledge. Soon enough I would be crafting necklaces as well, and many of the Tu'ulth would learn to produce slings and moccasins. For days we'd watch each other intently—as might a gaggle of five-year olds in a kindergarten class—learning from what we observed. For instance, I knew about certain medicinal roots, and they of others: how to stem an infection or withdraw various poisons from the blood; how to close a wound with sap and oil extracts, and, much to my surprise, they showed me their fishing nets woven from a certain stringy river vine. They would sink their nets with stones in the adjacent reservoir and, whenever necessary, raise them again, along with an astonishing quantity of wiggling fish. Thus, in the span of thirty minutes, they could capture a far greater number of fish than could a single man with a spear or club in three *days*.

"I'll admit that I found the Tu'ulth a very chatty people. Not until I'd begun to understand their language would I comprehend its most remarkable complexity. In my own village, I doubted I had ever known more than perhaps a hundred words. Yet, among the Tu'ulth, words tumbled from their mouths like over-ripened pomegranates from a shaken tree! In gratitude for my knowledge, they taught me many new sounds in short order and, after much confusion on my part, gifted me an extraordinary new marvel—the *verb*. Until now, my knowledge of basic objects had been simple. A rock. A branch. A fish. Things. *Nouns.* If I were off to hunt the long-eared tu'abi, to make such knowledge known in my village, I would grasp my sling, utter the creature's name and point in a direction. Certainly my village had words for hunt, for sleep, but these sounds were not strung together in coherent sentences. Our word for 'hunt' implied not only the search for fresh game, but also the kill and a meal afterwards. We used a completely different word if the hunt was unsuccessful and one came home empty-handed. But the Tu'ulth used a specific word for *hunt*, and with it a word for *boar*. They'd not simply point to a fire pit but communicate the need to *fuel* the fire with *wood*. Words to represent *go* and *come*. Rudimentary sentences! I can only tell you that I found this to be an extraordinary education."

"You remained with them quite a while," I said, aware of Reni's wistful expression.

"Yes, I did. Long enough to see their mu'ata die, and to see the new mu'ata perish many years later. And *her* successor as well. And eventually, yes, many others. As was their custom, they anointed the dead in a sweet seed oil, then wrapped the body in a thatched weave. The entire village assisted, humming a provocative dirge. It took me some time to decipher, but certain notes in sequence provoked certain memories for these people—song was their source of historical reference long before any written word. When the thatching was complete, the body encased, the Tu'ulth would carry the little buoyant raft to the river's edge.

"As the river's current ran quite swiftly here, the strongest of the Tu'ulth would cast the raft away from shore and we would watch until the woven sarcophagus had vanished beyond the mists downstream. A body could float for a great many miles in such a buoyant cocoon. Since no remains had ever been rediscovered by the Tu'ulth, they believed the river took the dead to a place they'd named *Tu'aku*. Much later I would perceive this place to be their version of heaven. A life after death.

"I must admit I had never before contemplated an afterlife. I consider the Tu'ulth to be the source of my philosophic awakening—although admittedly one that would not reach maturation for many centuries hence. But I suspect these people to have been among the first tribes among all of humanity to imagine a continuation of the soul or spirit. For a man who had only recently discovered the verb, contemplating an afterlife proved an extraordinarily profound experience.

"So, yes. As you so keenly intuited, I remained among the Tu'ulth. I *became* Tu'ulth. I taught them advanced slingshot'ry, and within a few months they had become quite accurate—especially the younger females, who were small and wiry and very good hunters. Much later, during the drought years when the invaders came, their keen aim helped save the island from being overrun and pillaged on numerous occasions.

"The island's isolation provided a superb natural defense. This was a time before knowledge of the bow or the arrow, and although I saw many of the raiders wielding blowguns fashioned from bamboo shoots, few were accurate at more than a few scant yards. The swirling river produced the most fickle of air currents, and we lost very few of our number over the years to the animosity of others.

"And it was I, myself, "Reni said with a roguish grin, "who realized that by utilizing additional lengths of rope, we could design enough slack into our bridges to render them virtually unusable. When the villagers sensed that hostility was near, we lowered our bridges into the water and raised them again when safety was at hand."

"How clever of you, dear," I marveled.

He smiled at me. "I'm ashamed to tell you how *many* years had passed before this thought occurred to me. But I was eager to remain with these people, to learn from them. They were fiercely egalitarian, a curious and gregarious people. My initial curiosity to travel wherever my feet took me had finally been exceeded by my need for community once again. Around my third, maybe my fourth century as a Tu'ulth, I became the patriarch. As far as I knew, I was the first male in the village to ascend to such honor."

"They did not fear you?" I asked. "Your amazing resilience?"

"On the contrary," he replied. "Being older than time, there burned within me the knowledge of time itself. I served as storyteller, apothecary, and hardware store. I functioned as their judicial system, and even today I'd like to think I was quite objective in matters of honesty and fair play.

"I still wandered, my earliest treks lasting no longer than several days, or maybe a few weeks at most. And I'd often return with some new marvelous invention or plant medicine. In those early years I discovered three additional river valleys and began to notice a pattern of life on Sister Earth. In those years before becoming patriarch, I'd discovered dozens of additional villages and, unique to each tribe, usually one or two new facets of burgeoning human development. I did my best to teach and to learn while among those tribes that accepted me, but I always found my way home again to my little island. And thus, for many hundreds of years, perhaps thousands, we prospered as a hub for discovery and knowledge.

"Hardships ensued of course; droughts and floods, sicknesses and misfortunes. Death was prevalent at every turn. The first time I died as a Tu'ulth, I'd eaten a large, delightfully moist fungi. Mushrooms had been a constant food source in my own valley and I had never known fungi to be inedible. Yet in this valley, and not far from our island, a toxic variety existed—a bright red, beautiful specimen. I staggered back to the village with an exquisite stomach pain. I vomited incessantly but felt the cold numbness of death encroaching. I managed to convey to the village that I was not to be sent downstream, then fell into complete paralysis, and eventually passed into that place between darkness and light.

"When I awoke several days later, I lay on a bed of animal skins, bathed and fragranced, and several women were humming a pleasant dirge around me. I opened my eyes and smiled, and they laid hands upon me with great excitement.

"I am loath now to admit how much I appreciated the Tu'ulth's joy upon my awakening that day, and upon those many times hence, returning from either death or a distant journey. After living for several generations among them—well, I'm afraid I became something of a willing celebrity. I confess that my prolonged life eventually created great admiration and I grew to relish my status among the Tu'ulth as *buka*—a traveler. And, oh, how they'd welcome my return! Imagine Clark Gable stepping out of a sleek limo at the premiere of a major motion picture. I felt a similar adulation returning to Tu'ulth, to shouts of wild abandon, tears and warm embraces from a people I dearly loved."

"And straight into the arms of some stone-aged Jean Harlow," I added with a playfully withering look.

When Reni said nothing, his mouth puckered like that of a hooked fish, I could only laugh. "I cannot be jealous of a woman who existed fifty thousand years before my birth! Nor of a man who existed long before the very ideas of love and marriage."

"True," he admitted, "although I hesitate to remark upon these matters."

"Even as a historical footnote? I am but a year shy of attaining my doctorate, my love. Your firsthand account of prehistoric mating rituals are not only fascinating, but also within my academic field. What *other* historian has ever had such a rare opportunity?"

Reni nodded uncertainly. "Well, yes—then one could view me as a suave, late-Paleolithic version of Gable, with my best gal Harlow in her finest pelts, the two of us feasting at the Brown Derby and dancing 'til dawn."

"Indeed," I replied.

"And you can understand why such fanfare can go to one's head. I might have been somewhat enlightened for my age, but I was still quite primitive."

"Nearly Neanderthal," I teased.

"To my knowledge, I've never met one," he replied after a moment's contemplation.

"Tell me," I asked, my voice earnest, "did it not strike you odd, even then, that you'd never sired children?"

"At least none that I know of," he said with equal aplomb. "But no, long ago I came to suspect my unusual condition had left me sterile—much to my, to our, current chagrin," he added. "For a child of ours would be the most exquisite of children."

"I agree, my darling," I said, my heart brimming.

"And yet I can only assume my barrenness serves as fitting retribution for eternal life. Had I borne children, who themselves might be gifted with apparent immortality, sooner or later this world would become quite overpopulated with my descendants."

"Still, you cannot be certain of your condition?"

"No, not absolutely," he said. "Interestingly, in my many years among the Tu'ulth, I felt a kinship with every child born, a sense of patriarchal pride toward the thousands of children born over the passing centuries. I was no more and no less a father than any other adult male among us. We hovered over our young, patient and caring. We taught all children—males and females—equally. And as the males grew older, we taught them the ways of the hunt and of the hunter."

"But not the females?" I asked, rather presumptively.

"Ah, but the women of Tu'ulth were too valuable to submit to the dangers of such an endeavor. Instead, they fashioned our pots and tended our fire. They were our healers, our sages and the true stalwarts of our society. In the middle years of my time with the Tu'ulth, our males pursued game, and found time to accomplish little else—although the rigors and rewards of their efforts were quite necessary.

"But no one among the Tu'ulth was *forbidden*. Those females who wished to hunt did so. Those males who wished to cook or mend or sing to the newborns did so. None met with disapproval for any contribution. Those rare times that the village found itself in peril from invading tribes, male and female fought most formidably, side by side, living and dying as one. This was simply the way things were.

"You should also understand that, during my time with the Tu'ulth, the notion of fatherhood was not yet within the bounds of our comprehension. At least—" Reni paused, his expression a lopsided smile. "—not by us males. I fully suspect that the females, who by then were tending the island's plentiful stock of boar and small goats, were fairly certain of the symbiotic nature of reproduction. And I believe our females had begun to select those males they perceived favorably. They mated most eagerly with the strong hunter, the fast runner, the intuitive thinker, far before we knew that we were being—" Reni grinned again. "—manipulated by their feminine wiles. For many generations, perhaps eons, I believe our women took advantage of their greater understanding about the complexities of reproduction. I do recall those days—long before our species knew of jealousy and possessiveness—as being quite pleasant.

"I also suspect that this veiled understanding proved a fundamental cornerstone to those burgeoning civilizations that would later emerge. While our males went about fulfilling their basic urges, the females shared a secret that I suspect many men, even today, have subliminally yet to forgive. But, you see, our females had mastered the knowledge of selective breeding."

"Modern civilizations are notoriously patriarchal," I agreed. "Egregiously so, if you'd like my opinion."

"Ah," Reni said playfully, "then blame *your* forbearers, not mine."

He ignored my squint and continued. "But suffice it to say that, in my time with the Tu'ulth, I remained oblivious. I recall only that we were a family, nothing less or greater than that. From time to time, a woman might choose a single male for any number of reasons, and she was in her full right to refuse any man for any number of other reasons. Any man who forced himself—well, to my knowledge, that did not happen."

"No slaves, no concubines, no prostitution? No wonder you miss it so," I said.

"Aye. By the time we had outgrown the island—and I believe this was quite a few centuries after I'd met the Tu'ulth—we had by necessity begun to form separate tribal hubs, purely based on proximity. These were not factions, but rather extended families, protracted clans living no more than fifty or a hundred yards in one direction or another. It was not uncommon for a woman to wander between families and choose several different men at different times in her life—no one thought her sinful or scandalous for doing so. Constant mating was essential, course. You must remember that, despite my fondness for the past, one of every three children did not survive their first year. Another third never reached puberty. Procreation was too important to the tribe to adopt the rigid values one finds today under the umbrella of Christian matrimony. One mated for the same reason one hunted fresh meat or stoked the fire, so that the family would survive."

"No doubt your longevity gifted you with ample consideration as a good catch," I said, albeit with some mischievousness.

"I don't believe my longevity was viewed as an asset in those days, although I did possess the wisdom of the ages and, as I said, I was eventually considered quite sage. I did not—" But Reni paused, belatedly aware of the implication. "Since you ask merely in the name of factual importance—yes, I *was* popular among the younger, or should I say the more *fertile* of our females. And yes, I suppose my popularity must have caused displeasure among our adolescent males, most of whom had not yet chanced the opportunity to prove their courage to the tribe. Many young Tu'ulth died heroic deaths—a selfless honor that I could not duplicate. If I were gored by a wild boar's tusk, or caught by the fury of a raging river, it proved only a minor inconvenience. Immortality does not make one necessarily brave, but indeed rather careless.

"Boundless time also makes one jaded and bored with the ordinary—and by now I had taken to spending lengthy periods away from Tu'ulth, once again investigating the vast world around me. I suppose I was as much a novelty as celebrity—and a bit of Kris Kringle as well. Upon my return from these sojourns, I typically brought gifts of both idea and necessity, new herbs and remedies, new *marvels* to impress the family.

"In time, the concept of wanderlust spread amongst the Tu'ulth. While I travelled alone in those early centuries, I was eventually accompanied by others seeking the same adventures as I. One of my truest friends—*Pa'u'ak,* as well as I can pronounce his name after all these eons—would also set off on solitary adventures. I knew him as a spiritual fellow, as the isolation of the journey provided a splendid opportunity to ponder life. I soon came to understand the apprehension of watching a brother wander off into the unknown. Upon his return, I would shout and weep in sheer joy, as did we all.

"I have long suspected that the Tu'ulth were among the first of the world's teachers—for we gave as well as took. We passed along the secrets of our success. For instance, it was Pa'u'ak, and not I, who brought back the first bow and quiver from a village far away. This was the most marvelous tool that we'd ever seen, much like the bow of the more recent Great Plains warrior. Flint tips were bound to a split shaft by sinew. Fletching was achieved by bird feather or by the bristled leaves of a most spectacular plant, a species that sadly no longer exists. The accuracy of this weapon surpassed even our slings, and so in a very real sense, the greatest tool brought to the Tu'ulth was not mine, but Pa'u'ak's."

For many moments Reni sat in silent reverie and I allowed him his memories without qualm. Finally, he said; "And yet it was upon Pa'u'ak's following journey that I last laid eyes on the fellow. He never returned, and I've always wondered what became of him. As I said, the true heroes are those who die but once. For many years afterwards, we delighted in telling stories of Pa'u'ak's fearless adventures, real and imagined. He eventually became a legend."

"Might your frequent travels," I wondered, "and your persistent youth, have elevated you to something of a living legend? Your longevity must have been whispered about by others in Tu'ulth? Your extended life and your friend's mysterious disappearance...might such occurrences have led to the basic tenets of a burgeoning mythology?"

"Indeed that is possible," Reni agreed. "But to the best of my recollection, the notion of a deity, of a superior being, was beyond our comprehension. Had the Tu'ulth concocted some cockamamie assumption of my divinity, I would have nipped *that* in the bud. And surely any assumption of my own divine grace—" Reni wrinkled his nose, "—strikes me as the epitome of egotism and arrogance."

"Traits that certainly don't define you in the least," I said. "And yet? Have you never found purpose in your remarkable condition?"

"I'm afraid I did not find reason to philosophize about my condition for many, many millennia. Believe me, had endless age itself advanced my knowledge beyond that of my ordinary brethren, I might have thought differently. But for most of my time among the Tu'ulth, my curiosity was my biggest, perhaps my only, asset. Even today, I'm quite aware that I don't possess the talents of an Albert Einstein, of Marie Curie or Alexander Fleming. Nor of Picasso or Hemingway for that matter—or even Lou Gehrig! I'm simply a man who can't seem to die, and for the life of me I can't comprehend *why*. So I hardly deem myself extraordinary."

"But you're wrong," I said emphatically. "It is your nature to *be* extraordinary with every breath you take."

Reni waved away the sentiment, but I saw that my comment had touched him. I pressed on. "Not once have I known you to flaunt your status, your wealth or your name," I said, aware that Picasso, Hemingway and the Yankee's Mr. Gehrig were indeed profiting from their remarkable talents. You could easily hobnob with the Rockefellers and Carnegies, but you would *never*. I know you so well, my darling. You shun the limelight, and all its superficial trappings. And you are hardly extravagant."

"A matter of self-preservation," he supposed with a shrug. But aware of my tenacity, of the fire in my eye, he leaned forward and said, "I find that the almighty dollar is hardly an adequate measure of a man's worth."

"Assuredly it is not," I agreed.

"I've always felt loathe to collect even a penny at the expense of another. Yet only a simpleton could live a life such as mine and remain a pauper. Imagine a single gold coin, invested wisely five millennia ago, and consider its earning potential from that moment forward."

I had never before considered the core of my Captain's vast fortune, nor had I ever been impertinent enough to ask. "Is it even *possible* for such prosperity to accumulate in perpetuity? Civilizations come and go, and with their demise, most of the value they represented. Is that not so?"

"Quite true," he admitted. "I once owned several million gold *dinaras*, as I had become quite successful as a cultural attaché during the reign of Sakari Chandragupta, during a time that many claim to have been India's imperial age. I grew quite prosperous until my fortune vanished when the Hunas sacked Bharhut in—well, in whatever year it was.

"Afterwards, as I recall, I spent a century or two wandering about the Indian subcontinent, although after Bharhut fell I was no longer an affluent traveler, but a rather impoverished one. And yet my subsequent adventures proved no less exhilarating. Occasionally finding oneself a pauper is good for the soul," he added with a resolute nod.

"And you've obviously recovered nicely in the interim."

"I have indeed, although I've had eons to learn the nuances of commerce. And, upon occasion, I've managed to invest small sums quite well." Reni stared out at the distant ocean, a peaceful cadmium blue in this hour of twilight. Finally he said, "Let me tell you a secret, my love. More often than not, I've despised having accumulated wealth. While I've never begrudged myself the fruit of my labors, money is a tool that I frequently use—and I won't hoard more than what I'd consider proper working capital. Or as necessary stockpile for those rainy days ahead. And yet I can't lie to you—while I disdain extravagance, 'tis far better to live in comfort than in squalor. And I do so love a fine burgundy."

"I've seen your books, dear husband," I reminded him.

"I know you've given freely to others far more than you've kept for yourself—much to my undying admiration. In the relatively short time I've known you, you've saved hundreds, even thousands, of people with your philanthropy, and I shan't *ever* allow you to reproach yourself for that."

He appeared uncomfortable accepting the compliment, as Reni was often quick to dismiss his own importance in peoples' lives. "Aye," he said reluctantly, "but I've seen the most perverse human suffering brought on by men of huge fortune and equally huge egos—men so blinded by wealth that they could no longer see nor feel the human condition. The greed that attaches itself to great wealth sickens me. There exist legions of once reputable men who've acquired vast fortunes, only to prey upon those who have very little. And the thought of an eternal being wielding both wealth and power is beyond terrifying to me. Therefore, a life of quiet and simple pleasure, of unnoticed servitude, of discretion, is all that I now crave."

"Oh, but how I wish there were a million others such as you," I said. I paused, suddenly stricken with a stark sense of uncertainty. "Tell me, have you *never* met another like yourself?"

"I did think perhaps once…" But he shook his head. "No, actually never. Although upon occasion I have speculated," he admitted. "Realize that, throughout those seemingly endless years of antiquity, I rarely divulged my condition, not even to loved ones. If others have been endowed with this gift, I suspect they've likewise remained suspicious and mute. And once humanity fell under the hypnotic influence of religion, to hint of oneself as being divine—even accidentally so—would have meant banishment, imprisonment, or execution."

"You've been reluctant to speak of your beliefs," I said, having known for some time my husband's predilection for agnosticism. Yet Reni merely shook his head, content to leave the question hanging between us. He was certainly *not* an atheist. I believed Reni to be the most spiritual of thinkers and well versed, I dare say, in all the world's religions. He could randomly quote from the Christian Bible and from the Persian Qur'an. He knew scripture from the Saqqara Stones, and what we know as The Book of the Dead, both of Egyptian heritage. He had mentioned to me of once studying the Vajra Sutra and spoke of a Druid mythology that predated the Mabinogi. I was also aware of Reni's fascination with the Mesopotamian work *Gilgamesh*, a four-thousand-year-old epic poem in which a warrior attempts to find immortality among the gods. Upon this extraordinary night, with Reni's secret safely uncorked, only now could I fully understand his interest.

And yet, of Judeo-Christianity I found my husband particularly suspicious. He once told me; "I do find it perplexing that the omnipotent Hebrew God once considered the world flat and declared that the sun revolved around our planet—and that the Almighty's opinion changed only with the advancing knowledge of mankind."

"Yet what of Yahweh's Christ child?" I asked. "Was he not the first to speak of love as a salve for the world's horrors? Was his word not cathartic, essential for all the peoples of ancient Earth?"

"I do believe that the time had come for people to listen to a greater voice. A higher consciousness," Reni replied after an uncertain pause. "Yet even Yeshua's good intentions could not stop the killing, nor the madness of wanton lust and endless warfare."

I did not at all comprehend such detachment! I had no doubt that Reni's cynicism toward both government and religion ran deep, but the core of his doubt remained deeply locked within his psyche's innermost recesses. In the coming years, he would often allude to having frequented the Holy Lands in those early, blossoming days of the Christian faith. How could he not have been transformed by such a healing power? What, indeed, had been the relevance of his personal observations? So *many* questions spilled into my brain on this fabulous night, and I knew it might take my entire lifetime to acquire my husband's eventual answers.

Reni lifted a finger and my thoughts scattered. "In the earliest years of our history—not of written history, mind you, but of the spoken word—and long before God was even a notion in our collective consciousness, wise men called *sy'amar* wandered from village to village, relating tales in either song or verse about extraordinary creatures or events thrust upon the unwary. I suppose one might assume these tales to be a precursor of modern religion. But the stories created by shamanic lore were not of gods or of superior beings, but rather of regular folk encountering the unknown. The early sy'amar spoke of a fledgling warrior who might suddenly converse with a cheetah, for instance—and from his conversation find a clarity of inner strength and spirit. Or of a young girl who took flight as a bird, soon returning to her village with newfound wisdom. We were beginning to understand basic morality, you see. And we learned to tell fictive tales to depict complicated or confounding issues. I believe we were beginning to comprehend the difference between right and wrong, to discover principles, even virtue. As a species, we were becoming aware of our own self-awareness.

"I suppose it was only natural," he said after a long pause, "that more rigid belief structures would eventually follow."

"A logical conclusion," I agreed.

"In those early years, these travelling sages might speak for hours and mesmerize us with their amazing accounts of mankind overcoming extraordinary obstacles. Eventually, the sy'amar would bring juices or crushed pulps in clay vessels to share with the village elders. Ingesting these plant extracts triggered a distorted sense of consciousness that brought such amazing tales alive. Over time, these shamanic medicines became special, and then sacred and eventually, long afterward, forbidden to all but a few. The shamans themselves were likewise eventually celebrated, and then revered. But these men bore little resemblance to their earnest predecessors.

"I believe the ancient sy'amar were the antecedents of our modern priests and clerics. Probably of our modern apothecaries as well," he added. "But once the strong and the wizened found distinction amongst themselves—*that* distinction became a precursor of both kingdoms and cults. Priests were acquired as assets by the wealthy and lavished with material fortune in exchange for their promise of an eternal afterlife. We lost the message and instead found the messenger deserving of our adoration. And with such adoration also came a sy'amar's ability to dictate wrong from right, or to determine the worthiness of any man brought before him. Those who had once hoped to bring all of mankind together had instead begun to push him apart."

"Was it not Napoleon who said, 'Religion is what keeps the poor from murdering the rich?'" I asked.

"Aye, 'twas his sentiment indeed," Reni agreed, nodding vigorously. "An astute proclamation. And no less true today than centuries ago. You realize that the world was, and remains, a particularly barbaric place. Modern civilized societies are no less adept at killing then were men wielding spears, and our weaponry has become far deadlier than ever before.

"And yet I look upon you, my love, still a young woman, and find a gentle creature, caring and empathetic toward all. How could this be? It's taken me a hundred lifetimes to reach that same state of grace. Shouldn't *I* be *your* most humbled disciple? One might think, over these many millennia—and by occasionally dying now and then—that I would have learned far more quickly."

"But here you sit," I replied, "a most generous and kind man."

"Atonement," he said with a tired sigh.

"*Poppycock*," I responded, somewhat unkindly, but not at all willing to tolerate such self-deprecation. I could only wonder how emotionally scarring, those endless years my husband had waded through such primitive times. Nevertheless, I found nothing but tenderness and compassion in this man I so adored with my every breath.

I should also admit that, over the course of these few scant hours, I had come to believe every word of Reni's tale. Captain Sebastian T. Renaud was not only a man incapable of wanton greed or anger, but also of hyperbole.

And yet his most recent comments tickled a question that had remained unspoken upon my lips. For a long while now we had spoken to each other in cathartic darkness. The time seemed fitting.

"You've died *many* times?" I inquired gingerly.

"Ah," he said. "More than I care to remember."

"I still don't pretend to understand this remarkable gift of yours," I admitted.

Reni spent a long while staring upward into the night sky. I followed his gaze, aware of the constellation Cassiopeia shining down upon us in ageless wonder.

"Nor do I," he whispered finally. "I've come to accept death as little more than a deep and grateful sleep. While I no longer fear its sporadic presence, I deeply loathe incarceration. A life sentence for me would be most unfortunate. I have been confined upon occasion, as a prisoner of war, of ideology, of petty whims, and from those episodes I have learned patience and meditation. Far worse than any prison, however, is my dread of venturing underground—the exploration of caverns for instance, or the prospect of mining. The notion of finding myself buried alive for eternity, undead, entombed like an insect in amber, seems a most horrific prospect."

"Oh, my," I said, feeling equally appalled at the thought.

"I also admit a curious fear of decapitation," he added. "I came within a heartbeat of my own beheading once, the executioner's blade a cold tickle against my neck and with only my wits to save me."

I instinctively put a hand around my throat, trying to imagine the sensation of my head suddenly uncorked.

"I have no idea of the consequence," he added. "Whether my body might sprout a new head, or if my head might cultivate a new body. Might I suddenly find two of me, but half-witted? I'm no longer afraid of dying, you see, but rather of *not* dying—of discovering my head and body separated for all of eternity. I'm not quite sure what my head would do without the rest of me."

"I'm not certain I want to hear about that moment of your life," I implored. "I do so adore your head exactly where it sits."

"No, no—quite right, my love. I promise to save that tale for another day, as I believe you'll find the adventure a most astounding one."

"Another day," I agreed eagerly.

"Fire hurts like the dickens," Reni continued blithely, as if somehow the notion of my husband *cooking* would prove somehow more palatable to me than his decapitation. "And it takes a good while for my body to shut down and to regenerate—meaning I scream like a bloody schoolgirl long after I should be dead, which scares the locals, and probably why I've not been buried afterward. In times of old, the wicked and the bedeviled were usually left for the wolves to devour. Twice I have been set aflame upon a pyre—centuries apart, thanks be to providence. Fortunately, both times I woke up in a pit somewhere, dragged into the woods and left for dead, although for whatever reason, predators have always given my flesh wide berth. Perhaps I've never smelled properly of rot or death, and even hungry wolves seem wary of a trap. On those fiery occasions I remained unconscious for a good week or two, only to awaken with fragile, baby-pink skin from head to toe, my cells still reviving, and with the least bit of movement quite painful. I took great care to avoid infection—without a clue then, of course, about bacteria or germs, yet somehow grasping the concept of cleanliness based on experience, aware that pollutants and contamination lead to painful conditions that only prolong healing.

"Drowning isn't pleasant either," he admitted after a thoughtful pause, "although I find it to be a relatively swift death. I was lost at sea once, rather recently, washed o'erboard during a nasty squall in the Southern Pacific. I was one of three navigators bound to an expedition led by the English adventurer Cook."

"Do you speak of Captain James Cook?"

"Aboard the *HMS Resolution*," Reni said with a nod.

I could not help but smile at the man's perception of the word *recent*.

"A rogue wave hit us amidships late one evening and over the rail I went, headfirst into the churning froth. I found myself bobbing upon the turbulent seas like a discarded cork. I attempted to tread water, but the swell was enormous and ragged, and I soon exhausted myself. During those tortuous hours I would repeatedly lose consciousness. I can't be certain, of course, but I think with each of these bouts of unconsciousness came a new death. Life would eventually return, and I'd sputter and choke and vomit forth copious amounts of the sea. I believe I died several times in those waters, the last few in delirium.

"I have no idea what might have happened had a shark found me. Might I have awakened in its belly in pieces? I shudder to contemplate such misfortune. However, after what must have been many days afloat, I drifted upon the shore of a tiny palm-swept atoll—a crescent of desolate sand that harbored no more than three or four acres of thick jungle foliage and a small hump of volcanic rock. Coming to my senses, I discovered that my fingers and toes had been nibbled to the bone, nothing but stubs." Reni put a hand in front of his face and wiggled his finely manicured fingers. "There was little I could do but watch the bone and tissue and skin gradually regenerate—and within a week I had regained the delicate use of my appendages. The healing process itched unrelentingly," he said, "although I found it quite fascinating to watch new fingers gradually emerge from old stumps. By then I was obviously well aware of my immortality. It was no more perplexing than waiting for a new suit from the tailor."

Reni glanced skyward, his gaze vacant, as if recalling a long lost memory. "I must tell you that over the centuries I'd discovered another curious facet of my body's remarkable regenerative properties—my ability to adapt to my environment, very much like a chameleon. Wherever I felt the chill of a long, harsh winter, my skin would become coarse and loose and thick. In the tropics, I would darken considerably, with only the slightest hint of sunburn. My hair on that blasted island soon grew a thick jet black, and within days the soles of my feet as tough as stone.

"A blessing, as I lingered on that speck of sand for a long time, years I suspect, existing upon a diet of coconut milk, sun-dried squid and sand crab before being plucked up by a Dutch schooner bound for the Indies. The vessel eventually harbored in Hong Kong—then known as *Ap Lei Chau*, although the Brits knew the place as Aberdeen Island. I had quite enough of seafaring by then and decided to venture inland to China—"

"And where you learned my language?" I asked eagerly.

"Ah, but truth be told, I had visited those vast areas of East Asia a millennium before, and already knew many dialects of Mandarin, of Cantonese and several Sino-Tibetan tongues, languages mostly long forgotten. So my first recollection of China is perhaps a thousand years prior, although I'd possibly wandered the same lands many times previously, before maps and borders had been created by men. I'd once spent several lifetimes upon the Mongolian plains, among the Tungusics and Khitans. I was quite handy with a scythe and sword, and my trusty sling of course—and I soon became an excellent horseman too.

"In those days, the Mongolian wilderness offered boundless freedoms. The Mongols were a quite self-sufficient and rugged people, much to my liking. We were also supremely loyal to our families. Our villages were very close-knit communities, yet self-sufficient and fiercely independent. We were known collectively as the *Shiwei*, our race a fusion of Chinese, Mongolian, Xiongnu and Siberian blood. For many centuries, the Shiwei and our sister clans occupied inhospitable swatches of northern Eurasia, vast tracks now occupied by Chiang Kai-Shek's China and Stalin's monolithic Soviet empire.

"Had we a cohesive leader in those days—as Genghis Khan would one day become, several hundred years hence—we would have comprised the largest nation of the ancient world. But food and resources were scarce, our villages scattered. Thus, we had little notion of any shared culture or firm boundary. Regardless, any stranger was considered a friend and any who roamed the Highlands or the Eastern *taiga* seldom left our village without a belly full of lamb and turnip stew.

"In the mountains we picked at shallow deposits of gold and silver and a crusty yellow powder highly prized by wealthier cousins in the South. We did not know it at the time, but we were providing sulfur to the emperor's alchemists—a rudimentary ingredient of a magical black powder that would soon change the course of civilization. As I would often travel south with the trade caravans, I found many opportunities to frequent the royal city of Chang'an—"

"*Oh?*" I said with sudden, bubbling excitement.

"A city with which you are no doubt familiar," he said with a gentle smile.

"But of course!" I exclaimed. For those of us whose lineage can be traced from those distant Pacific shores, China's ancient city of Chang'an holds a heartfelt connection, much as Mecca does to the devout Muslim or Machu Picchu to the indigenous peoples of the Andes. Long ago, the city's name had been changed to present day Xi'an, but historically Chang'an—the word itself meaning *perpetual peace*—is regarded as the cradle of our various and numerous ancestries. I had heard many stories of this sacred city as a small child. It was with great amazement that I realized that I sat before the single being in the world, in the *history* of the world, who could bring its memory alive.

"One day soon I shall divulge my knowledge of that great citadel, but for now I shall merely reveal that my first encounter coincided with the early years of the Tang Dynasty. Chang'an was the largest city in the world at the time, with a million people living within her walls. I saw much of the city in various phases during its resurrection, as centuries of previous wars had taken their toll. But under the Tangs' reign, I believe Chang'an to have been ancient humanity's crown jewel, brimming with artists and poets and scholars, and ripe with the promise of an extraordinary future.

"You realize that Europe had yet to rise from centuries of cultural and intellectual stagnation after the fall of Rome to the Goths. My presence in Chang'an would have transpired during the seventh and early eighth centuries of the Julian calendar. And while we in the West know so very little of its existence, this great city was both a capital and the heart of an empire far larger than even *Pax Romana*.

"But here I sit," he added with a troubled flourish, "presuming to tell you what I clearly need not. What you do *not* know, my love, is that while in the city, I became friendly with an officer of the palace guardsmen, a young man named Pi Q'an. This encounter occurred sometime in late spring, as I remember the blue Hydrangea blossoms cloaking every avenue, and cherry trees in countless gardens in full bloom. As was usual for Mongolian caravans at the time, we lingered for a month or two in the city before returning home. This gave us a chance to fatten our livestock, to repair our wagons and to miss the torrential mountain rains that made northward travel treacherous upon winter's retreat.

"One evening by sheer happenstance I found myself in Pi Q'an's company when a band of assassins attempted to kill prince Li Tai, the emperor's second son, who I believe was only eight or nine years old at the time. Although outnumbered, a handful of the Emperor's guards, and I with my sling, fought off these rogues in a brief skirmish. After they'd scattered, young Li Tai took great delight in heralding my assistance to his father, as my sling's accuracy had dropped three of these *xiōng shou* in their tracks. The emperor in turn insisted on personally expressing his gratitude."

"Wait—*what?* You've *met* Emperor Taizong?" I asked in utter incredulity. Many Eastern scholars considered Taizong among the greatest of all Chinese rulers. Reni might have just as casually told me that he'd lunched with George Washington.

"I'd like to think that we became friends," he said with quiet aplomb. "He was a remarkable man, and very learned. A great equestrian, by the way. And very much in love with his Empress Zhangsun. An outspoken woman. She used to write poetry and would sometimes read me verses of *jueju*— a lyrical style of the time. She was very philosophical. Deep. She once wrote a poem for me and had the verse etched into a glazed pot. I loved that vase. Stolen by bandits during— well, it's sorely missed, I can tell you that. The piece would look quite stunning on the veranda. Anyway, I think you'd have liked her. Empress Zhangsun, I mean."

I blinked, speechless, and could only wait in stunned silence for Reni to continue his tale.

"The emperor was often accompanied by a gaggle of mathematicians and scientists, and our many hours together were spent amid animated and somewhat boisterous discussions of one sort or another, theorizing about the nature of the soul, the world, the very universe. Do you know the man actually speculated that the earth revolved around the sun? This was centuries before Copernicus published his own theories. During such sessions, Taizong spoke neither as emperor nor teacher, but as a student among students, seeking only truth.

"As I mentioned, the emperor's chemists had already discovered the explosive quality of gunpowder, although its value as a weapon of war remained as yet unknown. At the time, Taizong's engineers used it to blast bits of marble and stone from quarries, a tool of convenience. Anyway, yes, the emperor and I often talked about science and art and the historical theory of warfare over tea. He granted me extended stay within the palace, for which I was most grateful, and I remained in Chang'an for quite some time as merchant and soldier, and eventually a *zhànshi*—a philosopher of sorts."

"I cannot believe you could have ever left such a remarkable realm," I said.

"Ah, but I did not leave of my own volition," Reni replied, his voice tinged with regret. "I remained in Chang'an for many years after Taizong's death. Poisoned, some say, although I do not have any evidence of such. His son, Li Zhi, was hardly the ruler his father had been. Cursed with poor health and addicted to the opium poppy, this new emperor faltered. His wife, the Empress Wu, would secretly assume control of the dynasty and would one day usurp her failing husband as supreme ruler.

"But Wu Zetian did not trust me. She tolerated my presence for many years, but as she grew older, she became increasingly angry with those of us who were critical of her ability to rule—as China had recently lost much venerable territory to invading Tibetans and the Khitan. Several of my comrades died in quick succession, and under quite mysterious conditions. Others were imprisoned. Aware that my good fortune was rapidly deteriorating, I made plans for a secret caravan to take forty of us to Luoyang, several hundred kilometers away.

"However, few secrets held fast in Chang'an in those tumultuous days. Before we could reach the city, our caravan was attacked by mercenaries and few of us escaped unscathed. I became a wanted man, my severed head worth a small fortune in Wu's hands. I took this as a sign to finally leave China.

"I set a course due west, and by horseback snaked a crooked trail through the war-ravaged Tufan lands, what is now Tibet, and into Khasmir; gingerly then through the warring Arabic Caliphate and into Bulgaria. I found absolutely no peace on Earth during that time. A century after Muhammad's death, Islam had begun to spread northward, encroaching upon the Byzantine and Turkish empires. The Avars and Slavs were at war with Bosnia. The Serbs fought the Croats. No friendship existed between those who *had*, and those who *wanted*. I wandered cautiously through the Balkan lands and into the crumbling Bavarian empire, a small kingdom busy battling the invading Frankish armies. Eventually I moved on to Paris."

"Paris?" I repeated with sudden excitement.

"Ah, but it was not the best of times," he remarked.

My brow creased. "Have you not known any kingdom to avoid collapse? To somehow find the will to endure?"

And yet I already knew the answer, for nations old and new came and went as plainly as the night followed day, as did sons of fathers and their sons after them.

"Regrettably, the very essence of any empire's greatness too often becomes the smoldering ember of its downfall," Reni said quietly. "Wherever prosperity flourishes, self-indulgence and corruption follow. All too soon the wealthy begin to hoard what they perceive to be their divine right to covet. The poor become enslaved and revolt festers. The rich bicker and argue about inconsequential things while their greed, plain and simple, eventually leads to social collapse. The lure of power, the lust for money, and the belief that one's own God is sovereign above all others, precedes the downfall of every kingdom that time has ever known."

"But certainly not our own?" I asked with sudden alarm, for although the blood of China ran through my body, my heart and soul had grown very fond, very protective, of my adoptive home.

"Have we not found a *different* virtue in our democracy? In our freedoms?" I asked.

"We're only as free as the wealthy are content, are we not?" Reni replied. "This nation is barely a century and a half old, and yet the prosperous minority is once again addicted to financial gains and losses—remaining all but ignorant of the plights of the many. Mr. Roosevelt's so-called Great Depression is nearly eight years old, and what have we learned?" Reni shook his head, as if in reply to his own question. "What I do know is that a century from now, this country will be far different from what it is today. Whether for better or worse I don't presume to even guess. But *different*, that is without my slightest doubt."

"I cannot fathom a world without this country," I offered, feeling oddly morose and quite on the verge of tears. Before I could stop myself, I said, "Perhaps *none* of us is meant to live forever, to witness the end of what we have striven so hard to sustain. To witness the death of so many friends and loved ones. I don't know how I could bear it."

"Aye, 'tis often most difficult," he replied with a wistful gaze. In that instant I sensed the weight of endless centuries crushing down upon my poor Captain. I felt immediate remorse for having spoken so thoughtlessly.

A single word my husband had uttered moments before echoed fiercely in my brain. To break the wretched silence between us, I reached out and took his hand in mine, and with a trembling smile said, "Tell me all about your time in *Paris*, my love."

"Yes, yes, Paris." Reni grinned at me with renewed exuberance. He'd promised me a holiday in France and Belgium come spring, and we had recently talked about our impending journey with great delight.

"The first time you saw that fabled city," I prompted.

"Ah, but I'm afraid you'll be disappointed. My first glimpse was not the medieval Paris of lore, neither a city of jousting knights nor swashbuckling musketeers, as those lofty times remained many centuries hence. In the middling days of the ninth century, Charlemagne's heirs had scattered the emperor's once unbeatable armies across

Europe. He had united a continent, indeed had sown the seeds of an eventual Renaissance, but Charlemagne ruled from Aix-la-Chapelle, his son Louis from Aquitaine, and Paris remained but a fortified bump on the Seine. Decades after Charlemagne's death, much of *Regnum Francorum* had descended again into untamed territory—Viking hordes to the north, Islamic marauders to the south, with Serbs and Basques and the insufferable Gauls hoping to carve away large chunks of land for themselves. The peoples in this region were predominantly illiterate farmers or herders, little more than scavengers. I remember riding through a smattering of impossibly impoverished villages on the road from Verodunum, passing ramshackle hamlets built of twig and mud, the meager populace destitute and begging for scraps of food, beseeching both God and king for salvation.

"I travelled with three others, soldiers of fortune from Avars. Confronting such poverty here, amid such fertile lands, proved heartbreaking. We ourselves carried little food to spare, although as I recall we had soon given up what morsels of cheese we shared among us and kept only three loafs of bread for ourselves.

"Ah, but I digress," Reni said, abruptly motioning with one hand as if to dismiss the whirling thoughts inside his head. "My first glimpse of Paris? I remember the city lost behind a gray mist, the morning chill wet and heavy. We passed beneath a stone gateway—a *barbican*, I believe the term to be, atop which several archers watched our progress. The bridge itself had been constructed of stone and mortar, arched across the Seine and connected to another fortified gatehouse that confronted us like some dark and ominous maw. Above the swirling fog I could see bits of the city's outer wall, fabricated of heavy rock and easily thirty feet high. I could also distinguish the shrouded forms of several stone towers above us, still quite crude by today's definition of a castle.

"We passed the guard unchallenged as we presented no obvious threat. I could smell an acrid smoke from many fires and hear the calls and shouts of men echoing about in the early dawn. A garrison lay before us, which I recall as being a rather tall building and also greatly fortified. We passed a second, lower rampart and finally discovered a large and functioning marketplace, a forge and stables, several churches and cloisters, even a cemetery—the true center of this island city. Although the island contained numerous churches and abbeys, I remember quite clearly one single cathedral, *Saint-Étienne,* rising near the island's southern-most bank, built of stone and wood and offering only a fraction of the splendor that its famous successor would bestow upon the city some three hundred years yet to come.

"I recall the city itself as being very cramped, the abounding houses tall and slender, constructed of clay and timber and peat, with thatched roofs, interspersed by jutting stone keeps here and there—miniature towers that stood in readiness should the outer walls be breached. The city seemed to me little more than a great and imposing fortress, as if the very existence of Paris served as little more but to ensure the survival of those who'd built it.

"And yet, by God, the place thrilled me. I soon learned that the island had, for many years, staved off repeated sieges by Norse pirates, who'd return each spring in ever stronger, more formidable numbers, as the Seine was proving a gateway to many riches and resources. Upon my arrival I had hoped to pursue my trade as a merchant, but as I carried no gold in my pockets, I could not afford to buy my way into any of the local guilds. I found myself soon enough indentured to a blacksmith of some renown in the city. Several years later, when Viking hoards lay siege one final time,

I helped defend my new home, equipped with a bow and quiver, my aim quite accurate from my perch atop the walls of *Île de la Cité*.

"Our eventual victory during that hot, rainy summer would ultimately break the back of the Vikings' will to conquer the island. And yet the uneasy truce that followed occurred only after an anxious king, still fearing these remarkable Norsemen, paid a tribute of much silver. Many of the invaders returned to their boats and continued to plunder towns and hamlets farther upriver, although others, weary of constant warfare, assimilated nearby and become part of the fabric of the landscape.

"With the prosperity of peace at hand, I at last found myself with sufficient coin to establish myself as a trader of exquisitely forged metals, including the Frankish broadsword—a tempered steel blade favored by the foot-soldier in many armies. I began to frequent the trade routes running south to Marseille and Cádiz, east to Athens and Constantinople and much later westward toward the fledgling Britannica. Despite Paris' conversion to Christianity during Charlemagne's rule, Moorish influence remained strong and continued to flourish. Many of our merchants hailed from the South; Al-Andalus or Morocco or Pisa. I found myself confronting exciting new tongues, including the rich languages of the North African coast."

"So not only did you speak fluent Mandarin, but French and Latin, and many of the African languages, as well."

"Dozens, I'm sure, although many haltingly. But, yes—*Mandarin!*" Reni exclaimed, tapping himself on the forehead. "We'd been speaking of your native tongue, hadn't we?"

"Albeit a long while ago," I said with a laugh. Already that evening, we had skipped through various millennia and many cultures. I would soon become quite accustomed to my husband's narrative routinely flitting between continents and centuries as might a fly between tasty morsels at a wedding banquet. Listening to Reni's stories over the years that followed felt like a carnival ride of continual twists and turns, of surprises and incredulity—and yet not once did my husband's tales disappoint or lessen my insatiable appetite for more.

"Both my Hellenistic Greek and Latin had endured for eons, of course," he continued casually, "as it was often necessary to fabricate either one's nobility or priesthood in those days of the Holy Pope's dominion over Europe. In Paris, we freely spoke Iberian—the language of the northernmost Moors—Darija, and Berber as well. I'm quite certain that I've learned and forgotten virtually hundreds of tongues. I eventually came to speak the King's auld English, although not for another few centuries. So yes, I easily juggled several languages during a single lifetime, as did those intrepid few who frequently traveled throughout *Mare Nostrum*—that is, our Mediterranean Sea. Sometimes, when bartering, one would wade through a multitude of tongues to reach accord. A merchant might speak in a Franco-Gallo tongue to an acquaintance who spoke Greek, who conveyed their intent to a trader who might speak Slavic and who'd translate words into Marathi, only to receive a reply in Lhasa. Such was the price of trade in those days, the difference between riches and failure."

Reni fell silent, as if reliving some precise moment. A fragment of history which I assumed, with some chagrin, would remain his for all of eternity. "I kept a home in Paris for many years," he said finally, "although I frequented my estate in Marseille far more frequently, and eventually found comfort in another modest villa in Constantinople—above a bordello, no less—for quite some time.

"I should admit to you that for centuries I had dealt in

weapons of war and, as a merchant of death, I had profited quite well. I crisscrossed the Mediterranean often, selling swords and various other blades in coastal ports, returning home with exotic spices, sugars and medicinal herbs, items still quite rare in the West at that time.

"Eventually, however, I could no longer ignore my own complicity in the bloodlust that had overtaken humanity. While in Constantinople, I chanced to discover a troupe of silversmiths from Nicaea who produced a remarkable array of products—jewelry and amulets, rhytons and flasks, intricately etched cups, bowls and vessels of extraordinary artistry. I was so taken by the beauty of these products that I sold my inventory of blades to a consortium of Ottoman traders and instead, began selling wares that would bring pleasure and joy, not death.

"I should also divulge that my revenues dropped precipitously, for in those days the worth of even the most dubious of crudely made swords far surpassed the price of the finest of artistic endeavors. And yet I was happy, and for many years our little guild thrived, selling our wares proudly throughout Mediterranea and Persia.

"Despite the conflicting proclamations of modern historians, Constantinople had remained largely an open city after the previous Crusade, with Muslims and Christians willing to co-exist. The Moors, Venetians, Egyptians, Romans and Greeks lived in uneasy harmony—and together, they excelled at nearly every endeavor. All things Byzantium flourished as the city became a haven for artists and musicians and writers from a hundred points of genesis.

"Ah, but greatness is fleeting, and Constantinople's enviable location between the Aegean and Black Seas—an open gateway between Europe and Asia—proved too alluring for the armies that would inevitably gather on the edge of one continent or the other. Ironically, I believe it was

Charlemagne himself who, many centuries earlier and having been auspiciously blessed by a Pope long dead, directly encouraged the rift between the two remnants of the Holy Roman empire. It was Charlemagne, I fear, who ultimately fueled the lingering feud between Christendom and Islam, a festering wound that has yet to heal itself.

"I still clearly recall the frenzy and fervor of the so-called Fourth Crusade. What began as a Christian assault on Jerusalem ended in the sacking of Constantinople. I returned to the city only months later to find my warehouses pillaged, my stock gone and my craftspeople dead or scattered. My own villa had been confiscated by a Venetian general and I remained hidden in the city for several days, waiting to make my escape. I could muster only a weary contempt, a keen hatred of kings and generals and the armies they led for little more than self-gratification, for the acquisition of foreign lands or the taste of gold and ill-gained profit.

"Under the cloak of a rain-soaked darkness, I returned to my small craft moored just beyond the pillaged palace of Boukoleon. With my trusted crew of three awaiting me aboard, I turned my eyes again toward the Mediterranean, its crystal blue waters a salve for that which burdened my soul. As it had done so many times before, the need for solitude once again beckoned."

Reni allowed himself a tenuous smile. "And so once again I abandoned my fellow man. You must realize, my love, that long before now I had lost my taste for bloodshed. I found no reward in victory, only a sense of deep despondency. The rampant slaughter of young men, of orphans and widows—for they were often butchered merely for the warmth of their blood on the hands of the victors—left me repulsed and bitter. I felt as if an unquenchable madness and lust for cruelty had descended over my brethren. I can't count the empires that blossomed and fell during those times, like autumn leaves dropping from a dormant tree; Brunswick and Cologna, Seljuk and Mamluk, Trier and Mainz, Savoy and Bohemia.

"I do believe that humanity suffered," my husband said, "when we began to thirst for domination over those endless lands that had once been ours to freely share. We indiscriminately inked dotted lines on our maps and threatened warfare should either neighbor or stranger dare cross these imaginary thresholds. At some point we began to believe that this world was ours to take, to own and plunder, when in reality we human beings are not at all unlike the fleas on a plump dog. I believe when Sister Earth tires of our madding itch, she'll shake us loose without a moment's hesitation.

"And so I remained sea-bound, content to sail upon the vast and comforting waters that mankind had so far found impossible to control. I called no single port or harbor my home. Indeed, the Mediterranean would become my haven, my passion, for many lifetimes. I eventually made my way around Cyprus and Malta and Majorca, taking fleeting comfort with the Hafskis and Maelukes, and later among the various peoples populating the smaller island states who felt no need to slaughter innocents. Thus, untethered by any loyalty to king or country, I was able to avoid the frequent wars that raged among so many nations.

"Equally important in those days when navigating the Mediterranean, one might choose, through either luck or providence, to be where *nigrum mortem* was not. The bubonic pestilence had first appeared near the borders of Mongolia and China, gradually following the trade routes both east and west. I myself had traveled with the Silk Road caravans many centuries before, unaware of the infected vermin hiding in our midst.

"When the Black Death swept through the Roman and Ottoman Empires, through Athens and Naples and then into Genoa, it did so quickly and without respite. It extended northward, to Strasbourg and Munich, Prague and Cracow. It ravaged Alexandria and Mecca to the east and, to the south, devastated Malila, Al-Marj and Tunis. This unfathomable curse would ultimately decimate much of the world over the next half-century. Indeed, throughout Europe, in Africa and Asia, very few kingdoms escaped its wrath.

"Yet somehow I did manage to stay one step ahead. I spent many years in Tangier, cocooned from peril. Later, with a small entourage, I fled to the Western Sahara, safe among the Berbers in Maghreb, before timidly visiting various small ports and oasis towns that had likewise escaped the infection. Understand that for many years I questioned whether we survivors were only prolonging the inevitable. It was a time of angst and trepidation among those I knew and held dearly, many of whom awoke every morning expecting all of humanity to end before sundown."

Reni offered me a feathered sigh. "The world did not end, of course, but merely recoiled in fear. Within a few decades, commerce would tentatively start anew throughout the Mediterranean, although the major ports of Marseille and Barcelona, of Naples, Alexandria and Damascus, remained shunned for quite some time. Little did we know that we ourselves, we far-reaching merchants, would continue to spread the disease among isolated coastal towns that had managed to escape the original infection. We knew nothing of microorganisms, those tiny creatures that so blithely corrupt a man's flesh and ultimately snatch away his life."

"The bacterium *yersinia pestis*," I said, as anti-bacterials such as tyrothricin and penicillin had been recently discovered and laboratory tests had proven promising.

"Aye, indeed I believe that to be the little bugger's name."

Reni stared out over the ebony sea for a long moment before he spoke again. "Soon enough, however, a semblance of normality resumed. Somehow, humanity had once again survived. It was during this fragile time that I began to seek new adventures upon uncharted waters—or at least those as yet unknown to me. My travels took me increasingly westward, into the Bay of Biscay, and soon further northward, into the Celtic and North Seas. I skirted the Norwegian Sea a few times, and my small ship was once briefly stranded upon an unknown rocky shore, far to the nor'west—possibly the Shetland Islands or Føroyar, or perhaps even Iceland, although I'll never know for certain.

"These frigid seas proved treacherous and unforgiving, however, and I positioned my sails to return me to safer waters, ultimately to the British Isles. For a lifetime or two, I explored the magnificent highlands of Scotia before meandering southward again. Soon enough I found myself at the gates of medieval London. Did you know I once saw a comedy of Shakespeare's, with the bard himself performing among the cast—at the Rose Theater in Southwark. Unfortunately, I was quite intoxicated at the time and don't remember much about the experience, I'm afraid.

"In any event, I decided to remain in England for a time, although occasionally I returned to Paris to secure additional funds for my continued survival. By now, you see, both circumstance and commerce had bequeathed me several lasting fortunes. Over the prior few centuries I'd been careful to secrete my wealth in various locations, in case I should ever find myself caught in the midst of some raging war. I have to admit that maintaining wealth was no great skill in those days, as the world had discovered the guilty pleasure of compound interest. My astounding longevity therefore assured that any principal, left in the capable hands of well-compensated bankers, would remain concentrated so that I could continue to prosper over the long term.

"I had long since perfected the pretense of becoming my own son, and eventually *that* man's son and then grandson, so I profited as the sole heir to my own fortune time and time again. To protect the ruse, I found it necessary to travel extensively—twenty years here, thirty years there. But commerce flourished in those days. Bankers had funded the Crusades after all, and bankers continued to finance wars and sporadic peace, bankrolling various Papal interests and several Jewish guilds. These same bankers had laid the financial foundation of the burgeoning Renaissance. I become a lender myself on the Venice Exchange and later in Florence, leaving trusted brokers in place during my lengthy absences.

"Yet 'twas never privilege nor excessive wealth I sought for myself—for the journey had once again become its own reward. And, oh, but how the journey had begun to thrill me! New ports, new peoples, new concepts and technologies. The sea provided endless routes and boundless opportunity.

"In those centuries after the plague, with humanity's numbers so drastically reduced, I thought that our incessant wars might cease, as I suspected the world's survivors too overwrought to find reasons to kill again. But that was not to be. During my travels, I would sometimes inexplicably find myself overlooking battlefields or skirmish lines, and on numerous occasions locked in mortal combat with men I did not know, nor with whom I had any grievance. Yet I understood that any stranger or rogue traveler might bring sudden death to a family or village. As a species, we had once again grown suspicious and reclusive—hostile in our persistent ignorance and prone to speculation and superstition."

I squeezed Reni's hand, as I could no more perceive my

husband raising a weapon against another human than I could imagine reaching up and touching the moon. And yet I realized humanity had barely evolved from its infancy, with mankind still as petulant as an unruly three-year-old. I could not perceive how a person of Reni's maturity and substance could have coped. I found myself quite curious in this regard. Recalling Reni's eager insistence in joining the European air war twenty years before, I said, "Did you *ever* have reason to fight for a just cause in those days?"

"Quite rarely," he admitted. "Although, yes, I did feel occasionally honor-bound to battle for, as you say, *a cause.* For the most part, however, I cared little about the rationale for war—those conflicting political whims and age-old vendettas in which neither side carried even the slightest hint of virtue. I would have none of it. Which is why I so eagerly continued to explore our world's endless seas, as free as a bird. We were not soldiers, intent on destruction. We were adventurers and philosophers; budding scientists, explorers of the unknown—very much like Mr. Edison, Admiral Bird or Dr. Goddard today.

"And that," Reni said, "is exactly how I found myself with Captain Cook, aboard the *Resolution* so many years later, our course set to span the globe—past Africa's Cape Agulhas and through the southernmost shoals of Australia, before venturing northward again along the rugged coastline of Alta California, so recently colonized by the Spanish. We sailed upward, past the Oregon Territory and into uncharted Canadian waters, then across the Bering Sea. Eventually we veered south and into the Pacific tropics. It was only then that fate found an opportunity to cast me adrift, and once again steered me toward the land of your birth.

"For many years I had eagerly anticipated my return to Chang'an. Yet I arrived to find the city ravaged, an empty shell of its former power and glory. The Europeans had by now arrived in increasing numbers, bringing with them the added curses of greed and conquest.

"While wandering amid the decrepit husk of this once great city, and later in Nanjing, I became aware of a lucrative slave trade between the East and the burgeoning west coast of the Americas. Such was this new world's penchant for unpaid workers and illicit sexual gratification. Small towns like San Francisco and San Buenaventura, mission settlements like San Juan Capistrano and San Diego de Alcala were already crowded with fur traders, gold panners, Spanish land-owners and frontier opportunists.

"I had known *quite* enough of slavery by this time. I considered the practice the most repugnant reflection of mankind's innate brutality. Despite my disillusionment with what Chang'an had become, and my disgust with this unholy practice of human trafficking, I need now only remind myself that being swept ingloriously from the *Resolution's* storm-drenched deck would eventually bring me to you, my darling."

I beamed and immediately my husband's pluck returned. He spoke with such a look of appreciation for me that my eyes welled until the tears streamed down my cheeks. Why Reni loved me so, I could not begin to grasp. But I felt eternal gratitude that he did.

"I did not spend much time amid the ruins of Chang'an," he continued, "before boarding a vessel that took me south once more. I soon found myself among the islands of Nippon the reign of young Tokugawa Ienari, a man who would one day own several hundred concubines. While the shogun himself accepted my presence in his court, many of his ministers treated my presence with contempt. The third time I was poisoned," Reni said forlornly, "I found enough incentive to move on."

"Oh, my," said I.

"Understand that mistrust ran rampant in Nippon. The many closely situated islands had known little but feudal war for centuries, as various regional warlords had attempted to wholly conquer the archipelago. As a foreigner with the shogun's ear, I was considered an ill omen—so I slipped from the palace one night and disappeared with little trace. I soon found myself island-hopping blissfully throughout Micronesia, leaving only when the Dutch and Spanish invaders had begun in earnest to conquer those island kingdoms. I spent a few idyllic years in the British Crown Colony of Fiji, where I refitted my small sloop, then finally set course back to the New World.

"For a long while I panned for gold in South America, acquiring a substantial bank account during my extended time in the jungles of Bolivia, Peru and Columbia. My patience and perseverance became so well-known throughout La Paz and Quinchia that eventually the miners called me *el Pato Extraño*—the Strange Duck. I gradually worked my way northward, up the backbone of the Americas. Mexico was becoming quite populated by then, although mired in revolution and shackled by desolate poverty. I eventually made my way into Texas, not yet a Republic—and one day I shall speak of the mission near San Antonio de Béxar—that hallowed place they now simply call The Alamo. I was not present for the battle but, by happenstance, came upon the smoldering ruins and pyres of the charred dead, only days after its defeat by General Santa Anna. The locals were talking in frenetic excitement about the heroism of the mission's defenders—a legend already in the making.

"As I spoke fluent Spanish, and with my skin darkened by years under the open sun, I was not bothered by Santa Anna's milling soldiers. Most of his army had already moved eastward and toward eventual defeat by Samuel Houston's forces. I followed the Mexican army at a safe distance and continued my way along the Gulf coast—lingering among the shameless and free-spirited Creole for several years, happily amid the many bayou dwellers south of Chalmette. I was intrigued by this land known as the United States. I'd heard much about the fledging nation and immediately liked the stock and spirit of its frontier people. They were an independent sort, although bound to a strictness and puritanical zealotry I admittedly found unappealing. Yet amid the seductive glow of candlelight or beneath the erotic lure of a full moon, I witnessed many of these puritanical dogmas cast away like soiled garments. Indeed, I discovered these fledgeling Americans to be a conflicted people who enjoyed passionate nights and suffered penitent mornings.

"I soon found it necessary to once again don a military uniform. My prowess as both marksman and equestrian allowed for my easy acceptance among the ranks. My patience for teaching others offered quick advancement, eventually as sergeant, and later as an officer. The allure of a nation at peace made for a soldier's dream.

"And yet," Reni added in a severe voice, "as a lieutenant in the First Louisiana Regimental Cavalry, I was duty bound to obey my superiors, and I was soon transferred from the frontier revelry of Fort St. Philip to a post in Antebellum. In Georgia, however, I once again opened my eyes to the prevalence of slavery—a most untenable situation for me. Even in this new country, amid cries of freedom and cheers of independence, humanity had not found its moral compass. I thought I had left the stench of slavery behind, long ago and half a world away, and I refused to tolerate such depravity here.

"Secreting several pouches of gold that I had mined in Mexico, I abandoned my post and purchased several families of Negroes at auction in Savannah. We proceeded west to Memphis and embarked by riverboat up the Mississippi.

By forging orders for myself and the Africans—who were kept chained below with the pigs and heifers—I was authorized passage as far as Missouri. I could travel no further with these people, since freeing slaves was a considerable offense in the South at the time. However, Missouri was decidedly fickle regarding the nature of slavery, and by offering several ounces of flake to the appropriate bureaucrats, I bribed our way into Iowa, which had become a state of the Union a few years prior.

"With a posse of well-armed northern sympathizers riding alongside, we reached Polk County under the cover of night. I acquired sixty-five acres of fertile farm land to establish a homestead for these gentle people, most of whom had spent their lives growing corn, rice and grain for the financial gain of their plantation masters. A pouch of gold purchased two dozen head of cattle, a dozen quarter horses and a hound who'd taken a liking to one of the children. A pair of golden nuggets, each the size of a ripe walnut, bought these people the promise of protection by the local garrison; by happenstance the commandant was a decent man from Massachusetts whose wife was a staunch abolitionist.

"As had become my way, after a few years of chopping trees and plowing fields in Iowa, I again grew restless, having discovered an entirely *new* continent to explore. And so I eventually parted company with these newly free people, our land bound by a mutual trust, and with the promise that I would always find safe haven there should I ever choose to return. I selected two mules and two horses and headed west toward the Nebraska Territory, which in those days extended northward to what is now the Canadian border. I ventured up the eastern slopes of the Rockies, into the Northwest Territories, for several years of blissful solitude.

"I bartered with the indigenous peoples that I occasionally met," Reni said, "quite aware that the basic skills of commerce had remained unchanged over many millennia. Warm blankets could fetch enough food for a winter, or safe travel among their lands, and medicinal knowledge—the application of various herbs and roots—could be had for the price of a knife or flint. I lived among the Siksika for a while—the Blackfoot—as I found their language easy to decipher and similar to languages I had not heard uttered for numerous centuries, once upon a time while wandering the high plains of the Kamchatkan peninsula.

"I eventually returned to the civilization of the *napikoan*—that of the White intruders—having made my way west to the Pacific coast and then south, soon finding myself in the lumber town of Portland. Apparently the Oregon Territory had become a state during my travels, and I gleaned news of America's horrific war and its bitter end. I felt immensely satisfied with the results, as freedom is the noblest of causes I can imagine, although the Union's wanton destruction of the South seemed unnecessary and abhorrent. I'd long ago learned that wars do not cease after the last gunshot fades. For generations, the hatred smolders. Wanting no part of such latent hostilities, I found myself with little desire to turn eastward again.

"In Portland, I also heard news of a transcontinental railroad having connected San Francisco Bay with the Atlantic Seaboard. I could scarcely imagine a twenty-eight hundred mile corridor that one could traverse in less than a week's time. Truly, such a marvelous achievement," he added enthusiastically.

"During the last century I'd witnessed the world around me so rapidly changing, expanding and modernizing as machines began to supplant and surpass the muscle power of mere men. Tools, laws, weapons and social norms—even those that had remained largely unchanged for eons—were quickly becoming obsolete, replaced by a ferocious quest for greater knowledge and more formidable powers.

"For those of you fortunate enough to live but a single lifetime, such dramatic change is not so readily apparent. And yet, to me, these were hectic, break-neck times. Dizzying, to say the least. The newspaper, the telegraph, the steam-engine, the electric light bulb, by God!—these were such *glorious* marvels. And so swiftly they came, invention after invention after invention."

"How it must have excited you," I said.

"Yes, and yet somehow not so," he countered with a good-natured smile. "Truth be told, I found myself terrified by such rampant innovation."

"Oh?"

"I'd long ago uncovered the weakness of the human race. For many millennia we had remained a childlike species, easily swayed by the sparkle of greed—give us too much, too fast, and we quickly lost our ability to adapt. To cope. And now, barely matured from those early times, we have begun to unlock secrets and pleasures beyond our ken. We have advanced too quickly. We have became spoiled."

"Have not these changes been for the common good?"

"Ah, but good for *whom* exactly? Think of the airplane. Of the radio or gunpowder. For every individual life improved by society's advancements, I believe that many more subsequently suffer. Think of a single bullet fired across a battlefield. If it strikes its mark, there's but one victor, one loser. The survivor in such encounter is not necessarily the strongest or the wisest but often merely the luckiest. And a bomb dropped from the sky can instantly decimate a hundred brave and heroic men."

"But I'm not sure how the radio—?"

"As equally guilty in modern warfare as the repeating rifle," he said, his voice strident. "Only a century ago, battles were fought on great, open plains. On distant hilltops, generals largely would peer through binoculars and base their strategies solely on what they perceived. Skirmishes were often mercifully swift, won or lost in a single afternoon and with casualties counted in the hundreds. But equip those same armies, those same generals, with field radios and very quickly the rules of engagement were altered, enhanced. New orders could be issued at whim, with entire battalions shifting, adapting, in the course of minutes. Consider the Battle of Somme, not yet twenty years past—over one hundred thousand men falling dead within a scant twenty-four hours. I don't necessarily see progress being made."

"Is progress itself to blame?" I wondered. "Or merely our inability to use that progress wisely?"

Reni's eyes glistened. "You're right, of course. One doesn't blame the brush if the artist is blind."

I beamed, as it was a rare instance when I could successfully counter my husband's logic.

"Now," he continued, pausing for the smallest sip of brandy. "Where was I?"

"Stuck in Portland," I sniped, still smiling. "And apparently quite afraid of the future."

"*Hush* now," he said affably. "Yes, yes—Portland. Contemplating the puzzles of this newfangled existence. And from that bustling mill town I hastened my travels southward, much of the time remaining within spitting distance of the Pacific, admittedly enthralled by its vast, rich expanse. I remember quite distinctly coming upon our own magnificent bay early one evening, and of standing upon the creaking dock of the Cavallo Point ferry station, staring across the channel at a flame-flickered city of brick and wood, very few structures rising more than two or three stories. Even then, San Francisco had consumed much of the peninsula. Many great sailing ships stood at anchor and, even from that distance, I could feel the bustle and commotion of its lifeblood. I saw no trace of grandeur—no castles or great cathedrals—and I found the lack of pomp and circumstance both alluring and invigorating. A *working man's* city, I realized. I felt an immediate peace in its presence."

Reni smiled at me, a wholly gratified expression, yet one tinged with weariness. "And so I remained. I rejoined the cavalry at Fort Point—wearing a blue uniform, not gray, and under an assumed name. I had no trouble concocting a new tale of my own past, and I eventually parted with several plump nuggets of gold to secure a position of prominence. The occasional skirmish aside; brief melees with the indigenous peoples to the east or with small bands of marauders from the south, I eagerly made San Francisco my home. Once again, I'd begun the foundation of a new life for myself. A new life..." he repeated in a whisper, staring again out over the vast blackness of the ocean. However, his attention did not return.

Aware of my Reni's fatigue, and of the late hour, nearly dawn, I suggested that we retire, despite my longing to hear more. My Captain eagerly agreed and within minutes he lay gratefully asleep in my arms. It seemed to me that a great weight had lifted from his soul. I clutched him tightly and wept quietly in the darkness, feeling as if I held a boundless treasure that was mine, for but a moment in time, to keep.

At one point during his restless sleep, Reni muttered two scant sounds. *"Mei Xing,"* he whispered, my name sufficiently tender upon his lips even as he slept. I closed my eyes and drifted into a most peaceful slumber, feeling profound gratitude for having at long last discovered the secret buried within my husband's long-suffering soul.

THREE

RENI HAD BEEN DEEMED TOO 'OLD' to serve his country in December of 1941. He had recently grown a beard and streaked his whiskers in barrel bleach to appear as if we had begun to age naturally together. My husband remained both a philanthropist and a manufacturing baron, with ten thousand employees producing airplane parts and medical supplies for the military. Thus, Reni wasn't expected to serve and die—he was expected to produce and prosper, and in that regard he proved himself quite successful.

He would tell me several times during those years, and with a resigned acceptance, "War makes casualties of the young, politicians of the old, and wealth for the merchants of its trade. It has always been so, and I doubt it will ever change."

We relocated shortly after the war, as far from California as we thought necessary. By now, we found that we could no longer distance ourselves from the past by a few dozen miles. Technology was advancing at a hectic pace and Reni was a man supposedly fifteen years my elder—nearly sixty years of age. Newspapers, photography, radio and eventually television were proving far too invasive for his liking. Too soon, friends and neighbors would have been struck curious and perhaps fearful of my husband's freakishly healthy youth and longevity. And, long before, Reni had admitted to me that he now feared only the unfettered fears of others.

Before leaving the Pacific coast, he'd abdicated most of his business concerns to a board of trusted friends and we moved to the isolated, rocky coast of Maine, close to the New Hampshire border. As he had done so many times before, Reni altered his identity by hiding in plain sight. In Maine, Sebastian T. Renaud changed his name to S. Thomas Renaud, toggling between the two names he'd chosen for himself a century before. Amid the relative isolation of northern New England, and once again clean shaven again and spry of step, he publicly became my son, the only child of my late husband, who we claimed had perished suddenly of an embolism a year prior.

While some women might have recoiled at the pretense of being one's lover's *mother*, we took a great deal of delight in maintaining the charade. Reni's only concern was that one of the household staff might walk in upon us curled together in bed—naked as newborns!—and thus we designed a home of singular intent, with a separate wing and twin master suites, supposedly one for Reni and one for me. The bedrooms were joined via a connecting inner atrium, with both their outer doors faithfully locked from early evening to midday. None of the staff were permitted entrance to either until well after noon.

During our time in Maine, Reni would often commute to Boston, which served as the hub of his financial affairs over the next two decades. And I? After a short stint as a professor of history at Bowdoin College, I would soon become a visiting chair at Dartmouth University, a position I would retain during our lengthy stay in New England. And while I took great delight in this chapter of our lives together, all too soon we became aware of a flourishing slave market on *this* coast as well. Impoverished islands such as

Haiti and Jamaica, and politically unstable regions such as Honduras and Nicaragua, offered easy plucking for the world's Twentieth Century pirates and human traffickers.

Thus, I immediately set upon a blueprint for a second orphanage near Portland. Our school in San Francisco continued to flourish and prosper, driven by our continued pledge to help those who came to our country, shackled and abused, on either shore. We had acquired several agents by then, mostly retired policemen, who bought girls at secret auction or occasionally stole them away from their deplorable captors. We returned as many as we could back to their homelands, and educated others so that they too could one day thrive in America.

I remained in constant touch with The Muldoon School's trustees, as the telephone had made transcontinental communication relatively uncomplicated. When my beloved Lin Li died in 1958, she deeded me the ownership of her orphanage and school. And as providence would dictate, we found it convenient to return to San Francisco a scant dozen years later, still masquerading as mother and son. Our oldest friends had either passed on or moved away, and so our secret survived. We continued to thrive and love and cherish each hour of each day. The world spread out before us, as endless as the Pacific waves that once again beat upon our very doorstep.

In 1982, we returned to our home in Santa Barbara, which Reni had leased prior to our departure for the East Coast decades before. Over the many years since he had purchased several neighboring properties to eventually assure us the utmost privacy in the rugged foothills high above the harbor. Shortly before our return, Reni found it wise to again assume an even younger identity. My husband's face had once been a most familiar one around town and despite our years spent in Maine, he remained easily recognizable in historical photographs and newspaper archives. Even masquerading as his own son, Thomas Renaud would be a man nearly fifty years of age. Reni felt a younger version of himself to be appropriate.

By now I had matured into a matron of eighty-some years. In the mirror I appeared scarcely older than a woman of forty, and with the stamina, the desires and pluck of a woman half my age. Thus, back in Santa Barbara, I would have likewise found it difficult explaining my abnormally youthful appearance. Long ago, I'd realized my retarded aging process to be an unexpected consequence of Reni's own unique condition. He could offer no logic for my circumstance other than to acknowledge that the *aura* of his extraordinary gift had often likewise extended the lives of his closest friends and confidants. Over the eons, many of those nearest his heart had lived well beyond their predicable lifespan.

And so I became Mei Xing once more, the only daughter of Marcy Renaud, while Sebastian was compelled to become his own grandson—prolonging our ruse as mother and son. Thus, young and spry of step again, he would have no need to explain either his appearance or mine to the good people of Santa Barbara.

As a curious aside, I should note that there were many other indications of Reni's magical impact upon my physical being. I'd broken my ankle several years before, horseback riding in Connecticut, and within two weeks I walked again without pain. (Reni would have regained full agility, on his feet again within two or three days.) A long time ago, as a young apprentice cook in Miss Lin's kitchen, I had burned the back of my hand so severely as to leave a horrid scar. And yet within six months of sharing Reni's bed I noticed new skin flourishing beneath the dead tissue—and not long later the burn had vanished completely. Nor did either of us catch colds, nor suffer the viruses and bacterial infections, the cancers or tumors that commonly ravage humanity. For many years I wondered if I too might live forever, a most splendid eternity with the man I loved no less now than the day our gazes first met.

ONE MORNING I AWOKE and, with all the brazenness of a fox in the henhouse, I said to Reni, "Tell me about your brush with the executioner, dear husband, those many years ago. About almost losing your head. I've become quite curious, you know."

"Oh?" he asked, his expression somewhat startled. I wondered if he'd forgotten his promise to one day divulge the memory, as sixty years had now passed since Reni had first shared his secret. But a quick smile rose to his lips and confirmed his recollection of the moment. While we had talked of Reni's interminable pilgrimage countless times during the interim, he had steadfastly omitted this facet of his life.

"Are you certain?"

"I've been wondering for ages, truth be told." Indeed, my tolerance of accepting Reni's continual dance with death had gradually evolved over the years. Here he was, after all, quite intact. How could such a horrific tale end badly?

"Then the story might indeed interest you," he agreed, "as it has a direct bearing on the man that I am today."

I nodded vigorously. "Please, do tell." I took Reni by the hand and led him to the upstairs veranda; our usual milieu for his lengthy soliloquies. Caressed by the morning's gentle Pacific breeze, I curled into my favorite wicker chair with Sophia, our long-haired Birman, purring contentedly on my lap.

Reni smiled and said, "I was once a citizen of the Roman Republic."

I found myself quite surprised by the remark. "You've mentioned Rome only in the vaguest of personal terms over the years."

"Aye, as was *your* wish, my love—as my time in Rome leads directly to the blade against my neck. Although those days weren't the proudest of my previous lives, and I've been in no hurry to divulge such memories."

"I'm more intrigued than ever," I admitted.

After a thoughtful gaze toward the horizon, Reni said; "I first ventured upon Roman soil during that expansive bout of imperialism in the early years of the Republic. My arrival occurred a good two centuries before the reign of Gaius Julius and the eventual rise of ambitious Augustus.

"For several lifetimes prior, I had spent my time upon the Caspian Sea, near what is now considered the Baku Archipelago. 'Twas where I first learned to master a sail, and where I developed a love of the open sea that exists to this day. I gradually drifted northward, sailing across the Black Sea in a *gauloi,* a primitive yet sturdy merchant vessel. I traded my boat for several horses, traps and supplies before continuing farther into the boundless wilderness that parts the Soviet Union from Eastern Europe. These were cold and uncharted regions, thickly-forested lands that provided sanctuary for nomads like myself."

"The Proto-Celtic tribes," I offered. Reni smiled, nodding, as usual delighted by my historical ability to trace his meandering journey through time.

"Yes, love, quite right. And I soon found comfort in a fortified village along the banks of the Vltava River, so far as I can determine, in what is now Czechoslovakia. I dare say we were little more than a melting pot of roving vagabonds, a rugged and unwashed people who valued bravery and bold adventure. We were numerous but scattered, unorganized as a single nation or people. We did share a similar mother tongue, eventually becoming the people who would migrate across Europe over the next several centuries; the Saxons and Vikings, the Germanic tribes, the Franks and Cossacks. And, aye, the Celts of Britanni too. But these earlier tribes were largely roving and unstructured, all but unknown by today's historians.

"We constantly bickered and tussled amongst ourselves. We traded salt, meat and pelts, dug shallow mines for gold and ore, and built primitive forges. We knew the strength of iron and our blades were most formidable. We cremated our dead and worshiped numerous gods. My clan was quite superstitious, and we would sometimes torch a lodge or sacrifice an elk based on the whims of our mystics. We believed in a world of spirits, above and below, and we prayed to our gods for signs about this and that and just about everything. We worshipped a god of smoke and one of fire, a goddess of northern winds, a deity for each animal in the woods. A goddess of beetles! We fermented beer and consumed hallucinogenic fungi; all in all, we were a generally unappealing and unruly sort. We also lacked the leadership that had already begun to coalesce the various populations of Macedon, of Mycenae and Persia. I fear that we were a people destined for obscurity.

"For several decades we clashed with expeditionary forces from the south—the Carthaginians and Etruscans and then the Greeks, who ventured into our lands in pursuit of resources and slave labor. Their forces may have been better trained, but they lacked sufficient numbers and were inexperienced in the fine art of *cath-coillaire*—deep forest warfare. We would often decimate an enemy's ranks unseen, our archers hidden amongst the tangle of tree branches. We would taunt our foes from wooded hedgerows behind moss-covered peat bogs. I recall once watching a legion of heavily armored Aeolians—or perhaps Corinthians—charging toward us upon a foggy glade, only to sink helplessly into the swamp without so much as a drop of blood spilled during the encounter. For many years, all who came were soundly routed.

"But, of course, the clock ticked. Tactics changed. *Publica Romana* grew, both in size and in power. The Roman generals did not often repeat their mistakes. In those early days of the Republic, the famed armies of Marcus Fabius Ambustus gradually whittled our numbers and captured many of our scattered villages. Yet the generals continually underestimated the harsh cruelty of the Northern regions. Despite periodic victories, when winter fell the invaders would inevitably flee back to their warmer kingdoms.

"But Rome had begun to intrigue me, as whispers of its sophistication and wealth persisted. It was a place where free men shared philosophies about the meaning of existence. Once, long before, I had come to know and appreciate such forward thinking—in Tu'ulth, later in Tjenu and for a short while in Mideia. And how I hungered for such keen conversations again! One morning before dawn and accompanied by a league of young adventurers, able warriors and horsemen one and all, we set forth to observe for ourselves this burgeoning empire.

"We were eighteen cocky Celts, fierce and strong, fearful of neither man nor beast. We ventured southward from Raeti to Veneti unscathed, then from Mantua to Felsina. We passed through large swatches of Etruscan territory, although that empire had begun to scatter upon the winds. Eventually we made our presence known to the Roman garrison on the outskirts of Velusna, bringing as tribute six wild boar that we had slain and cleaned the previous day.

"Just like that—" Reni snapped his fingers. "—the new world embraced our presence! One of our number spoke a halting Raeatic and explained in earnest to the Centurion at the gate of our desire to serve Roma.

"Becoming a minion was not difficult in those days. Kneel and kiss the consul's golden ring—while reciting some silly verse of allegiance and loyalty—prove to the *praetor* that you could suitably wield a sword and ride a horse, and one was granted the privilege to fight and likely die for the glory of the Republic. The fact that we had arrived upon our own mounts and were laden with impressive weapons meant decent quarters and good food for the lot of us, as only the most destitute were shuffled off to the Roman infantry, and typically to a quick death.

"And so we were assimilated. We trained for many months and learned basic commands in Latin, then later embarked on lesser skirmishes to the north or east or south. As a soldier in early Rome, one accrued wealth by plunder and through plucking items of value from the dead. We did so without reservation. In those days, Rome was not yet *Italy*—the land crawled with Samnites and Umbrians, the Messapians and Frentani and, farther south, the Greeks. Alexander of Macedonia had begun to expand his empire to the east, although his influence was felt as near as Napoli. Had his armies turned west instead, how history might have changed. But Rome had not seized Alexander's attention—the generations of hatred between the Greco-Persian peoples defined much of Mediterranea, and Rome's presence, by comparison, remained insignificant. And yet," Reni said with a twinkling eye, "unlike most others burgeoning empires of the day, Rome managed to thrive.

"You should realize, of course, that I did not set foot in the vaunted city itself until many years after my arrival, and by then I had long parted ways from my Celtic brethren. I suspect that many of our number died nobly in battle, and others eventually of old age. Only one other, to my knowledge, became wealthy and prospered, as did I.

"My own fortune came as a cavalry officer during the

Battle of Sentinum. I had been elected *decurion*, akin to a squad leader, and during the campaign I led an impressive patrol of *equites romani*. We managed to capture the brother of the Samnite general, a man named Gellius Egnatius as I recall—his camp in full flight with a caravan filled with gold and treasure. For my effort, and for the bounty that found its way into the hands of the Roman Senate, I was granted the deed to a splendid plot of land south of Genoa. Almost overnight I became the master of thirty hectares, my new domain a hillside vineyard overlooking the Mediterranean Sea. The vineyard's Carthaginian owners had wagered their prosperity on the enemies of the Republic, and their land had been snatched as a spoil of war.

"But I soon discovered the vintners to be decent, honest people who had produced fabulous wines for several generations. As I knew nothing about the grape, other than the wonderful dizziness it bestowed, I recognized a viable enterprise in the making. When the Carthaginians realized that I would not subject them to slavery, but instead wanted knowledgeable partners to revive my new estate, they eagerly accepted themselves into the House of Renniscato— the name a fabrication, of course, and one I had arbitrarily chosen upon immigrating from the north. It also marked the beginning of my current lineage, come to think of it."

"Has it significant meaning?" I asked anxiously, aware that I too was inexorably anchored to the House of Renniscato.

"At the time," he said with a smile, "its root was a tongue-in-cheek equivalent of *in your face*. Up your nose. Not quite offensive to Romans, which was not my intent, but rather a name representing the absurd incarnation of my new lifestyle, my sudden prominence as *nobilitas*—a sort of neo-patrician—although I lacked both the aristocratic blood and proximity to Rome itself to become a darling of the Republic. In those days, understand that estates such as mine, scattered amid the outer territories, were either allied to the Republic or else brutally dissident. As I recall, several battles were fought by Rome's allies within half a day's walk from the vineyard, and whenever the Republic's armies retreated, I could loudly satirize my own Roman aristocracy.

"I do seem to recall shouting *De Mors de Roma!* as the Etruscan or Ligurian armies marched past our fields, while freely offering our best undiluted wines to those who asked for refreshment. My hillside villa became a favorite stay for an assortment of occupying generals to take respite. Allied with none, amiable host to all, the vineyard thrived.

"Within two or three generations, the Republic inevitably extended its reach and, after a series of horrific battles, Genoa became an important Roman trading port and municipality. In the resulting peace, I found the tending of grapes much to my liking. The following century passed in idyllic splendor. As the vineyard flourished, spreading from thirty hectares to over ninety, I became fully immersed in my own importance. I paid tribute to prosper and accepted tribute from those seeking the same. And, for the only time in my life, I owned slaves."

Reni hesitated long enough to cast me a troubled glance. I realized now why he'd been reluctant to reveal this facet of his life. "When in Rome, dear," I offered gently—a familiar expression of the day—and patted his hand, meaning every word. I had long ago learned not to confuse the present moment with those centuries I had not witnessed for myself, nor to condemn the ignorance of my ancestors, as one day I hoped *our* best efforts would not be so utterly reviled by our descendants.

Reni kissed my fingers most appreciatively and said; "In those times, in Rome—we pronounced it *Ruma*, rolling our R's—one was either slave or indentured, farmer, shepherd or craftsman, merchant or aristocrat—which meant service of some import in either the military or government. Survive one's tenure, as either slave or soldier, and one was allowed to grow fat and happy, which I'm afraid is what became of me, a fat and happy owner of fertile lands and impoverished men. For the first time in all my many millennia upon the planet, I experienced *leisure*. Upon my whim, my Carthaginian partners directed the overseers who directed the field foremen who directed our slaves—mostly prisoners of war or else offered as tribute by those who courted the favor of the Roman senate.

"Please understand that I was not a harsh master," my husband added fervently. "A saying persisted in Genoa in those days; *Better a slave of Renniscato than a prince of Populonium.* And, aye, I was fair and just. But still an owner of men and women, to dictate their fates as I desired. Each morning I awakened to the gentle strains of a lute. Thrice daily I was bathed by my servants and often travelled my fields in a silk draped oxcart, lest the hot sun fatigue my eyes. Every evening I dined on boar or pheasant or baked *lavraki* and drank my wines in excess. Looking back, I realize that for the longest while there seemed little else that mattered in life."

"Your longevity did not cause curiosity?" I asked.

"It was whispered about," Reni replied with a nod, "as to why the gods should anoint a man with such permanence. Rome may have been advanced in its day, but science ran amuck with *magick* and superstition. I was considered a charismatic—blessed by the gods rather than cursed—although I'm certain the plump taxes I routinely bestowed upon the Republic fostered that perception. Let the fools in the Senate ponder my agelessness, and let their sons and daughters gossip as well, as I felt cocooned within the sanctity of my own wealth and privilege.

"So you see, Rome had changed me," Reni said, "as I'm sure its song had altered many an honorable man. When an empire burns so brightly as to blind those who have built it—aye, probably 'tis time to get out of the light."

My husband nodded assuredly to himself and added, "Rome eventually revealed to me that abundance is the curse of civilization. With abundance comes greed and the lust for the power to create even greater wealth. And I—well, I'm afraid I'd come to such a conclusion a bit too late for my own good, as I had succumbed to the allure of all that glitters—hook, line and sinker.

"Ah, but I digress," he added, his lips playing with an alluring smile that hinted that change was in the air, that lessons were to be learned. "I was eventually able to purchase a fleet of sailing vessels in Genoa and to acquire still more land on which to harvest grapes. By then I owned a winter villa in Frascati and often vacationed near the *aleatorium* in Pisae. Upon my lands I built a small hamlet complete with stables, pubs and a market—and of course a temple honoring *Baccus*, our god of revelry—where my servants might dwell in relative ease when not tending the vines. But as to my rapidly accumulating riches—I soon owned all that I could possibly want. What remained of my ambitions? To build distant homes I'd seldom visit? To fatten the local politicians even further? To possess the moon? When a man owns too much, the mind grows weary or else obsessed by the curse of plenty. Judgment suffers. Morality fades.

"One afternoon, while drunk on the grape, I ordered a servant whipped for having accidentally ruined a barrel of my favorite *mulsum*—a sweet mix of wine and honey. Yet no sooner had the first lash snapped—the poor lad and I both screaming in simultaneous agony—did I awaken to the man I had become.

"I immediately set the fellow free of his indenture, with

a small purse filled with a token of my guilt. But more importantly, I set myself free that day as well. With a single stroke of the lash, the shroud of drunken apathy had lifted from my soul.

"For so many years the House of Renniscato had traded wine and grapes and honey for luxuries I had never before experienced: Spices from Mesopotamia; livestock from Harrapan; delicate wood carvings from Cyrene; silk, apricots and exquisite silver works from Chang'an; and marvelous perfumes from Bahrata. And during these years, all of Mediterranea had lain at my feet. I'd freely sampled the pleasures of this newfound world but had allowed others to unlock its secrets. Even though I owned a fleet of *corbita*—sturdy cargo ships—and stock in the caravan trade, here I sat among my grapes like a plump bump. Yet all the while this, this—this *freedom* had been mine for the taking.

"By mere happenstance, the vineyard's overseers were making preparations to join the spring caravan in Sardeis, barely a month hence. I announced, to great astonishment, that I would accompany our merchants on their journey. For a fortnight, I busied myself with the tenacity of a man suddenly reborn, as frenzied as a baby sparrow about to take flight. I fasted on spring water and fresh fruits, vigorously walking the boundaries of my vineyards daily, allowing the various toxins to bleed from my skin.

"Soon enough, I found myself on the road, in the company of Lucian de Vinea, our vineyard's chief arbitrator, and twenty-three of our best *venditores*, with their apprentices and servants. I recall the date very well—the year 584 *Ab Urbe Condita,* our second calendar month of *Aprilis*—the new grapes mere promises on the vine and the warmth of the compassionate Sol radiating splendid promise for the new growing season."

"The sun god," I remarked.

"Aye. And do you want to know a secret?"

"A secret of yours is worth half a dozen chapters in any history book," I admitted.

He laughed at the realization. "Our Roman deities weren't what many of today's scholars assume. Remember that the Romans had pilfered their gods largely from the Greeks—and those deities were not necessarily revered with the same sense of respect or piety. Nor are Rome's ancient gods understood in the same way we might grasp the meaning of a *Christian* deity today. Rome's gods were considered purveyors of fortunes. One prayed for good fortune, not bad fortune, because we presumed that righteous belief could alter the future, much like an airline passenger, caught in a thunderstorm and praying *'I hope to God the plane doesn't crash.'* Or a gambler muttering, *'Please, just one more lucky seven.'* But one did not expect an omnipotent power to take heed or actually intervene in the outcome of any moment. Throw a penny in a pond and make a wish. That was the extent of our belief system.

"I must admit, if one were superstitious enough, one consulted a *haruspex*, a reader of omens who might dissect a pig's liver or poke through the entrails of a goose to reveal a more personal divination—whether that be a diagnosis or a glimpse into the future." Reni smiled. "We needed such sages to walk among us, to care about us, because we sensed our gods to be utterly aloof and esoteric, and not particularly interested in which way the winds of fate blew."

"So your gods were...a *coping* device?"

"Indeed. We'd simply made familiar that which was otherwise incomprehensible. The Macedonians may have been truly devout; but to us, the gods were interpretive assumptions to so many unanswerable questions.

"But, yes—ah, my adventures as a man newly reborn," Reni continued, collecting his thoughts. "And so, my vintners and I travelled by road to Genoa. Once there, we boarded sailing ships for a twelve-day sea voyage around the toe of Italy and east to Smyrna—the town which I believe once stood near the port of Izmir, at the tip of the Turkish peninsula. Safely ashore, I purchased sixty wagons and the oxen to pull them. We filled fifty-four carts with wine-filled *amphorae*—terra-cotta vessels as tall and thick as a sumo wrestler. Another six wagons carried our provisions and tents. Later, on the highway to Sardeis, I hired a dozen Apollonian mercenaries to see us through to Bharuch, on the west coast of present-day India. The Apollonians, while expensive, were considered the most knowledgeable and fiercest of defenders against the indigenous desert peoples."

My husband's eyes gleamed. "I must intrude upon my tale one more time. I'd concocted a splendid plan, you see. Before leaving Genoa, I'd set in motion the arrangements to eventually assume the identity of my own non-existent nephew—the first time I'd ever considered the ruse of becoming my own progeny. The caravan was set to return in two years' time, heavy with riches. Yet I secretly planned to linger in the East for a decade or perhaps two, with grand adventure once again my only goal. I would one day reappear in Genoa with the appropriate documents and government seals, announcing that my beloved uncle had died in a distant land. Upon my late benefactor's final request, I would return to manage the vineyard as the sole heir to the House of Renniscato."

"How brilliantly conniving!" I marveled, unable to conceal my glee.

"We arrived without mishap at the caravan station outside Sardeis, an enormous grassy plain called *Campo Aequitas Campo*. Countless tents and campfires filled the meadow, rich with the scent of charred wood and roasted goat. Anxious merchants milled about with fully stocked wagons and hundreds of baying beasts of burden. Bartering had already commenced among those waiting to embark on the journey. Such was the frenzy and power of the moment. In the center of this encampment, a single marble obelisk rose a hundred feet above the fray. Chiseled into its surface were the names of many distant locations, and numbers in *milliarium* to represent their distance. Babylon—MCL. Alexandria—MMX. Rhagae—MCDL. A dozen other destinations were clearly marked, as the main caravan would splinter several times before our journey's end.

"At dawn, a dozen blaring horns filled our ears. We broke camp in a murmur of hushed excitement. "Our trek to Media would soon begin, and our numbers would eventually stretch several miles in length. Our strength was in our solidarity, each man bonded by sacred oath to all—and by forging such kinship we easily outmatched both pirate and thief. We gradually made our way through Phrygia, Cilicia and Assyria—selling our wares quite often upon the road."

"Persia's Silk Routes," I said, for the ancient pathways to the East had been well documented.

"Aye, although in the day, known to me as *Viae Rhagae*—the Way Through Rhagae. Current day Tehran," he added. "Past the Caspian Gates we rolled—a series of enormous stone walls standing farther to the north, built within the ravines and gorges separating the kingdoms of Persia from the unruly barbarians. You realize these lands would not see Muhammad's armies and the spread of Islam for another five hundred years. Even so, in those days, Rhagae was already a sacred city, the capital of Mazdaism, a religion that had guided the desert peoples for a thousand years. Zoroastrianism, I believe, scholars have since named it."

"After Zoroaster," I said, "one of the first of the early prophets who believed in a single god, a supreme being who created not only mankind, but the entire universe."

"The locals knew him as Ashu Zarathushtra, I believe," Reni replied with a nod. "But, yes, a shaman who foretold the coming of a messiah. One who would release the people from Roman bondage. A common wish in those days, as I recall. I myself had only a passing knowledge of the desert religions, but I remember Jews and the Sumer, the Himyarites and various Egyptian and Greek mythologies mingling freely in Rhagae. The various gods were far less hostile, it seemed, when money and wine flowed freely through the desert lands.

"But allow me to continue," Reni said, furrowing his brow. "Yes, yes—we soon left Rhagae in our rearview mirror. Our caravan eventually reached the great grain silos of Herât—a massive desert oasis—although Alexander had renamed the region after himself centuries earlier. Our wares dwindled as we forged eagerly ahead, our caravan's destination either Kabul, at the base of the Himalayas, or south to Barygaza, a port city in Gujarat. Others continued ever eastward toward China, deep through the Ganzu Corridor. And indeed, several days later, we eventually found our great caravan splitting into three factions, my wagons among those venturing south toward the Indian Coast—to the farthest reach of Alexander's once great conquest. Word of our wine's marvelous qualities had preceded us, and within the month we had completely depleted our wares, our vendors quite excited by our success.

"At the port town of Lothal I sold our wagons—all but one—and entrusted my fortune to Lucian, as my exhausted troupe would board a merchant fleet to sail over the Arabian Sea and north through the Red Sea, to the port of Clysma. From there, via a series of shallow canals and overland camel routes, they would eventually board Roman boats at Pelusium for their final leg through the Mediterranean. With pouches filled with gold coin, they would soon return to great favor and fanfare in Genoa.

"I watched with sadness as the fleet's sails disappeared beyond the horizon, and then dismissed my Apollonian guards, keeping only two of their best warriors to accompany me. By fortune, I chose brothers—Argos and Salthesius—who proclaimed fidelity to me once again for the journey ahead.

"I had promised Lucian I would return to Genoa within a year's time; a promise I did not intend to keep, of course. With my secret safe, I set out on the road to Mathura, deep within the Mauryan Empire, now northern India. This was a land quite unfamiliar to me although, earlier in my journey, rumors of the region's wealth and beauty had proliferated. I found these whispers to be quite exciting. I eagerly set out with the remaining convoy of merchants who'd yet to exhaust their goods."

Reni gazed at me with a most exquisite expression. "You must realize that, by now, my soul had once again found peace, as I had filled my senses with an exuberance I had all but forgotten as a citizen of Rome. Mind you, I had not completely forsaken the privilege of my station, as I remember having hired a small Mauryan entourage to accompany me—freemen, of course—although I recall many nights of pampered sleep in a pointy Assyrian tent, with woven blankets beneath me and wine in my belly. Upon waking each morning, I chose my day's mount from a selection of fine, fresh Arabian stallions.

"We left the peninsula of Gujarat in late spring, with the days initially promising warmth and sunshine. However, soon thereafter and well into the rugged Kalagarh foothills, a torrential rain began to fall. The downpour continued relentlessly for many days. We knew of Mediterranean storms, of course, but understood little of the treacherous monsoons—and quite often the wet season arrived early. After a belabored week of plodding northward into the rain-soaked mountains, our party was forced to turn back, as an avalanche had completely obstructed the route ahead.

"Our guide, a man we'd hired in Jaipur, indicated an unmarked trail leading westward, one we had passed only a few days before that eventually descended through the rugged highlands and into a dense jungle. He assured us that we would soon again find ourselves upon the sands of the Persian plains. The trek was inhospitable, he explained, although the route would directly pass by the polis of Pumaessia, which he claimed some called the City of Gold. After a brief, yet passionate, discussion among our troupe, we chose to follow this trail."

"A golden city?" I asked. "I'm aware of such mythology surrounding the Tibetan city of Shambhala. Of Kalahari in Southern Africa. And also of 16th century Conquistadors in the New World seeking El Dorado. But I know of no such city in Persian lore. Although, wait—wasn't King Midas supposedly Assyrian? I recall that the Greek historian Herodotus spoke of the man's greed, of his golden touch, although I've always assumed Midas to be little more than a fable."

"Aye, a cautionary tale," Reni agreed. "But the ancient lands of Assyria lay only five hundred miles from Pumaessia—the kingdom of Pumaessia itself perhaps as old as the ages. Who knows where truth ends and legend begins? I can only tell you that the mention of this golden city ignited our fantasies. It reputedly stood high in the mountains above the Rajasthan Desert, somewhere near today's Indo-Pakistani border. Yet those few among us who'd already known of its existence had also heard whispers of a great evil residing in its midst. Yet such is the nature of greed as to dismiss caution.

"Many of the merchants were thrilled with the potential to finally exhaust their goods—and evil be damned. I, of course, relished the excitement of confronting the unknown once again. I remember our guide from Jaipur assuring us that the rumors were merely to keep the city's identity a secret." My husband offered a feeble smile. "Which made perfect sense at the time.

"The road to Pumaessia was arduous, and although we soon left the torrential rains behind, we lost several of our number through mishap. Those who'd previously offered song and prayer to Fortuna, Rome's goddess of good fortune, now began crying aloud to Clementia, goddess of mercy, beseeching that our lives might be spared from the fates. Yet each of us knew Fortuna to be a fickle and jealous sort, and who took as easily as she gave.

"One morning, we came upon an expanse of high desert plateau, with fierce mountains rising in the north and south. In the distance, vast plumes of steam drifted upward from a volcanic cone—a most troubling omen to many among our ranks. Yet the plateau proved thankfully flat and straight, and we proceeded swiftly, with no further calamity.

"After several miles of travel, I became aware of a tall peak, ablaze in a golden luster, equal in brilliance to Sol itself. 'Pumaessia!' our guide called repeatedly to us, lifting his hands toward the distant beacon. Those in the caravan grew tense with excitement, our prayers for salvation quickly forgotten. Another two days passed in what I can only describe as 'a torment of the purse', for the burden of empty pockets can sometimes far outweigh the heft of gold or silver. Our party advanced slowly; our wagons creaked with disrepair and our animals looked gaunt. We passed several small villages nestled among the foothills, although the people here existed in such poverty that the caravan did not stop, for surely there could be nothing of value here to barter or buy. Nor were any ramshackle doors open to us. We did not see a single soul, nor a single curious face watching us pass from within the shadows. I wondered how a city of gold could exist amidst such desolation. I began to question what might lay ahead and shielded my eyes against the glow that now radiated from the mountaintop as would the flame of a hundred pyres.

"Finally we encountered a large crack between an enormous slab of black rock, and within this crevice we discovered a narrow path barely the width of a wagon. Uncertain of its terminus, we sent two able equestrians to scout ahead. They returned a short while later on their lathered steeds, babbling with great excitement, confirming that this road indeed snaked upward to a set of golden gates. We could see little of our destination from our present position—a glint of a wall, the merest glimpse of a spire—as the city lay tucked beneath the cliffs that towered above us.

"As no gate or soldiers barred our way, my companions viewed such providence as an open invitation. I admit that I had grown quite curious as well. And yet a brooding doubt lingered within me, as I had lived long enough to suspect that which presents itself with such casual abandon. We numbered three dozen wagons, with two hundred men among us. In our midst, we also claimed over a hundred head of oxen and camels, and many equestrian mounts. I suggested that we leave our stock and half our party camped upon the open road, our wagons circled and our sentries on high alert. Should the others not return within a day's time, we would assume that some unkind fate had befallen them. Yet not a man among us expressed willingness to remain behind. And so I capitulated. Against my better judgment, I found myself advancing upward along the narrow corridor.

"We made languid progress, our animals exhausted and our souls oblivious to their pain or to our own precariousness. For two or three miles we meandered between jagged walls of sheer rock, until we came upon a plateau of green pastures and swaying palm trees. The thick clouds shrouding the higher peaks obviously graced these scant hundred or so acres of highland with plentiful moisture. A series of slender falls cascaded into a small lake of crystalline water, and many of our number cheered its presence.

"At the farther end of the plateau, we encountered the city's outer wall. Gold of course. Four massive columns framed an elaborate archway—the *porta praetoria*—whose two doors, chiseled from black rock, stood generously open, beckoning to us. As if the city itself eagerly awaited our arrival.

"Quite soon I gazed upon a black cobblestone courtyard through the open gateway—as one can't produce *all* things shiny in a City of Gold—lined with various shops of wood and trimmed stone on either side of the plaza. I could see the upper balconies and turrets of a large palace, Assyrian in design and mostly gold as well, but also ornately decorated in quite striking designs of white and black marble.

"I suspect most of what we observed—the walls, the spires, and the palace itself—consisted of solid stone beneath a golden leaf façade, and as such I assumed this place to be a bastion of great strength. And yet, for the amount of gold needed to even *surface* such an area was nothing short of breathtaking. The city-fortress of Pumaessia was not large by Roman standards. I'd judge the walled city to have been no larger than one of our metropolitan football stadiums, the palace itself encompassing a third of that expanse. The palace itself easily stood five or six stories tall, with three golden towers of unequal height—the pinnacles of which we had occasionally glimpsed aflame from the valley floor.

"Within the main plaza stood a palm-shaded courtyard, and from a stone fountain rose a bubbling geyser. Directly behind the fountain stood a statue of a man upon a tall pedestal. The golden figure stood bearded and stern-faced, his features Persian in style; his face framed by a square beard

303

and tightly curled hair, and atop his head a tall, drum-shaped crown. The crown blazed with an array of large oval rubies, easily thirty or more, and quite striking in the sunlight. At his feet lay a ram and a lion, the two beasts gazing adoringly upward. The man held a glistening scythe in one hand and, in his other, the golden likeness of a man's severed head.

"I cast a backward glance toward the green meadow from whence we'd come. I could have kicked my mount into a fast gallop from whence we came, but even as I debated such a retreat, I took note of a dozen or so archers staring down from their ramparts above the archway. So I remained in my place near the front of the caravan, which had fully encircled the courtyard and its gurgling fountain. Those around me had gone into a silent reverie, as if blinded by the sight of such opulence. I believe only myself and my two Apollonian bodyguards had as yet taken note of the soldiers' somber presence.

"A ram's horn blew from within the castle's highest tower. Twin palace doors, elaborate golden slabs twice my height, slowly groaned open and a procession of somber looking men—*ascetics* presumably, temple priests—wearing turbans and robes of simple black cloth, emerged from the inky shadows. A wizened, toothless fellow in front carried a simple wooden staff, which seemed conspicuously unpretentious here amidst the splendor of the city. This feeble parade moved without haste toward the plaza, and finally stood before us.

"In a quavering voice, and in a tongue unknown to my ears, the old priest said; 'Welcome to the House of Pumaessia, weary travelers. The most splendid hakim of Pumaessia, Sabihkar en-Qadir, son of Qadir Pumaessia al-Qadir, grandson of Zor Pumaessia Qadir Zor, begs to honor your presence with a magnificent feast, worthy of the immortal gods.'"

"Realize, my love, that these words were translated haltingly to me by Argos. I can only paraphrase to the best of my recollection. However, as this forlorn little procession bowed humbly in our honor, my colleagues had alternately begun to babble and weep in celebration of their good fortune. With a final backwards glance and a shiver of trepidation, I dismounted and stood ready to confront our fate.

"THE MOST SPLENDID HAKIM OF PUMAESSIA made his appearance at dusk," my husband remarked, and upon his lovely face, a puzzling assortment of emotions passed within the span of mere seconds. I believe this was the first time I'd ever seen fear cross Reni's brow, and its fleeting appearance startled me.

"We had entered the palace hours before," he said, "following the ascetics, finding ourselves confronting a great hall. It was an enormous, cavernous space littered with pillows and veils of draped silk, an ornately textured room of dark woods, inlaid gold and black marble, polished smooth enough to mirror one's reflection. The hall was not only magnificent in length and girth, but astonishingly I could see no ceiling. Lighted by the flames of a thousand candles, the walls appeared to vanish upward into utter blackness, as did several dozen thick stone columns. I noted many Pumaessian soldiers standing rigidly amid the shadows, so still and silent as to appear to have been cut from stone as well.

"Three long tables had been set with goblets of rich wine, and with golden bowls filled with dates and figs and olives. Unsmiling Pumaessian servants preceded us to our seats. We followed with great delight, like children in a playground filled with favorite fantasies. I happened to notice that our guide from Jaipur was nowhere to be seen, the man having disappeared somewhere within the cavernous darkness. Quite curious.

"Eventually, the hakim Sabihkar appeared, greeting us warmly in very proper *Latium*—the tongue of aristocratic Rome. The hakim's unannounced entrance, essentially presenting himself as an equal among us, was quite unusual for a king or sultan; uncommon even for a patriarch among strangers. He wore no bejeweled dagger nor any visual indication of his status, and apparently he felt no need for bodyguards to shadow his every move. He was a slight young man, smiling and gregarious, and he strode among our number in simple white robes, a shawl of light blue around his shoulders. His ebony hair, tightly curled to his shoulders and thick with rich oils, was otherwise unadorned. I immediately noticed a resemblance to the golden figure in the courtyard, although the hakim appeared to be a younger man than the one represented by the statue. Thus I assumed the hakim to have inherited his throne.

"Sabihkar was immediately applauded by every man within our party, those twenty-five merchants and their respective servants and escorts—as all of us, trader and servant alike, had been invited to feast this evening. The merchants sat together at the smaller central table with the sultan seated at the table's head in a simple chair, no different or greater than any other in the room. Those of us who were not merchants, myself included, as I had no longer had wares to sell or trade, sat at two long servant's tables on either side of the sultan's main table. Much of our evening meal was punctuated by various finger-snapping and impatient gestures from the merchants as their numerous young attendants hopped incessantly to perform some task or another at the whimsical beck and cry of their masters. The merchants, soon giddy on ale and *badeh*—a sweet desert wine—took great delight in these needless theatrics, the way one might showcase the quick obedience of a trained monkey for the amusement of others. While our host took notice of this formality, he appeared otherwise unconcerned.

"About this time, a most unusual exhibition occurred. Raising his goblet as toast, Sabihkar announced his honor of introducing the Queen of Pumaessia. The merchants offered our host a rousing cheer, no doubt awaiting a woman of exquisite beauty. But for the longest moment we saw no motion amid the shadows of the great hall. Quite faintly then, we heard the squeak of rope, a groan of soft metal and from the darkness above us, the shadows parted to reveal a large *avarium*—an enormous, golden cage—slowly descending to a place beside the hakim.

"Grand spectacle was not uncommon to the citizens of Rome, but so bizarre was the queen's entrance that we watched, transfixed, without a whisper among us. Centered within the cage, a ring of surrounding candles revealed a young woman, quite beautiful and draped in the finest of diaphanous silks, sitting *asana*—I believe what Americans term the lotus position—cross-legged and straight backed, her eyes closed as if in deep trance. Her long golden tresses spilled about her shoulders and arms, reaching to the very floor of her gilded prison. She did not smile, nor even acknowledge those who had begun audibly clucking and clicking their delight at such an unexpected pleasure.

"I observed the girl's skin to be porcelain white, as if forever untouched by sunlight. Understand that, living in northern Italy, lighter skinned, blonde-haired people were not unfamiliar to me. Yet a fair complexion was far less common in Rome and, deep within the Arabian deserts, an even greater rarity. I could understand the hakim's appreciation for such a prize, of one so radiant as to reflect the very hue of his kingdom. I also took note of the young woman's age. Despite the bright rouge of her cheeks and the cherry red fullness of her lips, she was but a child, perhaps on the cusp of womanhood, yet still no older than twelve or thirteen years of age. Not at all a woman by today's moral standards, and yet it was not uncommon in those days for a man of wealth and privilege to wed one so young.

"The cage halted abruptly, hovering perhaps a foot or so above the floor, such that our seated host could gaze upon his queen at eye level. The sultan reached out to lovingly tap one of the vertical golden bars that held her captive. The child made not the slightest of movements, nor opened her eyes, despite the surrounding festivities.

"Sabihkar smiled proudly and proclaimed; 'My perfect queen.' And then he said, 'The queen of my father and of his father before him. Of his father and that man's father as well. Behold, the beautiful *aeternum regina,* my magnificent beloved.'"

Reni paused and regarded me with an arched eyebrow, as I had already leaned forward, stiffened in rapt attention. Long ago I had studied Latin at my husband's bequest, and I pulled the necessary words from memory.

"The eternal queen," I translated, my heart pounding.

"Aye," he replied.

"But in what context? He spoke of his grandfather? And of that man's grandfather. *Could* she have been?"

"Questions that dizzied my own brain, all those eons ago," Reni said. "And yet? Might he have spoken metaphorically or rhetorically of his own eternal love? I could not be sure."

"Go on," I said impatiently.

"I have nothing else to divulge. The girl did not speak that evening, nor give herself away in any manner. Except for the slight rise and fall of her shoulders as she drew breath, she might indeed have been a marble figurine. But even in her quietude, I could not take my eyes from her. Nor indeed could the young hakim, for he continued to stare upon her with unbridled passion. I couldn't help but wonder, to a man whose wealth is a city of gold, what sway might this child have over him?"

"An attribute gold could not purchase," I allowed.

"Precisely. If the girl indeed shared a gift such as mine, her lifetime of captivity would pass in relative swiftness. Her captor would age and eventually rot, his death both her salvation and best revenge. However, the opportunity to pose these questions did not present itself. All I could wonder—did Sabihkar covet that which he could never have? Not at any price?

"The hakim observed his caged queen with a long, silent pause, during which a respectful but uncertain hush fell. At last, he looked away and gestured for the merriment to continue—although the gilded cage remained at his side, swaying gently above the floor, as if the child's companionship in this manner was not at all unusual.

"The evening progressed, as did our party's drunken ecstasy. Sabihkar did not appear displeased by such boisterous revelry, or else he overlooked our churlish behavior with weary acceptance. You must understand that during Rome's early expansion, all who were not born of Roman lineage were frowned upon by the Republic's illustrious citizenry—the Greeks treated with polite tolerance, the Egyptians with pity and the peoples of Arabia, Bharat and Bactria with quiet disdain. I myself had suffered cruel whispers for decades, until my eventual wealth excused the transgression of my foreign birth. However, those cultures unfortunate enough to touch upon the Republic's expanding borders either assimilated or languished while Rome's elite reveled in their own decadence and depravity. That evening, behind Sabihkar's silent acceptance, I couldn't help but wonder if the young sultan's contempt festered.

"And yet, I could not help but assume that Pumaessia's extraordinary wealth would have been well known among Rome's strategists. The hakim likely paid a healthy tribute each year for the privilege of our indifference to his existence. He had every right to resent those who profited from his sweat. And I had no doubt that those of us seated in Sabihkar's tonight were somehow representative of Rome's most egregious offenses.

"Ah, but I digress," Reni said with an apologetic smile. "Suffice it to say that Sabihkar had thus far remained a polite and gracious host. I'd noticed him seldom sipping from his goblet of wine, and thus remained quite in control of his senses. I had discreetly taken my cue from the young sultan; both my bodyguards, as I myself, had remained sober and ever watchful as well.

"However, the festivities continued apace, and eventually I began to question my own instincts. How foolish would I be to reject this man's hospitality, only to leave, unsatisfied and regretful, come morning? Had we not been treated graciously? Did not a trio of musicians weave sweet, mellifluous tunes from the rafters above? Nor had our goblets lacked for want of wine. We had feasted upon an assortment of melon and pomegranates, tangerines and figs, followed by platters of duck and quail, and finally upon a tender brisket of boiled goat. What miniscule cost would it be for a man who ruled a city of gold to share his prosperity for a single evening?

"Even so, I found that I could not shake this impalpable sense of apprehension," Reni said. "The evening wore on. Hours passed before our host finally stood and clapped his hands sharply. Silence fell. The most splendid hakim of Pumaessia, Sabihkar en-Qadir Pumaessia offered a taut smile and in a loud voice proclaimed; '*Kaíre pollá! Kaíre pollá!* The festivities will now begin, and in which you are each to take a special part!' The young king seemed amused by his own words and once again clapped his hands. From the shadows, a phalanx of young women emerged—had they been waiting all that time?—wearing flimsy gray togas and their young bodies dappled and alluring in the candlelight.

"I could not help but count their number. Twenty and five, the same number as those seated at Sabihkar's main table. And as if by silent cue, the women moved toward a merchant and took each by hand. The drunk and cheerful men willingly accompanied the women to the large scatterings of pillows that lay strewn about the floor."

"I *see*," I snarked. As a historian, I knew well the exotic histories of various empires—with Rome being neither the most nor least notorious among them. The Republic's sexual proclivities had been scrupulously studied by modern scholars, including myself. Although I must admit academia wasn't so much on my mind as much as the jealous realization of my husband encountering such a delightful opportunity.

Aware of my expression, Reni smiled and said; "It was not unusual for a host to offer his wealthy guests a selection of slaves for their gratification, especially after much wine had been consumed.

"I'm certainly glad you'd chosen a seat at the *servant's* table."

My husband laughed. "As am I," he admitted, although his expression grew quite serious. "For several minutes, the young hakim regarded the decadence with great delight, the man finally allowing himself the smallest sip of wine. By now all of the merchants had found suitable cushions and, as was typical in the day, lay prone—some continuing to eat and drink while Sabihkar's women, naked now, straddled their loins and writhed in quite provocative ways.

"As copulation was often not considered a private affair in millennia past, those of us still seated watched with fascination or amusement or else continued to feast ravenously. Many of those young men at our table, indentured by providence or debt, had never before been party to so magnificent a banquet. Argos, Salthesius and I also quietly observed the bacchanal, not from any sense of voyeuristic pleasure, but rather with wary apprehension.

"A sudden movement from within the shadows caught my attention. Yet I barely had time to notice, for what happened next transpired with incredible swiftness. Three swordsmen emerged, bathed in candlelight and dressed entirely in black. Each held a curved bronze scimitar upright and near his cheek—similar to a ball player cocking a bat at home plate. Fascinated, I watched three swords glint as one, heard the chilling whir of metal and, in amazing unison, saw the swordsmen cleave the heads from the necks of three young women in the very act of servicing Sabihkar's guests.

"For an instant, the headless, glistening bodies remained upright, the half-naked merchants immediately horrified by this abrupt display of madness. A warm, red mist spewed out upon the revelers, extinguishing several candles. One poor woman's head tumbled forward into the lap of her lover, the man unleashing a most hideous scream. Try as he might to jump up from the soft pillow, the weight of her body upon his loins and the wine in his belly prevented him from rising."

Reni cleared his throat. "I shall spare you, my love, from a more detailed account. Note that the two Apollonians and I had sprung from our seats in unison, aghast to witness such barbarism—its intent solely to impart terror among our number. Although we had not brought weapons nor armor to the feast, Salthesius, at my left, drew a short blade that he'd concealed in the sleeve of his garment.

No sooner had he done so than a host of bowmen hidden in the darkness above us unleashed their arrows. Salthesius fell dead across the table, his body bristling with feathered shafts. Shouting his despair, Argos reached for the blade in his brother's hand. And only by wedging myself between them, an act of sheer brute strength, did I manage to keep the weeping warrior from meeting a similar fate.

"The merchants' screams continued for several moments, punctuated with the laughter and applause of our host, as Sabihkar seemed pleased by the reaction of his horrified guests. He reached down, snatched a woman's detached head by the hair and lifted it as one might display a trophy. In a macabre display of madness, the sultan touched the head's grimaced lips with his own.

"The surviving women, standing with their heads bowed in submissive silence, retreated slowly again into the darkness. I couldn't help but realize that each of these slaves must have known that some of their number would die this evening in a most gruesome manner. Yet none had raised an alarm or revealed a modicum of fear, so brutally powerful was the sultan's control over his people.

"Once again aware of his frightened audience, Sabihkar flung the severed head into the darkness and absently wiped his hands against his tunic, leaving a crimson smear. 'Time to pay the price of your supper,' he called out to those of us cowering among the shadows.

"'You there, vendor,' he said and pointed to one groveling guest. Two of his swordsmen, massive, muscular mountains of flesh, moved to lift the poor man, shivering with fear, to his feet. The third swordsman stood beside Sabihkar, his stained blade held at the ready.

"'What is the value of your life, my friend?' the sultan asked.

"The trembling merchant did not appear to understand

the question.

"Our host paused and pondered the impasse with thoughtful deliberation. 'What do you offer me to spare you from a similar fate?'

"The man glanced at the headless bodies on the floor, and said, 'Whatever your wish, master!'

"'A worthy reply, yet not necessarily informative,' the sultan replied.

"'I have a pouch fat with gold and coin, sayib!'

"'Gold?' Sabihkar laughed, appreciating such irony. 'What need have I for gold?'

"The merchant opened his mouth but found himself unable to respond to such solid logic.

"'Have you a villa? Property in Roma?'

"'I hail from the woodlands of Neapolis. But yes, yes— a splendid villa! Fat with sheep and slaves!'

"'Yet far too distant to my liking,' the hakim replied with a sniff, and before the man could again speak, a swordsman struck such a blow as to slash the wretch from shoulder to pelvis. Sabihkar quickly back-stepped as to avoid the gruesome contents of the man's displaced organs.

"The hakim turned toward our table and said; 'This man's servants are now my servants. Those unwilling to work my mines may join their master's journey across the Styx.'

"Sabihkar gestured to another merchant and the mad repartee continued. Another merchant quickly fell dead, decapitated, and then a third fell, the poor fellow's head also removed from his torso. The fourth merchant, who apparently owned a sizable home overlooking the Tiber and nestled within the city gates, found himself in Sabihkar's favor. A scribe appeared from the darkness—a Roman, no less!—who then began to draw up a contract on parchment that would deed the merchant's villa to the hakim.

"I had by now guessed the nature of Sabihkar's wicked game. A king of the Persian wastelands is a far cry from a lord of Rome. And among the aristocracy, those whose families had ruled the city for generations, one could not simply buy into their midst. A land deed, however, represented not only wealth but prestige, as one would not presume to sell to another of lesser status. The hakim was amassing a powerful presence a whisper from the city's heart and soul.

Shortly thereafter, I would glimpse the contract bearing a formal seal of the Roman Senate. I recognized the red wax crest, the stamped impression of an eagle's head. It was in that moment I realized that Sabihkar was not acting alone in his treachery, but merely served as the tail of this snake of corruption that appeared to slither back to the Senate itself.

"'*You*, merchant!' the hakim said to another among us.

"Before long, all but six of our caravan's merchants lay dead, most of them having been separated from their heads. Those fortunate enough to live within Rome's walls had been spared, although I assumed their futures remained far from assured. The hakim was no stranger to deceit, and in the course of those frantic moments, I had begun to contemplate my own fate as well—to toil for an eternity in Sabihkar's mines, or surrender my head? Neither option appealed to me in the least.

"His slaughter complete, the hakim cast a cursory inspection upon those of us who remained. Inevitably his gaze fell upon me. I realized my robes were not those of servant or slave and, flanked by my Apollonian bodyguards— one who now lay dead—I noted the curiosity in the young sultan's eyes.

"He pointed. 'You are also a merchant, no?'

"'An adventurer,' I replied, as I had already realized my

estate in Genoa would provide nothing of value to this man.

"'And of what worth is that to me?' he asked with a regretful shrug, one of his mountainous warriors approaching from the shadows, his blade held high.

"I had yet to formulate any coherent reply and felt my life tilt as if unbalanced by a strong breeze. Yet, caught in a flicker of candlelight behind Sabihkar, I again took heed of his imprisoned queen's golden cage. A flash of inspiration passed into sentience and, with no other die to cast, I said, 'I have traveled to the far ends of the earth, sayib. I have seen wondrous sights unknown to the merchants of Rome, or the scribes of Babylon, or the shamans of Bhutan.'

"The hakim did not appear to be impressed. Aware that I had but few seconds remaining, I said; 'For instance, high amid the ice mountains of the Yuezhi, there exists a valley in which civilized man has yet to explore. I have visited the birthplace of your beautiful queen, sayib—a place whose people are graced with perpetual youth.'

"At which point Sabihkar's snapped his fingers several times in quick succession. His brute had already positioned his blade against the side of my neck, as if to anoint the exact spot upon which to strike. Needless to say, we both stared expectantly at the hakim.

"'Permit me my life and I can procure ten or twenty or even fifty such women,' I said quickly, aware of both the young man's suspicion and his growing interest. "I swear to you upon the gods of Olympus.'

"'You will draw me such a map, *rafiq*?' he asked cautiously. Imagine such perversity—this man already calling me *comrade!*

"'Respectfully, I will not.'

"Sabihkar laughed. 'You are a shrewd one, are you not? However, are you clever enough to take me to this marvelous place? To assure your own survival?'

"'As you wish,' I replied, quite ready to take my chances upon my horse, putting countless miles between Pumaessia and a land I knew only in my imagination. 'It is but a fortnight's journey from here. I shall personally guide you, sayib. Soon, you will have an entire harem filled with such beautiful queens.'

"Yet perhaps I had capitulated too quickly. Squinting cautiously, the hakim appeared to suspect a ruse. 'Beware the man who offers that which has not yet been asked, hmm?' He gestured toward the rock-hard, black-draped bladesman standing with his sword at my neck. 'Rather, I think that you will lead three of my most abled *gladitores* to provide proof of this land you speak. You have until *Ayah* shines plump and full again in the night sky to prove yourself worthy of my benevolence. If such a place does exist,' Sabihkar said, 'I will reward you with the weight of each of these women in gold. If not, you will die a horrific death, one painful morsel at a time.'

"Under the circumstances, I could not help but feel that I'd bargained well, and I nodded my consent. My eyes once again fell upon the girl in the cage, who now regarded me in a most confused manner.

"'I have one further condition for your continued life,' Sabihkar said. 'Your sword hand, if you would be so kind. Show it to me.'

"I cautiously raised my right hand.

"To his waiting bladesman, Sabihkar said, 'Cut it from his body.'

"And he did, you know," Reni added with an awkward frown, twisting his right hand in idle circles, as if somehow recalling its temporary absence. "The gladitoris stepped forward and in a heartbeat his weapon had severed my hand at the wrist. I fell to my knees with a gasp, the wound gushing freely—and I bade myself utter no other sound, my jaw clenched and my gaze full upon the young hakim, bathing him in utter contempt. I barely noticed the swordsman moving to apply a tourniquet of tightly wound silk. I willed myself to remain conscious, death's blackness hovering over me like a comforting shroud.

"'My apologies, rafiq,' Sabihkar said wistfully; 'but only a scorpion denied its barb does not sting.' From the shadows appeared a physician, a man bearing dried herbs and gauze and a metal rod, its rounded tip glowing bright red. He seared my spurting artery with a simple touch, then proceeded to wrap the oozing stump tightly.

"And yet, with my sudden loss, I also realized the means of my salvation. For I would soon have a tactical advantage that they could not begin to comprehend."

Aware of Reni's unique ability, I could barely contain my excitement.

"The next morning, faint from loss of blood and my arm throbbing in pain, I began this improbable journey with the hakim's three hulking gladitores. Even with my missing hand, they did not chance their fates with me incautiously. They lashed my ankles to my stirrups, one man keeping ahold of my reins, so that escape would not be possible.

"I navigated our route the best I could, keeping my blood-caked stump within the folds of my garments, as if hiding my shame. They took no notice of this act and for three days we meandered northward, into the wet mountains and toward the Mauryan Empire, from whence I had journeyed only days before."

"How long?" I asked anxiously, cutting to the chase. "How long until you could wiggle your fingers?"

Reni tilted his head, his eyes sparkling, my husband appreciating my anticipation. "For an entire week I endured the indifferent silence of my captors as I pointed out unmarked trails that took us farther northward, into a cold and inhospitable topography. The rains had subsided, but the sky remained gray and the high-altitude chill proved nearly unbearable. I had been allowed my own mount, my furs and possessions—all but my knife and sling and the pouch of gold coin that I had brought with me from Genoa. The gladitores fed me well, as the hakim did not want me dropping dead from loss of blood. And so each evening I was thrown a shank of lamb, and thus subsisted. Each night I was chained, cuffed left-handed by a ring of forged iron to one of the hakim's swordsmen, wrist to wrist, and slept no more than three or four hours before being tugged awake. We moved forward at a frenetic pace, pushing perpetually upward into the mountains.

"I'd managed to keep my regenerating hand well swathed in my garments, conscious of the mushrooming stump and the five tiny nublets that pushed the flesh outward daily. By the end of the seventh day I could move my small, newborn fingers, slightly and painfully, yet neither the bone nor baby-soft muscle proved strong enough to grip a blade. Each day upon my horse, I would clench and extend my new appendage until the muscles ached and my fingers trembled.

"I had no idea of our whereabouts. I can only guess that we had moved into what's known today as Kashmir or Jammu. By our twelfth night on the road, my entourage had begun to grow agitated by my endless and utterly random selection of trails. I feared they had come to suspect my deceit. That evening I overheard their whispers, and while I did not comprehend their tongue, I well understood their menacing gazes and their harsh tone of contempt. I could only imagine them forging a plan to slay me and return to their golden kingdom, telling the sultan that I had attempted to escape. I realized that the time had come to end my charade.

"Early the next morning, as one of the brutes knelt to unlock my iron cuff—another gladitoris watering the horses and the third de-watering himself—I waited until the man's attention had focused upon the lock, which I had discreetly caked with dirt. In my newborn hand I clutched a jagged length of lamb's tibia, a remnant from my previous night's supper. As the cuff fell away, I withdrew my hand from my coat and plunged the bone deep into my captor's throat.

"Even mortally wounded, he could only gaze in wonder at whatever *magick* had transpired, ogling my pink and quivering hand with a final moment's confusion before falling dead at my side. Unchained, I quickly unsheathed his sword, and with an excruciatingly painful, two-handed grip, I swung the scimitar at his companion's neck. He, too, fell with a perplexed expression. Even as his uncorked head tumbled to my feet, I could see his eyes gazing curiously at me, locked upon the unexpected appendage that had struck him down.

"The third bladesman fell with the same wide-eyed confusion. I stood exhausted, relishing the sweet silence of my liberation."

"*Bravo!*" I cried. "And good riddance to that damned city."

"Ah, but I could not," Reni said with a frown.

"No...no, of course," I realized, as my husband was not one to walk away from injustice.

"Full moon—*ayahdul*—was still two weeks away. I had much to do, as revenge had become my only goal. Not for personal gain, but to rescue my surviving brethren who now toiled in the hakim's mines. Nor could my mind release the image of the girl in the golden cage. I promised myself her freedom.

"I lashed together the four horses and took all but the naked bodies of the dead gladitores, trusting that hungry predators would make quick work of their flesh. I backtracked for several days until I recognized the road to Gujarat and from there returned without incident to the port of Lothal. As anticipated, I found my former Apollonian mercenaries still encamped, awaiting a new purse to buy their way back to Persia.

"And so I shared my tale about the young hakim's deceit, recounting the death of their comrade, Salthesius, and the likelihood of Argos' imprisonment. I also described the City of Gold in great detail and watched their fascination turn to insatiable hunger, like embers ignited by a fierce breeze. I used half of the coins I'd found in the gladitores' possession to once again buy their allegiance and told them, as quickly as possible, to raise an army of one hundred warriors—the most cunning and brutal they could find— swordsmen and axemen and archers. In return, I promised them a city of gold."

Reni smiled at me, a most delightful expression. Even though I did not doubt that the memory of a brutal retribution lay behind the grin, I could not help but return the smile, so eager was I for his story to continue.

"I was maybe two weeks tardy in my reappearance at the gates of the hakim's lair, as Ayah's fullness had come and gone again. I can only imagine the sultan's agitation as he waited and grew increasingly anxious as to the fate of his men. Imagine too, one bright morning, Sabihkar's sudden excitement, horns blaring atop the golden spires, as our caravan wound up the mountain road toward his glistening city. Not any caravan, mind you, but five wagons of golden-haired women, cloaked and veiled—all with long tresses of sunlit hair that fell freely around their shoulders. Behind the wagons, on fine Arabian stallions, rode a gaggle of holy men from the far north, hooded in robes, their heads hung in humble reverie.

"At the head of the procession," Reni said, "rode my three biggest Apollonians, wearing the clothing I had removed from the hakim's gladitores, their scimitars glistening at their sides. And, preceding them by a length, only myself—dusty, dirty, and convincingly slumped forward, as if I'd barely enough strength to remain upright on my saddle.

"Another horn sounded from within the city walls and the golden gates slowly yawned aside to receive our party. Into the fortress we rode, slowly rounding the courtyard square. The hakim himself emerged from a doorway, smiling and surrounded by excited soldiers, none at the ready, the ruse thus far successful.

"*'Rafiq!'* cried the most splendid hakim of Pumaessia, Sabihkar en-Qadir, clasping his hands in anticipation. 'You had begun to worry my soul! The wealth of my city is yours to share!' he shouted, although I did not believe him for an instant.

"'The journey was difficult,' I said. 'But I have brought you fifty women from the city of Coronia'—a non-existent place whose name I had fabricated only an instant before. *'Behold!'*

"At that moment, several incidents transpired in spectacular unison. Another horn sounded from the city's spires, this blast far more ominous than the first. Several of the hakim's bowmen began shouting from the parapets in hysteria, pointing toward the mountain road beyond the gates. In the blink of an eye, my army began to spill from our wagons, their cloaks fluttering from their shoulders, their yellow hair—indeed, wigs of woven silk—askew. The hooded monks on horseback drew their knives and axes and charged toward the hakim's startled soldiers. The three faux gladitores drove their mounts forward, mouthing such feral screams as to scatter the defenders in confusion.

"Beyond the city gates a swell of warriors appeared— for I had not raised an army of a hundred men but one of a *thousand* or more, as whispers of plunder had rippled through Lothal. I could do little more than promise the spoils of Pumaessia to any and all who fought at my side.

"Panicked, the archers on the wall fired hastily, their marks untrue, and very few of our number fell. Several of the hakim's men then tried to close the gates, but the Apollonians dispatched them in short order. The mad throng quickly crossed the meadow and charged their way into the courtyard.

"Sabihkar had retreated in haste through the palace doors and into the main hall, mere steps ahead of a half-dozen arrows that would have ended his reign that instant. I kicked my steed forward, drawing my blade, and followed the man's flight through the doorway. In the candlelight, both movement and shadow danced in chaotic darkness. Soldiers darted to and fro in fright. Once again I glimpsed the escaping hakim and urged my mount into motion, the beast's hooves clacking loudly against the floor tiles—yet barely an instant later I reined sharply to a halt. Ahead of me dangled the golden queen's candle-strewn cage and, to my astonishment, the girl remained its prisoner still! She was standing now, clutching at the bars of her cage, her eyes rounded in terror.

"Do not fear me," I cried, raising my sword over my head. She shrank back and I swung my blade down upon the gleaming lock. It shattered and the golden door creaked open. But I dared not dally, as quite soon Sabihkar would be lost to me forever

"Remain here! I will return for you," I shouted in Latin and again in faltering Greek, our eyes touching for the merest of instants and, yes, I saw clarity in her gaze, the belief that I would not harm her. I bolted away, galloping madly through the murk, half-crazed by the adrenalin that grips all men in the heat of battle.

"At the back of the great hall, a stone stairway spiraled upward into the shadowed mezzanine. I watched Sabihkar clamber upward, the coward in full flight, without the tenacity to even help defend his own fortune. I slid from my mount and bounded up the steps after him, equally hobbled and shielded in the surrounding blackness. Leaping upon the mezzanine and to my utter dismay, I could discern nothing more than a maze of darkened corridors and abutting doorways. The cries and clatter of battle echoed against the stone walls below me, leaving me clueless as to Sabihkar's whereabouts.

"Suddenly, one of the hakim's remaining gladitores stepped from among the shadows to confront me. Our swords clashed and, even today, I remember the fury of the resulting duel. The man's scimitar nicked my flesh several times before my own blade found its mark with a deft plunge through his rib cage. He may have outweighed me by fifty pounds, but I surpassed him by countless centuries of combat, and I'd merely had to bide my time to triumph. But I'd lost many precious minutes before the man fell, and with neither light nor map to guide me, I knew that further pursuit of the hakim would be futile.

"I returned again the great hall, intent on fulfilling my promise to the caged queen and aware of jubilant shouts from my army. My comrades had fought their way to easy victory, for most of the hakim's soldiers had not felt driven to trade their lives in service to such a cruel master. Many had surrendered with little struggle. A dozen of the hakim's prized gladitores lay dead amid the compound, but otherwise, this battle had proven mercifully swift.

"And yet, to my horror, the golden cage now hung empty. *'Where are you? Who has seen the child?'* I called into the murk, but to no avail. The warriors of both Lothal and Pumaessia, free to feast upon the spoils of war, cared little for my commands. They pushed and hurried past me, their arms laden with goblets, lamps and trinkets, while others stripped the golden veneer from the chamber's very walls. Their torches cast a macabre dance of red welts against the naked stone.

"Filled with a hopeless remorse," Reni said, "I could do little more than move into the sunlight and watch as my unfettered army scrambled as might a hoard of locusts, carrying away everything of value they could grasp. I saw the gold statue in the courtyard fall and, beneath a flurry of axes, find its way piecemeal into the hands of many. Even the outer walls beneath the parapets were being peeled of their luster.

"Within the span of a few hours my army had disband-ed. The last few vandals struggled through the gates laden with satchels of booty. Those soldiers who remained loyal to me—the Apollonians and a handful of others—had re-leased the male slaves from Sabihkar's mines and the wom-en from their various prisons throughout the palace. And although I continued to seek out the young queen, I found myself thwarted in my attempts to find her, as so many of the newly freed Pumaessians pressed against me, sobbing in joyful gratitude. I frequently found myself unable to move more than two steps in any direction.

"A great cheer rose from the Apollonians and I lifted my gaze to see my loyal Argos stagger through their midst, gritty and emaciated from his many weeks of chiseling ore from deep within the mountain. The man lunged toward me in great strides, parting the throngs as might a child wading through papier-mâché. He grasped me in such a manner as I thought my spine might snap, as such was his elation to discover that I had returned to secure his freedom.

"Within the hour we had opened Sabihkar's kitchens to those who had probably not eaten a substantial meal in ages. I noticed that the oldest among those working in the mines could not have been beyond twenty-two or twenty-three years of age. I would soon learn that most perished within a few months or years of their captivity. The concubines related the same tale; the hakim was a brutal masochist, raiding the local villages for any girl young and lovely enough to accommodate him and serve his lustful desires.

"I saw that enough golden residue remained scattered about—shiny tidbits here and there—for each slave to grasp a handful of prosperity, and I urged them all to take enough to start a new life. Gradually, huddled in pairs and small groups, they began to wander away from that wretched place.

"We spent the next few days scouring the city. I suspect the Apollonians believed that I sought additional treasure, and indeed we found several more of the Sabihkar's trunks filled with coin and gems. But I took nothing for myself, seeking only knowledge of the caged queen as my reward. I dreaded the moment that I might find her dead, but thankfully I did not. Still, I could not know if she'd escaped or had been taken captive, although I assumed the former. Those who had followed me to Pumaessia had done so for the prize of gold, not the company of children.

"On the morning of the fourth day, we finally made preparations to depart, and climbed upon our horses. We would have left that insufferable city in our dust, had we not heard the shouts from one of Sabihkar's elderly ascetics—the same toothless fellow who had first welcomed our caravan to the hakim's golden city. One of the Apollonians lifted his spear to strike, but I raised my hand, aware that none but the Sabihkar himself owned the misery that we'd found here.

"The old man pointed and waved, quite agitated, speaking so quickly that Argos shook his head, unable to decipher his words. And yet the elder's demeanor proved most curious to us. So we dismounted, following him cautiously across the plaza and once again into the great hall, empty now and filled only with ghosts. Through a stone doorway hidden behind a tapestry upon a far wall we found a secret passage that had remained undiscovered. The old priest, babbling still, led us down a series of ponderous stone steps, barely visible in the light of a few meager lanterns against the walls, sputtering and nearly consumed. *The gods save us from this tomb,* I thought, *should these fires flicker and die.*

"I had wondered how a City of Gold might have been forged amid such brutal peaks," Reni said softly, his eyes twinkling. "And here in the depths of the hakim's palace, I finally determined its secret. A vast underground cavern had been dug below the palace—a sweltering, miserable chamber it was, and dimly lit from numerous oil lanterns. Many thick stone pillars secured the weight of the substantial structure above.

"Numerous tunnels had been cut into the side of the mountain, enormous, cavernous holes that I could only imagine stretched onward for miles. Empty buckets, discarded oil lanterns and hand picks littered the room. I could discern other, smaller holes, drilled diagonally upward for great lengths, so that pinpoints of morning light glistened as might bright stars in a moonless night's sky. If not for these vents, I suspect the workers laboring here would quickly succumb to either a lack of oxygen or the feverish heat that permeated this underground prison.

"And, indeed, an iron furnace and smelting pot stood

like a great blackened beast at the far end of the chamber. A great rend in the earth parted the stone floor beneath the apparatus—an opening that funneled deep into the earth. This far into the cavern, the craggy granite walls, slick with steam, glowed and pulsated, eerily red, as if fueled by the fires of hell itself.

"I quickly realized that beneath the furnace flowed an underground river of lava. A giant rectangular vat, its flooring and walls hammered from roughly-poured iron, stood beside the smelting pot, easily a dozen paces in length and third that size in width. One could deduce the molten gold passing from the furnace and cooling as it oozed toward the far end. Wooden catwalks crisscrossed the vast empty space above the vat and a number of long, gold-caked stirring rods lay strewn on the hard floor.

"Immediately I knew that the army from Lothal had not found their way into these depths, for the vat contained a king's ransom of raw gold—a viscous goo at one end but which, after days of neglect, had gradually hardening into an immense, solid brick at the other.

"I also understood the old priest's excitement, for near the far end the vat—*inside* the vat—stood the most splendid hakim of Pumaessia, Sabihkar en-Qadir, son of Qadir Pumaessia al-Qadir and whoever else he might have been. The hakim was quite dead, his body from the waist down encased in solid gold. His chest, visible above the hardened metal wall, had been reduced to a gleaming skeletal remnant. His neck and jaw had been burned black from the heat and yet his face had been largely spared, his open eyes gazing horrifically upward. But here he stood, the remnants of him anyway, propped against the edge of the vat. His arms hung loosely over the edge, mostly unscathed, although his gnarled hands were encased in gold, as if during his fall he'd reached futilely downward to protect himself.

"He *had* fallen, of course, from the walkway above. The old priest pointed above the vat and I saw now that the catwalk's flooring had given way, leaving a ragged gap where several planks had once held firm. I could also see a small tunnel through the rock at the ramp's far end. An escape route of some sort, I assumed, cutting through the mountain. I could visualize the hakim retreating in a panicked rush, and whether thwarted by his own slaves or tripped up by Fortuna's wrath, I couldn't know. But the hakim had died a hideous death and, around me, the Apollonians mumbled their approval of his fate."

Reni offered a tired shrug. "And thus, appeased by this final triumph, I felt no further reluctance to leave the city. I left the Apollonians arguing as how to best extract the hardened gold from this subterranean basin. I can't be certain of their success, although I suspect they all eventually died wealthy men. Of course, they'd insisted that I claim a share in this newfound providence, but I assured them that I'd witnessed enough of gold's allure for a lifetime and, kissing them each on the forehead—to honor their devotion—I returned to the outside world of blue skies and fresh air."

"And your young queen?" I asked, for I suddenly felt as if I had lost a daughter that day. "You never found her?"

"Nay," he said, sadly shaking his head. "Nor can I blame her. The allure of freedom had proven too great. And for the last two thousand years, she has provided me with a fair share of restless nights. I admit that I sometimes still keep an eye out for the child. Granted, she may be long dead, her immortality merely an illusion of the mind. But every now and then, a young woman, her tresses long and golden, will pass on a busy street and I will stare intently, wondering if it might be her."

"If she is one such as you, darling, I know you will one day find her," I said, nodding with certainty.

Reni smiled in return, reaching to take my hands, but I suspected that these were but empty gestures. The sadness of his gaze spoke my husband's truth. And sitting there, I could not comprehend such measure of heartbreak, stretching without end over the boundless sea of time. So I waited patiently, without words, and when he was ready, my Captain resumed his journey.

"I did not look back at the hakim's castle that day, for what was there to see? A barren rock fortress amid the upthrust peaks of an inhospitable range? I found myself once again on the road that would take me to Mathura, quite content to be alone for the first time in ages.

"I soon found myself upon a steep passage through the mountains that I had never before encountered. As the last of these scraggly peaks dwindled behind me, the path forked ahead, leading both west and east. I realized that I did not, *could* not, return to Rome. The young hakim's evil had left a stain on my psyche and I sought only the solace of an isolated world. Mankind had once again failed me, or perhaps I had failed humanity, and I sensed the need to purge myself of the ugliness that abounded in those of us who lacked a soul.

"And so I turned eastward. I would travel for many years without a compass or the company of another, until one day I found myself on the Tibetan Plateau, a land of snow-capped peaks and grassy vales. My presence there predated the nation of Tibet by centuries, of course. In those early times, the region remained a largely unnamed and ignored wilderness, a cruelly inhospitable, unimaginably beautiful land.

"Amid those desolate lands I found a ramshackle village nestled at the foot of an unassailable mountain. Atop this enormous peak lived a small enclave of holy men, gifted thinkers much like the sy'amar whom I had honored so many millennia before. I inquired among the villagers, and discovered these men were disciples of Buddha, as Prince Siddhartha had passed this way some four or five centuries previously.

"But their collective knowledge was not easily obtained. The holy men lived in obscurity, as most days the peak itself remained concealed above a thick shroud of fog. They seldom, if ever, left their mountaintop. Some in the village wondered if they even existed. Yet peasants would travel dozens or hundreds of miles to bring food and robes, tools and kindling, items which were hoisted on a wooden platform up the rocky face on immense pulleys made of rope and iron.

"I asked among the villagers if I might speak to these holy men. Instead, I was guided to an empty hut, one of maybe thirty or so dismal structures, quite threadbare and meager. So I sat down to wait, as had several others who, like me, shared an uncertain desperation, seeking impossible answers from those above.

"Weeks and then months passed. The same gracious people who brought the holy men their sustenance also brought us food. In return, I would share my knowledge of ancient herbal medicines, of farming or hunting. I felt as if I had come upon a people as gentle and ancient as my own unforgotten Tu'ulth.

"Amid such desolation, in this land of paltry joys, I discovered the time and space to forgive both myself and humanity for our past sins. After a year or so of waiting, I became so content in this realm that I forgot my intention to seek guidance from above. I stopped looking upward with angst and anticipation, and one day shortly thereafter a rope ladder descended. Tied to the bottom rung, a simple scrap of rice paper, my name scrawled in charcoal. I had been invited.

"I had found forgiveness in the village and quite soon, amid the clouds, I would learn an even more profound lesson—*acceptance*."

"Oh?" I said. "But is not forgiveness the greater virtue?"

"I don't believe so. Forgiveness carries the swagger of ego, the power of subtle dominance," my husband replied. "Acceptance is to see others for who they are, and to see myself for who *I* am, without prejudice or pity. It acknowledges that whatever our fates, each is intrinsically woven into the fabric of all that exists. All that will ever exist."

He smiled at me. "So *that* is what I learned atop the mist-shrouded mountain."

"You became a disciple?" I asked. "Of the Buddha?"

"I was told that I did not have within me a living *vijja-carana,* and therefore could not follow the Buddha's path as did they. This was not a rejection, mind you. One of the holy men, a man we would today call a *bhikkhu,* explained that my purpose was not among them, but rather that I sought a separate peace. I was like a man attempting to *see* a savory aroma, or who wished to *hear* the color blue. To find my way I had to correct my perceptions, as I had far greater value on the path that had been destined for me.

"And then he told me, this most wondrous disciple of Buddha—he told me I was *yatri-samaya.*"

I cocked my head.

"A time pilgrim."

"*Méimén!* He told you *that?*"

"With no more inflection or amazement than if he were informing me that I might be a brick layer or a grocer."

My pulse raced. "Did this man reveal more to you?"

"I pressed him further, of course," Reni said, his eyes twinkling. "He replied with a question of his own. He asked me the precise number of footsteps I had taken since my birth. I had nary a clue and told him so. The bhikkhu smiled and said; 'Then how should I know either?'"

Reni laughed at the memory and whatever annoyance I might have felt passed in a flash. I recognized myself as a creature of impatience, hardly upon *any* bumpy road to enlightenment in that regard. In that instant, I could harbor only a swell of gratitude that my Captain had found his own acceptance, for an endless lifetime of unanswered questions is a burden I could not even fathom. If Reni was content to allow—no, to *accept* his fate, then perhaps I too could learn a modicum of such tolerance. I chose to mirror the quiet joy I saw in his eyes.

"I have no idea how long I remained with them," Reni added blithely, "although I recall that the young priests I encountered upon my arrival were wizened elders when I departed. Had I not been deemed ready to confront my fate I certainly might have stayed forever. But the good monks felt otherwise."

"You mean they *threw* you out?"

"Aye, in a manner of speaking. None ever spoke as much, but I knew the time had come, and I knew that they knew. So early one morning I tossed the rope ladder over the edge and climbed down through the clouds.

"I wandered once more through the Himalayas, into Bhutan and Nepal and India—and for the first time in my life I travelled without the worry of being here or being there, nor where I might go afterward. I moved from moment to moment, from place to place, and found myself enchanted with every step. I gazed again upon the high deserts of Persia and, no longer perturbed by Rome's expansive presence, pushed west toward the Mediterranean coast. Within a month I stood upon the outskirts of the Empire. Rome could no longer call itself a Republic, for greed and the lust for power had undone yet another test of democracy. I was no longer angry, and yet I did not linger. I could not hide my sorrow at all Rome had become, of the glut and avarice that such mighty empires represent. And," he added with a weary frown, "I believe I might have mentioned as much in passing.

"I quickly discovered that criticizing Rome's emperor or the empire itself was not a trivial offense. I found myself unwelcomed in Mesopotamia or Judea or Cyrenaica, all under Roman rule by now. And I could not fathom returning to Genoa, nor what excuse might I use to return to a home, to a land, I had not seen in well over a century. Assets and taxes and profits and bureaucracy did not appeal to me in the least. And so I continued to wander, through Alexandria and Khartoum, into the central core of Africa—what are now the nations of Sudan and Kenya and Zaire.

"Journeying ever southward, I lingered a lifetime upon the sands of the great Karoo before setting out to sea on little more than three hollow logs lashed together, with a sail of woven lambskin. I island-hopped past Madagascar, weaving up through The Seychelles, The Maldives and Sri Lanka—idyllic oceanic oases—before returning to India again, like a fallen leaf, borne upon the swirling winds of providence. All the while, I remained true to myself, making and losing fortunes in what seemed like a blink of an eye—regretting neither poverty nor wealth. Whenever I found the need to travel again, I'd bequeath my estates, my recent fortunes, to whose who had far less. I passed through Sindh to Zabul and then into Kashmir, into the Turkish Himalayas and eventually found myself on the vast plains of Mongolia."

"And then to Chang'an," I marveled.

He laughed. "Yes, yes! Truly, we have come full circle. Amazing how five or six centuries can pass in the time it takes me to speak these words. My most cherished memory of those times is of awakening every morning a new man, caring not about yesterday or tomorrow, nor the weight of my purse, and choosing one direction or another without regard to my destination.

"For many of those years afoot, I lived without a home or want of one. I ate when I was hungry and, if I could not find food, I would ask. Do you know something? Nine times of ten, I was fed with sincerity and open hearts, and by people who had next to nothing to share. Whenever I encountered a village in need I would stop and offer my knowledge—for I had forty or fifty millennia of experience within me, and I'd like to think I made a difference in people's lives. And why I found such happiness upon the vast Mongolian plains, as the indigenous peoples had little and wanted for little more. I felt as if I belonged with them, not so much seeking the external as mastering the internal. But always and everywhere," he added, "with a quick glance about for the golden queen.

"I had, of course, long before accepted the probability that her immortality had been but an illusion. I no longer yearned to find her, but instead acknowledged that if our chance meeting was meant to be, then it would be. Enlightenment is very freeing in its own way. I remember one of the holy men telling me that enlightenment was like a lover who whispers in your ear, but when you turn to embrace her, she's no longer there. The whisper itself becomes the lover and you are free to acknowledge or dismiss this fact as truth. Her absence makes her no less real. Yet as her whisper transcends reality, you eventually become her, and she you."

"Oh, my," I responded, my head dizzied.

"As I said," Reni remarked. "Heady stuff. One day baffling, the next day not."

"And *is* she real?" I pondered. "The girl in the golden cage?"

"A question only the Almighty would know," he said with a weary sigh. "And the one thing I am certain about the good Lord, he so seldom reveals such secrets."

Reni's comment surprised me, as my husband was not one to blithely reference any belief in divinity; not even in passing. Although we'd often and freely talk about the world's religions with a theoretical detachment, only once could I ever remember delving deeply into Reni's own beliefs. And *that* conversation had transpired many years previously, not long after we had relocated to the sparsely inhabited shores of Maine. And yet, our discussion had remained close to my heart ever since. It is a conversation that I feel I must recount here.

As I RECALL, Reni and I were travelling by rail from Boston to Chicago at the time, as his business ventures often took us far from home. Embarrassed as I am to reveal such an irrational fear, I did not enjoy air travel in those days. Ever observant to my needs, my husband had booked a private coach aboard the *Lake Shore Limited*.

Smoking his burl wood Calabash from the Russell Pipe Co. and eyebrow deep in the *Globe*, Reni had barely spoken since leaving South Station earlier that morning. I'd hardly touched my breakfast, my cheek pressed against the cold windowpane as I watched the world speed by in a splendid blur. Only recently acquainted with the blustery northeastern states, I found great curiosity in the flurry of white-steepled, cross-topped churches that proliferated across the rolling green countryside, sometimes with several such structures visible at a single glance. My curiosity grew until I was finally unable to sustain my silence.

"Do you believe that God exists?" I blurted, without even the courtesy of preamble. I glanced across the dining table to find Reni's newspaper dipping oh so slightly, the dear man peeking at me with what I believed to be a hint of trepidation.

"God?" he repeated with uncharacteristic uncertainty.

"Do you find the question difficult?" I chided.

"Not the question, per se. Although I suspect the answer to be somewhat complicated."

"Touché," I allowed with a smile.

"God," he said once again, folding the paper and tapping his pipe gently against a crystal ashtray.

"I don't believe you've ever mentioned your personal beliefs."

"Haven't I?"

After a heartbeat of stubborn silence, my gaze unrelenting, Reni sighed and said, "Truthfully? I don't believe the human brain capable of comprehending the reality of an omnipotent being any more than I believe a field mouse capable of understanding the workings of the internal combustion engine. However, as I sense my continued procrastination to be futile—yes, I'll admit to the probability of a consciousness far superior to our own. One that perhaps spreads the seeds of sentient life across the entire cosmos. If you're asking whether or not I believe in a *being*—a wizened and often grumpy elder, sitting among the clouds and recording our each and every peccadillo—no, I doubt that very much. Mankind has a habit of anthropomorphizing a great number of mysteries, and our assumption of a humanistic God, one with fingers and toes, a bad temper and a questionable ego, is likely one of those inclinations."

He leaned forward enthusiastically. "And yet the concept of a supreme being is one that I believe is instrumental to our ver—"

"But that was not my question," I said, undeterred.

"Ah, quite right," he replied, taking ample time to relight his pipe. "The truth is, I'm afraid I've seen too many wars over the eons, witnessed too much savagery in this world to believe that we are an intentional creation of divinity. A benevolent being would not have bestowed such barbaric tendencies upon us, upon our bumpy road to—to what exactly? Enlightenment? Some sort of sacred metamorphosis? And I've admittedly pondered the conundrum for quite a few millennia. Still, a base premise remains unanswered in my mind. Is an absent God a merciful one?"

I must have allowed the slightest slip of a frown, for Reni's demeanor immediately softened. "Forgive me, my love, if my lack of faith strikes you as impudent. I've been scolded many times in the past by my more reverential brethren. Then again, I've had a distinct advantage of witnessing the relentless, vicious nature of human beings in their ageless pursuit of power and wealth. If there *is* a God, I wonder whether or not that being has long ago turned away from humanity with regret and sorrow."

After a contemplative silence, I said, "You will not be angry with me if I disagree? That I might continue to seek such answers for myself?"

"Angry at you?" Reni's eyes glistened. "I would be angry if you *didn't* follow your heart in these matters. My lack of faith is not an excuse to judge you, nor to critique any rational being seeking a purpose to life. Truth be told, I envy those who do find faith. Perhaps it's my obstinate persistence in this world that has embittered me. Unable to die, I question whether the concept of God is remotely relevant to me."

I had never before considered the notion of an afterlife from the perception of an immortal being. How callous my question must have seemed. "I have dishonored you," I admitted shamefully.

"Hardly, my dear. Not for a single instant. After all, does the shadow dishonor the sun?"

I shook my head, immediately confused. For a moment, Reni appeared equally confounded. "A wise man once spoke those words to me, eons ago. I thought they might suffice, although I've never been able to fully interpret their meaning. But, no, perhaps not."

He watched a plume of aromatic smoke drift upwards from his pipe. "Please understand the God we worship today is far removed from those deities we worshipped in eons past. Admittedly a much nicer being. Far less angry," he added with a smile. "The absence of human sacrifice, of self-flagellation and mutilation is a vast improvement over our attempts to appease our gods of antiquity. And yet I'm troubled that the God we worship today—I'm speaking of the same God worshiped by both the Hebrew Abraham and the prophet Muhammad—appears to favor the strongest army, or the fattest purse. I have difficulty believing in a supreme being who's created such an immense and diverse universe and, having done so, who harbors such petty favoritism of the mighty over the meek. Given omnipotence, wouldn't such a being bestow equal blessings on the wealthiest and poorest alike? Upon the strongest and the weakest? Upon believers and non-believers? I think that such a benevolent architect might personally *hint* of what lay beyond for the righteous mortal, for what better way to temper the brutality of our existence than the promise of a cheerful eternity?"

"Then you *do* believe in an afterlife?" I asked.

"I believe the two concepts can separately exist. God or no God, I believe that what we perceive as death may be nothing more than a transition, a portal—a link from one realm to another. After all, where does the soul reside? Where lies human consciousness? No surgery has ever uncovered either profundity within the physical realm. Are we a manifestation of our own thoughts, our bodies merely borrowed frames of blood and bone? If so, whatever exists for us after we expel our last breath here on Sister Earth will be rather exquisite."

Reaching for my Reni's hand, I said, "An afterlife you may never embrace!"

"A thought that has preoccupied me for many years, I fear." Again the dear man smiled, although in a somewhat tepid manner. "To me, death is a Siren I indeed may never know—and believe me, I've often dreamed of its seemingly impossible reach. Perhaps one day I shall close my eyes and at last make its acquaintance."

I nodded, silent again, content to stare at the passing countryside, mulling over my husband's haunting words. I have not forgotten their impact upon my psyche. Only in that instant did I recognize Reni's extraordinary condition not as a blessing, but as a curse. And I? I could not imagine a more horrific fate.

We did not discuss the matter further. Although I had been raised in adherence to Miss Lin's Buddhist beliefs, Captain Muldoon had been devoutly Catholic, and not shy in expressing his own opinions during my more formative years. His words had not been lost on me, and I had come to find both tranquility and enlightenment in the written words of the Christian God as well as in the philosophy of Buddha. But to confide my beliefs to Reni would, I feared, only torment him further.

And so I held fast to my secret that morning aboard the *Lake Shore Limited*. Cocooned that same evening in the warmth of my husband's embrace, I quietly wept for Reni's eternal vigil. And every morning since, I've prayed for Reni's soul. I can only assume that a benevolent God looking down upon us all would excuse the cynicism of such a complex being and instead view my husband's life as one of wondrous purpose and wisdom. Because any afterlife without Reni at my side would be, I suspect, little more than a perpetual hell.

As I CONTINUED TO WADE through the years with Reni at my side, fewer and fewer of his astounding stories remained unfamiliar to my ears. Yet I knew that much had been lost over the centuries. Many gaps speckled his memory, "Like holes in a brick of Swiss cheese," he'd sometimes remark. "Entire lifetimes that I can no longer recall."

Other times were, in my husband's opinion, simply not worth mentioning. "Of those many moments that I've witnessed and remember in great detail," Reni told me, "also realize how many anonymous hours passed by in mindless stupor; endless days planting fields or chopping forests or building cities, stone by stone. I acknowledge that the bulk of human lives drift by without a second thought. A pity, and yet also very much our reality."

As if to punctuate the remark, he lifted a finger. "Did you know that I was once held captive by Pyotr Alexeyevich? A tall man and a fine sailor, quite cunning and maniacally ruthless in his rule over Mother Russia. I had been a cavalry officer—a feared Cossack—in Peter's army for a year or two, as marauding bands of Ottomans had previously pillaged and burned the town I'd chosen as my home, a picturesque village nestled in the Carpathian Mountains, in the current nation of Romania. Several of my friends had been wantonly executed, and my decision to wage war had become a personal retribution. As Alexeyevich's army, stationed a few hundred miles north in Kyiv at the time, fought the same enemy, I felt myself firmly entrenched on the side of my perceived righteousness. And so I enlisted.

"I served with distinction during the battle of Azov. By happenstance I gained the Tsar's approval and found myself assigned to the court of the royal palace in Moscow. At the time, Peter shared power with his half-brother and sister— this being quite a few years before he declared himself emperor, after Ivan had died of mental illness and Sophie, his older sister, had been banished from power. A vile woman, Sophie was, and one who made several brazen attempts on Peter's life. The family was quite dysfunctional, as I recall."

"Indeed," I marveled. "And yet name one powerful family that isn't so?"

But Reni could not and shook his head forlornly. "For a while Peter and I were close in the way that a monarch gains familiarity with those who advise him on a daily basis. This was before he'd begun the construction of *Sankt-Peterburg* as Russia's newfound capital, as he'd yet to wrest the Baltic from the Swedes. He would, of course, capture their stronghold at the mouth of the Neva River a few years hence.

"I remained in Peter's graces for some time as a tactician, and I must confess the Tsar's lavish lifestyle became as addictive as any narcotic. While the Russian peasantry knew nothing but brutal hardship in those times, the nobility knew little of want or need.

"Yet even amid the regal splendor of the Tsar's court, I did not repeat the mistakes of my past in Roma. I remained quite moved by the plight of the impoverished, and I admit to secretly feeding many of those living along the barren outskirts of our city's walls. A cavalry officer's wage was often far greater than the accumulated prosperity of an entire peasant village, and by then I had few personal wants or needs of my own.

"Ultimately, misfortune did befall me in Peter's keep. During one of the Tsar's numerous battles against the Turks in the south—as he was eager to conquer all who might infringe upon his expanding empire—I was called to lead a cavalry charge east of Narim. During the skirmish I was struck down by a volley to the chest. Unbeknownst to me, my body had been carried from the field of battle and viewed by Peter himself. I awoke days later in a large pit partially filled with frozen corpses. I healed and made my way back to our picket lines, under the pretense of having escaped capture by the Ottomans.

"When I reappeared in Moscow several weeks later, Peter was quick to suspect my unholy resurrection, as were his many elderly Orthodox ministers. I found myself unwelcomed in either the Tsar's kingdom or apparently God's. Despite my many honors, I was imprisoned in a stone cell barely three *arshin* square, an area less than nine by nine feet, and forbidden to speak or look upon others. I remained in that room for nearly thirty years, fed little but potatoes, carrots and water. I was released from captivity some years after Peter's death, when nobody could recall my offense. For the totality of that dreadful time, I had but one narrow loophole to view the outside world in its passing—and how very slowly did those days amble by.

"My point being, to speak in any great detail of such misadventure would prove regrettably vacuous, as my only memories were of racing cockroaches and of watching Moscow's skies advance from blue to gray, then gray to blue, again and again and again. I don't think I uttered a word during my isolation. Sanity prevailed only because, sooner or later, I assumed my prison walls would crumble."

And so I did not press my husband for those times he chose to ignore, nor did I wish to hear any more of humanity's unforgiveable brutality. The most splendid hakim of Pumaessia had filled that particular vessel *quite* full, thank you very much. I had no desire to further understand mankind's senseless cruelty, back in those dark days when the worth of a human life was a mere pittance.

And yet, even the smallest of moments, the slightest of glimpses into Reni's past, were invaluable to me. For instance, he had admitted to me, many years before, of taking three wives during his endless journey through time. In my boundless love, I harbored no room for jealousy—nor could I scarcely expect a man of his age to have never before wed. And yet I could not help but feel gratified that the prior Mrs. Renaud had been born centuries before me. I'm sure Reni had taken lovers, had even made conquests, in those pagan epochs of the past, given that the notion of marriage for love remains a relatively new cultural tradition. But I did not doubt his love for an instant. Long ago I'd realized that time spent regretting the past meant squandering the precious moments of today, and I refused to wallow away a single instant.

THERE DID YET REMAIN an integral part of my husband's extraordinary journey hidden from me—if only because of my own selfish fears. Decades ago, Reni had told me: *'In those distant ages there were no seasons, nor night and day, as our planet did not rotate around the sun as it now does...'*

Fearful for my own sanity, I had been unable to listen at the time. But I felt now that the moment had come. To deny *any* truth Reni might reveal, to keep even a single secret between us, had become unthinkable.

Time's meaning had changed for me, you see. The world had begun to spin more rapidly around us. Man had landed on the moon and satellites probed our sister planets. Sicknesses had been cured and science had transformed us into a most curious species. Much of the world's wisdom lingered as near as one's own personal computer. As we entered a new millennium, I found myself likewise entering my centennial year of life.

Although the mirror continued to lie to me, I could no longer deny the crinkle of lines about my eyes or the single lock of white that shocked my hair—although Reni appeared oblivious to my encroaching maturity, confessing that his love for me increased daily. Of course, my husband had yet to age a day, and remained exactly the man I had first encountered back in 1915.

Early one evening I took my Captain's hand and led him to the veranda. Pouring us each a snifter of cognac, I said; "I am ready."

I expected some confusion on his part, a quizzical look or frown. Instead, Reni merely smiled. "I've expected this moment for quite some time," he admitted. "Shall I finally reveal to you the world of my birth?"

I laughed. "You have not forgotten my petty impertinence, all those years ago?"

"I knew your curiosity would eventually prevail. And I am thrilled, as this is a secret unlike any other."

"Even greater than your own remarkable life?"

"Far greater, my darling."

"Then tell me," I begged.

"You're certain?"

"Quite positive, yes."

After sampling a small sip of cognac, he did so.

FOUR

"I WAS BORN INTO A WORLD whose sky knew no transition between day and night. We understood nothing of seasons, nothing of change." Reni gazed upward for perhaps a full minute, and I knew him to be reliving that lost epoch. Eventually, composed again, he continued. "We knew nothing of our own infinitesimal existence within the universe because we knew nothing of our universe—nothing of planets nor stars, nor of the astounding darkness through which they cast their brilliance. As I'm certain you've surmised by now, our heat, our light, came not from the sun that we know today."

I managed to offer my husband a subtle, silent nod.

"When we first spoke of my curious life all those years ago, I could not fathom from whence our planet had begun its journey. I surely would have confounded both of us in my attempt to explain to you any scientific principle. But over these last several decades, science has offered me various tantalizing clues.

"I've never mentioned this to you, but when we lived in Maine, I once travelled by rail to New York to meet a man, a psychiatrist by trade, who had recently published an extraordinary vision of our planet's prehistoric travels. He'd concocted a theory very similar to my own experience and we exchanged a pleasant afternoon of speculation and conjecture. I came close to revealing the truth of my longevity, although America at that time was quite paranoid with regard to Communists, anarchists and radical idealists. Unorthodox behavior was not tolerated, and in those days I feared imprisonment should I divulge too much of myself and somehow be discovered.

"However, he and I spent several hours in deep, shared contemplation. Our assumptions were not identical, but close enough. When we parted, I believed that I understood my distant past with a far greater clarity.

"Since that day you and I first spoke of my life, so very long ago," Reni said, "I'm convinced that, in the time of my youth, Sister Earth existed as a moon orbiting our sixth planet."

I found myself unexpectedly stunned, unable to speak. When my voice returned, I said, "A moon of *Saturn?*"

"Yes, yes," Reni said, quite excitedly. "Once upon a time, a larger, hotter Saturn was our *sun*. Our *Mu'at.*"

"And what you wanted to tell me all those years ago?"

"Aye, it is. Looming eternally overhead, unmoving, a milky blue presence that consumed most of the sky. Our Mother was a constant companion, an eternal comfort. And lit from within! Not nearly as hot or bright as our sun shines today, although Mu'at radiated sufficient energy to sustain her children."

"Mu'at," I said curiously. "Similar to mu'ata, your tribal word for *mother.*"

"Even with our primitive minds, we understood that Mu'at had somehow birthed our world—indeed, she was the mother of us all. But we were not an only child, for Mu'at had also birthed Luta'u and La'u'ata, our sibling planets, whom she held in much closer proximity."

"Siblings? You've never mentioned such mythical belief before."

"How could I, my love?" he countered gently, and

much to my chagrin. "But also remember that we had not the slightest concept of mythology in those days. We had no past to mythologize and no heavens to dream upon. Cocooned within Mu'at's ever-radiant aura, we'd never known a night sky. In our souls, perhaps in our very DNA, we understood that Mu'at provided us with life itself. So our assumption of this perpetual presence as *mother* was not borne of mythology, but rather of intuition."

"But you did know of two other planets," I parried.

"Ah, but not as planets, of course. Both Luta'u and La'u'ata—literally *first brother* and *little brother* in the language of Tu'ulth—remained fixed overhead and likewise did not move from Mu'at's warm embrace." Reni smiled. "In scientific jargon, our three planets shared a geo-synchronous orbit. The three planets moved in perfect alignment, as would three knots tied upon a length of string, pulled taut and circling a fixed point."

"La'u'ata eclipsing Luta'u, which eclipsed Mu'at," I presumed.

"Exactly. Little La'u'ata was perhaps thrice as large as our moon appears in the sky, and Luta'u barely half-again larger, and thus we saw only the outer rim of Luta'u's surface. Big brother would occasionally glow and I've recently assumed that poor Luta'u's proximity to our mother must have proven staggeringly hot. Certainly too hot for life as we know it to exist."

"And La'u'ata?" I asked.

"I've recently wondered if others like us had found a home there," he replied. "But I have no clue as to the planet's distance from us, nor its distance from Mu'at. Nor could we see any real surface features, as we were always viewing La'u'ata's dark side."

"Which means there once existed a dark side to *our* planet as well?"

"A perpetually cold and uninhabitable hemisphere," Reni confirmed with a nod. "In my later wanderings as a Tu'ulth, I would occasionally venture toward what I would now consider our solar meridian—a vertical divide which separated light and dark earth. A harsh and frigid wind thwarted my various attempts to travel any great distance beyond Mu'at's comforting glow. I eventually trekked far enough to discover my first icicle and to experience the brisk joy of rubbing one's face in snow, but *cold* was an alien concept to me, and I did not enjoy its lingering embrace. The distant glacial plateaus I eventually confronted were sheer and impenetrable, rising easily a mile above me, and above which hung a blanket of fierce, dark clouds, swirling in perpetual anger. Had I continued, I might have eventually discovered the starry night sky, but I dared not lose sight of Mu'at. Such was her impression upon my psyche at the time."

I must have appeared pitifully dumbstruck by Reni's words, for I could not fathom my husband retreating from *any* obstacle. To hide my disappointment, impudent as it was, I said, "Tell me more of Mu'at's sway over you, my darling. Of Luta'u and little La'u'ata's significance in your life."

Reni studied me briefly, then reached down and plucked a book from atop the squat table between us. I had not been aware of its presence before this instant, but I saw that he had selected a volume of astronomy from his extensive library. How could this man have so cunningly anticipated our conversation this evening?

He slid a loose photograph from its pages, an image of an ancient cave etching—a petroglyph—depicting a crude circle within a circle within a circle, and with many rays (or so I interpreted) extending outward. I had seen similar photos littering my husband's study for decades, of similar prehistoric markings spanning the globe. The few times I'd inquired about them, Reni had muttered unspecific rhetoric about *anthropological research*—intent, I now realized, on discouraging my curiosity. I had never puzzled together the importance of these images in Reni's life.

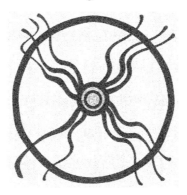

I took the photo from his hand and studied the grainy image, scratched into what appeared to be a granite slab. Scribbled across the bottom edge, the caption read: *Cork, Ireland — Discovered 1949. Presumed Paleolithic.*

"Mu'at?" I said, touching the outer circle. "Luta'u. And La'u'ata, the smallest circle in her midst."

He smiled. "Aye. I suspect Mu'at's three children had remained in precise alignment far as long as *homo sapiens* walked the Earth. Perhaps far longer."

"And the protruding rays?" I asked. "Might these represent lightning? Were these spokes of energy the key to your exceptional life?"

"I've recently begun to suspect so," Reni replied.

"But you don't know how. Or why?"

"Nary a clue. Lightning storms were a complete mystery in those days. Every so often, for whatever reason, La'u'ata's big brother Luta'u would grow churlish and petulant above us. A magnificent violet aurora would sometimes pulsate for great stretches of time. Streams of electrons, what we would now call *plasma trails*, would often leap across the sky in giant, rotating spindles. Occasionally these electromagnetic storms would reach as far as Sister Earth."

"One that would eventually knock you from the precipice," I presumed.

Reni nodded. "I believe that all life on our planet originated from these charges, triggered by a precise combination of chemical and electrical soup that Mu'at had concocted for our benefit. Whether we are the by-product of far greater sentience than ourselves or an accidental coalescence of random electrons and atoms—that I cannot answer."

"A mystery far older than you, my darling."

"And we humans do so hate an unsolvable problem," he agreed with a smile.

"So what became of our loving Mu'at? Of Luta'u and La'u'ata? How did we get *here*?" I asked in frustration. "How did we lose sight of our Eden?"

"What is Earth if not a giant spaceship?" Reni replied.

The notion had never occurred to me before.

"And I do have a theory..."

I held my breath and waited.

"Eventually it became time," Reni said in a stoic voice, "for Mu'at's children to grow up."

"FOR HOW LONG I REMAINED among the Tu'ulth, I cannot say. Perhaps a thousand years or more, as I had no perception of time in those wonderfully endless days. I realize how such a comment might seem—" Reni shrugged, only slightly apologetic. "—totally beyond comprehension. A thousand years is not exactly a drop in time's bucket. At least not in humanity's construct. But I swear that I cannot parse those passing centuries any more accurately than an adult attempting to recall each individual minute of an idyllic childhood summer. I can only tell you that, among

the Tu'ulth, I filled my waking moments with contemplation, yearning to understand all I might survey. Had I any
conception of mathematics, of geometry or geology, I might
have proven myself far more useful to the ages. But alas, I
had neither the skills nor the awareness.

"Although I would encounter many villages nestled
within the various, hospitable valleys we found, I never
grew weary of returning to my little island. Sooner or later
I would grow homesick, as would any man bound by the
love of his family."

"What a wonderful place it must have been," I remarked.

"Indeed," my husband said with enthusiasm. "I believe
humanity was becoming civilized, Tu'ulth serving as a central hub for knowledge and commerce between the few valleys that we'd explored. We knew nothing of economies or
currency, of course, but we traded freely with one and all
and, in that regard, lacked for naught.

"Somewhere in the midst of those countless centuries, I
became aware that our tribe's incessant wanderings—as my
journeys had inspired many of our number to venture forth
as well—had left deep and distinct trails in the once opaque
white silt of the upper earth. We had long before now chiseled several wide stairways into the canyon walls, and our
many treks to *aka'uha*, the vast empty highlands, were no
longer viewed as dangerous or sinister.

"Where the planet's surface residue had been scattered
by our countless treks to-and-fro, a soft, reddish-brown layer of soil had revealed itself for the first time in Lord knows
how many eons. Before long slivers of vegetation sprouted
from this newfound loam. Within the span of a single lifetime, venturing forth between river valleys became as easy
as following the roads that spun like green ribbons in many
directions from Tu'ulth. Moreover, much of the growth pro-

vided fruits and flowers we had never before known. Trees eventually dropped branches and kindling for those who stopped to build fires for rest and nourishment."

"You had built a paradise," I told him.

Reni hesitated, lost in the bliss of those memories. Slowly then, his smile faded. The most pitiful expression emerged upon his face, an ominous countenance that sent a shiver through my body.

"Ah, but why behold thee a mote in your brother's eye?" Reni said, paraphrasing scripture from the New Testament, staring toward the nocturnal horizon.

I waited in silence.

"Something occurred," he said finally. "Something quite different in a world where *difference* was a largely unknown phenomenon. After one long slumber in my beloved Tu'ulth, I awoke and stepped from my thatched yurt, gazing upward into the warming face of Mu'at, intending only to wish her my love. I happened to notice a faint spark of brightness in the sky, one that lingered quite close to our mother. Infinitesimally tiny, it nevertheless blemished the sheer pristine blueness that had forever lain like a comforting carpet overhead.

"I was instantly transfixed by this incongruity. I pointed to others and very soon all of Tu'ulth had turned their gazes upward, babbling with great agitation. But nothing out of the ordinary occurred and the spark remained fixed for— well, certainly for the equivalent of many weeks or even months. Some pondered that Mu'at might be giving birth again, or that an insect had flown upward to torment our mother. Many in the village tried to shout or wave away this unwelcomed intruder, but to no avail.

"The speck remained and became familiar and yet we could not shake from our collective psyche the trepidation triggered by this phenomenon. We would sleep and awaken and peer immediately into the sky. When again fatigued, we would look upward and wonder anew before we slept.

"Gradually the spark grew larger. Even so, its position remained static to our perception, barely a finger's breadth from Mu'at's shining round face. As this offending morsel grew in brightness, we named it *B'ziz,* our word for any flying insect. Despite our misgivings, catastrophe did not strike. Sickness did not befall us. Mu'at did not abandon her children in fear. We gradually grew accustomed to this new presence in our sky and eventually I grew restless again and eager for adventure.

"I suspect that many months had passed since I'd last ventured any significant distance from the village. Such was my love for these people, for my little island home. Soon enough, however, I decided to set out on another exploit and chose five of our tribe to accompany me. I had intended this journey to be an extraordinary one. I had already explored nine additional valleys to the west, and I yearned to scratch another mark upon our map of the world. I sensed that the discovery of a tenth valley—a number of some importance to us, in that *ten* signified the maximum quantity that we could comprehend—would represent a most spectacular achievement.

"For several days before I set off, we prepared and feasted, and the village came together in celebration. I realized that I would likely not lay eyes on our elders ever again, and that our many children would have grown to adulthood before my return. As was my usual practice, I would choose one of my companions to return home every so often to inform the village of the success of our travels. I suppose one might consider the strategy a primitive equivalent to a letter dropped in the mailbox. But I, as always, would be the last to return, often with an accompanying caravan, bringing with me any new and as-yet unseen marvels that the world had to offer.

"And so we departed, the six of us moving smartly up the canyon's stepped walls, buoyed by the enthused shouts of our brethren. We continued with panache until their joyous voices faded. We headed westward, and gradually slowed to a seemlier pace for such a long journey, smiling at each other quite often, elated in these first moments of our quest.

"Yet even lost within our own excitement, I was aware of each in my party casting frequent glances into the sky. B'ziz was now half the circumference of my thumbnail and as round as Mu'at herself. And yet Mu'at offered no premonition of danger—as always, a self-assured and reliable mother.

"Within a span of several weeks we had bridged three adjacent valleys. We had become quite familiar with many of the villages we encountered and were often remembered and embraced as friends. And yet we did not tarry. We promised to return one day, fully laden, with new and exciting gifts from afar.

After an arduous but otherwise uneventful journey, we eventually passed the seventh and eighth valleys, and finally we moved into the unknown wilderness beyond the ninth. Mu'at had shifted very slightly overhead, although we had come to accept this odd phenomenon in our longer travels away from Tu'ulth. To this day, I cannot fathom the breadth of our trek. Had we walked the equivalence of Manhattan to Pittsburgh? To Columbus or Chicago? I simply have no reliable references.

"By now, we had moved far past the familiarity of our tree-shrouded roads, slogging once again through the white, flat starkness. Soon enough we came upon the tenth valley, our little party whooping and laughing with delight.

"And what a discovery it was! We stood overlooking a

forested valley quite extraordinary in its girth, the opposite canyon wall quite distant. We could see a number of rivers flowing toward the sea, and several wide lakes, each gleaming a crystal, aquatic blue. For a great while we sat at the canyon's lip, pointing and chatting, taking sufficient time to relish our new find, still ripe with its allures and mysteries. Finally, we slept with giddy exhaustion, knowing that when we awoke this new land would be ours to explore.

"Our normal course of discovery had been to follow the canyon walls toward the great sea. Although this trek might mean many additional hours of traveling before we reached the delta, we found it a wise precaution, as we could take better stock of all we surveyed on the valley floor beneath us. As we no longer feared the shoreline and tidal pools, we welcomed its rich bounty. We would bloat our bellies with many tasty delicacies and would bring many more as tribute to the villages we'd soon encounter. And by carefully marking our way, we could also—if necessary—beat a hasty retreat back to the shore.

"Also, as I mentioned was my usual custom, shortly after the youngest among us had taken sufficient nourishment on the unblemished white beach, we hailed his farewell and bade him a safe journey home. While young Ba'ura's dismissal might have seemed unkind, his return to Tu'ulth would be eagerly anticipated. Should fate treat us unkindly in the tenth valley, the Tu'ulth would at least be aware that we'd arrived. The lad's fireside tales of our great adventures thus far, some true and some likely embellished, would capture the hearts of many females and bode well for morale. Ba'ura would be the envy of all his younger brothers.

"I do remember however, watching the others call out after the boy's departure, of glancing upward at the now familiar B'ziz. I reached out toward the heavens, my thumb extended—quite startled to realize the spark had grown larger than my thumbnail, its aura a bright halo around the tip of my finger. Moreover, a faint purplish ring had appeared around this once insignificant speck. An omen of some sort, I presumed, although I could not fully appreciate its significance.

"So we began our exploration of this rich valley, and the first few villages we encountered were both inviting and generous. I wish I could relate more, but my memory is vague. What I do recall, a moment etched for eternity in my brain, is the solitary young woman in our party, Na'u—our word for *flower petal*—smiling broadly and giving this crack in the earth a name."

I waited.

"'*Vu tah ka'yat teh*,'" My husband said. "Roughly translated, the 'Valley of our Rebirth.' A name, I'm afraid, that would prove harshly prophetic."

"We remained within vu tah ka'yat teh for some time— many weeks, I would surmise. Yet since our arrival, we would often gaze skyward and B'ziz would be perceivably larger. The valley's villages appeared increasingly agitated, and yet in a world otherwise unchallenged by suffering, what significance was this tiny speck in the sky?" Reni pondered his own question with a thoughtful gaze. "Imagine somebody pointing a loaded pistol in your face."

I did so, and instinctively reacted with a wince.

"Now imagine you'd never seen a gun before and did not know of its capacity for harm. How would you respond?"

"Quite differently," I admitted.

"Aye. The sky above had begun to change ever so slightly. Although I had never known reason to fear for Mu'at's safety before, I was aware of the halo around B'ziz becoming increasingly prominent—bright red, gradually blending to orange and then increasingly yellow. Even more confusing, we'd begun to see a small variation in our mother's face. A slight bluish bulge appeared, as if Mu'at were leaning toward this interloper, intent to accept it as her own.

"We had soon visited a dozen or so villages in this new valley, staying sometimes a week or more, teaching and learning from one another. The last few tribes however had proven increasingly hostile, even injuring one of our party with a stone hurled from a slingshot much like our own. We retreated back into the jungle, aware that Mu'at's displeasure might be clouding the minds of those we sought to engage. We talked about returning to Tu'ulth and continuing our sojourn only after B'ziz had disappeared from our collective consciousness.

"We had all but agreed to such course of action when the first earthquake struck. The ground began to tremble, a strange and drunken turbulence that did not diminish for several minutes. Most disconcerting."

I put a hand to my mouth, remembering my own earthquake, and my lost sisters, all those years ago.

"We had never before felt Sister Earth move beneath us," Reni said, "and we gazed upon one another in terrified silence. Once the ground had stilled, we agreed that we would abandon our journey immediately and return to the river's mouth. We also agreed to stay clear of those villages that had so recently welcomed us. We knew that fear could warp a man's perception, and we did not want to be condemned as the harbinger of this terrible thing that grumbled beneath our feet.

"The ground shook several times before we again reached the coast. Even more troublesome, B'ziz appeared to be growing far more quickly in the sky above us, seemingly expanding with every upward glance. The colors surrounding her had expanded as might a bloody stain, and vast tendrils of purple lightning arced angrily between

Luta'u and the intruder.

"'Luta'u is protecting her mother,' Na'u said to me, and I could not find a reason to disagree.

"When we reached the shoreline, the great sea's waves danced and crashed in ways we had never before seen. Much of the white sand we had first encountered had washed away, leaving deep, ragged trenches in the beach. We did not linger as before, but quickly made our way up along the canyon's edge, back upon the fragile shell of the earth.

"We returned to our original point of contact atop the cliffs. The youngest remaining among us, a lad named De'oji—likely the smartest among us as well—had plunged the tip of his spear into the soil where we had first come upon the valley. Spying it now, I let out a yell of great relief. Yet we'd barely reached the mark when the next quake stuck, throwing us willy-nilly to the ground. We stared at each other in fear and bewilderment, with barely an instant's respite before the sky pulsed with a series of blinding lights. Mu'at had now fully reached out to B'ziz and had engulfed the intruder in angry flames—truly a terrifying sight. Even tiny La'u'ata had moved away from his brother overhead, the two planets misaligned as never before, Luta'u blazing with rage.

"A thunderous din tormented our ears. I could not determine from where such sound emerged, but I suspect now it was a sonic boom of sorts; a giant, echoing thud that rocked the foundations of our very souls. The ground no longer shook, but instead lunged violently to one side. We thrashed and tumbled like scraps of paper in a swirling wind. I watched, horrified, as two of our number were flung over the edge of the canyon, flailing like insects as they fell. I reached out with an anguished cry but they were gone—hurled into the valley below—and still the ground shook. A fine white mist rose from the earth and bathed the angry sky in pastel hues.

"A'bu, *a'bu!*" Na'u cried in alarm, crawling on her hands and knees. Only she and young De'oji remained of our party. I snatched my gaze from the heavens and followed Na'u's gaze toward the sea. A great wave of water had risen, sweeping into the mouth of the valley. It moved inland with incredible swiftness, obliterating the villages we had visited, leaving only a swirling, frothy wake of destruction in its path.

"The ground had stilled and so we began to flee from the canyon's edge, fearful of likewise being cast over the cliffs and into the maelstrom below. In those moments of crazed panic, I forgot my extraordinary ability, and I dreaded death as would any mortal.

"We ran until we finally fell, exhausted. The earth's dusty residue had begun to settle again and covered us in a ghoulish white powder. Behind us, I could barely see the canyon's edge, a thin, ragged line against the western horizon. Enormous columns of steam vomited upward from the canyon floor, hissing and sizzling with intensity.

"'*We must leave this place,*' I called out—words to that extent—pointing eastward, toward the ninth valley, and even though the earth intermittently rattled and hummed beneath our feet, we began to run again.

"Yet I had barely spoken before the cataclysm occurred. I cannot arguably even call it a quake," Reni said softly, "but rather a great rupture from far within our world. We were tossed along the ground with extraordinary swiftness, falling not downhill but sideways, like marbles rolling and bouncing down an incline. A great and continuous grumble rose from below, a prolonged screech and crack of splintering rock. The ground beneath our feet buckled and I caught fleeting glimpses of distant mountains being born and torn asunder, collapsing again. Far ahead, I spotted an enormous wall of fire burning high into the sky. I can only assume these flames had burst from beneath the floor of what had once been the ninth valley. Surely this was mankind's first glimpse of hell.

"Had we been closer to the flames we would have been immediately incinerated. But given our distance from the inferno, we felt only an expansive rush of hot wind slash at our faces and extremities. Seconds later giant boulders, glowing a deep molten red, began to rain from the heavens. Most of this fiery debris dropped upon the broken plains far away, but several boulders fell dangerously close, their impact throwing us once again off our feet. I flailed for Na'u, who had tumbled as I had, and who struggled to stand mere steps away. I glanced behind me, where I had last seen De'oji. The boy had likewise risen to his feet. In that instant—our gazes fusing in a way I shall never forget—an enormous slab of rock, easily the size of this house, fell and pulverized the earth where he had been standing.

"I pulled frantically at my remaining companion and we made our retreat, back again toward Vu tah ka'yat teh. By some miracle no debris fell upon us. Quite close to the canyon wall, we found sufficient cover beneath an up-tilted shard of solid granite—a place that, not long before, had been utterly flat. Without room enough to fully stand, the cavity's thick roof nonetheless offered sufficient protection from crackling heat and falling stone. We crawled as deeply as we could into the meager space and waited for death to claim us. Na'u sobbed for breath and for the longest time we huddled together, shivering, as the world shook and belched and screamed in agony around us.

"Giant rocks like flaming meteors continued to pepper the terrain for quite some time. Eventually the barrage subsided, and I found the courage to creep toward the cavern's jagged mouth and gaze upward. Much to my horror, I could no longer find Mu'at in the clouded sky above us. I could do little more than shrink back beside Na'u, our backs pressed desperately against the warm rock. She trembled in terrible fright, unable to speak, to move. I wrapped my arms around her, such an inept attempt at protection, although the gesture sufficed to comfort us both. We remained there, numb and unmoving, for what must have been hours. Thick smoke gradually darkened the sky until eventually I could no longer see even a faintest hint of light. For the first time in my life, I knew the fear of relentless darkness.

"When the clouds cleared sufficiently to reveal the heavens, a wondrous vision emerged. Mu'at appeared far above the distant western horizon and had engulfed much of the offensive B'ziz. Great arcs of electricity danced between the two orbs. The intruder clung to our Mother's side, pulsating a fiery angry red, and perhaps badly wounded, as B'ziz oozed a trail of glowing blood that partially encircled Mu'at.

"Nearly as terrifying, little La'u'ata had been pushed completely from the grasp of his older brother Luta'u, rendering the planet wholly visible to us for the first time. It was a sight beyond comprehension to me."

"Venus?" I asked. "And Mars?" Trying to piece the puzzle together.

"I have often speculated so," Reni said with a nod.

"And the mote in Mother's eye...*Mercury?*"

"That part of B'ziz that would ultimately break free of Mu'at's grasp," my husband affirmed. "I cannot be certain, of course, but yes, it seems plausible."

I nodded, content again to sit quietly. To listen.

"Only recently have I come to understand a theoretical explanation of what had transpired above us that day—that a small, rogue planet had grazed Mu'at, and in doing so had dislodged Sister Earth and her brothers from our mother's gravitational pull. The collision would indeed prove to be a fatal blow, for Mu'at would lose her luster over time—not in the blink of an eye, but slowly, as if the fire in her belly had sputtered, with insufficient fuel left to burn.

"I've recently read about brown dwarves and sub-stellar objects; large, gaseous bodies lacking sufficient mass or combustion to burn brightly. I suspect that whatever sort of celestial body Mu'at had been, she'd sacrificed too much of herself to protect her children. Indeed, she had loss much of her own mass considerably since the collision. But in the resulting carnage our planet had been orphaned, as had our two brothers. An enormous amount of stellar debris accompanied us toward whatever future B'ziz, that cosmic knave, had chosen for us.

"Our journey between *there* and *here* would take—well, I have no idea, to tell you the truth. Absolutely no perception," Reni added with a rueful shake of his head, "as I shall explain shortly. But on this first day of our terrible new world, all that I had ever known and loved seemed but a fading dream.

"Na'u and I had lost a good deal of our provisions, yet neither of us dared move from our protective lair until we could no longer ignore our hunger. Na'u had badly bruised her thigh and a rock fragment had sliced through my shoulder, although I had already begun to heal. Still, my hunger was not unlike any mortal's, and I knew I could not let Na'u suffer much longer, as death would soon claim her.

"Weak as I was, I eventually ventured forth into this hostile new reality. I could move only a few paces before stopping, wheezing for each breath. I had fastened a pelt over my nose and mouse and yet, still, my mouth and nose continually filled with an evil-smelling, viscous dust. Not far from our lair, I discovered that a portion of the canyon wall had crumbled, providing rather precarious access to the canyon floor. Each morning I would pick my way through the carnage, attempting to forage the various fruit that had been ripped from shattered trees, or to snare a variety of snakes and lizards that darted about in the rubble. Although the waters had receded, the wave's force had left utter destruction within the valley. I dared not traverse the ooze-coated floor, as a single false step might have plunged me into the muck to be swallowed whole. I can only imagine, had I sunk into the slime, fully engulfed, that I might still linger there today, like some insect forever trapped in amber, my mind fully capable of thought and fear and pain."

"Good Lord," I replied, horrified.

"And yet I had no choice but to scavenge for our survival. I did so furtively, as eventually did Na'u, neither of us losing sight of the other, or venturing too far from the safety of our cave. We lived in constant fear of this new reality, of darkness, of night's inevitable return. It's difficult to explain such terror when day and night are as obvious to humankind as—" My husband smiled weakly. "—as night and day. But my primitive mind could make no sense of this new paradigm. How to *cope* with such an unknown phenomenon? Each morning, Mu'at would appear upon one horizon and cross the sky, much as our sun does today. And yet she would rise over a different peak, one morning far to the left, the next morning far to the right, and the following morning, far to the left again. Each morning our mother would appear the tiniest bit smaller in the sky. I realized, deep within my soul, that Mu'at was dying. She would disappear again and again behind the horizon and the loathsome night would return to blanket the land.

"'She runs and hides from the darkness,'Na'u surmised, a comment that seemed quite plausible at the time."

"Earth's axis must have been terribly thrown off kilter," I assumed.

"We were spinning through space as would a billiard ball, having been struck with a good deal of polish," Reni replied with a nod. "Thus, each evening the stars scattered anew, like sparks from a distant bonfire. Mu'at would eventually return, bringing the light of day, her face streaked with debris and dark clouds. Around her midsection, a trail of blood remained, a glowing crimson smear that scattered across the heavens, grander than any sunset you could imagine."

"The birth of Saturn's ring," I said with sudden clarity.

"Indeed, I believe so. One of countless new horrors our primitive brains were forced to accept. For many months, the night sky would confound me with its strange wonders; meteors and auroras and molten smears beyond comprehension. Giant plasma arcs would stretch across the sky. At night they would appear in fiery colors and sometimes resemble cosmic snakes or spiders, and occasionally winged, fire-breathing lizards."

"Oh?"

"Quite often," Reni said, "our mythologies arise from that which we find inexplicable."

I nodded silently, but I very much felt as if one such mystery had been unleashed within my soul. Had our infatuation with dragons begun so very long ago, birthed out of such cataclysmic destruction?

"Both Luta'u and La'u'ata were often present," Reni continued, "as they accompanied their sister on our escape though the cosmos. They remained her bright companions in the night sky. For quite some time, Luta'u continued to glow as would a hot ember. Nearest Mu'at, I now suspect the planet had been incinerated during the collision. I can only hope that sentient life had not forged a home there.

"I'm sure many of my remaining brethren were driven mad by observing such chaos filling the heavens, although I'll admit that I found the proximity of our brother planets comforting. I've since come to realize how fortunate we were that our own planet had broken away from her orbit around Mu'at, as our dying mother was rapidly failing.

"Our days were quickly cooling and, of course, at night the temperature would plummet. Those places where the ground had splintered remained hot, as molten rock continued to spew upward from the depths. I'm firmly convinced those of us who survived did so by huddling near lava flows, or else finding underground vents that radiated sufficient heat. Honestly, I'm amazed any of us manage to persist during those terrible times."

"But you survived," I reminded him and, struck with a sudden new realization, I said, "You and Na'u were not unlike Adam and Eve."

Reni smiled, an expression that appeared to mask a great deal of sorrow. "Since I could not reproduce, the world would have sadly lacked a viable forefather. But survive, aye, that we did. We were fortunate; within our shallow cave, a single fissure had opened beneath our feet, a long and jagged crack, barely the width of my finger. Steam hissed forth with sufficient warmth, and with adequate oxygen, to sustain us. I believe this constant flow of mist continually purged our small cave, ventilating what might otherwise have become a lethal atmosphere for us.

"For a long while our only moisture came from ice that accumulated at the mouth of the cave each night. We captured what we could in several crustacean shells that had washed up on higher land. The sea itself, once brimming with life and forever lapping upon our crystalline shores, had turned a murky black, its odor quite repugnant. Volcanic mounds dotted the once pristine waters, vomiting fire and smoke. Once sufficient strength returned to me, I searched for the rotting carcasses of dead fish along the shoreline, and we would cook and consume what we were able to save by steaming the flesh on the rocky floor of our cavern.

"I'm not sure how long we remained, huddled near the precipice overlooking Vu tah ka'yat teh. Months, probably. Gradually, moss and lichen flourished within the cave and thorny weeds eventually sprouted upon the broken plain, as life can be tenacious when it must. Somehow, I instinctively knew that if such fragile flora could survive in such heinous conditions, so could Na'u and I.

"And yet we continued to suffer frequent quakes," Reni said, "and sometimes many in quick succession. Late one evening the ground shook very harshly. With a grinding scream of shifting rock, the fissure beneath our feet closed. Too quickly a black chill fell around us, before we were even aware of our peril."

"Na'u?" I asked gently.

"Neither my body's heat nor the warmth of our pelts could sustain her, and within the darkness of our small cave, I felt her life flee from my arms. I had little time to mourn her loss as I sensed my own body succumbing to the same numbing chill. A baffling yet quite comfortable warmth crept through my extremities—I felt dreary, yet strangely euphoric. I realized that Na'u must have likewise experienced such rapture, with death perhaps no more painful than an enviable sleep. I closed my eyes and drifted into the nether world. For a very long time I lay frozen while, around me, Sister Earth found the courage to survive her remarkable trek.

"WHEN I AWOKE, as if from a protracted dream, I experienced both muddy thought and exquisite pain. For the longest time I found myself unable to move or even open my eyes. A multitude of small tics and spasms wracked my body, as if a hundred trillion cells were angrily awakening within me, one by one. I repeatedly drifted in and out of consciousness, crossing between life and death many times. And yet whether over a matter of hours or days or even years, I simply don't know.

"As I lay in groggy repose, I soon became aware of a familiar hiss. The narrow fissure in the rocky floor had again opened—moist, hot air escaping from some deep volcanic pocket—and I understood that Sister Earth must have recently shaken, reviving me as if I were a bear waking from a winter's hibernation.

"I was eventually able to open my eyes. I lay without moving, aware of a tepid yellowish glow emanating from the cave's elongated mouth. Strangely enough, the cave's opening struck me as far smaller than I remembered; only a fraction of its former size. Much of the interior had been filled by bits of shattered rock and thickly packed soil, and the cave itself seemed tilted in a precarious manner.

And yet the encroaching daylight played over my bare legs with a curious tingling sensation. I watched small vapor clouds rise from my skin. The pelts that had once so capably warmed me had fallen away as would long-dead petals from a broken flower, and I noted how their skin had rotted, little more than brittle lumps of fuzz. No trace of my beloved Na'u remained. I could only assume that she had found Tu'aku—eternal paradise—and with that knowledge, I experienced tremendous joy.

"For many hours I could do nothing but move my eyes to and fro. When I felt ready, I forced myself to make the smallest efforts to rise. After several futile attempts I began to drag my stubborn body toward the mouth of the cave and into the warming light.

"What I saw perplexed me. Little beyond the cave resembled the inhospitable, volcanic world I remembered. Much of this new landscape lay draped in a mossy green carpet, and not far away, thick forests had sprung to life.

Beyond the broken tenth valley, mountains rose where none had been before. How curious! I've since to come to realize that time had reshaped the surface of Sister Earth during my frozen repose. And yet, nearby, I recognized several large outcrops of black rock, although softened and more rounded than the jagged terrain that I remembered. Countless holes in the porous rock had filled with water, as if recent rains had flooded the planet's surface.

"You can't imagine how this discovery thrilled me—fresh water so very near my reach! And had I been able to move with dexterity I would have bound forth from the cavern at a full sprint. However, I crept from the cave with all the elegance of a banana slug, my lungs gasping for air, until eventually I found myself under a clear sky, able to sip at the sweetest water I've ever tasted.

"Over the next several days I managed to regain a modicum of muscle strength. Each morning I would crawl toward the dawning light and watch a new, unknown glowing orb peek above the distant peaks. Was *this* to be our new Mu'at? She seemed such a small, timid mother. Each day I would plead for her to remain, to resume her rightful place in the sky above me, but she ignored my cries and crept across the sky with reckless abandon. Darkness would inevitably appear once more and, fearing another frigid death, I would cocoon myself within the misty warmth of my cave and wait.

"I did not venture far from my shelter for the longest time, for I had grown fearful of all that I surveyed. In the distance, mountains continued to belch steam, occasionally exploding without warning and spewing spatters of molten lava high into the air.

"And so I lingered. Day would follow night would follow day. I was pleased to see, after my long sleep, Luta'u and little La'u'ata still passing through the sky far above me, although if mother Mu'at also swam through the heavens I no longer recognized her, as no object appeared larger than our moon does today and, in fact, that new orb—" Reni gestured toward the horizon, where a half moon glowed above the inky Pacific, "—had somehow made its appearance in that ancient, turbulent sky while I had lain unconscious. We made our first acquaintance when I awoke from my cave, and I have often since pondered her presence. Perhaps she had been hiding far above Earth's dark side for eons, an unknown little sister.

"If memory serves, the moon slowly spun, as did we all, and appeared somewhat larger than she does today. Conversely, our sun was perhaps half its current size, offering only the slightest of creature comforts, providing no more warmth than that of a chilly November morning. Survivable, but hardly pleasant.

"I dared not move far from the tiny cave that had so long been my domain. I was eventually able to traverse an acre or two, but I did not trust myself to venture further. I was so completely baffled by this new world that confronted me. And I might have remained emotionally chained to this fragile existence forever, had not a curious occurrence jolted me from my complacency. One afternoon, near the farthest extent of my explorations, I stumbled upon the edge of a rocky gorge, in which several rather large pools of lava bubbled and spat beneath me. I stood mesmerized at the edge of the precipice, staring down into a swirling cauldron of liquid fire. In that moment I felt the full extent of my loneliness, the unbearable weight of my dear Na'u's loss. I truly considered throwing myself into the abyss. I had never before, nor ever since, contemplated the absurdity of suicide, but what an odd remembrance, those few heartbeats of surrender.

"I don't know what saved me from that terrible fate, although I do remember the sudden cry of some predatory bird high overhead. Such a forlorn sound, and yet one that reminded me that I was not alone in this world. Other creatures had similarly suffered and still they endured, calling out to an empty world in blind faith and with boundless hope.

"In that instance I found the strength and will to once again explore this new and broken world, to uncover whatever secrets it might hold." My husband's voice no longer trembled, as if the memory of his salvation, eons ago, had vanquished the lingering sorrow from his soul. "By God, I resolved to spend my life searching for humanity's survivors. Certainly there must be at least one other still alive. It was my—what is the expression?—my come-to-Jesus moment. Although many weeks would pass before I felt strong enough to embark on such a strenuous expedition. Despite my aching lungs and addled brain, I pushed myself to forage and produce sufficient supplies, pelts, and tools that would satisfy my needs. Each day I expanded my comfort range, first by wandering a quarter mile, and then a half, until soon I had fully weaned myself from the security of my little crack in the earth.

"And then, one morning, I simply left. Truth be told, I believe I was inwardly seeking some sign of Tu'ulth. And I don't suppose I've ever stopped looking."

Aware of his inference, I said, "Have you *never* found any vestiges of your beloved tribe?"

"I've spent many lifetimes actively seeking even a hint of my people's fate," he said cautiously. "Perhaps it is for the best that I've never found a trace of them."

"Perhaps," I agreed, although not yet convinced, for I knew the pain of uncertain longing.

"For many years, I did harbor hope that I would one day rediscover my little paradise, thriving and unblemished. I held that belief most dearly, as it fueled my resolve to survive. I suspect I wandered alone for many years, possibly even decades. I continually felt impending madness come and go during this time of *Mu'a'atabi*, the endless days and nights passing in utter isolation."

"Wait," I said, and repeated each syllable cautiously to myself. "Mu'a'atabi?"

"A word, an epoch, unto myself. Mu'a'atabi was a waking nightmare that would not end. In my heart, in my soul, the word represented both our Mother's absence and a time of great sorrow, of loneliness and fear as I confronted a world alien to me. Truly the lowest depths of my depression."

"I cannot *fathom*…" I said, a hand at my throat. "So many years without glimpsing another soul, so many years wandering in isolation."

"A drop in the bucket, as we immortals like to say."

I saw behind my husband's attempt at levity and did not believe his stoicism in the least.

"During those years," Reni said, "I meandered far greater distances than I ever had among the Tu'ulth, for returning home was no longer an option. I did not know if parts of our world had been spared such cataclysmic incineration, and indeed I would eventually discover deserts of soft sand and seemingly ancient forests of pristine beauty. I observed fresh water lakes brimming with fish, and also mountain ranges that appeared far older than those that had been violently upthrust during our recent brush with oblivion. Had these vast regions been spared beneath thick layers of ice? Had ocean floors risen and fallen? Had jungles re-rooted and sprouted during my hibernation? I had no idea—and still, to this day, I do not understand the magnitude of what transpired during my long sleep.

"But as my travels expanded, I began to comprehend the grand magnificence of our Sister Earth, and how insignificant my own existence as I walked upon her surface. I once believed that this planet existed for the benefit of me and my own, but I soon realized that I was but a flea scampering about the hide of a mastodon. Had I known that those infinite specks of light in the night sky were the countless stars among countless galaxies, I'm sure I would have gone completely insane. Such immense vastness was inconceivable to me. But for many centuries to come I continued to assume the darkness twinkled with sparks of a distant *oht*, burning far above me, floating upon some cosmic breeze.

"One moment a master of my tribe; the next an idiot savant," he added, most forlorn.

I could not find the words to console my husband, and my heart ached. And yet Reni was not one to allow his pessimism to fester unchecked. Quite unexpectedly his gaze sparkled.

"And then my love, one morning as I moved through a moist riverbed—a rocky outcrop to one side and dense jungle to the other, the now-familiar yellow sun radiating its vague warmth against my back—I glanced up to see a small child standing on a high ledge maybe fifty yards ahead of me. Slender waterfalls dribbled from the ledge on either side of this apparition. The boy was quite naked and dark skinned, the top of his head matted with a black furry mop. I stopped in my tracks, startled, half-convinced the child to be a mere illusion. I raised a hand in greeting, but he did not move. I rubbed my eyes and again peered toward the ledge, but the boy had vanished.

"*Had* he been merely a mirage?" Reni asked, his amazement as vibrant as if this were a recent memory. "I began to run toward the ridge, but on closer approach I realized that the child had been standing far above me. By the time I was able to reach his perch, all traces of the boy had vanished.

"Slightly above the ledge I came upon a great flat apron of black stone. Mountains rose in the distance and several small streams slithered along the smooth rock, toward the path that I had so recently trod. Several caves pocked the far end of this enormous slab. You can't believe my excitement at finding several small, wet footprints glistening against the stone. I had barely taken note of them when the child reappeared at the mouth of one dark cavity. He pointed at me. A second child appeared from the cave and a third. A woman finally appeared as did a man—all naked, dark haired, dirt-smudged, little more than the skeletal remnants of a species I had once known so well.

"I called out but received only haunted silence in return. Others began to emerge from the caves; another half-dozen children and several more women. A second man emerged, missing much of his left arm, and then a third. These people seemed grossly malnourished, barely capable of standing, yet the men held clubs aloft with obvious animosity. They grunted with great effort, sounds that conveyed far more fear than fierceness.

"You must realize that I had fully equipped myself by now. I had stitched together pelts and leggings, fur boots, even a hooded vest that I could pull over my head during periods of rain or wind. I carried both sling and bow at my side, and a flint-tipped spear of great length. In a knapsack woven from skins and rope, I carried food sufficient for several days of travel. Should these beings be hostile, I could thwart their best efforts in a melee, and with no more effort than a bison dispatching a hoard of angry rabbits.

"And yet I had not seen my human brethren in—in more years than I could ever know. I fell to my knees and let forth a great wail, one that revealed the depth and breadth of my loneliness. I dropped my spear, my arms open wide, my demeanor both submissive and accepting.

"Had they desired, they could have easily fallen upon me. But in my vulnerability, they sensed a despair even greater than that which had hollowed their eyes and emptied their stomachs. One of the women moved curiously forward, and in her arms I saw an infant. I saw what she could not yet see, that the child was quite dead, the skin already retreating from its lips, its fused eyelids sunken inward and tiny nose shriveled. Another women approached me as well—younger and quite reluctant, although I recognized compassion in her gaze. I smiled at her, an expression that trembled with apprehension. She touched me on the forehead and uttered a single sound to the others—a sound neither hostile nor fearful—and they approached. Very slowly I unslung my pack and dropped it before me. Fruit and strips of cured meat fell upon the rock and they looked as if I had brought life itself. For indeed, I believe I had.

"They spoke in grunts, in mono-syllables, primitive sounds to my ears. But the children, unfettered by caution, lunged at the morsels of food that had fallen free, snatching up tiny fistfuls of fruit and nuts and bits of sun-dried meat. When I showed no sign of anger, the young woman who had touched my face smiled at me, and I began to cry. She put a hand on my shoulder and even though I found myself among a nascent and simple people, I realized I would no longer feel the sting of loneliness. I had found a new family. A new start. And I, I had nothing but time to heal."

"MANKIND MIGHT HAVE SURVIVED a near collision of planets," Reni said after a reflective pause, "but our collective innocence did not. Our ragged and largely inhospitable landscape had made life arduous. Hunger would reign for many lifetimes and we became scavengers, subsisting on meager provisions as we rooted for food during the daylight hours and huddled around insufficient fires at night. Although jungles and forest lands once again repopulated the earth, even the trees seemed vengeful now—thorns, oozing poisons and razor-edged bark proved hostile, their fruit scarce and bitter. Smaller animals had become far more skittish and evasive. Those larger animals that had once been no threat to man had become predators and would often raid the tribe to snatch an infant or unwary child. Sister Earth had grown harsh and uncooperative without Mu'at's love and blessings. And in return, her children had become resentful of their mother's demise."

"Humanity's fall from paradise," I said quietly.

"Aye. And for many millennia thereafter, various religions would promise its return."

"No one alive could remember the world as having been such a marvelous place," I reminded him.

"Quite right, none but myself. Only the fabled stories of our past prevailed, the myth of what once *might* have been. For countless generations, whispers propagated throughout all of mankind's survivors, spoken by mothers and fathers to sons and daughters, heralding a lost epoch that would one day be ours again, if only—" Reni frowned. "Ah, but nobody knew the key. Not even I. How does one return to the womb? Yet the ceaseless whispers continued to promise an end to our pain and suffering."

"Couldn't you have explained to these new generations? Did you not try?"

"Even as I grew to love these people—we were *Arth*, a word they could easily enough pronounce once they understood the concept of a sound to represent themselves—I understood our inherent differences. These gentlefolk had long ago grown fearful of their own rather harsh existence. They would recoil at any unexpected movement, dreading every quirk or sudden shift in life. A thunderstorm or the howl of a passing wolf would often petrify them, and they would shrink back into their dark caverns, refusing to confront an obstacle, a predator, a freak of nature—much to their own detriment. Several generations would pass before I was able to reach these people at any emotional depth, before I attempted to explain the truth of my reality. Yet even then I was met by derision and suspicion."

"They did not believe you?"

"Some did. Others did not. But Sister Earth's harsh new reality had unlocked many new characteristics in my fellow beings; jealousy and envy, scorn and belligerence—an illogical and often fatal hatred of themselves, of their neighbors, of their entire species. To my chagrin, those who *did* believe me could not cope. Tell a starving man that food was once rich and ripe for the taking—or explain to a freezing man that an endless heat had once radiated from the skies like a soothing blanket. I soon realized that my past, true or fabled, proved to be an unbearable torture for the Arth. And I could not fault them for their resentment. So eventually I fell silent."

I nodded, quite heartbroken.

"I believe," Reni said, "that during those many centuries or perhaps millennia that I lay in frozen slumber, the whispers of our lost utopia had become the obsession of an entire species. I suspect fireside tales became superstitions, which became myths, which became cults, which became religions—all founded on loss and lack, and upon our new-found fear of the unknown.

"But, of course, I eventually broke through their superstitions. By showing strength in the face of adversity, they likewise learned to endure. But teaching patience, I taught them to flint a fire or sew skins into a garment. Even so, my first few decades with the Arth proved frustrating. I could not teach the adults simple tools like the sling or the bow. They proved completely inept at hunting for their survival, although they were not without emotion or a yearning to understand. I mean no disrespect to the Arth, as these people represented the forebears of everything we've become—but I felt roughly akin to a college professor approaching a gaggle of wide-eyed kindergartners. Thus, it became far easier to lead, to point and command. Gone were those days when every single Tu'ulth was neither greater or less than another, and when earnest discussion, and every voiced opinion, was heard. Despite my love for these people—you must realize why I eventually began to search again for traces of my beloved Tu'ulth, as foolish as those journeys might now seem."

"Yes, I do understand," I replied, "for you could not forget what had been taken from you."

"Aye. In my own way, I was no less naïve than the Arth," he said. "I was seeking a past that did not exist for me either. The survival of Tu'ulth had become a figment of my own imagination. By assuming its continued endurance, I was creating my own mythology.

"My initial forays into the surrounding wastelands were very short. As I was the only hunter amongst this new tribe, they continued to teeter on the brink of starvation. They gathered berries and nuts, but they'd yet to identify a single poisonous plant or flower, even after a number of their brethren had perished from eating the same forbidden fruit. By my fourth or fifth generation among the Arth, we could wield a bow or axe with skill and dexterity—and, Good Lord, it was a start! And much later, when the great snows came, we were adequately clothed and healthy enough to flee south as a unified people, as we understood the direction of both ice and of heat. We remained one step ahead of what I can only fathom to have been a rather significant ice age, one that would linger for centuries, consuming much of the northern hemisphere.

"But as its frigid approach was gradual, we escaped its rage, laying the foundations of many new starts before being driven relentlessly south, time and time again.

"As a tribe, we'd also begun to retain knowledge—the awareness of building huts and pottery, of basic tools and uncomplicated words. We remained a simple and nomadic people, and such knowledge was handed down with great joy and appreciation to each generation. But as no home was permanent to us, we learned to live and to rely on very little. Time and time again, we fled ahead of the relentlessly creeping arctic chill.

"One day, after a trek of enormous endurance, we crested a peak and found ourselves staring into the depths of a deep and remarkable valley, a vast land of green forests and blue rivers. Even the clouds seemed unable to pass above the ragged mountain tops on which we stood, and sunlight flooded the world before us with warmth and bounty. We could see a multitude of birds fluttering like black clouds above the distant vista, and many of our people wept. I had never known a land of endless forests, and yet this is what presented itself here, as far as the eye could see. I wondered if this amazing place had somehow escaped damnation, unscathed here for all of eternity.

"Our entire tribe numbered no more than fifty or sixty by now, barely a third of those who had set out on this treacherous journey south. We eventually descended, past the lingering foothills and into the valley's embracing balm. I truly felt that I had again found paradise, and after a few weeks of scouting the terrain we settled near a sizable lake. For years we worried that we might again be driven from our home, but fate proved kind to us. The massive mountains to the north held the advancing chill in check, and so the Arth settled and prospered, generation after generation. The people gradually forgot the hardship and pain of our exodus, and the foundations of our community survived."

"A *new* paradise," I remarked happily.

Reni nodded. "The trees blossomed with many types of previously unknown, brightly colored and delightfully edible fruits. Our lake provided a bounty of plump fish. Wild game that resembled tiny deer roamed the forests in great droves. Strange and wondrous animals abounded—some of them dangerous, although the Arth no longer feared such beasts. Indeed, by now, we had become a tribe of relatively keen hunters. By now I had begun to wander and I soon discovered vast meadows to the south, shaded by groves of tall trees and where various herds would come to graze and populate. Several rivers ran east to west and, overhead, the yellow sun burned hot—I dare say nearly as hot as it does today, as the orb had grown gradually but increasingly in size and brightness since I'd awoken from my hibernation. I wondered if this new mother was coming to claim us; one who would be as kind and gentle as our old.

"And so I would soon come to know peace and joy again. For several lifetimes we lived amid the forests of *Lahm*, and we prospered. Cataclysms would occur of course—a distant volcano would spew lava, or the earth would now and then rumble beneath our feet. Sleet and ice would sometimes fall from the sky or an occasional meteor would strike nearby with a resounding thud. And yet no calamity struck with the ferocity of what had torn Mu'at from her children. We persevered. We eventually thrived, our little tribe soon numbering a hundred or more. We became cautiously human again.

"I would soon discover other small villages scattered throughout this new land, although the vastness of our valley provided a great deal of tribal isolation. And with such isolation came an innate distrust of strangers.

"Very few villages consented to my attempts at friendship, and I was often turned away with shouts and sharp stones. Yet I remained optimistic, or perhaps nostalgic, for

I continued in my attempts to invoke peace and harmony among my brothers. However, I was met with suspicion no matter where in the valley I chose to roam.

"Understand, too, that I use the word *valley* somewhat erroneously. Although mountains rose to great heights in the north, our new home lay amid so great a depression in the earth that its width and breadth appeared boundless. Even from the highest northern peaks, I'd been unable to glimpse distant pinnacles nor adjacent canyon walls to the east, south or west. Indeed, I suspect many decades would pass before I'd wandered sufficiently to discover a looming southern range. Beyond those ragged cliffs, a dense, steaming jungle loomed, a foreboding land we eventually named *Ta'ay Bah*—Hot Rain. Mosquitoes hovered in great numbers, thirsty and brutal, beasts as large as your hand. Spiders as big as a plump house cat. Snakes as large as—well, *very* large snakes. This was a foreboding land so impenetrable, so inhospitable that I attempted no lengthy journey there, but always turned back to my fruitful valley, so much of which I had yet to explore.

"During my frequent travels beyond our village, I'd found it necessary to appoint a leader in my stead, as my new tribe responded not to democratic discourse but to direct command. I would choose as wisely as I was able, many times over the next few hundred years—a woman or man who exuded great confidence and ability in maintaining our people's needs. Alas, I remember clearly only the last of these, a capable young fellow named Slut, who had—"

I could not help but smile. "*Slut*, you say?"

"Indeed, a word meaning *wise* in my ancient tongue. Slut had proven himself a strong hunter and a sensible, cautious sort. I had planned to be gone a long while, a solitary trip, my heading due east by so'east—a difficult trek, as the rivers in our valley typically ran south or west, and I had concentrated my previous journeys on those areas that seemed most hospitable. But my curiosity had gotten the better of me, and I found myself once again ready for the unknown."

"Adventure being the last opiate of the timeless," I surmised.

"Indeed," Reni replied with a warm smile. "I once again felt nestled in the bosom of Sister Earth, but alas, such respite was not to last forever. The endless opportunity for adventure may be a wondrous gift for an immortal—but change serves as an equally constant challenge, and one which never remains too long in slumber."

"THE INVADERS CAME and took my people shortly before my return from one such lengthy sojourn. I had been aware of dark, drifting smoke for the last mile or two of my homeward journey. Hastening, I soon found the village in smoldering ruins, utterly deserted. Several of our bowmen had been slain, as had many of the barbarians—all of whom had been stripped naked and left where they had fallen in battle. Poor Slut had been impaled, gutted and left hanging over the smoldering embers of a fire pit—"

"Good Lord," I said.

"—which I can only assume was retribution for his determined defense of the village. Until that moment I had been completely unaware of the existence of these marauders, despite my many previous wanderings through the valley. Nor could I extract important clues from the slain assailants. I acknowledged them to be powerfully built young men, their skin a dark copper—several shades darker than our own. I further noted that the invaders were adorned with many tattoos about their neck, shoulders, upper chest and back—fearful, demonic masks that glowered viciously outward in all directions. I'm sure that, in combat, such horrific markings might prompt an opponent to hesitate before striking, thus losing any hope of a tactical advantage.

"They were a shorter, stockier people than the Arth. Their hair color was similar—dark brown, but cropped short and coiled into tight, oiled ringlets. Those invaders who'd fallen had been pierced with multiple arrows before death had snatched them away from this existence.

"I soon discovered several blood trails at the edge of the village, no more than a day or two old, leading into the forest. I'd missed this tragedy by a matter of hours. Mad with rage and sorrow, I gathered what few remaining supplies I could find and, as nightfall remained several hours away, followed the trail eastward.

"They were easy to follow, for their great numbers could not be easily hidden, nor did they have any reason to fear retribution. These people were apex predators in a world of easy prey. For a long while they chose to follow a dry, meandering riverbed. I tracked them with haste, stopping for only brief snatches of sleep, until one evening I came upon these butchers. The raiding party had bivouacked in a flat meadow beside the dead river. I heard them long before I ever laid eyes on their camp, as they proved themselves a loud and boisterous lot. I would later learn that these people had long ago discovered the fermented grape, and that night they drank their fill. I secreted myself in the thick brush above them by hiding behind a jagged ridge line running parallel to the dead river.

"I stared down upon the barbarian camp with a great, frothing anger, noting the many campfires and numerous crude tents made from the pelts and skins of large animals. And their horses! I had never before seen a man mount such an animal—as this was not the creature I remembered from my past, small and skittish, but a large beast of magnificent, powerful bearing. It carried a man on its back as easily as

I might carry a rabbit in my hand. I watched in awe, confused and amazed.

"I could hear vague wisps of mischievous laughter from the warriors, a sound that eventually silenced as the night progressed, although even in their slumber I was forced to hold my position. Too many of their number remained alert in the darkness. I soon realized that this night would be lost to me.

"I crept cautiously back and forth along the ridge, continuing to search for weakness. I eventually realized that the raiders existed in numbers I did not comprehend—to this day, I assume I saw well over one hundred men—and easily triple that number of prisoners among them. They held not only captives from my village, but from others as well. The prisoners were not bound or chained, yet the males had been separated from the women and children. A masterful tactic, I realized, as I intuitively understood that the men would not dare chance an escape and jeopardize the safety of their families.

"I also realized that these people were not merely marauding warriors, but rather an army of *soldiers*, a word that did not yet exist in the era of Tu'ulth. These men did not merely wander together in large numbers; they moved with order and a unity of purpose as well. I marveled at their level of coordination—the way a single-celled organism might react upon encountering a complex, multi-cellular creature for the first time. Imagine our modern armies someday confronting an entirely robotic enemy moving in a precise, symbiotic unity, and you might understand my amazement that night.

"I could do nothing more but linger and wait for the sun's eventual rise, snatching snippets of sleep now and then. I followed their numbers over the next several days and, each night, I would look for some way to free my people. Yet their bright fires and perimeter guards discouraged any foray into their midst. Such was their cohesion night after night. Eventually, after a journey of many days, the invaders began to set a rear guard, likely as they approached their homeland.

"'Twas only through an innate sense of precaution that I avoided detection on several occasions, although my good fortune proved short-lived. Early one afternoon I found myself confronting a barbarian scout who'd secreted himself in a bushy thicket beside the trail. The man, smaller than I, his skin darkened with the inking of many tattoos, sprang from his lair, moving unlike any warrior I had before encountered. And yet I managed to parry his first blow—more luck than skill, I'll admit. The man was quick and agile, merciless in his resolve and fearless in combat. Despite the many small wounds he inflicted on me, eventually my axe cleaved his neck and he fell, mortally wounded.

"As had been the way of the Tu'ulth, I knelt beside this stranger, my enemy, my hand upon his shoulder so that he might not leave this world alone. I chanted the tale of Mu'at's love as life fled from his eyes, leaving only emptiness upon its retreat…"

Reni fell silent, and I watched his emotions wrestle with age-old memories. My husband began to chant in a half-whisper, no doubt the same words he uttered so many millennia before—sounds that inadvertently released a stream of tears down my cheeks. I lowered my gaze in respect and waited patiently for Reni to return.

"I knew," he said finally, exhaling a soft sigh, "that this man's death would not go unnoticed. Even in victory I felt a rush of trepidation. I assumed that others would come in search of their comrade. I will admit that I truly felt *fear* in the presence of these people. I considered the fate of poor Slut; and I realized how he must have suffered at their hands. Were I to be captured, I presumed that a similar death awaited me. A temporary experience perhaps, but the pain is nonetheless real."

"You had never before known such an evil," I offered, wiping my eyes.

"Quite true. Nor did I know what to make of their brutality. I'd not yet begun to fathom how much we humans had changed during our long journey through the darkness, or to what extremes we had learned to forge our own survival. The descendants of those who survived the apocalypse had become cunning, mistrustful and angry since our planet's abrupt orphanage. I can sit here now, pondering the endless eons of wars, the greed and avarice and fear that has saturated our species, and I believe our core essence—our very soul—had brutally changed on the day that our worlds collided. We had become uncivilized. We had discovered our capacity to behave barbarously toward one another, a trait that, as a species, I fear we have not yet dismissed.

"I took from the dead warrior those items I considered useful and, hoisting him over my shoulder, carried him deep into the forest. I found an area of soft soil and buried his body. A granite ridge rose nearby and provided a vantage point over the forest, so I climbed up and slipped into a crevice to wait.

"As dusk fell, several men appeared and surveyed the surrounding area with great concern. I observed their movements and watched them discover the unmistakable signs of our bloody struggle. Yet they remained unsure of their colleague's fate. Might he have fallen to an adversary, or had he become prey for a hungry animal? Taking no chances, they chose to linger in hiding, long after darkness fell. I made neither movement nor sound, remaining vigilant until the first signs of dawn. Yet, come morning light, I discovered that they had vanished.

"But where, I did not know. As I did not underestimate their cunning, I waited until the following day, and eventually yet another. These were a crafty people, and my singular advantage, as always, lay with the passage of time.

"On the third morning I set out once again to reclaim my people. I had grown progressively concerned for my tribe, and increasingly agitated by my inability to have formulated a method of rescue. Yet I had no other strategy but to follow their trail. *That*," Reni said with a timid smile, "was the extent of my guile.

"Eventually, the forest thinned, until I found myself standing upon the lip of a golden meadow. Far to the mountainous north, an extraordinary waterfall plunged for hundreds of feet, creating a great blue lake. A meandering river cut a swatch between the forest's edge and an immense, rolling plain upon which grew what I now suspect to have been wheat. Of course, I knew nothing of grain at the time; I saw little more than a tall, cumbersome grass that swayed in a passing breeze with hypnotic allure.

"In the distance I spotted a bridge spanning the river. I had seen many bridges before, yet I had never encountered one so formidable as this. Its decking had been constructed of split logs which lay flat upon a trestle of sturdy pilings. A wooden tower, built upon stilts, loomed at far end of the bridge, a confounding erection that rose some twenty or so feet above the ground. Upon this raised platform, beneath a roof of wicker and fronds, I could see three men. I had climbed countless trees in the past to survey my surroundings, and thus I could easily understand the purpose of this structure; although I marveled at the idea of creating an entire *tree* on four spindly legs. I had never considered such a radical concept before.

"These people," my husband said again with an arched eyebrow. "They were different than us. They were dangerous. The invaders were more knowledgeable than me, and that realization terrified me. Since I remained well hidden within the tree line, I felt at no immediate risk of being seen. I watched and waited and, as daylight waned, I decided to maintain my vigilance until darkness had fallen. Long ago I had learned to swim quite well among the Tu'ulth, to glide quietly through the waters, and so I moved downstream until the bridge was no longer visible. Under the sheen of our three moons, I crossed the river in silence, cutting a wide swath around those waiting for me in their manufactured trees.

"The next morning I wove my way through a sea of tall, endless grass that grew as high as my brow and provided excellent concealment. Eventually I stumbled once again upon the river, which had snaked due east. Yet my attention was immediately drawn to a new curiosity. Adjacent to the river's edge, the grasses had been cleared, the land purposefully flattened to benefit travelers—a road!—unlike any path I had ever before seen. This trail was not merely of hardened dirt, worn bare by countless steps, but rather a created surface tamped and deliberately inlaid and hard-packed with stones and sand. Even as I attempted to pluck free a pebble, I found that I could not do so. I marveled at its simplicity, flat and wide and quite pleasant beneath my feet. A traveler could move quickly along its surface without glancing for vines or thorns or the occasional python that often hampered one's pace.

"Another two days upon this glorious roadway led me through hill and vale, with the flowing river as my constant companion. Late into the second afternoon I found myself cresting a knoll that overlooked a vast, sloping meadow. In the distance, my eyes followed the meandering river until, near the horizon, the waters pooled to form an enormous lake. Rising from the still, blue waters, I observed a large island, and built upon the island stood a city of phenomenal size and complexity. A *city*," Reni repeated breathlessly. "I had never seen a city before this moment. The vision of such a sprawling metropolis left me dizzied and breathless, a discovery beyond all comprehension. From amid the multitude of structures, a large pyramid, black as night, rose high above all else. The top of the pyramid was not pointed, cap-stoned like many of those in the Mideast, but flat, more similar to the pyramid at Chichén Itzá, its uppermost platform cluttered with strange and curious objects.

"I could formulate no words, as I had no comprehension of *pyramid*—nor of half the sights that presented themselves to me. For the longest time I stood in the middle of the road and simply ogled that distant island in awe and wonder.

"Imagine such a place," Reni said with a quiet reverence, his voice resonating with a memory that had lingered throughout the ages. "I speak not of an island as Tu'ulth had been, a swatch of land that one might easily traverse in a matter of minutes—but rather an isolated dominion that contained the equivalent of fifty or even a hundred villages. Not only were the structures too numerous to count, but they completely filled the island, verging against the very edge of the surrounding waters, as if every morsel of the island had been snatched from nature. I could see several bridges crossing the lake at various points; great wooden spans of the same impressive bearing as I had glimpsed earlier from the forest's edge.

"I eventually found it prudent to once again conceal myself among the tall grasses, where I might continue to study the city in relative safety. As night fell, I detected many dozens of small fires being struck, their collective, hypnotic glow casting a reddish radiance that pulsed with its own living heartbeat. I neither ate nor slept that night, as the city—which I would soon come to know as *Crüz*—lay like a brightly lit ruby beneath our three distant moons."

My husband's words thrilled me. Reni had never before offered any specific location in the primitive world, and yet I could only infer the island-city to be an unknown predecessor of the Pharaoh's Egypt, and the river undoubtedly the budding Nile. Although flowing *east*? I pondered this strange notion. And my brain still throbbed at the thought of Earth's three moons overhead, as Luta'u and little La'u'ata had continued to accompany their big sister across the cosmos. Despite my many questions, I forbade myself to utter a sound, content to trust my Captain to divulge each facet of his story in its own time. And yet how frustratingly slow his words seemed to come that evening.

"I had but two choices," Reni continued, "to move forward toward inevitable capture or else return alone to my abandoned village. Peering at this island fortress, I had little doubt of my failure should I attempt to liberate my people. I held as likely a chance of success as might an angry lemming confronting a pride of lions. But how could I turn away from such a wondrous city? How could I live without knowing more?

"I anxiously awaited dawn, all the while contemplating how best to make my initial approach. As the sun crested the distant hills, I was struck with a sudden inspiration. The warrior I had slain in combat shared similar features with me. A smaller man, but only by inches. The rear guards I'd observed had worn skins similar as my own, although each had tied a woven band of rope around their left bicep, stained with the color of many berries—significant markings, I assumed, although I knew naught of their purpose.

"I had taken the dead warrior's armband, his spear and also his knife, whose blade had been shaped from hammered metal. The biggest differences between us remained the tattoos inked across his shoulders and back, and the shortness of his well-oiled hair. To a man, I'd seen these marauders uniformly shorn. Using the edge of his knife, I set about cutting the long, tangled strands of my own hair that hung to my shoulders. A challenging and painful process, I must say. Yet when I was finished, I realized my cleanly shorn scalp granted me a far greater ability to see peripheral movement. A distinct advantage in combat, I realized.

"I had neither the knowledge nor ability to tattoo my own body, although I withdrew two handfuls of dark river mud from the water's edge and lathered my shoulders, neck and chest. From a distance, I hoped that such stains might resemble such intricate markings.

"And so equipped, I pressed forward with great trepidation. As I edged closer through the sloping meadows, I observed many people working in close quarters—some using spears to systematically pierce the earth, with others on their knees and tending closely to several bare swatches of land. Confounding behavior, to say the least.

"That was my first introduction to agriculture, of course. Although watching from afar, the commotion seemed such an illogical waste of effort. I knew nothing of seeding or of harvesting, although I would have my first taste of unleavened bread quite soon. And what an exquisite pleasure it would be! But at that moment I was simply confused by those toiling in the fields. Many appeared barefoot and naked, save for a short pelt around the waist. Others wore skins wrapped around their knees and still others about their shoulders. As I've mentioned, nudity was not uncommon, so I assumed these garments were somehow necessary for their labors. Indeed, I became aware of several people carrying wooden yokes on their shoulders or strewing seeds from waist pouches, and I began to sense an orderly pattern underlying their labors.

"All too soon, the bridge and adjacent guard tower loomed before me; fifty paces, then thirty, then barely a dozen steps remaining. The structure was similar to that which I had confronted from the edge of the forest several days before—a simple platform tower atop four sturdy wooden legs. A knotted rope provided access from below. A flat roof provided shade, while the split log sides provided protection from the slings and arrows of approaching adversaries—although the very idea of attacking a city of such magnitude seemed preposterous to me. Perhaps the tower had been erected to *prevent* escape? If so, my entrance to the city might well proceed without incident.

"A trio of guardsmen stood leisurely atop the platform, and one by one their heads turned to heed my arrival. I hadn't the slightest of notions as to the consequence of my actions once I reached the bridge. As I said, I hoped that my casual gait, my armband, and my newly shorn scalp would allow for my crossing without challenge. However, I had discreetly slipped several small stones into my hand, and my sling remained within easy reach. I had no plan beyond that.

"One of the guardsmen lifted an arm—in greeting, I presumed, although I noticed a short bow firmly in his grasp. His arm lingered above his head and I deduced that he might be waiting for some specific reaction from me. I could think of no other gesture but to raise my arm in return, holding the dead man's spear likewise above my head.

"The guards regarded each other with some confusion. The fellow with a bow withdrew an arrow from his quiver and notched the weapon. Another leaned forward and called to me in an exotic tongue."

Reni paused, frowning. For the longest time, he lingered in a wordless stupor, as if listening to the distant ocean's hypnotic murmur.

"Darling?" I asked at length, as I had never before witnessed such uncertain silence.

He offered me a curious look and said, "And I? I *understood* his words."

"Oh?"

"Not fluently—but he had spoken in words eerily similar to my long-dead tongue."

"Of Tu'ulth?" I remarked.

"Aye," he said. "Tu'ulth and yet *not* Tu'ulth. Imagine hearing medieval English as Shakespeare might have spoken. Coherent and yet somehow foreign. I stared at the three guards as would a simpleton. But as I made no aggressive movements, the bowman repeated his salutation. Something, I recall, about the river's perimeter and whether or not I belonged betwixt the gonads of a wild boar!

"Scarcely able to think straight, I nonetheless believed it best to respond, my own words comprehended or not." Reni shrugged. "I called to the guards that I had overslept. Words to that effect, as oversleeping is a relatively modern term. Rather, that sleep had not easily released me from its clutches. And then I waited.

"I could see a mask of confusion cross their collective brows. I lowered my arm and once again moved forward. I half expected the bowman to draw back his weapon, but he did not. They continued to warily observe my progress as I crossed the bridge.

"Once again upon solid ground, I could do nothing but stand in a stupor, trembling, hearing words and voices around me and contemplating their enormous significance. Might the Tu'ulth have once lived among these people? As captives or warriors? I could make not one whit of sense of my situation."

Only because my husband's gaze so fervently searched my face did I allow myself to speak. "Could you not believe that *this* is what the Tu'ulth had become?"

"A race of barbarians? Of slavers? No, that was not possible. These people shared none of the peaceful demeanor, nor the open friendliness the Tu'ulth exhibited to one and all. Not from that moment to this could I ever accept such a possibility."

Gently, I said, "Have you *no* idea how long you'd spent in your frozen slumber?"

"I have so often pondered that very question. How could my body have lain in stasis for a year, or a dozen years or even a hundred? Such a reality seems utterly absurd. And yet, a simple logic prevails: If one can remain frozen for a day, then why not a year? If a year, then why not a hundred years? And if a hundred, why not a thousand or ten thousand, or a hundred thousand? I simply have no clue as to the duration of my hibernation."

"Certainly time enough," I cautioned, "for the world to have changed so dramatically around you. You cannot know what events transpired while you slept. Nor can you blame yourself for what your people might have become in those unknown generations since your last council."

He remained adamant. "No, I'm sorry. This is simply not how the Tu'ulth could have evolved."

"But why?" I pressed.

"Because my people could not have become *savages*," he replied sharply.

In all my years of loving Reni, I had never known a harsh word to leave his mouth. I winced, although I did not take his anger to heart, for my husband's frustration had not been directed at me, but rather toward an incomprehensible mystery from his past. I was merely a conduit for the questions that had haunted him too long.

And yet, horrified by his own reaction, my Captain reached for my hand. In perfect Mandarin, he said, "I apologize for my ill temper."

I smiled with all the gentility I could muster. *Oh, but how I loved his man.* "None is necessary, I promise you. I share your frustrations! I'm certain there must be an explanation. You said that you did not fully recognize the language. That is encouraging."

"Indeed. Many of the words I overheard were foreign to me. Others sounded similar—but of course, standing fully upon the edge of Crüz for the first time, my head pounding, I could barely sort through my confusion."

"Then tell me more," I pressed in earnest.

Reni closed his eyes and once again summoned his memories. "I pivoted at the water's edge, a slow pirouette, taking stock of my surroundings. Upon the sloping shoreline rested many wooden canoes, little more than hollowed logs. A multitude of small fish hung on poles or lay in hemp nets, drying beneath the hot afternoon sun. Scores of naked children stood knee deep in the lake, holding sharpened sticks, ready to thrust these spindly spears at some passing morsel. Such was the fertility of those waters that fish abounded in quantity to feed a city of such size! Within a dozen steps from the gently lapping lake front, mud and clay huts proliferated, much like they do today upon many shores.

"I suppose even ancient man knew the value of location, and on Crüz," he said, "the waterfront represented both food source and sunlight. Yet many structures were so tightly pressed together at the shoreline that walls had fused together—the world's first condominiums, perhaps. Many of these huts possessed funnel-shaped rooftops that emitted plumes of smoke, accompanied by the aroma of burnt wood and roasting fish. I glimpsed inside several huts and saw men and women sitting cross-legged upon woven mats, gutting fish or weaving hemp nets, cooking fish stew and freshwater blue crabs atop small clay ovens.

"I became aware of several narrow, dirt-packed streets fanning away from the bridge. Each of these avenues were crowded with huts, cramped plazas, and small corrals filled with braying goats, or else crammed with pigs, rabbits and foxes. I stood and gawked, taking in the many confounding sights and sounds. The people who passed me, even in close proximity, did not regard me with either fear or suspicion. A stooped man with a stick, herding a flock of geese toward the lake, wandered by as if I were nothing more intriguing than an old tree stump. Encouraging.

"As I continued to scan the island, my eyes again swept over the bridge tower and, to my dismay, I perceived that the bridge guards had continued to observe me from their perch. I'd lingered for no more than a minute or two, but I now thought it prudent to move along, to bury myself amid the throb and bustle of the city.

"I must note another curious discovery as I began to wander inland. At some point I became aware of a wall girdling the innermost part of the island—an extensive barrier fashioned of mud and brick and stone. The wall stood no more than twenty or so feet high and yet dwarfed by the massive pyramid it enclosed. I would soon discover that the wall completely encircled the structure, with only a single, gated entrance providing access within. Quite soon I would learn the name of this inner sanctum: *Savo Crüz Savo.*

"So much of Crüz lay before me, inviting and, indeed, breathtaking, that I did not immediately feel any great curiosity to explore what might lay behind the wall. Truth be told, the pyramid's size frightened and confounded me, so I remained content to roam about the city streets and collect my thoughts.

Reni took a deep sip of brandy. "Once I realized that

I was able to move comfortably about the city unchallenged, my attention returned to rescuing my people. But how to locate the Arth? With no plan or precise destination in mind, I meandered about the dusty streets for the remainder of that day, lost in the mud and stone labyrinth that was Crüz. I listened to scatterings of conversation and marveled at the many simple advances previously unknown to me: the potter's wheel, the hand loom, and the humble wooden bucket—much sturdier, yet far lighter than the clay pots of my youth. I also glimpsed exotic new tools and weapons that appeared to have been crafted with hammered copper or cast in bronze. I gradually began to comprehend some of the more complex conversation and, by evening's approach, I no longer felt like a total stranger. As darkness fell, I saw flames sputter from many hollow stones. I knew nothing of lamps or lamp oil, but recognized that the Crüzians had indeed found a marvelous way to hold back the night."

"Why do our libraries not hold evidence of such early progress?" I wondered aloud.

"Our books only acknowledge the past that we know. Should we someday stumble upon the bones of Crüz, I believe we'd excavate a city whose influence rivaled that of Mesopotamia, Babylonia, or even the Old Kingdom of Egypt."

"But no such evidence has been found," I said with a huff of dismay.

"Aye, none."

"And yet you've hinted that Crüz existed many millennia before the reign of the pharaohs. It's difficult to believe the ancients had progressed so remarkably."

"Then prepare yourself, my love," he said with a gentle laugh.

I nodded fervently and beckoned him to continue.

"Later that night, I managed to catch a partial night's

sleep in the warm straw of a corral, my presence an annoyance to a number of sheep. At sunup, I once again took to the streets. I had very little food left, only a small number of berries and yellowing mint leaves, so by midday I had grown quite hungry. I continued to wander, drawn by the afternoon's cacophony of sounds and a breeze that carried the tantalizing aromas of cooking foods. Before long I came upon a deli and—"

"A deli?"

"Indeed, of a sort. A street vendor. The man, wearing nothing but a loin pelt and a *sa'utche*—a rodent's skin covering his balding scalp—sat cross-legged behind a small fire pit. Inches above the small flame, I spied a half-dozen measly game birds and several pats of bread. I stood there wondering what I might barter for a morsel. Yet as I eyed his offerings, I immediately became aware of the fellow's unpleasant expression. The man glanced repeatedly at my armband and finally pushed a single grain patty at me with a clucking sound, a dismissive hand gesture that I immediately understood."

"The policeman on the corner, eyeing a grocer's shiny apples," I presumed.

"Yes, precisely. The man did not understand my intention of making a fair trade, although apparently a soldier's life offered certain privileges. I did not quibble, but instead strode away with my prize—nothing more than a palm-sized wafer of bread, half blackened by heat, smelling of ash and still quite warm. And yet I held in my hand a wholly unknown foodstuff! *Bread!* I sniffed, most curious—and salivated, although I still had no idea what I grasped. I took a bite and to this day I remember the taste and texture. 'Twas a bit like chewing leather…although the morsel hinted of rosemary and other herbs and its taste immediately delighted my mouth.

"Sufficiently satiated, I began to roam once again, my gaze increasingly drawn to the massive pyramid whose broad base remained largely hidden behind the stone and mud-patched wall. The wall surrounding the entrance was fortified with mortared stone—mortar being another baffling novelty to me—and the gate itself constructed of heavy logs lashed together and further strengthened by bands of roughly forged copper. Soldiers stood on either side of the gate, suspiciously eyeing any who approached.

"But Crüz was a busy place, and I could not linger long without attracting the wary eye of the guards. People did not linger idly in the streets but moved with an air of necessity and intent. I'd begun to comprehend that this was a city not yet complete as I'd already seen much under construction, both within the island fortress and along the outer banks of the river as well. To gawk was to invite suspicion, and so I shuffled past with some supposed purpose, back and forth, back and forth, several times that day.

"Only once did I observe the gate lowered to the ground, and from within! Hoisted by a sturdy rope-and-pulley system—another feat of *magick*—I found myself awestruck by such a mechanical miracle. Despite my fascination, I decided to bide my time.

"By happenstance, on the afternoon of the following day, I did find a way into Savo Crüz Savo. The shrill howl of a ram's horn announced an event of some importance and, ever observant, I watched as a procession of servants and mules approached through the street—some thirty or so workers—carrying large wicker baskets of rice and grain and other supplies. Two armed soldiers led the way while several others brought up the rear of the column. With only a heartbeat of hesitation, I nevertheless stepped into line behind the last of them, hoping that my colorful armband would provide me with the price of admission."

Reni smiled. "And for about two minutes, the ruse worked. I found myself wandering amid a sparse collection of ornate dwellings, nestled within an oasis of palm and date trees that flourished amid a number of small ponds. This place seemed a man-made paradise designed to please the eye and tickle the senses. I suspect the inner city covered perhaps a dozen acres, with the pyramid's base consuming perhaps half of that space.

"As I believe I've mentioned, the structure was like that of Sakkara, or the Mayan pyramid in Chichen Itza—its four sides not smoothly sloped but squared at intervals, a series of smaller blocks placed increasingly higher upon larger blocks beneath. The stone was unlike any I'd before seen, a glistening, black marble. A wide, centralized stairway—not of stone but of ornately carved wood—rose from the base of the pyramid to the top. The pyramid rose perhaps two hundred feet above me, the tallest structure I'd ever encountered. Several squat, rectangular buildings clustered around its base—as did a covered courtyard supported by numerous stone columns—a bazaar of some pedigree—that bustled with the ebb and flow of many Crüzians wearing colorful, flowing robes; either bartering their wares or buying goods.

"The few shaded streets I glimpsed were constructed of brick pavers, as were numerous pedestrian walkways. Arched bridges crossed stone channels flowing with water, evidently piped beneath the outer city from the surrounding river. I must mention that the dwellings within these walls were not those same tiny, muddy, thatched-roof lodgings I'd seen outside the wall. These were larger structures, with wooden framed doorways. The external walls were decorated with cut tiles formed from sun-dried bricks and dyed in various hues, colors that blended together in what I can only describe as dizzying patterns of artistic beauty—earthen reds

401

bleeding into a dusky violet, and dark, rich purples melding into deep blues. Yellows to ochers. I found such potpourri of hues and colors utterly entrancing, as I had never before known the concept of *design*. Even my beloved Tu'ulth knew nothing of such kaleidoscopic beauty.

"Although such extravagance seemed quite foreign to me, I instinctively recognized an exclusivity here—a state of privilege, given the cramped and pedestrian functionality of the outer city. I did not know the meaning of this social disparity, but I was not blind to the experience of spaciousness in contrast to confinement, of abundance in contrast to squalor. Those Crüzians who lived within this inner sanctum wore woven cloth—not coarse-weave pelts or animal skin, but fine flowing garments. These people were clearly more important than those beyond the wall, another concept whose logic I could not grasp.

"I had no comprehension of the social strata that cities—or at least *this* city—had developed to classify its own inhabitants. So complicated was this arrangement, so governed and espoused, that Crüzians identified each other by the colors of their cloth and ornamentation. Inside the walls one did not necessarily wear armbands, but rather necklaces or thin, bejeweled headbands to announce one's established rank. I would eventually come to recognize the various social classes within Crüz. Too quickly I realized that men of self-proclaimed power could rule and enslave those of less fortune or of perceived inferiority, whether a result of birth or mandate."

My husband smiled. "Ah, but such cultural pondering would come gradually, over the course of many, many weeks. In that moment, however, I felt little else but unabashed amazement. Unfortunately, my presence had not gone unnoticed. Several soldiers had taken a wary stance behind me. I was not aware of them until one, a large man, his armband significantly more colorful than my own, stepped forward to confront my backside with a rude poke with the tip of his spear. He spoke gruffly, and only half the words did I comprehend.

"I had no recourse but to mutter that I considered myself without a known direction, as *being lost* was not yet a notion. Hearing my words, the soldiers stared in what I could only describe as a startled silence. I'm not sure what might have transpired next had not another man in dark robes, and who by happenstance had witnessed the confrontation, intervened with a frenetic, keen interest.

"'*You, there! You!*' he screeched. I turned to see a rather elderly fellow, stooped and thin and hairless, and also quite angry. He approached with rickety haste, the soldiers lowering their gazes in subservience and allowing him ample room. Without warning he began to slap me vigorously across the face. 'You are not allowed! You are not *allowed!*' he scolded, his teeth worn and yellowed.

"The old man continued to strike me, his frail pummeling little more than a curious annoyance. 'I mean no harm. I am...a traveler,' I told him. *Ta ra'u tu ra'u.* How odd, but I remember the exact phrase—*Ta ra'u tu ra'u*—I walk many many," Reni recalled with a soft chuckle. "*Many* many being so greater a distance than many.

"Yet the man did not cease striking me, as my words seemed to infuriate him even more. I could not know that he was a temple priest—one of only eight such elders—since I had as little knowledge of priests or pseudo-religions as I did of class structure in those days. The man striking me was not a priest like we are familiar with today, but rather more of a jack-of-all-superstitions; part holy man, part magician, part alchemist, part astrologist, an herbalist, sage and fortune teller. After a final rain of blows, his chest heaving in exhaustion, he suddenly perceived that I was not Crüzian. He blinked several times, examining me as if only now aware of my subtle physical dissimilarity, touching my hair and the remnants of dried mud clinging to my shoulders. He tugged rudely at my armband, as if to question how I had come upon the piece.

"'I killed a man in combat,' I explained, as I had no knowledge of deceit in those early millennia, not even in so precarious a situation. 'And took what was his as my own.'

"Clucking irritably, the man reached up and pushed his fingers against my lips as if to stifle any further words. He grabbed my arm and pulled, pointing furiously toward the base of the pyramid, my assumption being that I was to accompany him. Still unaware of my crime, but sensing no real alternative, I grunted my agreement. With the soldiers closely flanking us, I fell into step behind the old man."

Reni paused for a sip of cognac and offered me a diffident smile. "And that is how I entered *Zhahrat*, a word which I would soon learn meant *holy place*—although I'm not certain if *holy* is the correct context. Sacred, perhaps. Exclusive, most definitely."

"And your crime, my love?"

"I assumed that my sin had been slaying one of their own. The man I had killed in battle had been a scout, a common foot soldier, and why the armband I wore did not merit my access to the inner city. In fact, the soldiers who surrounded me were known as *koru*, the Crüzian version of private security. An elitist guard. Neither my pilfered armband nor I belonged here among the illuminati."

"Another serious offense, I imagine."

"Oh, yes—quite so. Undoubtedly retribution would have been harsh and swift, had not my tongue completely baffled the old priest. One did not anger the temple priests, as they ranked only beneath *Tra*, the godking of Crüz."

"Tra," I repeated, rolling the name against my tongue.

"The old priest—whose name, as I recall, was Murah-kindra—served as a liaison between Tra and the people of Crüz. He and his seven brethren doted upon Tra as groveling acolytes. None other in the realm was permitted to gaze upon the godking, as that was a crime punishable by death."

"How silly," I remarked in haste, although I knew better and bit my tongue. I was well aware that many ancient rituals and taboos, no matter how absurd they might appear in current society, had guided and controlled humanity for thousands of years.

"Very few of us over time have not become addicted to our own beliefs," Reni remarked.

"I stand corrected," I admitted, aptly chastised.

"It was only on Murahkindra's whim that I found myself *inside* the pyramid. A dark, dank place indeed, uncomfortably humid and filled with numerous odors I found most foul; a combination of burnt sage and rotting meat. I was taken to large room, a sort of amphitheater, as I recall, alight from the glow of countless candles. The holy men, seated in a darkened half-circle around me, interrogated me for many hours."

"Interrogated?"

"A trial of sorts, I suspect. The language I spoke—the purity of my words and not the mutated, diluted dialect of the common Crüzian—was strictly forbidden except by the priests themselves and, even then, spoken only in prayer. Many of the words that spilled from my lips were completely unknown to those beyond the inner sanctum—*sacred* words, apparently. It was as if an uneducated peasant had suddenly begun speaking Classical Latin to a medieval pope. For the next several weeks, my interrogation became a daily regimen."

"And the language of Crüz?" I asked. "Did you ever discover its connection to Tu'ulth?"

405

"Not to this day," he admitted. "Nor could I offer any rational explanation to the priests. I thought it best not to divulge my endless string of lives to Murahkindra, as I had soon begun to suspect the Crüzians to be mistrustful and superstitious people. I could only divulge to them that I had learned the language in a small village, long ago and far away. Which was the truth, of course.

"I would spend many weeks, perhaps months, inside the belly of that monstrous building, although I remember little else of my time there." Reni paused and cocked his head slightly to one side. "When I was not speaking before the priests, Murahkindra kept me in a small square room without windows, lit from within by—well, by a faint glow that emanated from God knows where. I believe now that I was intoxicated much of time—*drugged* I suspect, as I remember being forced to drink a rather loathsome elixir on those mornings when I would be interrogated by the priests.

"Granted, despite my confinement inside Zhahrat, I did not find my fate a cruel one—I dined on ample food, my bedding soft. As the weeks passed, my interrogations shifted into less hostile dialogue. My mind gradually cleared. I believe the holy men understood that I shared their bewilderment and that my purpose in Crüz was not malicious—although I had not mentioned the Arth, as I continued to fear for my tribe's safety. I maintained that I was merely a wanderer, drawn to both the beauty and complexity of Crüz. Despite their earlier misgivings, my story did not waver. I think, in time, I simply wore them down.

"I was eventually permitted limited freedom to move about Savo Crüz Savo—but only within the inner walls, for the priests still did not trust me nor my tongue among the common people. And yet sometimes the smallest liberties are those most appreciated," Reni said.

"Did you never discover the fate of your beloved Arth?"

I wondered.

"All in good time, my love. Understand that I was allowed to roam the inner city provided I not speak under any circumstances. Perhaps only a hundred or so of Crüz's pampered elite lived within this sacred, inner sanctum, and most of them would avert their eyes or turn away when I approached. So I would often sit for hours, under a tree or out of sight, taking every opportunity to further decipher their language. I was not above the fine art of eavesdropping, you see.

"I must share here that the vast majority of the city's populace never set foot inside the inner city, not in an entire lifetime. Even those who brought food or supplies inside the walls were considered *mosh mo'aba*—the chosen of the chosen.

"By happenstance one day, while strolling beneath the midday sun—which the Crüzians had named *Khalam*— I recognized a young woman of Arth carrying a basket of clothing atop her head. I followed her to one of the small channels that flowed through the inner city—to a place where the water pooled and wide steps permitted access for bathing and washing. I called out her name, which was either E'eko or E'oki, as I recall. She turned and gasped, and for a moment we hugged each other tightly. I began to speak to her in our language, but she immediately put a finger to my lips and told me in halting Crüzian that none but the tongue of their captors was permitted. 'We are not allowed,' she explained, searching for words, 'our old voices.' She glanced around quite nervously, and only after assuring herself that we could not be overheard, we continued to speak, this time whispering in Arth.

"I anxiously asked E'oki about her family—about her husband and two small sons. She told me that her family had fared well, although others taken from our village had been separated and disbursed across the island. Still others had been integrated into neighboring villages as yet unknown to me, since apparently several Crüzian settlements lined the riverbanks farther eastward. Many of Arth's younger males had been sent to work the mines, she said. The mountains that rose downstream were laden with many essential resources; copper and silver, lime and salt. The thought of my people suffering underground immediately rekindled my initial hatred of this place, and I vowed to both myself and to E'oki to abet their escape.

"The poor woman gripped my arm tightly and shook her head. 'You must not! That we are slaves of this city, yes," E'oki told me, "but after five harvests spent in servitude, we will be allowed many liberties as minions of Crüz, and our children, and our children's children, will be born as citizens. It is for their benefit that we stay and toil, so that our sons and daughters will reap what we sow. To flee now and be caught—we would become sacrificial.'

"Harvest? Citizen? Servitude? I did not comprehend much of what she told me," Reni said. "Nor did I understand this word 'sacrificial.'

"'Every fifteenth day," E'oki said, "as Khalam descends into the forest, a priest offers three sacrificials to honor Tra's presence. The throat is opened, and the lifeblood is drained into a sacred vessel upon the alter of Zhahrat, as tribute.

"I was dumbfounded," Reni admitted. "I had only begun to comprehend the concept of slave and freeman and citizen, but now I was asked to understand death to appease...what? A king's ego? What sort of ruler would feast on the blood of his own people? I could not make sense of this. I will admit that during my entire stay in Crüz, I did not witness this ritualistic slaughter—but I did not doubt E'oki for an instant. The fear in her gaze was proof enough."

"So much had transpired during those eons you slept," I reminded him.

"Aye, and Crüz would prove to be a precursor of this modern world—a city so advanced, and yet conversely so primitive, as to lose its own sense of humanity! I feared that we had changed since our abduction from Mu'at's embrace. Our collective psyche had sunk to such depths of self-aggrandizement and depravity, with such self-loathing and despair, that I no longer knew the nature of my own species.

"And yet I could not deny that Crüz was unlike any place I had ever known. I lusted for all I could learn about this city. I would eventually discover a pervasive rule of law, a knowledge of philosophy and science that proliferated among the elite. I can't help but wonder if some within our midst were among the most educated men to have ever walked ancient Earth. Crüz's engineers and mathematicians had already cracked many secrets of algebra and geometry, and even certain complexities of astronomy. But how could that wisdom possibly coexist with such abhorrent barbarism? I could not fathom the dichotomy.

"Beyond our inner sanctum, however, the common Crüzian knew little but endless toil. They spent their days as miners or stonecutters, shepherds, farmers or carpenters. They remained largely uneducated, taught only a mythology steeped in fear—stories that no doubt guaranteed humble obedience. From E'oki, I learned that Tra had fallen from the heavens in a ball of fire, and within the framework of his fierce authority lay the blueprint for our species' eventual redemption—Tra's promise of our return to paradise."

"A common belief within many ancient religions," I offered.

"But there's more. Because Tra was not alone in the sky. The peasants of Crüz were assured that countless other deities lived among the embers that blazed in the night sky.

Beyond the inner walls, the people knew nothing of *stars*, of course. Nor did I, for that matter. But even the smallest child in Crüz understood that, if angered, any number of gods might descend upon them to take swift retribution. You can imagine the terror generated by the occasional meteor shower."

"I can indeed," I remarked, well aware that the Old Testament had its own tales of chariots of heavenly fire.

"And through such cursed fables did the average Crüzian remain enslaved to a single, ostensibly infallible master. They worked tirelessly and in complete subjugation—for no one wished to incur the wrath of a godking."

Reni paused, his expression pensive. "I often wish my primitive brain had been able to fully comprehend what lay before me. I'm afraid that the complexities of the city, and of its ruler, overwhelmed me. I believed E'oki, you see. How could I not? Tra had built a city unlike anything I had ever known. How could I doubt his divinity?"

"Then tell me more about this—this Crüzian ruler," I pressed sharply, my brow furrowed, my hackles up.

Reni smiled, aware of my sudden irritation. "'Tis only recently that I've come to appreciate the truth behind Tra's perplexing wisdom. However, I must warn you that from this moment forward, my story becomes somewhat...extraordinary."

"Oh?" I blurted, for I could not fathom any words more astounding than those my husband had already shared this night. "Please, yes, continue to astound me. Although permit me one impertinent question first? You obviously remained in Crüz for some time. Did you never attempt to escape?"

"Ah!" Reni's eyes blazed. "But I *did* escape—and no more than a month or so after I'd met E'oki. But I must reveal the precise sequence of events if you are to appreciate the magnitude of what would shortly occur. For Tra himself plays a significant role in this matter."

I nodded with a fierce and hungry curiosity.

"As I've said, by now old Murahkindra and the other priests had more or less given up on me, having grown weary of my repetitive answers to their relentless questions. I'm quite certain they considered me some sort of confused demigod. I've often wondered if Tra had ordered my survival for reasons I cannot comprehend. But I certainly had become a most privileged of unwelcomed guests. And until Murahkindra might determine a more suitable fate for me, Savo Crüz Savo remained my home. A most fascinating place—yet in reality, little more than a lavish prison.

"My one salvation during this time was of course E'oki, the *mosh mo'aba* from my village who passed through the inner city every few days to clean and mend the garments of the privileged few. Whenever we chanced to meet—sometimes quite briefly—she would attempt to answer my questions and I would attempt to answer hers. She became my solitary friend in Crüz and I still occasionally find myself fondly evoking her memory.

"It wasn't long before Murahkindra suspected that I had adequately mastered the tongue of the common Crüzian. But since I had caused no mischief nor attempted to escape, he decided to make me useful. He conscripted me among the engineers and architects as a *karita*, an assistant of sorts, a semi-intelligent lackey, fetching fat bladders of ale or water, passing messages and, as often as not, carrying an array of parchments and compasses and the ever useful *mo'ank*—an ancient precursor of the slide rule, although a more accurate translation would be *cubit rod*—in wicker sacks across my shoulders. Crüz was a city still very much under construction, you see—and the top of Zhahrat proved a common destination for a plethora of engineers. I would hustle up and down the steps of the pyramid many times each day," Reni said. "Realize that Khufu's Great Pyramid rises some five hundred vertical feet. Tra's Zhahrat rose less than half that height—but still, not an easy climb while laden with the engineers' various needs.

"I should tell you that, by design, the pyramid remained absolutely flat at the top, a polished platform spanning some forty by forty feet. The area was often cluttered with wooden tables strewn with the paraphernalia, charts and tools. I should also mention the presence of a curious vertical channel that extended down through the center of the building. A small, square tunnel, little more than a foot in diameter."

"What in heavens for?" I wondered.

Reni lifted a patient finger. "Oh, but there is yet one more secret I must reveal."

"I believe I shall have another brandy then," I told him, exasperated, reaching for the decanter.

"I must backpedal several weeks, to my first day of freedom beyond the inky chambers of Zhahrat. As soon as Murahkindra had permitted my release from the bowels of the pyramid, I gratefully stepped into the first warmth of sunlight I'd felt in a long while. Almost immediately, however, a cloud passed overhead, its shadow startling, and I peered upward. Floating above Zhahrat I observed a hot air balloon, a crude airship that carried several men in a lower bask—"

"*Wo tīng bù dong!*" I cried.

Reni lifted a hand, as if pledging a solemn truth. "Yes, I swear—a *flying* machine. I could not comprehend what I saw, of course, although I would eventually see it aloft many times, hovering like a bird of prey above the pyramid, filled with architects and engineers. And yet that first sighting filled me with a most spectacular dread. I felt all sense of rationality flee and actually dropped to my knees in agony.

I must have appeared quite the bumpkin, my jaw slack, my eyes cast to the heavens and—"

"Wait! You've admitted this city to be Neolithic, predating Egypt's Early Kingdom by several millennia. If so, then Crüz preceded the ancient Mesolithic cultures of China's Nanzhuangtou, of Mesopotamia and Early Assyria."

"Or more likely they rose simultaneously," my husband replied. "And I do have my reasons for believing so."

"But how could such knowledge have been possible?"

"Obviously, it *was* possible. I observed a balloon—our *pav*, the Crüzian word for *bird*. And undoubtedly built with Tra's guidance," Reni said. "As I've mentioned, I believe the godking's knowledge to have been unprecedented. I suspect Tra related the principles of buoyancy to the engineers, and likely oversaw pav's construction. Crüz's balloon was by no means some trivial, archaic contraption. The airbag had been fashioned of a finely woven material, cotton or silk I suspect, the color of wet sand. It was not spherical, as is the familiar design today, but rather an inverted pyramid, with bamboo poles connecting a topmost, triangular frame. An inner bladder had been stitched together, utilizing great quantities of sheep or goat's intestine, stretched thin and rubbed with some sort of dark, sweet resin that I remember smelling like rotten flowers, although I've never discovered from whence this ooze had been cultivated. Yet I'm convinced the resin provided some sort of heat retardant, a sealant that greatly prolonged the craft's time aloft.

"Carpenters had crafted a sturdy wicker basket, very much like the modern balloonist's cockpit—woven from a very tight, durable wicker that could sustain the weight of several men. The basket was large, perhaps six feet square. When tethered overhead, sometimes four or five engineers stood crowded together, taking measurements with some sort of ornate compass, a device that looked somewhat like a primitive navigator's sextant. I had no knowledge of this instrument's purpose at the time, although lately I've become quite curious. Still, all those millennia ago, such an invention seemed magical to me. I was never allowed aboard, of course—nor would I have volunteered. I had not the remotest desire to submit myself to the mercy of the contraption, as the thought of leaving the ground terrified me. I could not grasp the concept of hot air rising, nor of taking people with it.

"As I recall, three wood-burning fires in immense, pot-bellied copper stoves stood atop the pyramid, situated around the airship. When stoked, the heat from their fires funneled through copper tubing affixed beneath the airbag before a flight."

"These people knew of conduits?"

"Aye. Crüz's engineers knew about applied mechanics and crude metallurgy—although again, I suspect with Tra's guidance. Logographic script marked numerous scrolls of papyrus, although at the time I could not fathom their meanings either.

"As for the tubing, Crüzian workers hammered copper sheets extremely thin and rolled them into flexible heating ducts. By crimping them at various angles, one could create a permanent elbow joint. Thick resin would seal and lock the joint in place and engineers could even regulate temperatures with heat-release valves, large wooden plugs attached at various intervals. Of course, many of the workers lost fingers, eyes or noses in the inevitable steam baths resulting from so rudimentary a fabrication—but by carefully positioning these basic radiators beneath the airbag, the balloon gradually became buoyant.

"Incredibly, the craft could remain aloft for hours—tethered, of course, as *pav* was never designed for free flight—and pulled back into its cradle when a signal was given from the engineers above. I don't think I ever saw the craft rise more than a few hundred feet above the platform—still, an astonishing feat considering the height of Zhahrat itself. I recall it taking a dozen or so men to tug and wrestle the craft back atop the pyramid after each flight, although I do believe there existed some sort of heat-release patch located near the top of the bag as well."

"What a thrilling experience it would have been," I said. "How unfortunate that you never found yourself floating above the city."

"Well, not *voluntarily*," Reni replied with a wry smile.

"Oh?" I said, bursting with curiosity.

He lifted a finger, a soft smile tugging at his lips. "As I mentioned, the top of Zhahrat was quite level."

"Yes, yes," I said eagerly. "Flat. And a square hole perforated its core. A necessity for the balloon's tethering, I suppose?"

"Not in the least," my husband replied. "Rather, the housing for a—well, a lightning rod. I should mention that the most precious metal in Crüz was *bota*—silver—mined from the mountains to the east. The entirety of the city's silver belonged to the godking. To hoard even a speck of silver for oneself was punishable by death. While gold was plentiful and used to lavishly adorn the city's privileged few, the possession of silver was prohibited for all but Tra himself."

He furrowed his brow, and I could only wring my hands in silent frustration.

"Late one evening, I was directed to deliver several parchments to the engineers atop Zhahrat. It wasn't uncommon that the engineers worked throughout the night atop the pyramid, as I'd come to suspect that they somehow measured the position of certain stars to pinpoint precise architectural angles. I sprinted up the steps, as I'd found standing upon Zhahrat, overlooking the city of Crüz, an exhilarating experience, an indelible memory to this day. Yet I had no sooner ascended that night, breathless, that I noticed pav drifting off the far side of the pyramid, the balloon having been tethered safely beyond the edge, little more than a shadow that flickered occasionally in the glow of the plump stoves' hot embers. In pav's place atop the platform, a silver obelisk now rose. The pillar, starkly smooth and without decoration, protruded easily fifty or sixty feet upward, its base firmly anchored within the channel that had puzzled me so."

I waited.

"Many of the engineers and the priests in their dark, hooded robes mingled together, speaking in rushed whispers. As the last colors drained from the distant horizon, the oil pots along the staircase and various lamps atop the pyramid were ordered extinguished. The trio of heating stoves were vented. I could feel palpable excitement flowing among the learned men gathered around me. Stars glistened overhead. The engineers gazed eagerly upward. Curious, I raised my eyes as well. Nothing appeared unusual for many minutes. And yet we watched."

Reni paused for the longest of moments. Finally, he said, "Then I saw what the others were seeking. A single, glistening light moved slowly against the myriad of stars. I watched with fascination as it approached and then appeared to hover directly overhead. With a hiss and sizzle of electricity, a single violet filament fell from the heavens and touched the top of the obelisk.

"If not for the composure of the others, I would have immediately fled down Zhahrat's steps like a man possessed with madness. I stood my ground on trembling legs, both terrified and mesmerized, watching that umbilical thread of light coupling heaven and earth, its arc dancing and jostling between the obelisk and whatever distant object that hovered above us. From within the depths of the pyramid I heard the slightest of hums, a vibration that tickled the skin.

"I don't understand," I said.

"Neither did I," he admitted. "Nor do I still. Not completely."

"But you suggest some sort of electrical connection? But with what? Certainly not another balloon."

"No. Much, much higher."

"An aircraft of some kind?" I pondered his words. "A *satellite?*"

"I simply don't know for certain. Nor can I be sure whether the stream of lightning originated from above or below, but assuredly a connection had been achieved."

I shook my head, dizzied by Reni's astonishing implications. He regarded me intently, his eyes afire. Oh, but I knew that look so well. At times, my husband was quite content feeding me puzzle pieces one by one, and only when I had connected the various aspects of his story would he divulge further information. Infuriating—yet also quite exhilarating. I was not his audience but rather an active participant in his revelations. Tonight, apparently, was to be of those nights.

"The obelisk was constructed of silver?"

"I believe so, yes."

"A material far more conductive than copper or gold," I remarked. "An obelisk of pure silver would have been far more likely to hold a stable electric current."

"Aye."

"And the humming you heard? I assume you speak of a vibrational frequency?"

He nodded. "One that changed pitch and frequency every few seconds."

"You were undoubtedly witnessing a controlled charge of some sort. The presence of a battery perhaps—one located deep within the pyramid?"

"Or a generator," he replied.

I mulled the possibility, still dizzied by the implications. Eager for further details—as my psyche does not easily tolerate unsolved puzzles—I said, "Please, dear husband, continue."

"Atop Zhahrat, the temple priests continued to peer upward, although the engineers had busied themselves in their charts and crude instruments. The wisps of conversation I overheard made no sense to me. As the others were preoccupied, I found few chores heaped upon me throughout that long night, and so my attention remained locked on the electric bolt that danced and arced as if alive. For many hours I stood transfixed.

"Shortly before dawn, the last of the priests finally descended Zhahrat's many steps, and the weary engineers began to gather their tools. A single hooded figure had remained, pacing back and forth at the edge of the platform, his eyes still turned upward at the night sky. Taller than the others—standing a full head taller than I—he was slightly hunchbacked and walked with the help of a wooden staff. As I gazed upon him, his silhouette edged in a soft violet glow from the electrical charge, his eyes dropped from the heavens and he turned to face me."

My husband paused and took a moment to brush a piece of fuzz from his pant leg before he spoke again. Finally, he said, "This priest—he was not like us. His body was deformed, his face disfigured. And yet in that split instant, I recognized a—an intelligence in his eyes far beyond my own. Funny, but I do not have the words to explain my comprehension with any deeper clarity. He seemed neither displeased nor threatened that our gazes had met, and he merely turned toward the pyramid's steps."

My mind raced. "Had you laid eyes on the godking Tra?"

"Aye. I believe I had."

"And without repercussion?"

"His thoughts were obviously elsewhere. No sooner had he began his descent than the flow of current ceased. A loud *crack* pierced the night. Darkness once again flooded my senses, and a hushed murmur drifted among the few engineers who likewise remained atop Zhahrat.

"There was much yet to be done, however. Lamps were re-sparked. I watched the workers begin the arduous task of disassembling the silver obelisk into many smaller segments and of returning pav to its dock, guided by the rust-colored face of La'u'ata—whom the Crüzians knew as Rhyan, by the way—emerging from behind the distant northern peaks. My work was far from over however, and I ultimately made several journeys up and down Zhahrat's long stairway, descending with tools and returning with bloated skins of fresh water. It wasn't until dawn's first light that the chief engineer signaled to the others that the night's objective—whatever strange occurrence had transpired there—had been accomplished.

The remaining engineers muttered a weary praise to Tra and began handing me satchels of tools for one final trip down Zhahrat—when quite abruptly the city began to shake. First, a long, undulating tremor, followed by an enormous jolt. The tremors returned. Several of the engineers wobbled and fell to their knees, while others cowered back from the perilous edge of the platform, lest anyone fall to their deaths.

"For several minutes—*minutes*, mind you, an eternity it seemed—the earth continued to quiver. Below us, many Crüzians staggered from their homes in the murky twilight, calling out to Tra for mercy. Just as abruptly, both silence and stillness returned. Dust rose from the streets in mighty plumes. I did not see a single brick fall, nor soul perish, and a great cheer erupted. Crüz had been spared, our cries heard, and each of us rejoiced.

"I now understand the quake's epicenter had been quite distant," Reni said. "I believe that some twelve- or fifteen-hundred miles away the earth had been torn asunder. But we knew nothing of seismology in those days, and so we returned to our early morning chores, to begin this day anew." My husband paused to stare off toward the Pacific.

"And?" I pressed eagerly.

"And, for three days, nothing happened."

Again, I waited.

"As I recall," he said, "the experiment was repeated each night during that period. Slightly different times, I recall. I never observed Tra again atop Zhahrat, and I remember my sense of relief, for the sight of the godking disturbed me in some subliminal way, and I hoped never again to lay eyes on the man.

"On the morning of the fourth day, I awoke as usual with the first morning light. I remember that much needed to be accomplished before nightfall. I also knew the engineers would be frantic to complete whatever chores Tra had assigned them.

"I should mention," Reni said, "that several smaller earthquakes had occurred over the past few days. Tremblers that sent slight, but increasingly stronger, vibrations beneath our feet. Nothing as terrifying as that first quake, however. I do not remember sensing any trepidation from the engineers and thus I felt no foreboding myself."

"Did you not consider these quakes to be a result of your experiments?" I asked.

"Aye, I did indeed, but heaven knows why. I was far from the smartest man in Crüz on that day. Still, I've often pondered this unintentional consequence, the correlation between Sister Earth's rumble and the bright light that pierced the sky that night.

"By mid-morning however, we became aware of swirling dark clouds forming against the western horizon. Not long afterward, we observed enormous flocks of birds taking flight, their vast number appearing as a black stain above the distant forests. Our gently flowing river became increasingly swift and bloated, jumping its banks here and there, flooding our pastures and croplands and soon splashing frothy waves upon our island's crowded shoreline. Many of us atop the pyramid stared intently, first with curiosity and then concern. Eventually I became aware of a strange vibration underfoot—not a quake, but a constant, tingling sensation, quite unusual. By the time Khalam had reached its zenith overhead, we could hear a deep grumble, an ambient sound unlike any I'd ever before heard.

"I happened to again be atop the pyramid, having filled several bladders of water from the aqueduct below, when several of the engineers began chattering incessantly and pointing wildly toward the horizon. Cautiously, I scanned the tree line and observed a thick, rolling fog advancing quite rapidly. Almost immediately I recognized the mist for what it was—not a cloud, but rather a wall of water, filling our entire valley from one edge to the other. Judging from the wave's height above the distant treetops, I believe what many of us had already realized, that the advancing wave was far higher than our perch upon Zhahrat.

"The engineers began to call out to those in the streets beneath us. Within Savo Crüz Savo, panic quickly erupted. I stood immobile, staring in fascination until the gradual roar of approaching water shook me from my stasis. By sheer chance, my gaze fell on the tethered balloon no more than a dozen steps away. The fire pits had been well stoked, and pav stood full and eager again to be aloft. Without an instant to spare, I bolted for the aircraft, pushing my way through the absorbed engineers as one might part a cluster of small children. I took several great strides before turning to shout to the others. Yet few heard my voice—such was the howl of the swirling winds and the thunderous roar of the approaching wave.

"I did not understand. Were these not educated men, aware that their only hope of survival lay above? I watched several of them began to flee *down* Zhahrat's steps—an insane decision! But I could not tarry. I kicked the heating ducts from their positions beneath the balloon and climbed into the gondola. I snatched a short blade from its sheathing, as there was insufficient time to unknot the many tethers. Hacking at the cords that bound the craft to Zhahrat, I'd managed to cut all but few strands before the chief engineer, a gnarled and burly bull of a man, finally realized my intent. He pointed at me, calling out as he did so. Had he been able to roust the engineers from their fear, together they might have wrestled me from the basket.

"Instead, he charged the balloon with an incensed cry and flung himself aboard. At that instant, the last lashing parted, and the aircraft shot upward with a jolt. I dropped the knife and grabbed one of the support lines attaching the basket to the bloated pouch above. I had never before felt the lift of flight—such an extraordinarily dizzying sensation."

My husband paused briefly and emitted a soft sigh.

"By now, several of the engineers had begun running toward the basket. But *pav* had already risen out of reach. Their fingers clawed at the empty air beneath us. Angered that I had not attempted to wait for the others, the chief engineer turned to me and drew his blade. He ordered me out of the basket with a snarl. What? That I should jump of my own volition? I managed a caustic laugh in return.

"In an adrenalin-charged rage he lunged for me, ignoring all rules of sane combat. I merely stepped aside, pulling his arm forward. Driven by his own momentum, he tumbled headfirst from the basket. I heard his scream's descent, the sound quickly consumed by the roar of the approaching wave.

"I saw that the balloon had not yet risen above the wave's frothing crest. I could not tear my eyes from the oncoming monstrosity. The approaching swell had snapped countless trees from their roots, creating a churning wall of wood and debris that would have surely pulverized me in a matter of seconds. I'm quite certain that I would have been minced into a million tiny bits, in a manner that would have utterly thwarted my regenerative abilities. And, indeed, I believed in the moment that such would be my fate. However, a thick rush of displaced air preceded the water's advance, and suddenly I felt pav push upward with incredible speed.

"I was flung to the floor of the basket and felt the crushing weight of my own body as the contraption swiftly rose into the heavens. I reached out with some difficulty, clutching at bits of cord—such a frightened old lady I'd become inside this apparatus! As the wave passed beneath me, I heard and felt its destructive impact upon the city, a sound unlike any I have ever heard since, dwarfing even the harshest shrieks of our modern machinery. I pressed my face against the wicker flooring and, smothered by the black cloak of my own fear, I could only assume that the entire earth had been consumed by the raging waters.

"I don't know how long I remained in such a stupor, though it seemed an interminable duration before I chided myself to open my eyes and rise to my knees. The balloon wobbled back and forth as might an unbalanced pendulum, and quite disconcerting. A great, rushing wind whistled through the air around me and a cold breeze puckered my skin—a chill that I now perceive assured my time aloft for quite some time.

"Eventually I dared peek over the rim of the basket. As far as I could see, the entire valley lay beneath a vast ocean of frothing water. Whirlpools the size of city blocks pocked the caldron that bubbled and churned. I could see no sign of Zhahrat. Nothing of familiarity remained. Only the jagged mountains to the north appeared unscathed.

"I'm not sure how long I continued to float above the angry waters, searching for any signs of life below. Pav eventually began a slow descent, although I was still born on the breezes that pushed me along at a dizzying speed. I had no idea of my proximity to Crüz. Likely I had been blown dozens, perhaps even hundreds, of miles away. I simply had no clue. I'd hoped that by now the savage waters would have begun to recede, as they had done in the tenth valley so many eons before. But these waters did not retreat."

"Never?"

"I believe now that I was looking down upon the newly birthed Mediterranean Sea," he replied. "The quake must have ruptured the mountains far to the west, mountains that until that morning had kept the Atlantic Ocean at bay. But the quake opened a great rift, very likely the gap that today separates Gibraltar from Tangier. Uncorked, the waters rushed in and devoured an incredible swatch of fertile valley. Upon that day, I also believe the single most advanced city of ancient times was lost to the ages."

I pondered Reni's statement, until the magnitude of his revelation jolted me upright in my chair. "A *flood!*" I gasped.

"Aye."

"Could it have been? Was this the great flood of ancient mythologies? The flood of Noah, of the Babylonians and the Assyrians?"

"It was indeed of Biblical proportions," he offered. "And it greatly shaped the fate of those lands we now whimsically call the Middle East."

I deliberated further. "And Crüz?" I asked. "Might this have been the lost city so many have sought? Could yours have been the kingdom of Atlantis?"

"It was Crüz," he reminded me.

"A name unremembered by time," I said excitedly.

"Then I suspect it could have been. Mythology is such a complicated stew. Crüz may indeed have been Atlantis, as might any number of unknown cities that were crushed beneath the weight of the waters that day. Perhaps Atlantis is an aggregate memory of that catastrophic event, one whispered about by survivors from Marbella to Beirut. I can assure you that I have never before spoken of this cataclysm, although a few lucky others clearly survived the maelstrom. The mountainous tribes would have watched in horror. The myth of a great flood has obviously survived."

"How history is born," I said in awe to the night sky.

"And how easily great kingdoms perish," Reni parried, his eyes closed, either in memory or from fatigue; I wasn't certain.

My mind buzzed with many other questions, although the magnitude of Reni's words had stunned me into temporary silence. Yet I could not find the will to quell my own excitement, and eventually I pushed all thoughts of sleep aside.

"You could not have told me this remarkable tale before now?" I asked.

"Alas, I offer you not the slightest proof," Reni replied. "Had I told you before this night—and had you chosen to reveal Crüz to the world, it would have caused you only controversy and perhaps ridicule. Had you written about such heresy, your work would have been viewed as one of fiction, without tangible verification."

"*You* are my verification," I reminded him.

"And would you have subjected me to scientific scrutiny, my beloved?"

His tender reproach startled me, then forced an unwitting laugh from my lips. "Of course not, you silly man. You are a priceless gift that I dare not share with a soul."

"Like a stolen Renoir," he offered, "hanging tilted and dusty over the mantle."

"Precisely," I responded, my eyes glittering with appreciation for my Captain. "Although I have to ask—what harm can there be in the truth?"

"In a world unready to listen, truth is merely another illusion."

I could think of no adequate response.

"You should know that for many centuries after the destruction of Crüz," Reni said, "I feared those who might uncover my fate that day. I'm not certain why—superstition, I suppose. The risk of being considered a bad omen.

"As soon as pav descended, I hacked away the airbag and used the wicker basket as a raft of sorts. A wet and ungainly vessel it was, to say the least. I spent three days afloat until I reached a series of small islands, well in sight of the highlands to the east. Once ashore, I continued into the highlands, as far as I could distance myself from Crüz. I surrendered the tenets of civilization and for years I roamed through the sparsely populated, wildly rugged mountainous regions of what I suspect to be current day Syria or Turkey.

"As the new sun had grown steadily fatter and hotter in the sky, the glacial remnants of a great Ice Age had gradually retreated northward. Much of this newly revealed terrain remained covered by great lakes and swiftly flowing streams, rendering the land quite lush and fertile in those days. I enjoyed many years of solitude and solace, until the thought of Crüz at last became a distant, fleeting memory.

"I must admit that I sought out no other kingdoms in

those centuries between the destruction of Crüz and that day I would stumble upon Inbu-Hedj—the walled city that we now call Memphis, and long before Egypt's earliest dynasties. I was not completely alone all this while, of course, as I occasionally met other scavengers and recluses like myself, self-sufficient men and women who wandered anonymously through these lands. Yet inevitably, small tribes would come together and grow, and villages would become hamlets, becoming towns. Fearful of their expanding progress, I would shun those places that prospered. I would gather my few belongings and wander off again, venturing deeper into the wilderness in search of greater seclusion.

"I did not remain oblivious to the rumors of those emerging kingdoms, of course, of the stories shared in hushed whispers that told of distant, amazing splendors. I assume now that those whispers spoke of the burgeoning realms of Samarra and early Mesopotamia, but I harbored not the slightest interest in these tales. Strangely enough, while I had once hungered to learn of new discoveries and marvelous inventions, I now viewed mankind's expanding knowledge as both sinister and dangerous. Civilization required bloodshed and lust, entitled greed and forced servitude to succeed. I felt an abiding fear of those cultures that benefited the few while imposing despair upon the many. And so the centuries continued to pass.

"Ah, but of course, as always, my curiosity did eventually return. Although I suspect it best—" My husband stifled a sudden yawn, "—that we continue speaking of these times in the morning, as the brandy and my exhaustion have begun to cloud my thoughts."

"A bit longer—*please,* my love," I said, pleading like a small child. "I feel as if my head will perhaps explode if we stop now."

Reni smiled. "Very well. I know how you so hate mysteries. As I was saying, I spent many lifetimes as an *alnasik* —a hermit meandering about those splendid plains that would one day belong to the Canaanites and the Hittites. And I may have dismissed time, but time had not dismissed me.

"By happenstance one afternoon, a passing trade caravan stopped by a stream that flowed through a meadow quite near my yurt. I could not believe what I chanced to glimpse, camels and *elephants*—exotic, unfathomable creatures to me—and merchants too, a dozen or so tall men with coal black skin, their garments shimmering white, and who laughed and frolicked in the fresh running waters. None appeared in misery, nor did a single man among them appear in servitude to the others.

"Curious, I revealed myself. They were cautious but soon quite welcoming, offering me cheese and bread. In return, I presented one of my plumpest lambs for slaughter. As daylight waned, we dined in newfound friendship, and I tasted my first sip of fermented grape. An astonishing nectar! I recognized various bits of their language and invited their patience in teaching me more. For three days we ate and drank while I listened to many stories of their adventures. I knew, of course, of trading and traders, and remembered anew that distant time when I had once walked the world in search of similar exploits. Thus, come the morning of the fourth sunrise, I surprised myself by agreeing to accompany them southward, having been convinced that my plump flock would prove quite valuable for barter or sale.

"And that is how I first came to journey by camel along the Nile," Reni said, "and soon afterward to stand before the gates of Memphis, and later Thebes, still two or three millennia before those kingdoms united into a single Egyptian culture. And yet, to my dismay—"

My husband paused abruptly, somewhat reluctantly. Despite my excitement, I bit my lip and allowed him his silent contemplation.

"To my dismay," he repeated, his brow furrowed, "as my fellow travelers and I approached Memphis, my eyes beheld a troubling sight. Rising above the city's mud-bricked walls, I spied a black pyramid, larger even than Zhahrat, but otherwise similar. And upon its flattened top I spotted the distant, silver thread of an obelisk."

I gasped.

"Gazing upon this abomination proved a quite terrifying experience, as my memories of Crüz returned in a heartbeat, flooding my senses as if barely a fortnight had passed between this moment and that."

"And in Thebes?" I asked.

He nodded. "Another pyramid, aye. Larger still. But otherwise identical to the others."

I pondered Reni's words with a new rush of adrenaline. "I've seen no record of such structures," I said.

"No, no, all long since turned to dust."

"Merely a coincidence of archetype, or of architecture? Pyramids are known to have populated the ancient world. In China, the equatorial Americas, the Pacific Rim at one time or another."

He nodded somewhat obliquely.

"Tell me, did you find *other* influences of Crüz in these cities?"

"Yes, and one I believe you'll find of particular importance."

"Oh?"

"Many months later and quite by accident, I would catch sight of Memphis' pharaoh. I remember the man as standing quite tall, yet slightly hunched. He wore flowing garments and a veil that concealed his nose and mouth. And yet in those few seconds I observed him, I recognized the same oddly spaced, silver-blue eyes—quite similar to those of the Crüzian godking."

"How remarkable! There must be a correlation between these two disfigured rulers. And between the similar structures of Crüz and of Memphis and Thebes."

"It seems likely," he agreed.

As much as I adored the man, Reni could be quite maddening on occasions. "Did you ever see—" I hesitated and allowed myself a deep breath—"see *further* indications of electrical experimentation? Of lights dancing in the sky?"

"I did, during my many brief stays in both Memphis and Thebes. And later still in Alexandria. Often I witnessed multiple columns of violet light, many of them pulsing against the distant night sky."

"And yet this knowledge remains unknown to modern scholars! For what purpose? What more can you tell me of this phenomenon?"

"Very little, I'm afraid. Only in the last couple of centuries have we come to understand the nature of electricity." He sighed, a sound that lingered heavily in the air between us. "At the time, these so-called experiments seemed little more than a dance of the gods."

Once again, Reni yawned. Again aware of my husband's fatigue, I felt ashamed of my own zealous self-indulgence. "Forgive me, my love. Shall we adjourn for the night?"

He nodded gratefully. "As I find my thoughts scattering, I think it's best. We will resume our conversation at a future date."

"Tomorrow?" I urged.

"Soon enough, I'm sure. These secrets have lingered for many millennia, I'm sure they'll remain safely intact for another few days."

I nodded absently, aware that Reni and I had begun this evening's conversation in the waning sunlight. I observed the inky blackness around us, aware that even the moon had fallen from view, with dawn's approach only a few hours hence. The sputtering stub of a single lamp candle offered the last vestige of functioning light. I reached out and took Reni's hands in mine—and as I did so I noticed the texture of my own skin; the tiny crinkles, the veins, the encroaching traces of age contrasting the firm, smooth contour of his own supple flesh. For once, I was grateful for the shroud of surrounding shadows. "Come, take me to bed, my husband," I conceded. "Rest your tongue and I shall rest my mind."

"Agreed," he replied, standing and snatching up the lamp, its flame trembling as might a young lamb aware of a stalking wolf. Oddly enough, over the decades, I had continued to listen to Reni's tales by lamp light, as if the practical tools of modern times scarcely belonged here, among the sacred mysteries of the past.

As Reni and I made our way through the hallway, I said; "I have something to tell you, dear husband."

"By all means."

"For so many years I have wrongly envied your ability to thwart time. To this mere mortal, one too quickly grown old and tired, endless life seemed like such a magnificent gift. But I cannot fathom a lifetime of lifetimes without lasting friendship or camaraderie—or lacking that inner peace that husband and wife experience together. How I would relish helping you up the steps or fetching your eyeglasses, or finding your lost keys, as you have so often done for me! I have wronged you with my own naïve assumptions and jealousy. For this, I feel great shame."

Reni hugged me tightly and kissed the side of my head. "Poppycock. You have given this wanderer an oasis of unbridled love," he said. "And for that, I am eternally grateful. It's difficult to explain to you, who loves so easily, how *elusive* that emotion has been for me throughout the ages. To find love is something I'm not sure that you—" he smiled warmly, "—that you mere mortals can truly appreciate. One may walk for miles upon a windswept beach and so easily miss the one grain of sand that represents unconditional happiness. And yet I have found you. You are my singularity, my grain of sand, and my life now feels complete because of our union."

I, of course, felt tears tumble down my cheeks. Not tears of loss or yearning, but of rapture. I cried because joy itself could not contain me. My heart sang, as quite abruptly neither the past nor the future existed in the core of my soul. I felt as ageless as my husband and truly believed that even the separation of death would not, could not, distance or diminish our love. However selfishly, I knew that Reni was mine forever more.

THAT NIGHT, I struggled to sleep. My thoughts swirled in pandemonium—until a sudden realization forced me upright, fully awake. I had dreamt of ancient skies, once afire and filled with chaos. Of our planet glowing under the pale sheen of Earth's three accompanying satellites. For another hour I fidgeted beneath the sheets, impatiently awaiting morning's light and tortured by thoughts that would not recede. When I could no longer tolerate the confines of the bed, I snapped on a lamp and shook Reni awake with gentle urgency.

"Aya na'on?" he asked, for Reni would often stir with the remnants of some long-lost language on his lips.

I placed a hand against his shoulder. "Dear husband, my questions can wait no longer!"

"What time is it?"

"Dawn," I said. "*Almost,*" I amended quickly.

Although burdened with insufficient sleep, Reni nodded with resigned acceptance, rubbing his eyes with his fingertips. "What torments you so, my love?"

"You have so recently spoken of Luta'u and little La'u'ata in the skies above Tu'ulth, and again in Crüz, while accompanying Sister Earth on her long voyage through the cosmos. But whatever became of these bodies? You never mention them again in subsequent tales; not in your later wanderings among the Israelites or Persians, nor among the Greeks or Romans. No recorded languages hint of such bodies in our ancient skies."

Reni did not speak, but I could see the last vestige of slumber drain from his face. My husband smiled at me— but what on earth for? Had he been awaiting this moment? Anticipating such questions from me?

I fervently pressed on. "Last night you revealed ancient experiments with electricity, experiments that I can only infer either began or concluded far above this world of ours. Is there a connection between these experiments, and with the disappearance of Luta'u and La'u'ata?"

"Have you made coffee?" he asked.

I sternly *shhhhhh*ed him.

Aware of my urgency, his demeanor again grew serious. "I believe there is a correlation, yes."

"Might these ancient structures have served as some sort of electrical network? Each a component of an integrated effort?"

"Go on," he prodded.

"Overseen by Tra in Crüz? And subsequently by the godkings in Memphis and, presumably, in Thebes and Alexandria. And perhaps elsewhere, hundreds of years later?"

"If not longer," he amended.

"You've told me that Tra and the ruler of Memphis were exceedingly tall men, similarly disfigured. I'm aware that the Bible's Old Testament speaks of an ancient race of giants," I said. "The *Nephilim*. Scripture tells us that they were the sons of God and the daughters of mankind. Not completely human, if one reads between the lines. Biblical scholars refer to them as fallen angels. Might these god-kings have been the Nephilim?"

"Perhaps," he said.

"Damn your stoicism!" I cried out, my emotions fueled not by anger but rather by a sudden spurt of adrenalin. I grabbed for his hand and squeezed tightly, galvanized by Reni's ability to push me beyond the bounds of patience. "The godkings of which you speak and the Nephilim of biblical lore, were these beings not *human* beings?"

My husband's eyes glowed, as if lit from a fire within. "I don't believe so, no."

"Nor angels."

"Nor angels," he replied.

"An unknown species of Sapiens? Or, what? Might they have been visitors here on Sister Earth?"

"Ah," he said, his eyes blazing. I suspected that I had struck upon a terrifying truth. I felt joyful emancipation rising up through a numbing chill, my head suddenly floating as if tethered to a balloon.

"You could not have simply told me about such astounding occurrences?"

"How could I?" Reni replied in quiet exasperation, reaching out to brush my cheek. "Had you not been able to perceive this truth for yourself, my attempt to convince you would not have succeeded. Worse, you may have convinced yourself that I was merely delusional. Had you not been ready to accept my words, I could not have swayed you."

"And yet?" I asked. "You cannot be certain of these creatures."

"That they were from another world? I cannot, no."

"Then what *am* I to believe?"

"Only what you wish to believe. I offer no proof, merely a testimony beyond the reaches of time. That I have been able to share these words with another individual—you cannot image the burden that has been lifted from my soul. I feel as if I can breathe again."

I had not been aware until now of the tears streaming down my cheeks, dripping with abandon from my nose and chin. "What my rational mind cannot accept, my loving heart fully embraces. Of course I believe you," I said with a firm nod. "How could I not?"

"My dear Mei Xing," he whispered. "That you have listened is enough."

"But who were they?" I asked, absently backhanding tears from my eyes. "Why had these beings come to Earth?"

"I haven't the foggiest," Reni replied. "They were certainly not the benefactors of humankind. Not teachers or seekers of knowledge. My best assumption is that they were miners or salvagers; galactic foragers drawn to a planet brimming with abundant resources and an aboriginal people who would not miss what was taken. I suspect they discovered us somewhere along our unstable journey, not long after our world had been ripped from Saturn's embrace. These beings remained long enough, or else returned often enough, to eventually witness our frozen wastelands melting and our steaming jungles turning to desert sand. Our sun, shining as large in the sky as it does today, had become perilously hot. These beings recognized our planet's impending doom, and with it their own economic loss, should Sister Earth eventually be incinerated.

"And you believe they prevented such a catastrophe?"

"Aye," he said, "I believe they did. I believe I'd witnessed their earliest efforts in Crüz, and later their accelerated attempts again in Memphis and Thebes. By then the once-fertile lands of Egypt had begun to wither. The encroaching sands of the tiny Saharan desert had begun to claim those vast, marshy jungles that once carpeted Northern Africa. The godkings, using their knowledge of electromagnetics and plasma conductivity—or perhaps of something else entirely—gradually maneuvered Sister Earth into a stable orbit that would insure their prolonged use of our planet. Subsequently, of course, of our own survival. I assume they also cast aside La'u'ata and Luta'u and repositioned our current Moon to further stabilize our once eccentric wobble. Having succeeded in their task, I suspect they continued to harvest or mine whatever resources they desired.

"These beings did not flaunt their presence, nor expose their advanced technologies, as I'm sure any such overt exhibition would have driven our primitive minds to madness. During my incarceration within Zhahrat, I'm certain I must have glimpsed proof of their extraterrestrial origins, but so much I witnessed in Crüz I could not comprehend. I've wracked my brain in recent years, but I recall nothing that I could remotely describe as—as a computer, or a ray gun, or a rocket ship. And yet I'm certain some trace of their existence on Earth must remain buried somewhere beneath the earth, and I've searched for decades."

"Yet you've found nothing?"

"Nothing," he admitted. "Although—"

He closed his mouth. Seconds passed.

"Yes? Go on," I said breathlessly.

"Well, I've spent many years scavenging the Sinai Peninsula, seeking clues. I believe that the ancient Israelites, having either fled or exiled themselves from the pharaoh's Egypt, may have stumbled upon one of the godking's power sources—or perhaps pilfered it, wholly unaware of its purpose or potential—and worshipped it as a gift from

God."

He paused again, regarding me with what I perceived to be polite expectation. I furiously pondered his silence until a single possibility revealed itself to me. "*Arōn Ha'brēt?*" I asked, aghast. "The Ark of the Covenant?"

Reni smiled. "Ancient lore suggests that most who came into contact with the artifact suffered hideous burns and died horrible deaths. Only recently have I been able to formulate a logical theory. Death by electrocution."

"Millennia before our species had even grasped the faintest notion of electricity."

"Aye."

I continued to stare at my husband, utterly fascinated by his revelation.

"Even without proof, I do find the reasoning quite plausible," Reni said. "Tra's scientific knowledge certainly dwarfed what our greatest minds have yet to comprehend. Can you imagine the sheer amount of force required to nudge the mass of a planet from its course? The greatest endeavor in the history of the world—and yet, I cannot be sure. And now," he added with a playful shrug, "neither can you."

The gravity of that statement would not fully strike me until much later. But at that moment, Reni's words swirled about my brain, beyond my ability to fully grasp. I felt myself swimming through a most unpleasant delirium and, to this day, choose not to ponder too greatly upon this supposition.

"Whoever they were, these godkings," Reni continued stoically, "I don't believe they arrived here in any great number. Maybe only dozens of these beings populated our planet at any given time. Possibly they did not age as rapidly as we do—or maybe not at all, as they were certainly a highly advanced species. But they easily subjugated our primitive cultures throughout the world, until each of these beings had become the master of all it surveyed. They obviously needed our unwitting help in such an undertaking—as we ourselves dug the ore and helped construct much of the machinery necessary for our own planet's survival. Many thousands may have perished at hard labor so that one day billions could live."

"But these creatures, where did they go?" I wondered.

"Home, I suppose."

I blinked back my astonishment. "You mean…they simply *left?*"

"I believe so. They eventually filled their bins, or met their quotas, or exhausted whatever resources they had come to harvest. I suspect they departed with no more remorse than a farmer leaving behind depleted fields filled with weeds and rotting vegetables. Either they were unaware of their imprint on our collective psyche or else felt indifferent to our awe and thus ultimately to our reverence. Perhaps their species hadn't the slightest capacity to experience compassion or empathy. Cognizant or not, with their sudden departure they left an excruciating emotional void within our species. We had worshiped them as gods. As purveyors of infinite wisdom. And then one morning we awoke—" Reni shrugged again, this time indifferently. "—and found them gone."

"We had been wrenched from our mother's love," I realized, "and now we had been abandoned by our gods."

"Humanity had no understanding of their purpose," he agreed. "During their time here, I believe they had inadvertently taught us the skills of building a basic civilization, of writing and mathematics and science and rational order. Yet several millennia would pass before we could truly realize the purpose of these tools. Until then, we clung to our ignorance and our superstitions. After Mu'at's demise, our many mythologies revealed our genuine attempts to make sense of it all—our desperate efforts to find salvation and return to our so-called garden. When these beings came, we viewed their power and their knowledge as our means to salvation. When they left, we were reduced to little more than a race of hysterical infants, crying out for the love of a father who would likely never return.

"We continued to build pyramids," Reni said, "because they had shown us how. Yet we remained unaware that such structures had served a functional purpose. We built obelisks as they had done. And we also killed our brethren in sacrifice because—well, because *they* had done so too."

Until that moment, I had cautiously accepted my husband's respect for these creatures. But in that instant all admiration fled my soul. "How can this be!" I cried, sitting upright in bed, ignoring my nakedness in my zeal to express my most righteous indignation. "I don't understand. Why would they have *done* such a horrid thing?"

Reni shrugged and said, "Because I believe these creatures were carnivores."

I stared at him with revulsion, but he remained unapologetically stoic. "Would not one of our own expeditions—say a sailing ship lost upon an unfamiliar sea two or three centuries ago, hungry and chancing upon an island lush with wild boar or plump fowl—would not the captain and crew have butchered those unfortunate creatures to feast upon? And thought nothing of it?"

I allowed his words to penetrate and shivered. I crawled again beneath the sheets and pressed against my husband, hungry for his warmth.

"These starmen," Reni said quietly, stroking my hair, "they likely fed upon our flesh with no more remorse than we would experience devouring a lamb shank or chicken breast. The only difference being that humanity had already begun to grasp a sense of self-awareness, and so we confused our godking's need for sustenance with a presumed desire for sacrificial blood. When they abandoned us, we found it necessary—even comforting, I dare say—to emulate their actions. And with our blood rituals, we thought we might hasten their return. Or maybe we hoped to become the creatures they already were, intelligent and wise beyond our comprehension."

In that moment, I could no longer contain my pain. I began to sob uncontrollably.

"You must understand that these beings were not here as our saviors," Reni whispered, his voice warm against my ear. "But in rescuing our planet, and whether intentionally or not, they also rescued humanity."

"Still, they perverted our innocence."

"Ah, but I suspect we'd lost our innocence long before, amid the fire and brimstone of a dying mother. I don't bear these visitors malice," Reni said. "If we had not chosen them as gods, we would have chosen others. Which I suppose we eventually did."

"But what of the Vedas? Of the Sumerian cylinders? Of Tao Te Ching and the Old Testament? Are all these sacred texts a sham?"

"Not at all. Merely our struggling attempts to interpret what our primitive minds could not yet comprehend. We did our best to digest what we observed, and we invented stories to explain the inexplicable. But we did try to become a more principled species. We eventually established basic tenets of right and wrong, of good and evil. We began to sacrifice goats and sheep to appease our idols, rather than our sons and daughters. We began to forge a sense of our own morality."

"Then who was Jesus, son of Yahweh?" I asked. "He too was an—an *alien?*"

Reni remained silent, his hand gently caressing my hair. "No, indeed he was not," he said soon enough, his voice calm and his inflection soothing. "Eventually the time came for us to embrace a more compassionate God. And this time, I believe we chose one of our own."

I thought that he might elaborate, but Reni merely smiled at me, offering a heartfelt gaze that cleansed me of my trepidation. I felt myself succumbing to the warm embrace of my husband's love and compassion and, once again content to relax within his arms, I did not press him further.

FIVE

WE WOULD NEVER SPEAK of such strange mysteries again. Indeed, in the decades that followed, I would beg my Captain for no further details about impossible beings from a distant world. Nor did I ever again find reason to attempt to decipher the unwritten secrets Reni had revealed. To this day, an unfinished manuscript—*Lost Mythologies of Antiquity*—sits all but forgotten in a cardboard box in my closet. For who would believe me? And as for the questions that such a book would foster? I could scarcely unmask my husband's anonymity in pursuit of a truth that would likely be scorned and treated as nonsensical. And yet, how *else* to provide validation?

I have long since come to realize that we are a complacent species, suspicious of new ideas and the sudden disruption caused by change. I believe our resistance may be deeply embedded in our DNA, perhaps as a direct result of the loss of our Mu'at. Of our near annihilation. Humanity's existential fear—which so many seek to soothe through the rituals of our religious beliefs—may reflect a collective emotional wound that we've as yet been unable to heal.

Yet I did not begrudge us our long-forgotten past, for I found that I had very much fallen in love with the present. Each living moment contains its own wonders, its own ambiguities and mysteries. I cannot help but feel grateful for every explicit detail that had transpired since the dawn of time—because that endless stream of precise moments carries a direct bearing upon the here and now. And, indeed, here we are! We have survived the withering brutality of those dark ages. And as a species, we have thrived.

My husband and I continued to travel in the early years of this new millennium, snaking through the mountains of Peru and eventually touring the coastal splendors of Chile. As Reni had never given up his passion for those tall ships of swashbuckling lore, we ventured to Easter Island by gaff-rigged schooner that he himself piloted, and then through the Cook Islands to New Zealand. I sensed that Reni would forever feel enraptured by the snap of canvas sail, the slap of a cold wind and the creak of wet wood. With a hand-picked crew, we cruised to Indonesia and Malaysia and soon made our way to China, by way of Hebei Harbor—a gift beyond words, as I once again set foot upon the land of my birth.

We remained on Chinese soil for nearly three years, at times living in small mountain villages whose inhabitants had never before encountered a foreigner. (And how they laughed at my creaky, rusty attempts at Mandarin, while Reni—a sandy-haired *júwàirén*—spoke several dialects with absolute perfection.) Eventually we travelled north and then west, and then south again, every so often my husband pointing toward a mountain, a valley or an ancient ruin, describing a memory that would set my soul ablaze with wonder and awe.

Eventually, of course, we returned home to California, inspired by our travels but also bone weary and exhausted. Once again I would linger with a glass of port or snifter of brandy and, buoyed by the warm breezes, stare out to sea for hours at a time. The distant horizon represented eternity to me and I would bask in the endless possibilities that lay ahead.

By now, I think both Reni and I had begun to suspect that our journey together was nearing its conclusion. Although his stories would persist, my husband was cognizant of my encroaching decline. Thus, he would share only the most whimsical of memories, snippets of historical irrelevance that often brought me moments of unmitigated laughter.

For instance, Reni recalled his time with the famed warlord Tokugawa Ienari, a young shogun from Japan's turbulent *Edo* period. Tokugawa had been educated for many years by a much older samurai named Hōkuburakki, a distant cousin of Emperor Kōkaku. By the time Reni found favor in the teenage Tokugawa's court as *sutōriterā*—a storyteller—Hōkuburakki was already a scarred and weary veteran of many skirmishes. Having been blinded in one eye during a battle, the old warrior had replaced his own missing orb with a porcelain substitute. Yet Hōkuburakki suffered allergic reactions to his beloved saké, and whenever the man sneezed, his porcelain eye would pop free from his head and skitter across the floor. The teenaged shogun found this to be the most hilarious of misfortunes. While his court attempted to ceremoniously ignore Hōkuburakki's predicament, Tokugawa would laugh hysterically until the missing eye was returned to its rightful socket.

Another of my favorites? Henry VIII's daughter, adolescent Elizabeth—soon to become England's famous virgin queen—had once secretly married a nobleman named Bartheym. Their marriage occurred several years after Thomas Seymour had been beheaded for making improper advances toward his future queen (or so alludes one of the more accepted theories for his execution). Yet shortly before her rise to England's throne, Elizabeth had covertly declared to Bartheym her eternal love. She had also gifted the young lord a ruby-studded gold ring as a symbol of her devotion. But no sooner had Elizabeth risen to power than she annulled her own marriage, and audaciously asked for the ring's return.

Lord Bartheym, in shock and anger, swallowed the be-jeweled band in protest. The new queen had the poor man tied to the mast of a small naval vessel wharved at St. Andrew's and ordered him force-funneled river water until the ring reappeared from one end or the other. Reni only knew of such shenanigans because he happened to be aboard that same ship, and had been assigned the dubious honor of searching for the ring—and finding it!—at the bottom of a chamber pot after its successful dislodgement from Bartheym's bloated bowels.

Such was the extend of Reni's narrative, and I absorbed each tale with the gleeful passion of an old woman sharing gossip at the corner market. Despite the scheming politicians and the endless wars, the poverty and anguish and apathy of so many, I had come to appreciate that humanity somehow shared a common need to find joy and laughter. And within my husband's ability to bring me such delight, no longer did I harbor the slightest fear of what the future might hold.

AND NOW, in these final hours, death beckons as comfortably as a warm breeze on a cold winter's night. I am ready, for my body has begun to ache with inevitable decay. Far more terrifying to me, I have begun to forget, to lose clarity on this plane of earthly existence. To lose my memory is to lose that which is invaluable to me—Reni's most precious gift. To honor him, and to honor myself, I have decided to move on.

Many years ago, I extracted Reni's promise that I alone

would determine my tenure here on Sister Earth. The dear man, with tears welling as he eventually acquiesced to my wishes, ultimately agreed.

Reni knows of an ancient herbal compound that, once consumed, will compel me toward a gentle and endless sleep. We will lie together, one last time as husband and wife, and I will drift into a deep euphoria. My heartbeat will gradually slow and then cease. I will dream my last moment in this world, and then begin to dream in the next.

As for my leaving behind my precious husband? I can only trust that the memory of my love will sustain him until he might again find another's adoration. He deserves both passion *and* compassion on his endless voyage through time, and I do not begrudge him another's affection. Someday, I believe my Captain will find ultimate peace. When that time arrives, my sister-wives and I will embrace, and together we will rejoice within the Oneness that I suspect will ultimately greet us all. *And, oh, the stories Reni will tell!*

For, eventually, all things must pass.

Even an eternal soul.

The Eternal
BOOK II
(The Future)

AN EXCERPT

البداية

BEGINNING

SHAKUR HUSSEIN RENAUD awoke to a distant cry atop the mosque in Pangani Dumali. He lay quietly, listening to the adhan—the first call to *Fajr*, the morning prayer—conscious of his own beating heart. The significance of this particular morning did not escape him. Exactly one hundred years ago to the day, a *Dhu'l Faqar* anti-terrorist unit had confronted him in the Kadhimiya district of Baghdad, opening fire without warning and stitching his body with synthal-methonium chloride micro-capsules. Moments later three men, their identities veiled behind black kefflyehs, dragged him in a paralytic stupor through the street and into a waiting skimmer.

Reni awoke several hours later, here in Tanzania, where he'd found himself the solitary prisoner in a lavish, centuries-old estate named بيردهاوس —*The Birdhouse*.

"For your own protection," Dr. Vipechi had explained, all those years ago.

He had come to like Dr. Vipechi, in spite of his captivity. He had been permitted full privileges within the main villa and in the abundant south wing—a choice of master suites, access to gilded baths and saunas, grand foyers and silk-draped, pillow-strewn lounging areas. He'd also been granted access to the extensive wine cellar, implausibly located next to the *masjid*—the estate's ornately tiled private mosque. Reni insisted on calling the room *the chapel*, if only for his own amusement.

The villa, a relic of a long-ago spurned elitist class, offered a holorium and a gymnasium—even a *book* library, filled with dusty, pulp-paged relics, that Reni would sometimes enter for no other reason than to deeply inhale the scent of old paper, like the warm hug of a fading memory.

He enjoyed the run of the villa's grounds, with its flower gardens, tidal pools, and a hillside gazebo where he could gaze upon the expansive turquoise waters of *Hind Mahasagar*. Such brief deception of freedom sufficed his needs, and somewhere amid these small moments of pleasure he found the strength to preserve his sanity.

They'd provided him with a manservant (whom he quickly dismissed) and a small housekeeping staff. A gardener. A chef. And, of course, the lovely Tia. His 'personal assistant,' Dr. Vipechi had explained, the old man's eyes twinkling. But Reni had known better. After a modest pretense of casual flirting and long discussions about art, philosophy and literature—which Reni appreciated, as the rituals reminded him of normalcy—Tia had become his lover. For years, each played the game of pretending that their affections might have been unarranged and spontaneous.

The illusion had sufficed.

He and Tia would often picnic near the koi ponds or play among the lush bamboo groves, next to a stream that trickled a crooked path through the hillsides and down to Peekinaw Bay. A pair of giraffes freely wandered the grounds. A family of spider monkeys, chattering incessantly in the nearby grove of Acacias, would beg for treats of rice cake or *tuatsui*. Sometimes, standing naked on the bedroom balcony and cooled by the sultry night's breezes, he and Tia would gaze across the pristine waters. They listened to Marsh owls call in the distance. And every so often they might catch a faint, ambient glow of lights from Zanzibar.

Yet even amid these splendid trappings, Reni remained a prisoner. He had been forbidden access to the compound's north wing—the medical facilities and plasma fusion reactors, the labs and staff's quarters, the data storage units. Nor, of course, was he permitted to leave the villa's grounds; not a single step beyond the meandering pink wall that snaked through the hillsides and meadows and wiggled between fringes of encroaching miombo woodland.

Reni found himself persistently shadowed by his captors, a small cadre of nameless young men, cloaked always in black and who followed at a respectful distance. Sometimes they remained unseen for days, although should the occasion for sudden escape present itself, he was certain that any number of these invisible *muhāribūn* would emerge as might bats swarming from a black cavern.

Over the next century he familiarized himself with every step within the grounds, an enclosure of some 52 hectares; slightly less than one-half square kilometer. Reni could easily observe the green, wooded hillsides beyond his captivity, a constant reminder of his incarceration. The wall itself was modest, barely a meter high. Climbing ivy had overgrown many of the protruding electromagnetic pulse-rods that towered above the wall at precise intervals. Often in the waning sunlight, the wall, a stippled terracotta the color of ripe peaches, reminded him of his estate in Frascati, some two and a half millennia before.

Reni could swim in the bay—another liberty—and often did so. However, fifty meters from shore, the plasma conductor implants in his skull would begin to hum, then squeal and, should he continue his course seaward, eventually his brain's electromagnetic circuitry would misfire.

He died once, nearly eighty meters out, having propelled his body seaward on sheer willpower alone, fighting the blinding waves of pain until he choked and spasmed, his lungs filling with sea water. They brought him back and left him on the beach, where he awoke two days later, spewing lather and aware that the punishment for such sedition would be severe.

Most mornings, mag-locked to a cot in Examination Room D—and always Room D, day after day, year after year—they took his blood, his urine and eventually bits of his body; sometimes hair samples, sometimes cell scrapings and DNA-taps, or deep core laser drillings into his organs or micro snippets of his brain. Sometimes they extracted bone marrow samples and fecal samples and saliva samples and isolated bacterial samples. He suffered through weekly MRI's and various electron scans. Radiation therapy. Occasionally they took larger scrapings of his spleen and kidneys, heart and lungs. After surgery, he'd often awake to find Tia, tears welling in her pretty almond eyes, tightly clutching his hand.

He had allowed their tests without complaint and Dr. Vipechi had responded in kind. "For humanity," he would often remind Reni, speaking in rusty French or Anatolian Turkish. Reni sometimes replied in halting Bambaiya Hindi, Marathi being Dr. Vipechi's native tongue. Somehow, they always managed to understand one another.

But Dr. Vipechi died sixteen years later, as had Dr. Proust a decade thereafter and Dr. Yn'kova several years after that. One morning, Reni awoke to find Tia gone as well. He had known for a long while that this day would come—Reni still the same, physically unchanged thirty-year-old specimen they had confined to the villa so many decades before. But Tia had grown older and increasingly insecure, tormented by her advancing age and convinced that her companionship alone was somehow insufficient to meet his needs. As if her love was somehow not enough to sustain him.

Silly notion.

Several other specialists had examined Reni over the following decades. Dr. Soob arrived at the villa two days after Dr. Kazari's departure. Unlike the others, Dr. Kazari had not been a medical consultant, but rather a Sharia-certified psychoanalyst. Reni had thought it best to cooperate—to an extent—admitting to the man that he remembered hazy fragments of his past, and that he held only vague, dreamlike memories of the preceding century. Dr. Kazari had attempted hypnosis almost daily, but without success. He scheduled weekly electro-neural frequency phase manipulations, cortex massage stimulations and medial temporal mirage enhancement, although by the end of his two-year tenure, the doctor conceded bitter disappointment with his failed endeavors to access Reni's deep past. Implants had proven useless. So had REM dream sequencers. Temporal distortion modifiers. For several months, Reni had seen the man only sporadically. He wondered if they might even be considering his release.

But Dr. Soob's arrival dashed Reni's hopes. A bio-engineering theoretician, Dr. Soob gazed upon Reni as one might regard a caged chimpanzee, marked and prepped for dissection. The doctor did not stand on formality, nor attempt even a superficial air of politeness or consideration. He rarely spoke to Reni. Even the house staff did not dare look directly upon Dr. Soob and would scurry away should they glimpse the man standing in a hallway or foyer.

Shortly after the doctor's arrival, the frequency of Reni's internal probing increased. His privileges and access to the villa grounds were curtailed, and Reni found himself confined to his bedroom suite between his extended visits to Exam Room D. Each morning, shortly after first prayer, he would be escorted to the north wing by a Dhu'l Faqar security detail, and electromagnetically locked into position on a simple nylon cot. Dr. Soob did not believe in the use of anesthesia, and his experimentation often lasted most of the day.

Reni would soon come to regard those many long months as his *year of dying*.

ONE

THREE DAYS AFTER RENI'S CAPTURE, in the waning years of the twenty-fourth century CE[1], a police detective arrived at the villa, waving a court-ordered *Writ-Of-Allah*.

As was customary at that time outside the sacred cities, the detective had dressed in western garments; a lightweight linen jacket (a purple armband honored the martyrs of the Jerusalem Crusade), a black Victorian *scarat*, and casual loafers. He wore a pale blue and black checkered *ghutrah* wrapped loosely about his shoulders. Only members of *al-Mabaheth* were permitted the symbolic color pattern that identified such individuals as sanctioned Protectors of the Believers of Allah.

Reni had been expecting the visit and arose from his seat in the garden, gesturing politely as the man approached from the villa.

"Kaif halak?" the detective asked pleasantly.

"I am well," Reni replied, also in Arabic. *Iana bikhayr.*

The man introduced himself as Sgt. Nassim Nassir, Colonial Investigations Division, then paused for a moment, studying Reni with a thoughtful silence. The detective nodded finally, apparently satisfied by whatever he'd observed. They continued their conversation in Arabic.

---

1   *Throughout much of Byzantinae: Year 108* ALAL *(Alsalam Alealamiu)*

"I am here to ask questions."

"I have many questions of my own," Reni replied.

"Oh?"

"I have been brought here against my wishes."

The detective spread both arms toward the distant ocean, sparkling beneath a cloudless sky. "This does not seem such a terrible fate, my friend."

"Still, against my will," Reni repeated.

Nassir smiled pleasantly. "Please, may we walk?" He gestured toward a stone pathway. Reni noticed the diode-studded fingerless glove fitted to the man's left hand—a recorder, comlink, and weapon if necessary, its touch an electromagnetic wallop.

"Of course," Reni replied. *T'abea.*

They strolled together down the sloping, well-manicured West Lawn, neither man speaking until Sgt. Nassir pointed at a sun-drenched bench near an imposing fountain. A dozen full-sized marble lions—prone, sitting, and rearing—purged cascading streams of crystalline water from their snarling mouths. A magnificent display of 22nd century Neo-Byzantine artisanship. This far from the main villa, the gurgling fountain providing a sufficient din, Reni became fairly certain that Nassir did not wish their conversation overheard.

To Reni's surprise, the man spoke in English. "As no doubt you have been advised, you are required to answer my questions truthfully, as required by Sharia law."

"In a forbidden tongue?" Reni replied in Arabic, suspecting a ruse.

"We are three thousand kilometers from Makkah. I doubt Muhammad will take offence."

"Yet only three hundred miles from the Sacred Tombs of Nairobi. Is it not a sin to presume the prophet's wishes?"

"Only two kilometers from the mosque in Pangani

Dumali. Four thousand from Jerusalem," Nassir comment-
ed with a nonchalant shrug. "Allah sees all and is not of-
fended by our feeble attempts to seek truth."

"Jerusalem is an open city," Reni reminded him, still
speaking Arabic.

"Perhaps...for the moment," Nassir said with a soft
smile. "But trust me, *sadiqi* Renaud, our words will not
anger Allah."

"Then by all means, ask," Reni said, speaking English
now. The language felt peculiar against his lips, a tongue he
had rarely spoken for many decades.

"Do you consider yourself a religious man?" Nassir
asked him.

"A spiritual man, perhaps," Reni replied. When he saw
that his answer was not sufficient, he said, "I have studied
Islam. Also Zoroastrianism, Druze, Ali-Illahism, Gnosti-
cism and Shabakism."

"Your passport states your religion as *Western Pantheism.*"

"Yes, it seemed...wise," Reni said, choosing his words
carefully. "I often travel the globe. It is one of the few religions that offends nobody."

"Or offends all, should one's conscience dictate," Nassir
parried.

"A fractal God—the belief that each of us honors the
same universal force despite our various sects, creeds and
moral ambiguities—does not strike me as highly offensive."

"Ah, yes, I've heard of this. *Pantheism* is also steeped in
mysticism, is it not? What is the Western phrase? In hokus
pokus."

"We believe that every living creature, every living cell
and each blade of grass—even the rocks around us, all are
inseparable from God," Reni replied. "Each and all are necessary and equal. I don't find such reverence mystical at all."

"Yes, I see," Nassir replied with indifference. "Tell me, sadiqi Renaud, you are a teacher, no? Of senior studies?"

"Yes. A professor of Cultural Sociology."

"In Alexandria, I believe?"

"And for a short while at the Universi— excuse me, the Grand Madrasa of Damascus."

"And before that, Barcelona, yes? And previously, al-Britannica?"

"Oxford," Reni replied, aware that the man's questions were posed merely as a formality. Obviously, Nassir already knew a great deal about him.

"You arrived in Baghdad eight days ago. May I ask why?"

"I sought information about certain artifacts uncovered in Delbaran earlier this year."

"Official business?"

"No, personal. I am a collector of certain pre-Mesopotamian artifacts."

"I see. Your father, Sinclair Hussein Renaud, he was also a professor of sociology?"

"Of anthropology, yes. In Paris. And later in Beirut."

"Your grandfather as well, no?"

"Correct," Reni replied with a nod. "Also a professor of anthropology. Tenured at the University of Brussels."

"And before that?"

He's testing me, Reni realized. Offering an apologetic shrug, he said, "I have no idea. The Pulse Wars, you know. So much knowledge, so much data, reduced to little more than fragmented bits of code, impossible to decipher."

"Ah, yes, the war. Subsequently, the birth of *Alsalam Alealamiu*. The triumphant end of Western domination."

"Certainly the end of Western interference," Reni countered. "But one must admit that the data loss was global. As was the socio-economic disruption, both financially and culturally. Wasn't it General Faheed A'mah who said, 'We are all now orphans of the world.'"

"I see that you are also a historian, sadiqi Renaud." The man smiled. "That is good, good. If I'm not mistaken, General A'mah uttered those exact words. But wasn't it he who also said, 'The past shall foretell the future'? Beguiling, wouldn't you agree? Perhaps you might humor me by examining an antiquated photograph I recently uncovered from a museum in Germinea. I'll admit that I find the image most fascinating."

Nassir leaned forward and tapped twice on his glove. A holographic image materialized from an embedded source projector, hovering in front of the two men, the graphic blurring slightly, briefly, wherever stray droplets splashed up from the fountain.

"Tell me, have you ever seen this depiction before?"

Reni studied the floating apparition—that of a centuries-old photo depicted beneath the stark headline of a British newspaper, worn and tattered and yellow-brown with age.

Reni's mind swam upward through a tidal surge of forgotten memories, gazing upon a pilot in an ancient war, the man wearing a practiced smile and flying jacket, a crooked leather cap, a pair of goggles jauntily askew around his throat. He wore a scarf, one that Reni fondly remembered as having been pure white silk, smelling faintly of lilacs. The man in the photo stood in front of a little Nieuport 15, a French-built biplane. The photograph had been taken by a man named Sheafe Smith nearly four hundred years earlier. A balmy Sunday afternoon, Reni recalled. The man had been a newspaper photographer, his camera a Kodak Autographical. Funny, Reni thought, the splinters of memory that remained intact.

"Yank flyboy scores hat-trick aloft," Nassir said, reading the headline.

Reni closed his eyes and said, without inflection; "American Captain Sebastian T. Renaud of the Royal Flying Corps ups his score to 14, the number of German aircraft downed since his arrival in Arras, France. The London Telegraph proudly salutes our brave American cousin."

"Ah! Thank you. I had trouble reading the words. The holox quality is quite irregular."

Reni remained silent.

"Your thoughts about the aeroplane's—what is the word—its driver?" the detective asked. "I find the resemblance quite astounding."

"Possibly a long-deceased ancestor of mine," Reni said with a shrug. "Or a coincidence. *Allahu a'lam.* The man's wearing a flying cap, much of his face in shadow. Personally, I don't see the similarity. And as you say, the original newsprint is muddied."

"Pardon?"

"Newsprint," Reni said. "A layer of black ink fused into pulped paper. Ink bleeds over time and can become unclear."

"You know of such processes?"

"My grandfather was an anthropologist, remember?"

"Yes, I *do* remember." The detective tapped his glove again. The image vanished. Nassir's gaze drifted to the distant ocean and lingered. When his attention returned, his expression had darkened. Reni sensed the man to be no longer in the mood for sparring.

"You continue to insist that you have no understanding as to why you were brought here?" Nassir asked.

"If my captivity has something to do with an antiquated photo—?"

"No, no, the image is—how do you say? Neither there nor here. It proves nothing. So then, one must assume that you were brought to Tanzania for another reason. Perhaps you should consider this affair more deeply, sadiqi Renaud. Did nothing unusual occur before your arrival in Baghdad? Nothing out of the ordinary? Please try to remember."

Reni stared toward the fountain. "I've travelled quite extensively of late. Kyiv-Putin to Mumbai. Thimphu to Dhaka. Istanbul to al-Madrid and to Cairo, only last month. By airbus to the ruins at Ashgabat and, eight days ago, to Baghdad. Wait, no. At the Cairo airport I was detained for several hours by security agents. I was directed to a private room but released with apologies later that same evening."

"And?" Nassir said.

"And?" Reni repeated obliquely. "Customs lags aren't infrequent. Nor are random screenings for *infidelitas*. I didn't consider anything—" He searched for the right word. "—awry."

"You passed a routine biometric optical scan," Nassir asked. "At the airport?"

"No, no, a DNA sniff. Apparently, Cairo's technology has finally caught up with the times."

"An interesting protocol, DNA sequence matching. Wouldn't you agree?"

Reni opened his mouth to reply—but instantly realized his blunder. He did not doubt that his expression, however briefly, had betrayed his own apprehension.

The detective regarded Reni's morphing mien with a taut smile. "Ah, yes. Perhaps *now* you understand."

"Might I presume that my DNA matched a previously collected sample?"

Nassir sat back on the bench, his legs crossed, his relaxed repose that of a self-assured man. "It seems you share the exact DNA sequence as a strand recorded in Roma, almost one hundred and thirty-eight years ago. A man, at the time, of similar age and bearing to yourself. The data lock clogged Cairo's opti-server for nearly an hour, the synapse relays searching in vain for a trace variance that did not exist."

"Unusual," Reni posed.

"Indeed. One might even assume impossible. Yet perhaps we might now contin—"

At that moment a digital voice drifted across the grounds, the call to prayer from a distant minaret.

"Ah, please excuse me," Nassir said. He stood, turned and then knelt on the grass, facing north, toward Makkah, to observe *Zuhr salat,* the second of the daily prayers to Allah.

Reni waited in silence on the bench, his head respectfully lowered, Nassir's fervent whispers of devotion soothing in his ears, occasionally lost behind the fountain's gentle splashes. After several minutes Nassir rose again, brushing absently at his grass-stained knees.

The detective turned toward Reni and, without hesitation, said, "The inevitable question is this. How can *you* be the man previously identified as Rafael Reniti—who presently would be one hundred and thirty-eight years older than you appear to be now?"

"I can't fathom," Reni said.

"Mindful of the edict of Sharia law, do you deny before the ever-present Allah being this man from the Roma airport? Perhaps even the same man standing in a photograph taken four centuries ago?"

"Being either of those men strikes me as quite implausible."

Again speaking in Arabic, Nassir said; "The prophet Muhammad implausibly conquered Makkah without bloodshed. And yet the Qur'an tells us it is so. So I must now ask for the absolute truth, under the impeccable watch of Allah."

The detective's looming silhouette shadowed Reni's

face. He was not afraid—Reni seldom found reason to fear—although the two possible paths of his future clearly defined themselves in those seconds of uncertain silence. He listened to the sounds of various birds in the nearby groves. He felt the caress of the warm ocean breeze. He nodded finally, squinting up into Nassir's tenacious gaze.

"In that case, sergeant, I can only admit to the improbable likelihood that we—the biplane's pilot and I—are indeed the same man."

Satisfied with the reply, Nassir nodded. "Thank you for your time, sadiqi Renaud. I have very much enjoyed our time together. I don't pretend to know how...." The detective, perhaps well accustomed to encountering the inexplicable, paused, his head dipping slightly. *"Ma'a Rahimak 'allah,"* he said and turned back toward the villa. Reni watched him leave.

He never saw Nassir again. That conversation had transpired a full century ago, Nassim Nassir most likely dead by now. Dr. Vipechi dead. Tia dead. And, for Shakur Hussein Renaud, far too much time had trickled away since his confinement within the villa's squat, terracotta walls.

END
(of Book II excerpt)

Made in the USA
Las Vegas, NV
14 January 2022

41382955R00280